For Chris, for being you and for making great tea.
Love you to bits, fella.

Prologue – December 2011

She pushed open the door to the bar and staggered out into the car park. The pounding in her head gained momentum as she swayed from side to side, trying to figure out which way was home as she balanced on her heels. She took a swig of the bottle she'd swiped off an empty table, wiping at her mouth as the lager spilled over and down her neck.

'Carole?' She moved a little further into the darkness. The bright lighting from The Potter's Wheel public house was far behind her now, the car park dimly lit for its size. Some way behind her the music became louder and then faded away again. She heard heels tapping, a woman's laughter, car doors slamming and an engine starting up. Then silence as it moved away.

'Carole?' she tried again. 'Where are you, you dozy cow? You said you'd only be gone a few minutes and that was ages ago. CAROLE?'

She froze when she heard a noise behind her. Swivelling round too fast for the amount of alcohol she'd consumed, she stumbled a step forward but stayed on her feet. She squinted into the dark but still she could see nothing.

'Look, Carole,' she snapped into the night. 'This isn't funny now. Come on, let's go home. You can crash at mine and we'll get the vodka out.'

But Carole didn't reply.

'Well, fuck you, Carole Morrison. I'll find my own way home. And fuck you, Terry Ryder. I don't need you to make me happy.'

She staggered back across the car park and round to the front of the building. In the distance, there were headlights. She wondered if it was a taxi and held up her hand.

'Hey!' The car rushed past her. 'HEY! Slow down! Hey! Well, fuck you, too!'

Another rush of dizziness. She retched and threw up. Wiping at her mouth, she sat down on the edge of the pavement and put her head in her hands. It was pretty ironic that she was in the gutter. It was where she belonged and she doubted anyone would miss her. Her daughter wouldn't, she was sure of that. Not after the way she'd slapped her during their last argument. Her husband wouldn't miss her, either. Twenty years married and it was more like a life sentence now. But she loved the bastard.

'Screw you, Terry Ryder,' she slurred. 'I hate you. You hate me. But we're stuck with each other. Can't live with you. Can't live without you.'

She heard another noise. She stood up and turned quickly, swaying as she tried to stay upright.

'Who's there?' she said.

Someone came out of the shadows.

'What the fuck do you want?' she said. 'And what are you doing creeping around like that? You scared the shit out of me.'

They were the last words she said. She fell to the ground easily with the first blow, not even having time to cry out in pain.

PART ONE
ONE WEEK EARLIER

Chapter One

The last week in November wasn't the best of times to be out on the streets of Stoke-on-Trent with nothing to snuggle into but a fiery attitude. In fact, any time in Stoke-on-Trent could be seen as cold to an outsider.

Like any city, it had its good points. Down-to-earth people who'd always offer a helping hand, a warm smile, a kind word – sometimes spoken in the potteries dialect – Wedgwood and Royal Doulton, Staffordshire oatcakes and the city's angel of the north, Robbie Williams. Like any city, it had its bad points. A run-down city centre. A multi-million–pound regeneration plan that had never materialised beyond knocking down properties and creating huge, barren landscapes of nothing.

And right now, it had a killer at large.

'He'll be here,' Detective Sergeant Allie Shenton said as she marched down the path towards a front door that had seen one too many fights.

'How do you work that one out?' Matt Radcliffe, the Detective Constable out in the biting cold with her, questioned as he followed behind with a quick step.

'You didn't notice the look on her face yesterday?'

'Not really. She was mouthing off too much. I –'

'She was spooked. Eyes flitting everywhere. She knows something.'

Matt shook his head. 'He's hardly going to be at one of the first places we'd look.'

'You reckon? His mother would stab me rather than tell me anything.' Allie confirmed her thoughts with a nod. 'He'll be in there, I'm telling you. And when I do find him, I'm going to stab him in *his* stomach and leave him to die. See how he likes it, the bastard.'

Andrew Maddison had disappeared two days earlier, shortly before the police were called out to Georgia Road, Hanley. His mother-in-law had visited to find her daughter, Sarah, lying dead in the back yard. She'd been there since the late hours of the previous night.

The door was yanked open and a middle-aged woman turned a caustic tongue on them. She smelt of cigarettes, lips pursed even without one, hair ratted, arms folded over a heaving bosom ready to burst out of the dirt-stained T-shirt she wore.

'I told you if I saw him, I'd let you know,' she snapped.

Allie pushed past her and into the hallway.

'Oy, you can't do that!'

Allie turned back to her. 'Where is he, Margaret?'

'I haven't seen him. I already told you that yesterday too.'

Allie pointed upstairs. 'Matt, you start up there. I'll check down here.'

It was only a split second before she caught a shadow out of the corner of her eye.

'Run, Andy, run!' Margaret yelled.

Maddison ran from the back room and through the kitchen. Allie and Matt followed close behind, Allie nearly turning an ankle treading over the mound of dirty clothes on the floor next to the washing machine and Matt banging his calves on boxes of lager piled up in the middle of the room. Outside into a tiny yard full of bric-a-brac and all Allie saw were a pair of white trainers as Maddison disappeared over the wall and into the back alleyway. She looked down at her shoes. Damn these heels.

'I'll get the car and radio through,' she yelled as Matt flung himself up and over the wall without a second thought to his footwear.

She ran back through the house, pushing past a disgruntled Margaret, and dashed to the car. She screeched off in the direction of the main road. If he got onto the Festival Park, they would lose him. If he headed towards the city centre, they would lose him. She had to get to him first.

Putting her foot down again, she turned right and raced along Etruria Road. 'Move!' she shouted at slow cars as they failed to see the flashing blue lights quickly enough to react. She glanced around as she flew through the traffic lights; neither Maddison nor Matt was anywhere in sight. She turned right and right again, coming out at the end of the back alley. But she couldn't see them.

She drove on up the street, braking but not slowing for the ridiculous number of speed humps, praying her lunch would stay down. She passed the last in a row of terraced houses – there they were, on the open waste ground to her left. Matt was hot on Maddison's tail but it was evident they were both tiring. Maddison's steps were faltering; his feet close to tripping him as he looked over his shoulder again and again.

Allie brought the car to a halt and, in her speed to get out, tangled herself up in the seatbelt. 'Let me go!' she cried, pulling at the black strips imprisoning her in the seat. Suddenly she was free and running towards them.

Seeing her approaching, Maddison slowed down and then stopped altogether. He dropped to his knees and raised his arms in the air. Matt pushed him forward and straddled him as Allie reached for his hands.

'I didn't do it. I love her!' Maddison yelled. 'I was drunk. I can't remember what happened but I didn't mean to –'

His words were lost as Allie pulled out her cuffs and clicked them on quickly. Then she bent forward and whispered in his ear.

'Not another word, you heartless bastard! Not another fucking word!'

It had taken the rest of that Friday evening to make even a small dent in the mound of paperwork that a murder investigation brought with it. Six hours before, Andy Maddison had confessed to killing his wife and was due in court on Monday morning. Allie, however, would be filling in forms and adding notes to files for far longer. Of course, it was always good to get a murder conviction, but afterwards there would be harrowing stuff to get through. Like talking to the couple's children about what would happen next. Two boys under five, who'd thankfully been in bed when the attack had occurred, were left without a mother, and with a father who would be sent to prison. Allie wondered how long it would be before she saw either of them in the station accused of their own crimes.

'Curry's here, Sarge,' Sam Markham shouted over from the far corner of the office.

Allie raised a hand in acknowledgment and then used it to cover up a yawn. Hearing laughter, she looked up. Perry Wright was messing about with Sam, squeezing her shoulders in an attempt to massage away the tension. But Sam kept on squirming out of his way. Allie smiled. She really was fortunate to have a good team of officers to command.

Perry was the longest-serving officer. Celebrating his fortieth birthday next year, he'd been in the force since he'd left school and didn't seem to mind that his sergeant was female and four years younger than him – he'd known her since forever. His athletic physique was down to playing rugby three times a week, his spiked hair, fake tan and snazzy suits down to his wife, who was ten years younger than he was.

At forty-eight, Matt Radcliffe was the old man of the gang. Easily over six feet, he towered over the tiny Sam, who was five feet four. Despite his age, Matt's short, thinning brown hair had only recently started to show flecks of grey, his olive skin early signs of fine lines. He sat hunched over his vindaloo as if it would be taken away from him if he hadn't demolished it in less than thirty seconds.

'Pass me some naan bread, would you, duck?' Sam held out a hand. Matt ripped off a chunk of his portion and handed it over. Allie gasped. Sam was honoured. Matt never usually shared anything to do with curry. Then again, this was Sam Markham. Allie would defy anyone not to like Sam. With a tiny physique and urchin features topped with a mass of choppy blonde hair, she could easily pass as someone who wouldn't put her neck on the line, but Sam was no pushover. She was a rookie detective, still on probation for another two months, having been in the force for five years after working as a social worker for over ten. She had a good heart, a great ear and a fine eye for drama unfolding. She'd also given birth to a daughter, Emily, earlier last year, to whom Allie had become godparent. So, too, had her husband, Mark.

Allie checked her watch: just gone ten thirty. It was too late to call in to see Karen so she decided she might as well head off home. If she was lucky, she could get in a little loving before the day was over. That would certainly take her mind off things here. Stretching out her back, she switched off her computer, plonked the files she was working on into her drawer and closed it with a satisfactory *clunk*.

'Great job, guys.' She stood up. 'I'm really proud of you all for cracking this case so early on.'

'It's the best part of the job, though, isn't it, Sarge?' said Sam.

'What, eating curry on a Friday evening?' Allie grinned. 'It was on the DI, this one, by the way.'

'Ooh, nasty Nick come good for a change,' Matt sniggered. Everyone ignored him, mainly because Detective Inspector Nick Carter was a fair boss. He just didn't see eye to eye with Matt over some of the old-school tactics that he continued to police with.

'There is something so satisfying about tying up a murder case, especially after such a brutal attack,' Sam continued. Then she blushed. 'Sorry, Sarge. I didn't mean –'

Allie waved the comment aside. She knew perfectly well that it wasn't aimed at her. And Sam was right. This work did have the odd moments of job satisfaction, as she had mentioned, but there was still the other ninety-eight per cent of crap to get through to find it. Allie was going to say that when Matt piped in.

'I'll second that.' He gave Allie a quick smile before raising a piece of bread in salute and dipping it into his curry. 'Especially after what that bastard Maddison put her through. I can't believe anyone could do that to another person. It's barbaric.'

'Sick,' Perry offered between mouthfuls.

Allie shrugged on her coat, loosening her long, dark hair from underneath the collar.

'You not having anything, Sarge?' Sam asked.

'Nope.' Allie picked up a brown paper bag. 'Taking it away, as they say.' Which really meant that she was going to try and sweeten up Mark with food when she got home. He'd be livid that it was so late again.

She stepped into the cold night, her breath bouncing out in front of her as she rushed towards her car. Thirty minutes later, she pulled into her driveway with a sigh of relief.

Home for the Shentons was a pre-war detached house that she and Mark had lovingly renovated. The former owner, a recluse for twenty-odd years, so the neighbours said, had died after spending hardly a penny on it. They'd had to rip out and replace everything. Electrics, windows, doors, flooring and central heating added. A downstairs bathroom, unhealthily found off the kitchen, had been moved upstairs into one of the four bedrooms. The kitchen had been extended and French doors fitted to add light as well as overlook a pleasant but small back garden. Over twelve years they'd created home sweet home, somewhere they could both chill out. But Allie had never quite learned how to switch off.

When she went through to the living room, she found Mark sprawled on the settee. He glanced at her as she walked over before his eyes settled back on the television.

'I have food,' she offered as her way of apologising for being so late. She bent over to kiss him but he moved his head to the side.

'Food!' she repeated, holding up the bag.

'Great.' Still he wouldn't look at her so she went through to the kitchen and dished the curry and rice out. She rejoined him moments later and they ate in silence as she caught up with the late night news. There had been two other murders in the country over the past week. One of them, the manslaughter of a German tourist in Kent, had been solved. The other in North London, a young lad known to have been stabbed by a rival gang member yet to be pointed out, remained an ongoing enquiry. As she heard where they were up to with it all, she wondered if her force would get a mention. But this was national news. The charging of Andrew Maddison would probably be a short snippet on *Central News* tomorrow.

Mark began to channel hop. 'Why so late?' He spoke without looking her way. 'Did you call in to see Karen?'

'No, I was catching up with my paperwork.'

'But you always call in to see Karen after solving a murder.'

'It was too late when I finished.' She nodded her head towards the television on the channel that he'd stopped at. Desperate to change the way the conversation was bound to be going, she continued, 'This looks like it will be good.'

The television went blank as Mark flicked it off. 'Paperwork is more important than coming home?'

'Of course not. You know –'

'We've been crossing like ships on the landing all this week.'

'That's a little dramatic. What time did you get in tonight, hmm?'

'That's beside the point.'

'No, it isn't. You got in, what, around eight? So in actual fact, you've been alone tonight for just over two hours.'

'I had to eat alone.'

'Really.' Derision dripped from the comment. 'No one to eat with on expenses?'

Mark stood up quickly, his lean frame towering over her; his stare would have been unnerving if she hadn't known him so well. After a moment, he chose to say nothing. The slam of the door as he left the room made her jump. Annoyed at his behaviour, she followed him through to the kitchen.

'It's not an excuse,' Allie said truthfully. 'In case it escaped your notice, a woman was murdered on Ryder's – Georgia Road. We've spent two long days proving that it was a domestic. We finally charged her fella with it this afternoon.'

Mark clapped in a sarcastic manner. 'Congratulations, Sergeant.'

'Look, we've got some bastard locked up for murder. You know how important that is to me after –'

'You can't solve every case, Allie. Just because –'

'After he'd beaten her to a pulp, he stabbed her in the stomach. Then he left her outside in the rain to die.'

Mark had the decency to look sheepish. Allie relaxed as she watched the fight in him evaporate. Despite the fact that he was nearly forty, with grey specks prominent in his dark hair and laughter lines crinkling around his brown eyes, he still had a cheeky boy image that made him look exceedingly childish when he sulked. God, he was handsome. She walked towards him.

'Doesn't it please you that we caught him?' she asked.

'You think I don't care when I hear about your victims?' Mark folded his arms. 'Well, I do. I'm sorry that some sick fuck beat his wife and then stabbed her but it doesn't stop me from missing *my* wife. It doesn't stop me from spending time alone when I should be with –'

Allie silenced him with a finger on his lips. She gazed into his eyes, fiery with rage. 'You make me so horny when you're angry.'

'That's not funny.' Mark pushed her hand away half-heartedly. She replaced it with her lips, moulding her body against his as the kiss turned from resistance to want.

'You never used to hate my job,' Allie told him when they caught their breath. Her hands reached down to undo the buckle on his belt. 'You used to love the uniform then, especially when it was teamed with pink furry handcuffs and I played about with your truncheon.' She slipped her hand inside his jeans.

'That's not fair,' he groaned.

'It's what I need.' She ran the tip of her tongue across his top lip. 'I run a tight ship at work and I demand the same respect at home. And if you can't follow orders,' she squeezed down hard enough to be pleasurable, 'then I'll have to take down your particulars.'

As Allie managed to switch off for a few precious moments of down time, in Stoke-on-Trent another murder was being planned.

Chapter Two

The next morning Steph Ryder opened one eye, squinted at the daylight and pulled an arm from beneath the thick winter duvet. That was one hell of a mad Friday night session. She tried to remember where she'd ended up and, more to the point, whom she had ended up with, but the visions wouldn't surface. Her eyes fell upon the empty whiskey bottle beside the bed. God, she'd give anything now to feel the warm trickle of heat as it travelled down her throat.

She could hear faint music – rap, R&B – which meant that her daughter, Kirstie, was at home. She turned onto her back, hoping for sleep to take her again.

'Wow, don't you look grand first thing in the morning,' a grainy voice spoke out.

Steph's eyes darted to her right as her mind caught up with the logistics. She sat up quickly, pulling the covers close around her naked chest.

'What the fuck are you doing here?' she snapped. 'Terry will kill you if he finds out.'

'But he won't find out, will he? Not from me, anyway.' Phil Kennedy grinned. 'I'm assuming you want me to leave pretty sharpish, though?'

Steph groaned and flopped back down. Oh God, what had she done? She had sworn she'd never get too involved and, so far, in all the time she'd been screwing Phil, she'd done just that. Thoughts rushed around her head, fighting with each other to make sense of the last few hours. She remembered being in The Potter's Wheel last night with Tracy Smithson for the monthly pub quiz. She remembered joining in with two other regulars but still they hadn't won, hadn't even come near to winning. But then ... nothing.

'What time is it?'

'Just gone nine thirty.'

Steph snuggled back down in the covers.

'Need a shower,' Phil said, as he made his way to the bathroom.

'Make it quick.' Steph sighed. Maybe this would turn out okay if she could get rid of him pretty sharpish. But wait – Kirstie! She darted across the room, her feet slapping on the parquet flooring in her speed. Across the galleried landing, she barged into her daughter's bedroom, ignoring kicked-off shoes and clothes strewn over the bed, make-up covering a large dressing area in the middle of a bank of wardrobes.

'Kirstie?' Steph pushed on the half-open door to the ensuite bathroom. But it was empty, save for a wet towel thrown on the floor for Jeanie, their cleaner, to pick up.

She tiptoed over to the window, feeling the tension leaving her shoulders. Except for her car, the driveway was empty. It looked like Kirstie had gone out without waking her – something she did quite often when she knew her mother had been out the night before. So with a bit of luck, maybe Kirstie hadn't seen Phil after all. And, as she spotted his car parked further down the cul-de-sac, she was more than thankful that he'd had the sense not to park too close.

'No one's home,' Steph remarked when she went back into the bedroom. Phil stood naked, towelling dry his hair. She felt the familiar feelings of longing as her eyes flicked downwards. 'Funny. I thought I heard music.'

'You did. I switched on the radio to catch the news.' Phil threw down the towel and beckoned her over.

'Why did you come here last night?' Steph needed to know. 'You could have ruined everything.

'I wanted to fuck you in his bed.'

'Slut!'

'You've got to admit it's a real turn-on. Look.' Steph stifled a grin as Phil's flaccid penis began to unfurl and stand to attention. He curled her slender fingers around it. 'I reckon now that I'm here we should make the most of it.'

'You have no fucking idea how much grief I'll get if he finds out about this, have you?' She shook her head.

Phil moved his hand over hers, urging her to move with him. She stared at him, watching his pupils dilate, hating herself for feeding off the danger of him being there. Loving herself for being able to have this man as well. Phil Kennedy carried off the mean and moodiness of a bad boy to perfection. His hair was fairly short, dark and curling slightly at the neckline, with the odd hint of grey here and there. He had a faint scar down the side of his face towards his ear, a sign of a deal gone wrong when he was learning his trade, and a chipped front tooth after someone had lashed out at him with a pool cue. His physique for a man in his early forties was remarkable. Steph knew she'd never tire of running a hand over his chest and rippled torso. Yet even though she loved him in her own way, he was still only a plaything to her. Sometimes she wished he would understand that.

Phil's dark eyes bore into hers. It was as if he sensed he could search out her soul. As he continued to move her hand up and down, he won. With his other hand, he pulled her close and onto the bed.

'This bed?' she asked as she ran a hand through his damp hair.

'This bed,' he repeated.

'Go fuck yourself, Kennedy.' Steph's tone was more defiant than she'd intended.

'You already have.'

In one fluid movement, Phil straddled her. She tried to wriggle from beneath him but he grabbed a wrist in each hand, forcing them up either side of her head. 'And you're going to fuck me again.'

'No, I'm not. You need to go!' She bucked her thighs underneath him but he stayed strong. She liked a fight. He knew she liked it rough. It was nothing more than role play.

Taking a breather as he moved down to her breasts, Steph threw her head back, laughing as she did. Fuck Terry Ryder, she thought. Phil was right. It was such a turn-on doing it here, on their bed.

Kirstie Ryder hadn't got up early to go out that morning as her mother had surmised. She hadn't actually got home at all from the night before. Instead, she had stayed over at her boyfriend's house. Luckily for her, she knew her dad wouldn't be back from Derby and her mother would be too hung-over to realise – or to care, even. But she needed to get a move on if she was going to get away with it.

'Fuck, my head's killing me!' She yelped as she lifted it up from the pillow. She nudged the life form in the bed next to her. 'What did you do to me, you bastard?'

Lee Kennedy turned towards her, a sly grin on his face. His dark hair was tousled, stubble on his chin making him look even sexier than Kirstie could have imagined.

'I didn't hear you complaining last night,' he said.

'From the state of the frigging brass band drumming away in my head, I bet I was in no fit state to say – or do – anything. What time is it?'

Lee looked at his watch. 'Ten past ten.'

'Fuck!' Kirstie shot up and then sat on the edge of the bed again as the room began to spin. 'I have to go. Now.'

'Don't fret, woman. It's only one night.'

Kirstie stood up, grabbed her T-shirt and shrugged it on. Reaching the bedroom door, she held on for dear life before turning back to Lee. 'I feel like shit and it's all your fucking fault. Why did you insist on that last line of coke? Why didn't you just take me home?'

'I thought you'd be better sleeping it off here rather than getting in trouble again.'

'He'll still do his frigging nut if he knows,' Kirstie shouted through from the bathroom as she sat on the loo.

'Why?'

'Oh, no reason in particular.' She wasn't going to tell him that she had a trip to New York lined up if she managed to stay out of trouble until Christmas. She knew he wouldn't understand. 'What time shall I meet you later?'

'Seven, if we're going to bed again.'

Kirstie came back into the bedroom and grabbed the rest of her clothing from the floor. It was surprising that she could find her belongings at all given the amount of Lee's things that were on the floor too. He might sport the latest in designer jeans and footwear but he wasn't a dab hand at looking after them. Items had been cast aside once worn, along with dirty cups, car magazines and a fit-to-burst ashtray. And the smell! She wished he'd change the sheets once in a while. Then she recalled with a grin the way she'd left her bedroom the previous evening, even if it did smell of perfume and deodorant rather than of teenage man.

Lee pulled back the duvet and patted the bed.

'Nice try, cowboy.' Kirstie pouted suggestively. 'You'll have to look forward to it later.'

Lee slapped her backside as he swept across the room naked.

Kirstie grinned again. Fucking hell! She still couldn't believe she was going out with Lee Kennedy, one of the bad boys of the

Marshall Estate. And, with both of them extremely good-looking, she knew they made the hottest couple ever. Wait until Ashleigh heard about last night and what they'd been up to. She would explode with jealousy!

She dressed quickly, trying to push all thoughts of her dad to the back of her mind. If he discovered that she'd been with Lee all night, never mind snorting drugs with him, he'd go ballistic. Not because she'd slept with him – at seventeen, she could sleep with whoever she wanted, which she did, and often. It was because he'd told her to stay away from Lee – she'd lost count of how many times – although she wasn't sure why. He seemed harmless enough to her, if a little rough and ready.

'Come here, bitch.' Lee grabbed her on his way back to bed. He kissed her roughly as she resisted.

'Leave me a-fucking-lone.' She tried to wriggle free. 'I have to go.'

Lee pushed her down to her knees. 'You're going nowhere until you've blown me away.'

'But –'

He shoved his erect penis into her face. 'Nowhere,' he repeated.

Kirstie sighed loudly. Knowing that he wouldn't let her go until she'd made him shoot his load, she ran the tip of her tongue up and down his shaft as he held her head in place. Might as well get it over with and then she could be on her way.

Once finished, she wiped her mouth and stood up, expecting at least a kiss of gratitude. But Lee got back into bed.

'See you later then?'

'Yeah, laters.'

Disgruntled with her dismissal, Kirstie turned sharply on her heel, making sure she slammed the door on her way out. Men!

Twenty minutes later, she cursed when she saw the black Range Rover parked in the driveway of her home next to the Mercedes that belonged to her mum. She checked her watch: quarter to eleven. Ah well, she'd have to lie if he collared her.

Once in the house, she stood in the kitchen, almost waiting for the study door to burst open and for her dad to rush out and go hell for leather. She squeezed her eyes shut. But ... nothing. She sighed with relief.

After texting Lee to let him know how much she'd enjoyed their night together, she made a cup of tea and two slices of toast and curled up on the settee. She switched on the television. *Oh, great*, she smiled, *a repeat of* Jeremy Kyle.

Terry Ryder did hear his only daughter come in but decided to ignore her for now. He had far more important things to think about than where she had slept last night. Besides, he'd been enjoying the peace and quiet.

The study was one of the things that drew him to The Gables. Of course any house could have a room changed to suit, but this one had been perfect as soon as he'd stepped into it. The decor spoke of class, of good taste. It spoke of money.

He sat behind a mahogany desk, polished to perfection by the cleaner twice a week. His pens were set out in a line, his notebook next to them – without a scribble as it would look untidy. Lined up on the bookcases in front of him were books that the previous owner had left, although he'd rearranged them to be colour coded. He didn't get spare time to read but if he had paperwork to catch up on, he'd sit in one of the two leather armchairs either side of the window and overlooking the garden.

Although he was considered a successful businessman to the people who mattered, there were parts of that business that he kept firmly under wraps. It was these things that caused him grief as he dealt with the many fuck-ups. Terry puffed heavily on a cigarette, hoping that he was almost rid of the recent headache he'd acquired. Before going to Derby overnight, clearing up the mess that Andy Maddison had left behind had taken him near on two days. The police had been swarming round Georgia Road as well as questioning him here, at home, twice. He supposed it was only fair, and routine. He was the landlord of the property where the murder had taken place. But he hated anything that could draw attention to him or his dealings, especially anything that could encourage the police to start digging deeper into his affairs. Or *any* deeper. Terry knew they wouldn't stop until they caught him good and proper. But so far, with friends in high places, he'd managed to stay one step ahead.

And now that Maddison was out of the way, he could pick a new tenant. There was no end of people waiting for a place to shack up on Georgia Road – Ryder's Row, as it was known locally – a fact that he was immensely proud of. Everyone wanted a piece of him. Everyone wanted to become part of his empire. Once the police gave the property clearance, he'd have the house occupied again – with a much more useful tenant this time.

Half an hour later, Terry heard the bed creak in the room above him as someone turned in it. Not for the first time he wondered if Steph was ever going to get up that morning. As it was nearing eleven thirty, it probably meant that she was so hung over that she couldn't get up. It wasn't unusual for her to stay in bed until after lunch because she knew that it pissed him off.

Lately her drinking had been getting out of hand. Her actions were certainly being talked about, if the phone call he had received earlier that morning while on his way back from Derby was anything to go by. Steph had been at The Potter's Wheel last night. Nothing unusual in that; it was one of her regular haunts. But the caller had informed him that Steph had left with Phil Kennedy. It could have been seen as innocent, if the caller hadn't told him he'd also seen them necking in the car park. And that he didn't like.

The harsh winter light cast shadows across the desk, matching his mood. Maybe it was a good thing that Steph wasn't up. She was better out of his sight right now or he knew there'd be another argument. But he did need to sort things out with her, and soon. Either that or he might easily slip his hands around her neck and squeeze until her eyes popped out of their sockets. She'd become such a liability, but he knew one false move would bring the police. Terry knew he couldn't hide everything, no matter how careful he thought he was. It would only take one silly slip-up and his life could be fucked up forever. He wasn't going to let any blonde tart do that to him, not even if the blonde tart was his wife of twenty years.

His mobile phone rang, the caller display showing the name Phil Kennedy. Talk of the devil.

'What?' he snapped.

'Problem at number three, Guv.'

Stoke-on-Trent had been renowned the world over for its pottery industry but, as technology had had a hand in lowering production costs, local pottery firms were closing on a regular basis and production moved abroad to take advantage of cheap labour prices. Terry had bought six small pottery firms that had gone bust. Born and bred a local boy, he'd opened a base of Car Wash City in each of the six towns. Number three was based in Longton, over in the south of the city. To the working public, Car Wash City did a roaring trade on car valets and wash-downs. But what went on behind closed doors was what the police were really interested in. And why there was a problem now.

'Go on,' Terry said.

'Looks like someone's had their hands in the till again. They're about two grand short on takings for the past three weeks.'

Terry ran a hand through his hair. 'I'll be there in an hour.' He ended the call and threw the phone onto the desk. Trouble at the office was the last thing he needed.

A light knock on the door and Kirstie came in with a mug of coffee. 'Thought you might like this, Dad.' She smiled. 'You've been working in here for ages.'

'Sorry, sweetheart, I have to go out.' Terry stood up. 'Where did you get to last night?'

'I stopped over at Ashleigh's.'

'You sure about that?'

'Yes, we had a few drinks in Stoke and then got a takeaway.'

Kirstie's smile was a bit too confident for his liking. Did she think he was born yesterday? She was a good-looking young woman in her prime, and Terry knew it would prove tough to keep Kirstie away from scrotes like Lee Kennedy, whom he'd seen her with a couple of weeks ago. Despite working for him, Terry couldn't stand the lad and had only taken him on because his father, Phil, had said he'd keep him in line. Lee Kennedy was eighteen, a cocky little bastard and a no-good layabout who would amount to nothing. Besides, no matter how much Kirstie liked him, there was no way Terry was going to let his daughter get involved with the nephew of one of his rivals.

Terry continued to stare, long enough to watch his daughter blush. Luckily for Kirstie Ryder, he had other things on his mind.

Chapter Three

The sound of Terry slamming the front door woke Steph up. She listened to him racing off in his car, wincing at the sound. Lord knows what the neighbours would think. There might only be ten houses in their exclusive avenue, allowing far more privacy than when they lived back on the estate, but she knew the curtains would still be twitching.

Lying in the foetal position, she pulled her knees up further to her chest. Now that she was awake again, more of last night started to come back to her. She remembered being in the car park at The Potter's Wheel. She remembered cuddling up to Phil to keep warm before getting into his car for a lift home.

Actually what she remembered was pressing herself up to him and shoving her tongue down his throat. Christ, how stupid they'd been. She prayed no one had seen them together. Tracy Smithson had gone home early when her husband picked her up at eleven thirty and she knew better than to shout her mouth off anyway. Like the drunken fool that she was, Steph had stayed there rather than have a lift home. She'd sat with the regulars for a while until she'd sauntered over to Phil, acting all casual as if they were catching up on chat. But it only took one nosy git to gossip and she would be for it. She had to get a grip on things.

She tried to focus on the bedroom. When they'd moved in, she hadn't wanted to change a single thing. But when the recent fashion emerged for bold, flowery patterns, she'd hired an interior designer and created a room to die for: pale green walls covered in large floral patterns, a vivid green rug at the side of the bed that matched the petals of the flower in the paper precisely. In their previous home, there hadn't been room for anything other than a bed and a small flat-pack wardrobe. In this room, she often did aerobics in front of the gigantic wide-screen television mounted on the wall. And that was just the bedroom – off that was an ensuite bathroom that was bigger than her previous living room. It was pure luxury.

Her eyes filled with tears. She'd been living in her dream home for ten years now, yet the minute she'd set foot in it she knew she'd ruin things eventually. Steph the fuck-up, she called herself. Having a powerful man for a husband, having money when she needed it and not having to get her arse up and out to work like most of the friends she'd lost wasn't enough for her. If Terry found out that Phil had been here, her cosy life as she knew it would be over.

Some mornings she hated herself so much that she couldn't bear getting out of bed. Let's face it, what had she? Her daughter hated her. Her husband tolerated her. She had parents and a sister living nearby whom she didn't have contact with. She'd mouthed off at them so many times they couldn't forgive her outbursts any more. And her friends were few and far between since they had moved there – if they had ever been her friends to begin with.

Wearily, she pulled back the covers and sat on the edge of the bed. She lit a cigarette, took a deep drag and stumbled across to the bathroom. Daring to take a look in the mirror, she gasped at her reflection. Christ, she'd need dark glasses to hide the state of her eyes today. At thirty-eight, weekly facials and monthly hair treatments went some way towards keeping age at bay but not as much as she would have liked. Her blue eyes seemed navy today, matching the dark bags underneath them. The blonde dye on her muddy brown hair made her skin tone look harsh. Still, once she had her make-up on, she supposed she'd look half decent. And the cigarettes kept her thin – no appetite.

Not bothering to shower, she wrapped herself up in a dressing gown and dragged herself downstairs to the family room. Kirstie sat at the breakfast bar, magazine in hand, cake and a mug of coffee in front of her. Steph swiped the mug from underneath her nose.

'Hey!' Kirstie protested. 'That's mine. Make your fucking own.'

'Do another one, Kirst, for your old mum,' Steph slurped noisily. 'I'm parched.'

'What's wrong with you? You look like fucking death warmed up.'

'Don't talk to me like that.'

'Whatever.'

Steph shook her head trying to rid herself of its fuzziness. She lit another cigarette and threw the lighter onto the black granite worktop, sucking in hard and then blowing the smoke out noisily into the room. As it cleared in front of her, through the window she noticed ice still formed in patches on the lawn and the greyness of the clouds and wished she'd stayed in bed. At least the family room was tidier than she'd left it last night. It looked like she wouldn't have to sit on the settee while Jeanie cleaned around her again.

'Has he gone?' said Kirstie.

Steph gasped and froze. The smoke trapped inside her lungs made her cough. Through watery eyes, she looked at Kirstie for signs that she suspected something. As far as she knew she'd kept her affair close to her chest.

'Has who gone?' she asked as if she hadn't a care in the world.

'Dad. He tried to wake you up twice.'

'Oh.' *Thank fuck for that.* 'Yes, I heard him screech off earlier, in a bit of a mad panic about something, no doubt. Did he say why?'

'Did he say why what?'

'Did he say why he tried to wake me twice?'

'Nope.'

Steph sighed with relief. It was looking like she'd got away with it. She was never going to let that happen again – ever. There was too much to lose. She took another drag of her cigarette, blowing the smoke out noisily again.

Kirstie looked up from underneath a heavy black fringe. 'Do you have to do that in here? It's fucking disgusting.'

'Oh, come on, Miss Holier than Thou.' Steph took another long drag and blew the smoke in Kirstie's direction. 'I'm surprised you haven't pulled it out of my mouth, the amount you steal from me.'

Kirstie pulled a face. 'I hope I don't look like that when I'm smoking.'

'Like what?'

'Like a puckered-up old witch. You have wrinkles on your crow's feet.'

Steph glared at her daughter. 'You're such a bitch.'

'Yeah, well I'm turning out to be exactly like my mother, aren't I?' Then, in a moment's breath, her tone was sweetness and light. 'Have you got twenty quid I can have? I need a sub until my allowance at the weekend.'

'Not even a please?'

'Don't know the meaning of the word.'

'I'm not made of money!'

'You're not made of money at all. It's all down to my dad. Look, I –'

'You should try making some of your own.' Steph leered at her pointedly. 'You could make a small fortune. Men would love your scrawny ass, especially in that skirt. It's far too frigging short.'

Kirstie stared back wide-eyed. 'I'm no fucking slag!' she declared.

'Different to what I've heard.' From the tears welling in her daughter's eyes, Steph knew she'd touched a nerve.

'You're such a nasty cow.'

'Takes one to know one.'

'And you're an embarrassment.' Kirstie slid down from the stool. 'Look, can I have the money or what?'

'No, you can't.'

'Fine! I fucking hate you, do you know that? You can stick your shitting money. I don't want it.'

Kirstie stormed out of the room. Steph followed close on her heel and grabbed a handful of her hair before she could leg it up the stairs. She twirled her round with so much force that Kirstie landed in the middle of her chest.

'You ungrateful little bitch,' she raged. 'Take a look around this place. Do you think you would have got this without me? Your dad didn't do it all by himself. Do you hear? Do you fucking HEAR?'

'And what part did you play in the money-making?' Kirstie's voice was defiant.

'Haven't you heard of the saying, "Behind every successful man, there's a woman"?'

Kirstie grimaced and purposely moved her head away from the stench of Steph's ghastly beer breath.

'You'd be better taking note of that, dear daughter, as you're going to find yourself in my situation one day. Married to a man who isn't around enough as he's too interested in money and his fucking reputation.'

Tears formed in Kirstie's eyes. Steph noticed them immediately.

'Don't start your whinging. You're big enough to dish it out. You should be big enough to take it back.'

Kirstie shrugged her arm, trying to release Steph's grip. But Steph's fingers tightened further. She squeezed harder, until they were hurting, but she never lessened the pressure. Finally, she pushed Kirstie away.

'Go on, get out of my sight.'

Kirstie stumbled but managed to stay on her feet. She ran up the stairs, turning back as she got to the top. 'I hate you, you stupid, bitch!' She sneered. 'I hope you rot in Hell!'

'Why, you little –'

Steph charged up the stairs after her. By the time she reached the landing, Kirstie had made it to the family bathroom. Steph heard the lock slide into place behind the door. She banged hard on it. 'Come out here, you little bitch,' she screeched. 'I'll kill you, I will. I'll fucking kill you!'

Moments later, breathless and hands stinging, Steph dropped to the floor in a heap. What the hell was happening to her lately? It was as if everyone she knew wanted to take advantage of her. First Phil and then Kirstie. Who'd be next, she wondered?

She grabbed hold of her hair and bunched her hands into fists, pulling harshly. Then a noise came from deep within and she screamed.

Chapter Four

Early Monday morning Allie parked the unmarked police car, switched off the engine and stared down the bank in front of her. Georgia Road was on the outskirts of Hanley. It wasn't a road that was frequented much after dark; it was busy during the day, though, due to the short-cut through from the estate to the city centre. To her left was the shell of unfinished flats. To her right were twenty-two houses in a row, all with identical floor plans. For anyone passing through, Georgia Road would seem to be a pleasant row of terraced houses. But anyone living in Stoke-on-Trent would be sure to know that they were owned by local property developer Terry Ryder and known locally as Ryder's Row.

There were frequent shout-outs to Georgia Road. Domestics were par for the course, a regular weekend trip. There were often loud parties but no complaints of noise. No one ever saw or heard anything that happened. So trying to question anyone there had always proved fruitless.

None of the door-to-door enquiries regarding the murder of Sarah Maddison had turned up anything. No one in Georgia Road had heard or seen anything happening at number fourteen, where Andy Maddison and his family had resided until a week ago. He'd even left the back door open and legged it, not thinking for one moment of his sleeping children upstairs. Although the properties had tiny walled yards, most of them with gates that fastened, either of his young boys could have wandered out.

It struck Allie as odd that Maddison hadn't abandoned the knife where he'd stood after the mist had dropped and he'd seen what he'd done. Yes, he'd confessed and was likely to be telling the truth because he was off his head on heroin at the time. But Allie still had her doubts that he had done it all by himself.

After arresting Andy Maddison last week, they'd found enough DNA at the crime scene and on Maddison's person for a conviction, as his wife had been beaten to a pulp with his fists as well as receiving a fatal stab wound to her stomach. But that was strange in itself. Sarah and Andy had been together for years – ten that Allie knew of, at least. And although they'd had their fair share of domestic call-outs, for that level of violence to occur, it didn't add up.

And the knife he'd used – possibly the middle size of a set of five missing from a kitchen drawer – to inflict the fatal wound hadn't been found. Neither had his clothes, or his shoes, which would be splattered with her blood. As much as she knew Maddison was a crack head, Allie didn't think he had it in him to use a knife on the woman he loved.

A lorry rumbled by and she looked to number fourteen again after it had passed. For all intents and purposes it was as if nothing had happened there now. Not even the back door had been forced to gain entry. She switched the car engine on and blasted the heater for a moment, rubbing her hands together. No doubt Terry Ryder would have another tenant in there soon, causing them more problems as they flitted from property to property playing the numbers game.

Although he liked to stay under the radar, doing the numbers was Terry Ryder's thing. It was part of a bigger plan so that the authorities didn't know who was living where. Apart from Phil Kennedy at number two, each hand-picked tenant flitted from house to house at Terry's say-so. The police knew it was part of a larger benefit scam – money laundering at its best. To the outside world there might appear to be three tenants claiming income support, but they would be using false names and identities.

And they didn't just stay in one property. Only one could be staying in each. The other two could be living with someone else, most of the time under their legal names, or living with partners but claiming single benefits of their own.

Allie sat forward and glanced upwards at the roofing. For once, she wished she was a super hero with x-ray vision. The row shared a communal loft space. Well, technically speaking it didn't, but the old-style terraced housing had only one layer of bricks between each property. In the lower edge of each triangle at the back, some of the bricks had been taken out to form a rat run from number two right through to number forty-four. Another way they scammed as to who was living where. It was usual for a tenant to be living at number twenty but never to be seen coming out of that front door.

Things like that had messed up the paperwork for a while but the fraud investigation team had cottoned on. It would take years for something to stick if they were to take Ryder to court, and this was only a small part of what the joint investigation was looking into; but it was a start. One of the many ways they were keeping an eye on Ryder and his crew. So until then, Allie could do nothing more than sit on her hands and watch that handsome-bastard lowlife get away with everything.

She let her mind wander to the first time she'd encountered Terry Ryder. She'd met him quite early on in the job when she was a police constable, about a year after Karen's attack. She'd pulled him over when one of his rear lights had been out on his car. Allie remembered it because at the time it was a top-of-the-range Porsche, black with sexy chrome work. A few smiles and charm personified and Allie had let him off with a caution. But she'd never forgotten him. Terence Steven Ryder, born locally in 1969. From the age of nine, he'd been raised in a children's home after watching his father beat his mother to death and then shoot a bullet through his own head. Through his years in care, he'd been in and out of trouble – petty theft, breaking and entering, stealing cars – but nothing major. At sixteen, he'd been saved by a local builder, Maurice Sterling, as whose apprentice he'd learned the trade that would make him his money. He'd married his childhood sweetheart, Stephanie Miller, and they'd had a daughter a couple of years later.

Six years after he'd started working for Sterling, Sterling's head had been splattered across concrete when he'd lost his footing on scaffolding thirty feet high. It had been early one morning. His hard hat had never been located. Terry Ryder had been twenty-two when he'd taken over his business. From then, he had grown from property to property and his stature had become grander by the year. Not all his dealings were legitimate but all of them were above board as far as the police nailing him were concerned. Still, they had time on their side.

Of course she'd remember him – what woman alive wouldn't? He was a charmer, blessed with good looks that models in Milan would cut off another's ear to have. *Chiselled features*, the fashion magazines would say. Just in his early forties, he had an impish smile and a perfect set of teeth, a strong Roman nose and deep-set blue eyes. He was tall and slim and wore the latest in designer clothes and accessories. He drove the best cars. He ate at the finest restaurants. He and his wife hosted a number of charity events throughout the year – one of which she and Mark would be grudgingly attending tomorrow evening. He was known as a man with a good heart yet a very bad soul. Allie often thought about him without realising. Just the mention of their charity, Ryders Dreams Come True, would remind her of a venue, a time, a smile, a touch. A police meeting would have her thinking of a shared joke, a double-entendre, a quick drink at a packed bar in the name of business. Terry Ryder didn't just leave a money legacy wherever he went.

A few years ago, he and his family had moved off the notorious Marshall Estate, Allie's regular patch, into one of the newer houses on Royal Avenue. Sometimes she'd catch a glimpse of him as he drove past in his midnight blue Mercedes soft-top or his black Range Rover, personalised number plates on both. Always she would be left remembering the image for quite some time afterwards.

Allie wondered. Could Terry Ryder be involved in Sarah Maddison's murder? She chewed on her lip for a moment before she drove away with her thoughts.

———⌣———

Terry Ryder watched Allie Shenton drive past in her car before he came out from behind the billboards situated at the far end of the road. He'd been doing his usual site check on land that he was interested in purchasing when he'd noticed her sitting there. A property developer from out of the area had bought a few acres for which Terry had put in a lower bid at auction and had built a block of twenty-four apartments. But none of them had sold, due mainly to the extortionate asking price in a city that was struggling to survive in the current economic climate. Had he been from Stoke-on-Trent, the developer would have known the land wasn't the bargain he'd originally thought. Terry had been trying to get him to pass it on to him for some time now, but at such a low price that the builder refused to sell. Instead the apartments stood empty, earning no one any money and making the area look even more derelict than it was.

He threw down his cigarette and headed off down Georgia Road, where he let himself into number two. Greeted by the sounds of grunts and the odd groan from the front room, he walked in as if he owned the place – which he did. Phil Kennedy was on the floor, straddled by a girl who looked young enough to still be at school. Even half clothed as she was, Terry could see a pretty young thing blossoming but young things weren't to his taste. Her eyes were closed as Phil pushed her up and down, but as she felt the tug of his stare, she opened them and screamed.

'Fuck! There's a geezer gawping at us!' The girl jumped up and off Phil in a flash and grabbed for her jeans and top, at the same time trying to avoid flashing him an eyeful.

Phil turned his head to see who had stopped him at the peak of his enjoyment and grinned when he saw Terry standing there. 'Yet again, you catch me on the job. How're you doing, soldier?'

Terry said nothing. The girl stood in the doorway trying to catch Phil's eye.

'Let me get rid of her,' Phil muttered. He pressed a small polythene bag containing a tiny amount of white powder into the girl's hand.

'Is that fucking it?'

When Phil said nothing, she snatched it from him. He followed after her flurry of curse words.

Terry sat down at the table in the front window. This house, owned by a man in his seventies, had been one of his first acquisitions; he'd purchased it at a knock-down price due to its disrepair. It had taken a lot to get rid of the lingering smell of death after the owner had been left to rot for eight weeks before someone called the police to report a break-in, but it had turned out good in the end. Downstairs, two small rooms had been knocked into one large airy one. Worn floorboards had been covered with laminate flooring. Old tiled and iron fireplaces had been restored and reset, light fittings updated and the Formica kitchen ripped out and replaced with state-of-the-art cupboards and gadgets.

Once he'd completed number two, Terry had purchased every house that opened up to him in the row. Over a five-year period he'd acquired, with a few helping hands and a few extra pushalongs, seventeen of the twenty-two properties. The other five had proved far trickier but eventually even they succumbed to pressure. Once one of them had been found dead after having a suspected heart attack, and the family had been paid a hefty sum to help out with funeral expenses, the other four emptied quite quickly and soon every property in Georgia Road belonged to Terry.

Number two was the only one in the row to be fitted out to this particular standard. That was because number two had been kitted out especially for his number two. Since Phil's older brother, Steve Kennedy, had been banged up for murder and Terry had taken the patch from them, he'd kept Phil sweet, making sure he got the best of everything. And up until now, Terry would have trusted Phil with his life.

Phil came back into the room, adjusting his clothing.

'Have you been able to get into number fourteen yet?' Terry asked.

'Not yet. I'll get to it as soon as I can. Just a clear-out, is it? Or are you moving someone in?'

'Moving someone in.'

'Want a brew?' Phil asked as Terry checked his watch.

'I'm not stopping.' Terry walked out into the hallway and opened the cellar door, slowing momentarily to search out a light switch before disappearing down the stone steps. 'Can you sort out a move-around?'

'Course.' Phil followed quickly behind. 'I'm already on it. We've moved Kris Mantell from sixteen to thirty-two, then back to sixteen. Sally Churchill moved from eight to twenty-four and I put Dave Russell in with her. No one's any wiser as to who lives where.'

Terry nodded. 'That's okay, then, if you've done the numbers.'

Phil breathed easy again. If Terry was asking him about the numbers, then he must be in the clear over his antics with Steph last night. Once he'd got home that morning, his mind had gone into overdrive at the sheer stupidity of his actions. He could have ruined everything but, worse, he could have ended up without his kneecaps.

As he stepped down onto the cellar floor, he saw Terry pick up a wrench from the aluminium shelving on the side wall. But he didn't have the split second needed to move in time before it was swung across his face. It caught him in the mouth, splitting his top lip. The force of it took him by surprise and he crashed backwards into a pile of boxes. Cigarette packs and the latest line in counterfeit T-shirts came hurtling down on top of him. He curled up in a ball waiting for the next hit. But it didn't come.

Terry stooped by his side. 'You think everything is a joke, Phil?'

"Course not, Tel.' Phil brought a hand to his lip and wiped away blood. 'I'm letting you know that everything is in order.'

'I'm not so sure that it is. Let me tell you what I heard this morning.' Terry shook his head slowly from side to side as he balanced on his haunches. 'Things that I never thought I'd hear about you. Obviously they might not be true. But, you never know ...'

Phil pushed himself up to a sitting position. He gulped. 'I don't know what you mean, Tel. I would never let you down, you know that. I'm your man, right?'

Terry remained silent for a moment. Then he stood up before continuing.

'Yes, you're my man, and to a certain extent that means that I will protect you. I will look after you and see no harm comes to you. But if I ever find you doing anything I don't like, I'll –'

'You won't!' Phil interrupted.

Terry glared at him. Then he drew his foot back, aiming for the chin this time. He felt an extraordinary sense of satisfaction when it connected and Phil's head jerked backwards before slamming onto the floor. He wiped the spittle from his face.

'Get yourself cleaned up. I've a job that needs doing and you're just the right person to carry it out.'

———

Lee Kennedy needed money. Keeping Kirstie Ryder sweet with cocaine and the odd perfume present didn't run cheap. But as long as it got him up to her house for a gander of what was what, he was prepared to take a gamble. There was no way he could stand back and be a pushover like his dad. Besides, he wanted into a world of luxury, too. It was where he belonged.

Coming from his base at number eighteen, stepping through the loft spaces, Lee had dropped down into number two moments before Terry arrived. At the sound of the front door opening, he'd pushed himself, unnoticed, back against the wall. Staying put for a moment, he watched a young girl storm out, followed by his dad. His dad came back in again and then he heard the cellar door open. Stealthily, he tiptoed down the stairs and hid behind the door.

A few minutes later, unable to believe what he'd heard, he'd dashed back up the stairs and onto the safety of the landing when footsteps alerted him to someone coming up from the cellar. He covered his mouth with his hand to ensure no sound emerged and waited for Terry to leave. Then he pondered his next move, trying to grasp how useful overhearing that conversation could be for him.

Fuck, what would Terry do if he knew he'd been earwigging at the top of the stairs? He'd kill him, that was for sure. This was big news, a dangerous job. Something he'd never thought would happen – not in a thousand years.

But, as he began to think about it more, Lee smiled. As quietly as he could, he crept up the loft ladders again. He was through as far as number eight when he heard Phil shout behind him.

'Oy! Get your arse back here.'

Lee's shoulders sagged as he turned around.

Back in the kitchen of number two, Phil tended to his cut lip over the kitchen sink.

'What did you hear?' he said without turning his head.

'I heard it all, man!' Lee became animated. 'Is he serious? He really wants you to do his wife in?'

'Yeah, I thought he said that too.'

'Are you going to do it?'

'Are you fucking crazy?' Phil dabbed a cloth to his mouth, pushed past him and into the living room. 'What if I did it and he changed his mind? That would be my life over.'

'Your life will be over if you *don't* do it for him. Why does he want it done now, anyway? He's been with her for years.'

'You know what they're like. It's a love-hate thing. One minute, they're all over each other. The next, they're at each other's throats like street fighters.'

'I don't know what he sees in the slag.' Lee dropped onto the settee. 'She's a fucking nutcase, if you ask me.'

'Less of the lip.' Phil clouted him round the head.

Lee flinched. 'All right, all right, keep your fucking hair on. I'm only going by what Kirstie says about her. So, it's this Friday then? At The Potter's Wheel?'

Phil didn't reply. If he didn't say it aloud, it wouldn't happen, right? Still trying to come to terms with what he'd been told to do, he shuddered. Fuck, *had* Terry found out about him and Steph? Was this some sort of punishment? Or some kind of loyalty test?

'You're not bottling it?' Lee frowned as he watched Phil's shoulders sag.

'Of course I'm not.' Phil pulled the cloth away from his lip to see if the bleeding had slowed. 'I just don't want to be there to pick up the pieces afterwards if he's full of grief.'

'Then get someone else to do it.'

'You heard him. He said it had to be me.'

'But why?'

Phil shrugged. 'I suppose he doesn't trust anyone else.'

Lee doubted that. From where he stood, there didn't seem to be any love lost between the two men. He knew that Terry Ryder had muscled his way in while his uncle Steve was away. Still, if the job had to be done, this could work to his advantage. He was glad he'd dragged himself down here now.

'Looks like you're screwed, then,' he said. 'Got any lager in?'

Without a care in the world, Lee sauntered into the kitchen and opened the fridge. Behind the open door, he smiled again. This could work out perfectly for him if his old man couldn't do it. Because whoever did do it could then be blackmailed. It was an easy way to make some money. And, if push came to shove, he'd kill Steph Ryder himself.

He pulled out a can and tore off the ring. He had some planning to do but this certainly called for a celebratory drink.

Chapter Five

On Tuesday morning, Steph opened her eyes a little in the darkness. Something had woken her. She yawned, scratching at her thigh as she felt a feeling similar to something crawling over it. She turned over, pulled the duvet under her chin and settled down to sleep again.

An arm wrapped around her waist and pulled her across the bed. What the fuck? But all was clear when she felt Terry's erection rub up against her bare back. She felt his hand between her legs, pushing his fingers deep inside her. She tried not to gasp, tried to focus on the clock. Fuck, it was ten past six. Far too early for this.

'I'm tired, Tel,' she said, her voice groggy.

'And I'm horny and need my fix.'

Steph closed her eyes but her body had other ideas as it began to awaken. She pressed back into his chest and her legs opened that little bit wider. She reached behind her, turning half on her side to accommodate him. He pushed himself into her, grabbed her thigh and began to move slowly with her.

She tried to turn towards him more but he pushed her back. Then he grabbed a handful of her hair, pulled hard and yanked her head towards him.

'Bleeding hell, Tel,' she cried. 'My neck.'

'I don't give a fuck about your neck.' Terry pushed her over onto her stomach and entered her from behind. With her face pushed into the pillow, she could hardly breathe but she knew she wouldn't complain. This was how Terry liked to play rough. This was how he liked to think he had the upper hand. She stayed that way for a while until suddenly, mid-thrust, she pulled away from him.

'You bitch,' he spoke hoarsely. In the dark, he had the upper hand. Steph tried to scramble away but he was too quick. He grabbed her hair again and threw her back onto the bed, picking up from where he'd started. She let him continue this time, grabbing hold of his buttocks, forcing him into her, deeper and deeper. When his rhythm quickened, she dug her nails into his back, feeling flesh turn to blood underneath them. He continued to move inside her. Faster, faster. She felt the waves of orgasm engulf her and she cried out into the dark. Moments later, Terry cried out too. His breathing laboured, he fell on her. They lay together in silence.

'You will always be mine,' he said into the darkness.

Steph stifled a yawn. 'I know, babe. I know.'

'I mean it, Steph. If I can't have you, then no one can. If you ever leave me, I'll scar you for life. You realise that, don't you?'

'Yeah, course.' Steph nodded, even though he couldn't see her. She'd heard it all so many times in the years they'd been together.

'And if I ever catch you, or hear that you've been with anyone else, I'll kill you. And then I'll kill him. Do you hear me?'

Steph's body froze underneath him. Had he heard something? Was someone watching her? Shit, she'd have to be more careful. She felt for him in the dark, brought his lips down to hers and kissed him. 'Now why the hell would I want anyone else?'

———

Steph hadn't intended on sleeping in too long but in the warm glow of post-orgasm, she'd closed her eyes again and another three hours had passed. Sleepily, she ran a hand over the empty space beside her and then sat up quickly. Disorientated, she blew the hair out of her eyes and focussed on the clock.

'Shit!'

She'd been hoping to fit in a flying visit to Phil on her way to the city centre. Terry was heading to Derby and this might be her only chance to warn Phil to be careful. She'd never make it now before her appointment. She'd have to go afterwards.

Within twenty minutes she was showered, dressed and dashing down the stairs into the family room. Terry sat at the breakfast bar, newspaper in hand.

'Have you seen my car keys?' Steph asked as she searched the work surfaces.

'What's the rush? What are you going to be late for? Hair? Nails? Spray-tan? Another important meeting in your oh-so-busy life?'

Missing the derisive tone, Steph raised her eyebrows. He must have read her mind. She was off to Powder and Perfume to get her hair done before she went to top up her tan. She splayed her fingers on one hand. Maybe she'd get her nails filed again while she was there. Roberto would always squeeze her in.

'Must look my best at the charity event tonight.' Her voice changed to a whiney tone. 'Do I have to go? Can't you say I was ill or something?'

'No, I want you there. It proves a united front.'

Steph rolled her eyes. Didn't he realise that everyone knew they didn't play happy families behind closed doors? Suddenly she spied the keys in the fruit bowl underneath the apples. What the hell were they doing there!

'I'm going to be so late.'

'You'd better run along, then. It'll take an age to get you looking half decent.'

'Ha, ha. You'd hate to see a white naked butt, or black roots at the top of my blonde hair, though, wouldn't you, Mr Perfectionist?'

She threw the keys in the air and caught them on their descent. 'I won't be long. Shall we do lunch at The Orange Grove?'

'Not today.' Terry checked his watch. 'I won't be back until teatime.'

But Steph was already out of earshot.

Allie slipped a black dress over her head, pushed her arms through and shimmied as it dropped to just above her knees. Visiting her favourite dress shop in her lunch hour felt like a delightful treat as the weather had turned nasty. The rain pelted down outside the Potteries Shopping Centre but Extravagance, which boasted one of the most charismatic changing rooms she had ever been in, made up for it. The walls were coloured with candy pink and white stripes, enough to look stylish but not sickly. A cream leather settee sat against the back wall. Under-floor heating ensured that toes were never cold while trying on strappy shoes.

She looked in the mirror and grinned. The dress was a halter-neck, showing off her shapely back and toned arms, and was low enough to make a statement and not a point at the neckline. It was pulled in underneath the bust and flared out lightly below. Allie held up her hair, stood on her tiptoes and twirled round.

Mary Francis, owner of Extravagance, was busy unpacking shoes from boxes at her side. In her late fifties, she wore a cerise two-piece shift dress and cropped jacket, thick cream tights and matching ankle boots suitable for the cold weather snap they were experiencing. Her immaculate hair was greying and cut in a trendy short, sharp style. Extravagance had been in business for seventeen years now, and was always Allie's first stop. Even though Mary's prices were often steep, Allie rarely made it to many more shops because of her fabulous stock. Besides, she liked having something different that she could wear over and over, despite the extortionate price tag.

'Where is it being held?' Mary asked. 'Tell me again.'

'The Moathouse. It's a black tie event.'

'Well, you keep out of Mrs Ryder's way. She's wearing even higher heels than these and she's bound to be unsteady on them from what I've heard.' Mary held up a pair of black, patent heels with a peep-toe. A slight platform sole would add further inches to Allie's five-foot-six frame – always a good idea as Mark towered over her at six foot one.

Allie had met the infamous Stephanie Ryder on several occasions but had never been to one of the charity events until now. And despite all their intelligence on Terry Ryder, there was no doubt he had a knack of making charity events rake money in by the bucketful. The last event, three months ago, had raised in excess of fifty thousand pounds and had included a live performance by local band Sapphire.

Allie slipped the shoes on, knowing instantly that they finished the outfit.

'Perfect.' She smiled at Mary before swishing the skirt a few times.

'Or I have these.' Mary unwrapped a pair of strappy black sandals from vivid purple tissue paper and held one up. The straps were covered in diamante, the heel still high but black to draw attention to the detail at the front.

'Mary, why do you do this to me?' Allie huffed affectionately. 'You know I can never decide if I'm given two choices.'

Allie came out of the shop twenty minutes later, clutching a paper bag containing the dress and both pairs of shoes – a fair few pounds added to her credit card. She was going to be the belle of the ball. Or at the very least, the apple of someone's eye.

Phil sighed when he opened the door to find Steph standing there just after midday. Christ, if Terry found out she'd been round, he'd be a goner. And she was the last person he wanted to see anyway.

But he knew he wouldn't turn her away.

'Oh, God.' Her eyes widened as she took in his new look. 'What happened to you?'

'Occupational hazard.' Phil cocked a half smile, even though his lip was swollen and cut and he had a huge purple-black bruise on his chin. 'Where're you off to spruced up like a Barbie doll?'

Steph patted her hair – now in a chignon after her visit to Powder and Perfume – as she stepped into the hallway. 'Charity do tonight. Do you like it?'

Phil smirked. You'd think by now he'd be used to Steph turning conversation around to herself.

They made their way through to the living room, Steph chatting ten to the dozen about what was happening that night and forgetting the real reason she'd visited. But after a moment, she stopped. All of a sudden, she felt awkward with him. She stepped nearer.

'What's wrong?' Gently, she touched Phil's lip with the tip of her finger. 'Are you okay?'

Phil wouldn't look her in the eye.

'What is it?' she asked. 'What's happened?'

'Nothing.' Phil shook his head.

She tilted up his chin, careful not to hurt him, and took a closer look. 'Doesn't look like nothing to me.'

'It was only a bit of business.'

Still he wouldn't look at her.

'It was Terry, wasn't it?' Steph gasped. 'Did someone see us together? Ohmigod, I'm so dead.'

Phil groaned as Steph went into panic mode. The last thing he needed right now was her suspecting anything. What Terry had asked him to do was wrong. He had to turn him off the idea.

Get him to change his mind. Because there was no way he could kill Steph.

He reached for her hand. 'It's some bloke I owe money to.'

Steph pulled it away. 'Watch my nails. I've only just had them done.' Then she sniggered. 'Some bloke gave you a beating? You must be losing your touch, old man.'

'Yeah, I must be.' Phil slouched down on the settee. He pretended to watch the lunchtime news on the television.

Seeing his forlorn face, Steph straddled him and put a hand on each shoulder. She could do something that would cheer him up. 'We do need to be careful though, don't we?' She kissed him gently on the lips. 'I mean, if Terry gets wind of anything happening between us,' she moved to his neck, 'we might have to stop seeing each other and,' her hand rested on the buckle to his belt, 'I wouldn't be able to do this anymore.'

'Don't. I'm not in the mood.'

'Precisely why you need something to take your mind off things.'

'No! You're not listening to me.' Phil grabbed both her hands to stop her. 'I said I'm not in the mood.'

'Okay, okay, don't get your knickers in a twist.' Steph sighed dramatically. 'Honestly, I'm only trying to give you a blow job. What sane man would refuse that?'

'It's all about sex with you, isn't it?' He pushed her to the side and stood up.

Steph pursed her lips. She hated it when he went all moody on her. 'Fine.' She got up slowly. 'You let me know when you're ready to see me again, then, huh? Because I can call and see you any time, can't I? Like, it's so easy to get away.'

'Steph,' he cried as she barged past him. 'Steph!'

She stopped at the door and turned back. The pained expression on his face made her relent.

'Terry's next in Derby on Friday,' she told him. 'I'll call and see you in the morning.'

'I have business to sort out then.'

She shook her head. There was no pleasing him at times. 'Fine. I'll see you whenever.'

She was out of the door before he could say anything else. Men! Why did they always think they were so important?

Still, what he had told her about Friday was perfect.

Chapter Six

It was nearing two thirty when Steph finally walked into The Orange Grove restaurant. It had started to rain heavily during the last hour and, mindful of her hair, she quickened her step and almost ran through the door.

The Italian eatery was owned by her friend Carole and her husband Shaun, and had been there for twenty years now. Situated off Piccadilly in Hanley, it was in the city's Cultural Quarter, a pedestrianised area that encompassed two theatres and a museum and tried to encourage its residents to enjoy a little class. Due to the economic climate, The Orange Grove was busy in peaks and troughs. A night out at the theatre could see the restaurant filling up quite quickly after a show had finished. No good acts, however, and the restaurant often had more staff than customers. Lunchtimes were particularly good for trade. Today, though, there were only two tables occupied. A party of six celebrating a fiftieth birthday were finishing a long lunch, and two women laden with Christmas shopping enjoyed a bowl of pasta, red wine and good conversation.

'About bleeding time,' a voice shrilled out.

Steph shook out her umbrella and pulled herself up onto a bar stool at the counter. Shopping bags fell at her feet. 'Chill out, woman. I had an emergency earlier.'

'Your life is one big emergency.' Carole sighed as she slid a glass of white wine over to her. 'I hope you have some gossip. It has been as dead as Barry White in here this week. I can't wait for the panto season to get going properly. December always brings in the crowds. If it wasn't for that, I don't know why we'd bother.'

'Honestly, I don't really know why you bother at all.'

Carole ignored her cynicism. 'Has that bug cleared up that you had?'

'Kind of.' Steph had been feeling off for a couple of weeks. Nothing too serious; sickness for a few days and thick headaches. 'But I've been to see Doctor Turner and he did some tests. I still can't shake it off altogether.' She pulled out a cigarette and stuck it between her teeth. Carole removed it immediately.

'Not in here, you don't.'

'But I need one before I –'

'It has been great since the smoking ban came into force. I can actually smell perfume and aftershave and not have to wipe my eyes all day because they sting. So you're not lighting up in here. Besides, it's the law and you're not getting me a hefty fine and a reputation.'

'I'll stand outside and freeze my nipples off,' Steph snapped. 'That okay with you?'

'Look if you've come here to snipe, then piss off. I'm not in the mood for you and your silly games. I need to –'

'I woke up to find Phil Kennedy in my bed on Saturday morning.'

Carole's eyes couldn't have widened any more if she'd used some mediaeval torture gadget. 'In *your* bed?' she whispered, glancing around madly even though no one was in earshot. 'Jeez. How the –?'

'That's the problem.' Steph sighed. 'I can't remember how he came to be there.'

'You blacked out again!' Carole's tone was accusatory enough without the crossing of her arms to indicate her disgust.

'Yes ... no ... hell, I don't know.'

'Where did you go?'

'The Potter's Wheel.'

'Who with this time?'

Steph raised an upturned hand. 'Is it my fault you let me down so much?'

'I have to work most evenings, remember. Work?' Carole laughed snidely. 'No, you wouldn't remember that now, would you?' She wrung out a cloth and wiped the top of the counter.

'If you can't make it and I want to go out, then I have to make do. I rang Tracy Smithson and she got a babysitter.'

'Tracy Smithson? The last time we saw her you slammed her up against the wall and threatened to bite her ear off if she so much as looked in your direction again.'

Steph snorted as she tapped a cigarette on the packet. 'Did I? I can't remember that either. No wonder she was so quick to get a round in.'

The eldest member of the table of six waved to get attention. Carole glared at Steph before heading over. 'Don't move. I want all the details.'

Steph grabbed the opportunity to go outside for a cigarette. As a double-decker bus lurched past yards away from her, she wondered why she bothered to light up at all. Flapping away the fumes with one hand seemed ridiculous with a fag in the other but she hated the stench of dirty diesel. Greedily, she took another drag and coughed loudly as she choked on it. By the time she regained her composure she had tears streaming down her face. She swiped away at them. Was someone trying to kill her off today?

Seeing Phil look such a mess had really given her the jeepers for a moment back then. But he'd assured her she wasn't involved. Terry had been fine since the weekend and they'd had sex again that morning. So even though Phil had been annoyed with her earlier, she knew he'd keep his mouth shut. He'd be too worried not to.

'Are you okay?' asked Carole as she joined her back inside a few minutes later.

'Only choking,' Steph explained her teary eyes. 'No need to do your agony aunt routine on me. My life isn't that bad.'

'Yes, it is.'

Steph snarled her top lip at Carole before grinning back. It broke the ice enough for them to continue.

'I can't believe you took Phil home with you. Terry will do his nut.'

'Phil won't say anything,' she said, more to convince herself.

'No? You must be mad to think that. He'll be bragging it all over Hanley before you know it. He's been trying to get one over on your Terry for years. Nothing better than screwing the Missus.'

'He won't say anything, I'm sure.' Steph decided to change the subject, although she made a mental note to push the point forward again the next time she and Phil met. 'So, you ready for tonight?'

Carole poured herself a coffee. 'Not really. I can see you are, though. Nice do.'

'Thanks.' Steph patted her hair, wispy tendrils hanging down onto what would become bare shoulders in a few hours. Then she held out a plastic bag decorated with Christmas baubles. 'I have this too.'

Carole reluctantly pulled out a long, red dress. It was strapless with one hell of a side split and she knew it would look fabulous on Steph. She watched her friend, eyes shining like a child's with a new toy, and once again wished she could have half of what she had. Steph Ryder was a lucky bitch.

'You got something new?' Steph interrupted her thoughts.

Carole shook her head, brown curls shaking frantically. 'I thought I'd wear my old faithful dress again.' Besides, she thought, nothing would ever make her look *that* beautiful. She looked away in embarrassment.

Steph immediately took pity, but for the wrong reason. She knew that Carole and Shaun had ploughed so much into The Orange Grove that there was never any spare money. She studied Carole with sympathy in her eyes. Carole was thirty-eight, a month younger than Steph but, to anyone who didn't know her, she seemed far older. Her hair was in need of a good stylist. She wore clothes on her plump frame that had seen better days – white shirt and black trousers – but they were practical for working in, she supposed. Steph glanced down at Carole's feet: she would never be seen dead in flat shoes, especially those.

For once, feeling sorry for her friend, she smiled encouragingly. 'Want to borrow something?'

'No!' Carole cried. She caught Steph's shocked expression. 'I mean, I daren't. What if someone remembers that you wore it first?'

Steph rummaged through some of the bags. 'I have loads of stuff that I haven't even worn yet, silly. A lot of them still have tags on. You should come and see.'

'Hmm, maybe, if I have time later.' Carole looked around, praying that someone would be needing her assistance rather than have to sit here feeling like a failure. But the only two customers left were putting on their coats, having settled their bill earlier.

'Ah, here it is.' Steph undid a bottle top and squirted perfume into the air. 'Smell this.'

'Nice,' Carole commented. 'Beats smelling of garlic all the time. What is it?'

'*Diamonds*,' said Steph. 'Well, they say they're a girl's best friend.' She held up her empty wine glass. 'Any chance of a top-up?'

Carole couldn't hold her tongue any longer. 'You are one ungrateful cow, do you know that?' She leaned in closer and whispered. 'I'd give anything to have what you have and you're prepared to throw it all away for that *freak*, Phil Kennedy.'

Steph shrugged. 'My life isn't all good.'

'No?' Carole sighed. 'Be careful, Steph. Terry won't stand your nonsense forever.'

'Oh, don't mind him. He's a pussycat. He'll do anything for his Stephanie.'

Carole bit lightly on her bottom lip. 'Yeah, right.'

'Go on, spit it out, woman,' Steph urged. 'What are you dying to say?'

'One of these days, you'll get what's coming to you.'

'Yeah, yeah. And I suppose you'll be there to pick up the pieces.'

'What's that supposed to mean?' Carole gulped nervously.

Steph glared at her, the easy nature of the conversation turning sour all of a sudden. 'You know very well what it means. I see the way you look at my Terry. The way you chat and giggle around him. The way you blush and throw yourself at him.'

'I don't do anything of –'

Carole saw Steph's eyes flick behind her.

'Hi, Shaun. Come to give this miserable cow a hand?' Steph stood up and gathered her bags. 'Honestly, she's such a moody bitch. Can't you cheer her up every now and then?' She grinned at Carole to show that she meant no malice and gave her a hug. 'See you later, babe.' She turned back as she got to the door. 'But leave the attitude at home, yeah?'

Chapter Seven

The door bell tinkled and in a flash Steph was gone. Her friend's words still ringing in her ears, Carole gathered up dirty dishes.

'What was she doing here?' Shaun asked.

Carole turned quickly to see him standing in the door frame. 'Showing me what she's wearing tonight,' she said.

'I suppose she came here to gloat. Tell you how wonderful life is for her and Terry. Make us feel like we're pieces of shit. Too poor to be in the same league.'

'Oh, don't start.' Carole's shoulders sagged. 'We're going to The Moathouse tonight, whether you like it or not. All the staff are on rota here and we need to network like crazy. Maybe there's a chance we can get someone interested in investing in the business.'

Shaun shook his head. 'I doubt that very much. They'll all be rich bastards. I bet they won't even talk to the likes of us.'

'Give over and pour us a brandy while I rest my legs for a minute.'

Shaun pushed two glasses up to the optics. Carole joined him at the counter as he placed one down for her.

'How's business been at lunchtime?' he asked.

'Steady.' Carole was glad to see the fight had left him again. 'Not busy, but not empty.'

Shaun sighed. 'Where the hell are we going to get Kennedy's money from?'

'We'll get it.' Carole placed a hand over his and gave it a quick squeeze. 'It's only a matter of time.'

'Time is what we don't have. The business is failing. We're in it up to here.' He patted his forehead. 'If the Orange Grove doesn't start to pick up again soon, we're screwed. We can't even make this month's instalment.'

Carole took a sip of the drink, relishing its warmth as it travelled down her throat. 'Phil Kennedy knows that one word from you about him fleecing the takings from Terry and setting up as a loan shark and he's a goner. So he won't come down heavy on us because if he makes a fuss, then we'll make a fuss, and I'm sure he'd prefer to keep his eyes rather than have them drilled out. Hang on to that thought.'

'Right,' Shaun huffed. 'When Phil has his hands around my neck squeezing my life away? Or when he's tied me to the back of his car and then dragged me all around the city? He's a thug, Carole, and I'm a mug for thinking I could risk everything by going to him for a loan. We should have filed for bankruptcy.'

Carole bristled. They'd worked hard setting up The Orange Grove. Yes, they'd made a few mistakes at first, meaning their debts had spiralled out of control, but things had started to get better eventually. And just as things had begun to get manageable, the bank had refused to provide them with any more finance. All they'd wanted was five grand to keep them in the black for a few more months and they would have been over the worst. Not wanting to show how much of a failure they were, they'd bypassed Terry and turned to Phil Kennedy. Pretty soon it had become clear they'd made a terrible mistake: the five grand had escalated into ten. Last month it had stood at over twenty thousand pounds. And the monthly payments had doubled, taking what little profit they had and more.

'You could always ask Terry for help,' said Carole.

'Are you mad, woman?' Shaun knocked back his drink and slammed the glass down onto the counter. 'He'd be so pissed off with me for going behind his back that he'd do me over in an instant.'

'Of course he wouldn't.' Carole shook her head. 'Terry's not like that. Not with his mates.'

'But I'm not really a mate. I don't even like him that much nowadays.'

Terry Ryder reminded Shaun of everything he hoped he'd be and everything that he wasn't. Now, when they met up, which was fairly regular due to their wives' friendship, it was written all over his face that he endured him. And although Terry was charming with it, he knew the feeling was mutual.

'I'm damned if I do and damned if I don't,' he added. 'My life is over.'

'No.' Carole shook her head again. 'There must be some way out of this mess. We'll think of something eventually.'

After leaving The Orange Grove, Steph arrived home and, armed with a bottle of wine, curled up on the sofa with two slices of cheese on toast.

Although Carole was her friend she'd really got on her nerves today. Sometimes she couldn't stand her constant complaining. She was always going on about how she had it so tough. Steph felt exasperated listening to her at times. She should try keeping up appearances. It was hard work getting tanned, having her hair perfected and her nails redone and shopping for clothes and charity event dresses—and that was without going to the gym to keep in shape.

Secretly, Steph knew Carole only went on like that because she was jealous. They'd known each other since junior school. On leaving high school with hardly a GCSE between them, and after her mum had kicked Steph out because of her anti-social behaviour, she'd moved in with Carole and her mum. Shortly after that, they'd shared a dive of a flat on the Marshall Estate. Steph remembered them being inseparable back then and could clearly recall the night she'd bumped into Terry. They'd been to The Place nightclub in Hanley, long gone now but forever in the memories of some. Steph had been blown away first by his bad-boy reputation and second by his good looks. Back then, his dark hair had been full and cut in a shaggy style. His tall and scrawny figure had thickened a bit but, even now, he was still fit for his age.

Carole had met Shaun a few weeks later but for all their thoughts of double dating, after a few meets it had been clear that the fellas weren't going to get on as well as the girls. But they'd all kept in touch.

To her dismay, Shaun had popped the question to Carole first, but because both of them were working in dead-end jobs, making barely enough cash to live on, they'd had no spare money for a big wedding. They'd married at Hanley registry office and twenty-seven family members and twenty-two friends had walked across to The Albion and taken over the lounge for a wedding meal afterwards.

Steph recalled how jealous she'd felt – and the hideous blue meringue dress she'd been made to wear as chief bridesmaid – and even on the day told Carole that she planned to celebrate in style when she and Terry married, even though he hadn't proposed to her yet. But she could remember in much more detail when, buoyed up by the occasion and the cheap champagne, Terry had dropped to one knee and asked her to be his wife in the middle of their wedding meal. Carole had burst into tears, accusing Steph of hogging the limelight on her big day.

Six months later, Terry had made an honest woman of her. They'd married in St Mary's church in Bucknall and hosted an evening reception at The George in Burslem. There was no four-night stay for her in a tacky guest house in Southport as Carole had had to make do with. Terry had whisked Steph off to Ibiza for a week of sun, sea, sand and what have you.

It was sad to think that Carole had been her only real friend throughout her life. Of course, there were a lot of hangers-on because of Terry's stature. Once he'd taken over after Maurice Sterling died, he'd begun to rake in the money, buying up old terraced houses in the city and over in neighbouring Derby for a few grand at a time, and making a tidy profit on each one as he sold them on. Some of the properties were never touched and still quadrupled in price during the property boom. He'd started to do the same with land, and as for his businesses on the side? Well, Steph reckoned what the police didn't know about was okay with her.

When they'd moved into the house on Royal Avenue, Steph had been thrilled with the envious look on Carole's face as she'd shown her around. Five bedrooms, four bathrooms, three garages, two living rooms and one ornamental pond became their strapline. It spoke volumes. She knew right there and then that she'd made it, especially moving off that scratty estate. Who cared that she wasn't doing anything to make any money? If Terry wanted a good-looking bird on his arm, then that would be her full-time job. But that was when it had all started to go wrong.

Her eyes felt heavy as she tried to concentrate on the television. What was that man going on about on the screen? She grabbed the remote and switched over to another channel. But minutes later, the wine bottle empty at her side, the room began to spin and she closed her eyes for a second.

Waking up with a jolt as she heard a door slam shut and voices in the distance, Steph opened her eyes and tried to focus. What time was it? Shit. She saw Terry throw his keys across the kitchen worktop, glimpsed a pair of black ballet-style pumps. Then a face appeared in front of her.

'Fuck!' she yelled, jumping up quickly. 'You nearly gave me a heart attack, you stupid cow.'

'Yuck.' Kirstie moved her face away as she grimaced. 'You're pissed again.' She picked up the near empty wine bottle. 'Have you drunk all of this in one session?'

Steph snatched the bottle back and immediately wished she hadn't as the room began to spin. She sat still to gain her wits. Glancing over towards the kitchen, she saw that Kirstie was now helping Terry to put a few bags of shopping away. Thank God. Kirstie must have been to Tesco. She'd forgotten to place an order online in her rush this morning.

'I fell asleep,' Steph said by way of explanation when she'd dragged herself over to join them. She pulled herself onto a stool and rested her head in her hands.

'I gathered that much by the state of you.' Terry's tone was accusatory, to say the least.

Steph sighed. Shit, she'd forgotten she'd had her hair done. She didn't dare look at the state it would be in now. Hopefully she'd be able to salvage it later.

They stared at each other for a moment before he turned away.

'Kirstie, get me a glass of water, girl.'

Kirstie ran the cold water, thrust the glass under the tap and then pushed it over to her. Terry opened a drawer and slid a small box of headache tablets along the work surface.

'I can't believe you're drunk again,' he muttered. 'You show me up tonight and there will be trouble.'

'I am not drunk,' Steph corrected him. 'I've slept it off.'

'You're drunk,' he repeated.

'Whatever you say.' She tried to salute him but in doing so lost her footing. Kirstie caught her before she slid off the stool completely.

'Jeez, Mum, you're such an embarrassment. It's barely teatime.'

Steph held on to her head as she tried to support herself on the stool again. 'I must be coming down with something,' she replied. 'I haven't been feeling too good lately. As well as being sick, I'm having headaches. I've been to see Doctor Turner. He reckons they might be hormonal.'

'More likely you were suffering from a hang-over each time,' Terry retorted.

'Don't start on me the minute you come through the front door.'

Terry laughed, and not a happy-go-lucky laugh – more an evil-sick-to-the-back-teeth-of-you snort. As Kirstie left the kitchen area to sit in the family room, Terry grabbed Steph's chin and squeezed it hard.

'Everything I do is for us. I made you but I can break you too.' He snapped his fingers loudly next to her ear, causing her to jump. 'You'd do well to remember that.'

'Don't say that, Tel.' Steph tried to pull away but he squeezed her chin harder. 'Gerroff me!'

'You stink of alcohol. You'd better gargle a gallon of mouth-wash before this evening.' He jabbed a finger so close to her eye she thought he'd have it out.

'I'm sorry,' she managed to whisper. 'I'll make it up to you.' For a second, she thought he was going to hit out at her. Then his grip loosened and he dropped his hand. In a flash, his trademark smile was back.

'No,' he shook his head slightly, 'you'll always be a selfish bitch. There's no way back for you, my darling.'

The chill in his voice matched the foreboding she felt as he turned and walked away.

Steph rested her head on the worktop again, this time too stunned to move. That was the side of Terry that she didn't like. Most of the time she had the put-up-with-Steph-no-matter-what-she-did Terry. Sometimes, like today, Terry showed a glimpse of the man behind the reputation.

But fuelled by the drink, complacency took over. Fuck him, she thought. He was always spouting off that he'd had enough of her, that he was going to do something about it if she didn't buck her ideas up. Didn't he realise that by now she knew they were empty threats?

He'd come around. He always did.

Chapter Eight

Allie fastened the strap on her shoe, stood upright and gave herself a final once-over in the full-length mirror. Realising her sexual allure, she pouted before grinning, loving how the new dress made her feel. She went downstairs, putting out of her mind the thought that she was making so much more of an effort than she would normally do for such an occasion as this.

'Wow, you look hot!' Mark whistled his appreciation when he saw her. He took her hand and kissed it lightly, and then placed it on the bulge forming in his crotch. 'You look that hot!'

Mark was wearing the black suit that she loved, thin lapels and trouser legs reminding her of the fashions when they'd first met. Along with it, he wore the lilac shirt she'd bought for him that morning, black tie fastened in a perfect knot.

'You don't look so bad yourself. The suit, I mean.' Smiling, Allie pulled her hand away before walking off. But Mark pulled her into his arms.

'You don't expect me to waste it, do you?' he complained.

'You can keep it in your pants for now, Mister.' Allie gave him a quick kiss. 'I am not making a mess of my make-up purely to satisfy your needs.'

He slipped a hand up her skirt. 'Dick tease.'

She slapped it away playfully. A horn beeped.

'Saved by the hoot.' She bit his bottom lip playfully. 'But hold that thought for later. Come on.'

Following Mark out into the dark, she caught a whiff of his aftershave and, as he held open the car door, she recalled the night that they'd met. They'd been dancing around each other in Valentino's nightclub, she with a group of her friends, he with a bunch of his. After a few up-tempo beats, the music had changed and a somewhat-worse-for-wear Mark had grabbed her around the waist and pulled her into his arms. A few dances had turned into a few dates. A few dates had turned into a few more and their relationship had grown from strength to strength. Recently returned from university and not at all liking the fact that she was back at home with her parents, Allie had jumped at the chance to move in with Mark. He'd had a small terraced house in Green Street, not far from where she worked at the social services office. Life had been perfect for twenty-one-year-old Allie and not even what had happened to her sister had marred their relationship. If anything it had made it stronger, more reassuring and, well, right.

The Moathouse hotel was situated on the site of the former National Garden Festival Park, now a retail area for the city. Allie loved pulling up outside its grand entrance: it made her feel stupidly regal. And this time of year, both inside and out looked particularly special. A huge Christmas tree sparkled in the reception area, decorations blowing slightly as the doors opened to the outside every few moments.

The chatter of people out for a good time could be heard as Allie and Mark made their way through and into the reception venue. Christmas carols played in the background. Helium balloons bounced around like marionette puppets in the centre of every table, catching the eyes of some of the younger guests. A net attached to the ceiling was full of many more. Red table cloths draped to the floor over twelve round tables; white serviettes popped out of glasses, denoting the colours of the charity logo as well as their premier football team. At the back of the room, Signal 1, a local radio station, had set up their equipment on the raised area, ready to take over once the ABBA tribute band had performed.

Allie glanced around, then spotted a hand waving to get their attention.

'There's Nick,' she said to Mark. 'I'll head over.'

'Suppose I'd better find my team first.' Mark worked for a major UK bank, one of several sponsors for tonight's event. He'd been there for twenty-two years – since he'd left university – and for the last five years had been regional commercial manager. He gave her hand a quick squeeze. 'I'll catch you in ten.'

Allie slalomed through the tables to where Detective Inspector Nick Carter and his wife, Sharon, were seated. Wearing a navy blue suit with a pale grey stripe, Nick stood up to his full height of six foot three as she got to them. In his late forties, he was of medium build with the beginnings of middle-aged spread, with blonde hair thinning slightly at the hairline. He wore a genuine smile that reached his hazel eyes as he leaned towards her slightly.

'I made sure we were put on Ryder's table,' he whispered. 'You never know: one of these days, he might please us and slip up.'

'Yeah, right, and all our Christmases will come at once,' said Allie wryly. She turned to his wife. 'You look gorgeous, Sharon. Good holiday?'

While Sharon enlightened Allie about the delights of Hawaii, more and more people came into the room and soon the sound of chatter was heard above the music. Mark joined them minutes later.

'I see we've been put on the naughty table.' He shook hands with Nick before pulling out a chair. 'To what do we owe this displeasure?'

Before anyone had a chance to say anything, a ripple of applause started and guests began to stand as it reached them. Allie got to her feet but she didn't clap. Mark did. Hypocrite, she mouthed at him.

Terry and Steph Ryder stepped into the ballroom as if the toastmaster had announced the arrival of a bride and groom. A frisson of heat passed through Allie as she caught a glimpse of Terry in his black dinner suit, the cut giving away its expensive price. The white scarf hung strategically around his neck finished off the look. For many of the people present, she was sure he lit up the room far more than his wife.

Steph Ryder, gripping onto her husband's arm, wore a red floor-length dress, the provocatively high side split revealing tanned and toned legs — Allie spied the black strappy shoes and made a note to compliment Mary Francis if they had been her choice. Over the strapless, sequinned bodice Steph wore a white fur shrug, matching gloves completing the perfect Christmas outfit.

'Good evening, everyone,' Terry greeted as he glided over with his wife. As introductions were made, a couple rushing in behind them scurried to their seats, the woman stopping to give Steph a quick kiss before checking place settings and plonking herself down.

'Sorry we're late.' She held a hand to her chest as she caught her breath. 'Haven't missed anything, have we?'

'Only our grand entrance,' Steph replied stonily before sitting down across the table from Allie.

Allie frowned slightly at Steph's tone. She couldn't believe it when Terry introduced the late couple as close friends. She watched as the woman, Carole Morrison, lowered her eyes and fussed in her handbag. She was plump with brown hair, deep red lipstick looking bold but striking teamed with the short, black dress she was wearing. Her husband, Shaun, looking uncomfortable in his suit, sat with a thump. His fair hair was still wet at the collar and he wore a scowl. Allie caught his eye and he gave her a nearly-there smile. *Great*, she thought, *someone who doesn't want to be here. That'll make for a lively atmosphere.*

The small talk associated with that kind of occasion started.

'I asked to sit next to you, Detective Sergeant,' Terry addressed the table once the starters had been served.

Allie nearly choked on her goat's cheese and cranberry parcel starter. She glanced over at Nick, who raised his eyebrows discreetly.

'Yes, I was curious to meet the member of Nick's team who caught the nasty bastard who beat and stabbed his wife to death in one of my properties.'

'It was a team effort, Mr Ryder,' Allie assured him. She took a granary roll from the wicker basket in front of them and broke it in two.

'It was nothing of the sort.' Terry turned his head towards her and smiled, his eyes seeming to drink in her beauty for far longer than was appropriate. 'A team is only as good as its leader. And, please,' he ran a finger along her forearm, 'call me Terry. "Mister Ryder" is far too formal.'

'But Nick is my superior,' Allie replied. 'And this is a formal occasion.'

Terry's laughter rang around the room. One or two people looked over in their direction. 'But you're off duty now, surely?' He picked up her glass and refilled it with wine. 'Unless you're one of those officers who are never off duty? Anyone else need a refill?'

Allie felt as though she had been chastised in the most delightful of ways. She gulped a mouthful of wine as Terry stood up to pour. Mark coughed. She caught his eye, instantly noticing his discomfort. But there were also heated glares coming from Mrs Ryder. Allie continued with her food, grateful that they were all eating so that the conversation would be short.

But Terry continued after he was seated again. 'Dreadful business.' He shook his head. 'I can't believe it happened in Georgia Road. It goes to show that no matter how hard you vet tenants you can often miss some important details. To think that I housed a murderer ... Well, it shocks me. Saddens me, too.'

Allie swore inwardly as she listened intently to his speech. She felt like clapping her hands afterwards. It sounded like every word had been rehearsed. She just couldn't work out why he was doing it for their benefit. He knew as well as she did what the police force thought of him, despite hiding behind a charity bearing his name that offered treats to vulnerable people.

'It was quite nasty, by all accounts,' Carole added to the conversation.

'I believe so,' said Nick. 'I was on holiday when it happened.'

'Maybe she had something to do with it, though. They say there's no smoke without fire.'

'Carole!' Steph cried. 'How could you say that someone deserves to be murdered? You always have to lower the tone, don't you?'

'I didn't mean to.' Carole put down her cutlery. 'I think there are two sides to every –'

'If you can't say anything interesting, then zip it.'

'Do you always have to be nasty to my wife?' said Shaun. It was the first time he'd spoken since they'd arrived. 'You could do with zipping it for a change.'

Steph huffed. 'I was only saying –'

'Well, don't.'

'Children,' said Terry, his warning tone evident.

'Do you always have to show me up?' Carole snapped at Shaun, a blush rising from her chest.

Allie and Mark exchanged glances as an uncomfortable silence descended.

'I hope he gets what he deserves in prison.' Steph seemed determined to get in the last word. 'She must have been in some pain during that attack. And,' she turned to Terry as she picked up the wine bottle after knocking back in one what he'd just poured, 'despite my husband's praise....' She then turned to Allie with a look of pure poison, '... How long was that sort of thing going on that you lot should have dealt with, rather than let a so-called domestic get out of hand?'

At the mention of pain, Allie paled. She looked down at her plate, trying to calm her breathing as Karen's battered face swam before her eyes. She'd been fifteen minutes late – that's all.

'I'm sure we did everything we could, Mrs Ryder.' Nick sensed Allie's discomfort and tried to take the heat off her. 'Sometimes we offer help and get it flatly refused. These things are always easier to blame on the police. But sometimes we have to walk away and, unfortunately –'

'Some sick fuck murders his wife.' Steph filled her glass again. 'Yeah, I get it.'

But Terry took it from her. 'That's enough for now, my love.' He smiled sweetly at his wife. 'We don't need talk of doom and gloom on a night when we should be celebrating.' He stood up, threw his napkin onto the table and rubbed his hands together in excitement. 'Talking of which, let's get some pockets emptied before they serve the main course.'

Spying a chance to escape, Allie excused herself and headed for the sanctuary of the ladies' toilets. Once in there, her breathing became laboured and she tried to calm the panic. *Pain.* One word. That was all it took, and it felt like yesterday that she'd learnt the terrible fate of her sister. Karen had been twenty-five, four years older than her, when she'd been raped, beaten and left for dead one winter evening. Her attacker had never been caught and even though she'd known it wasn't her fault, Allie still carried the guilt round with her. It was hard not to. Even after fourteen years.

After a few minutes, she pulled herself together and emerged into the corridor to find Mark seated on a leather couch. His look of anxiety had her eyes filling up again. She dropped down next to him.

'Are you okay?' he touched her arm gently.

She smiled, thankful for his concern. 'Yes, I'm good.'

'Do you want to go home?'

Allie knew how important this event was for Mark's employers. There was no way she would slope off due to the taunts of a drunken woman. And besides, Mark had made it perfectly clear over the years that the career she'd chosen would always bring back memories. He'd said so during many a heated discussion.

She shook her head. 'No, we'll stick it to the end.'

'Are you sure?' Mark kissed her lightly on the tip of her nose. 'Because I'm happy to leave. That Ryder bloke is getting my back up. He can't keep his eyes off you.'

Allie gently squeezed his thigh. 'It's business chat, that's all.'

'Yes, but –'

Allie pressed a finger to his lips.

The rest of the evening went as uneventfully as it could, seeing as one of the hosts became more inebriated and could hardly stand by ten o'clock. Steph held onto her husband for dear life as first the auction was held and then the raffle was drawn. After the main course came the awards for the year's best fund-raisers and then a few tear-jerking awards to children of courage. Finally, after a dessert of champagne ice cream or Christmas pudding, the formal part of the evening was brought to an end with a round of applause for the Ryders, a huge bouquet of Christmas flowers for Mrs Ryder and an explosion of applause to make ears ring as the balloons were released.

As the merriments went on around them, Terry only had eyes for Allie. It became so obvious that Mark threw quite a few sarcastic remarks over in his direction. So it was a relief when it was finally over and they could say their goodbyes. Before the band had belted out the first line of 'Waterloo,' Mark had marched off.

'What's up with him?' Sharon asked Allie, oblivious to the atmosphere at the table. 'He's usually a good laugh. Did you two have a row before you came out tonight?'

Allie smiled faintly at her and Nick. 'Actually, we didn't.' She raised her glass in salute before knocking back the last of her drink. 'But it looks like that will probably change before the night is out.'

She said her goodbyes, all the time feeling Mark's stare as he waited for her by the door. She'd hardly got to it as he pushed her out into the foyer.

'What's wrong with you?' he snapped.

Allie's feet were aching in her new shoes. She could hardly keep up with his pace but for the grip he had on her arm.

'I could ask the same of you,' she said through gritted teeth.

'What do you mean? I wasn't the one who was getting leered at.'

'I wasn't getting leered at. I told you. It was –'

'I don't know how you –'

'Going so soon, Sergeant?'

They turned swiftly to find Terry striding towards them. He held out his hand, first to Mark and then to Allie.

She smiled as she met his eye. 'Yes. Early start in the morning, I'm afraid. But it was a lovely evening. Thank you for the invitation.'

Terry held onto her despite the glare he was getting from Mark. 'And Mark, did you enjoy the evening too?'

Mark turned on his charm as if he had an invisible button to do so. 'Yes, it was an excellent event, thank you. I do hope the sponsor did a great job for you too.'

'Absolutely.' Before he had finished the word, Terry's eyes had already returned to Allie.

'Can you order a taxi for me, please?' Mark asked the receptionist.

'There's no need for that,' Terry exclaimed. 'I can give you a lift.'

'Thanks, but we can get a –'

'I won't take *no* for an answer.' Terry clicked his fingers at a guy sitting on the sofa engrossed in a Mark Billingham paperback. 'You can use my car and driver.'

'Thank you,' said Allie quietly.

'Thanks again for coming and have a safe journey home.' Once more, Terry's eyes lingered on Allie before he burst into laughter. 'You'd better have a safe journey home with my driver. If anything were to happen to you—now, that would be a crime!'

Allie smiled and turned away quickly to follow Mark's disappearing form.

Mark had left the outside light on while they were out so that at least the house was welcoming on their return. Allie thanked the driver as he pulled up outside their home. She raised her eyes to the sky as Mark got out of the car before it was properly stopped. Watched him stride up the path, his shoulders hunched, ready for a fight.

He left the front door open for her and continued through into the kitchen. Allie closed it quietly and reached down to her feet, slipping off her shoes. Sighing with relief, she walked through to him.

Mark went to speak, then shook his head. He opened the fridge door.

Allie was astonished. 'Surely you're not hungry after all that food?'

'I could have choked on mine the way that Ryder was gawping at you.' Mark pulled out a bottle of lager and slammed the door shut. 'By the look on his face, he wanted you for his dessert. Laid out on the middle of our table. I was half expecting some waitress to appear with a bowl of strawberries and a can of squirty cream.'

A delicious memory of her and Mark and a lazy Sunday afternoon came to Allie's mind but she brushed it aside.

'Don't be ridiculous.' She sighed. 'The man's a charmer. He rakes money in for charity by being that way.'

'His wife was a right bitch, too.' Mark flicked off the bottle top. 'God knows how much wine she knocked back. I suppose that came out of the charity pot as well!'

Allie rubbed at her neck and sighed. 'Let's not do this now. It's late. We're both tired and we'll end up saying things we regret.'

'It was wrong, Allie. And you made me feel like you were his for the taking.'

'I never did!' Allie retorted. 'You know my role. My boss was there too. I have to keep him sweet.'

'He's one of the biggest crooks in Stoke!'

'*We* know that. That's why we're investigating him.'

'Oh, right. And you're doing that under his watchful fucking eye?'

Allie sighed. Booze talk. 'I'm going to bed now. Are you coming up or are you staying downstairs in a strop?'

Mark glared at her. What was it with men tonight, giving her the eye? Terry Ryder's flirtatious manner had nothing to do with her. She hadn't been comfortable with his actions either. He could have been a little more discreet in company but she wasn't going to let that spoil her night.

'The guy's a creep!' she added. *Although he does have the most amazing eyes.* 'And it wasn't my fault that we had to sit at his table.'

'Table?' Mark balked. 'I'm surprised he didn't pull you into his lap!'

Allie turned and left the room.

'Grow up, Mark,' she snapped. Then, before she realised how childish she was acting, she switched off the light and left him in the dark.

Chapter Nine

The next morning, Steph woke alone with yet another headache. She rummaged around underneath the mattress until she found the bottle of whiskey tucked away. Well, hey ho. Hair of the dog. She slugged back a massive swig and wiped her mouth with the back of her hand. God, there was nothing that tasted quite so good.

Her eyes focussed on the clock. Half past ten. She hadn't even heard Terry get up. She wondered where he was as she pulled herself out of bed, back first, followed by lolling head.

Shit, she felt rough. What the hell had gone on last night? Walking across the room like an extra from a zombie film, she negotiated the bathroom and flopped down onto the toilet. Every muscle in her body ached. As she ran a hand through luggy hair, she noticed the beginning of a bruise on her thigh. She prodded it. Ouch! *Stupid cow*, she chastised herself. It looked sore enough to hurt without testing it.

What day was it? Tuesday? Wednesday? What the hell had she got up to get a bruise like that? She grimaced. More to the point, who would tell her what she had got up to? Because for the life of her, she couldn't remember. She tried to cast her mind back.

Had she visited Phil first thing or was that the day before? Either way she couldn't recollect if they'd messed around or if she'd only called to pick up more booze. Oh, yes, it was coming back to her. He'd been in a mood because he'd taken a thumping off someone. Well, she'd sort out that when she next saw him.

Steph got such a kick out of having an affair with Phil. On several occasions, she'd thrown herself at Shaun, Carole's husband, but it had all been in vain. No matter how many times she'd cornered him, pressed her body close to his as she rubbed at his balls through his trousers and tried to kiss him, he hadn't been persuaded to try out the rest. Still, his loss, she reckoned.

Thinking of sex was making her horny and her head wasn't up to it. She ran her hands over her face and then spotted her red dress, crumpled up in the corner of the bathroom. No doubt she'd left it where she'd struggled to get out of it before staggering to the bed and passing out last night. She groaned loudly. The Moathouse – last night, the charity event. Oh, God, she'd screwed up again.

It all came tumbling back then: insulting the Mayor and his wife in front of their daughter and son-in-law; falling down on the dance floor and having to be hauled to her feet by Carole; cursing loudly when the deejay refused to play any more records because it was late. She remembered puking up in the car park. Oh, God, she remembered it all now. And wished that she hadn't.

Head in her hands, she started to cry, big fat wails of self-pity. Despite all the beauty treatments, even she knew she'd let herself go over the years as the drink took hold. Alcohol had turned out to be her closest friend. Even this early in the morning, she had to taste it. There was nothing like it for her, not even sex, as much as she liked that. It was all about the buzz, the confidence it gave her, the memories it blocked out. Yes, she craved it but she relished losing herself more. It was a never-ending circle. The life she led wasn't worth being a part of on some days.

Finally, after showering and dressing, she dragged herself downstairs. She opened the study door but the room was empty. Terry must have gone out earlier. Kirstie would be out at college, too. Thankfully, she had the house to herself.

As ever, Terry's desk was tidy, neither a scribble on the jotter pad nor a pen sitting on it. The chair was pushed under the desk just so. She ran a finger idly along its surface as she moved past it, relishing the silence in the house as her head pounded.

Through the window she noted his car had gone and that, weather-wise, it was another depressing day. God, she hated winter. It would be December in three days, time to start thinking about Christmas again. Shivering slightly, she pulled her cardigan closer around her. Looking down, she spotted a single piece of paper crumpled up in the waste bin. She fished it out and straightened it on the desk. It was a yellow Post-It note. There weren't many words written on it but it was certainly Terry's handwriting.

It read *20k – this Friday.*

Steph paused. There wasn't anything she could deduce from that limited amount of information. She wondered how long it had been there. Twenty grand? What was that referring to? Could this Friday have been last week, meaning that's why the note was in the bin? But Jeanie had cleaned in here earlier that week, surely? The only time she didn't get into the room was when Terry was working in there and didn't want to be disturbed.

Through the open doorway, Steph jumped as she saw what looked like the figure of a man.

'Oy, you!' She peered around the door into the hallway but there was no one there. She paused. Was her mind playing tricks? No, she had definitely seen someone.

Grabbing the baseball bat from behind the study door, she raised it high and barged into the family room. Lee Kennedy was on his knees but he stood up quickly. Kirstie, who was by his side, let out a shriek.

Bat held high, Steph paused as she took in the scene before her. Lined up on the coffee table were two rows of cocaine, cut and ready to use. Lee had a rolled note in his hand. She watched him wipe evidence away from his nose.

'You stupid bastard!' she hurled at him.

'Fucking hell, Mum!' said Kirstie. 'Put that down!'

'What are you doing home today? You should be at college.' Steph glared at Lee. 'And what the fuck are you doing in my house? You've been told to stay away from her.'

'No, I haven't. Your old man told her to stay away from me. No one told *me* anything.'

'He's my boyfriend, Mum.' Kirstie stood up and moved to his side. She took his hand. 'Now, put down the fucking bat.'

Steph frowned. Was Kirstie really going out with Lee? She searched her brain for clues. Memories. Anything to make sense of things. She remembered Terry going ballistic when he found out that she'd dated him and telling Kirstie to end it. But she'd just said that Lee was her boyfriend. If he was, then Terry must know about it. Which meant that she should know about it too. Jeez, her mind was well and truly mashed.

Still hanging onto the bat, she shook her head as she spotted the lines again. No, Terry would never allow that. Not in his home. He might deal in drugs but they weren't welcome here. And hadn't Terry warned Phil, too, to keep his son away from Kirstie? So what the hell was he doing providing her with cocaine? In an instant, she blamed Lee for everything and charged towards him.

'You sneaky bastard!' The bat came down on top of the coffee table. The lacquered glass shattered, spraying tiny diamond particles into the air, a white puff appearing for a moment. Kirstie screamed as she moved away. With all her might, Steph pulled the bat up and, ignoring the particles digging into her bare feet, ran at Lee.

Lee had seen some wild women in his time, but Steph Ryder was by far the craziest. No wonder Terry had turned on the mad bitch.

'You're scum, you are!' Steph yelled. 'You have no right to be here with your filthy habit, Kennedy. Fuck off out of here, NOW!'

'Mum!' Kirstie tried to pull her away. But Steph was too strong. She hit out again. Lee retaliated in the only way he could.

'Back off or I'll spill everything.'

Steph stopped, bat in the air.

'Spill everything about what?' asked Kirstie.

'She knows what I mean.' Lee stared at Steph, glad to see that he had the upper hand for now.

Steph stalled as she caught her breath. She might be bottle blonde but she wasn't stupid. As far as she was aware, no one else knew.

Unless Phil had told Lee.

Or had Lee seen them?

Or maybe he was calling her bluff?

'Will someone please tell me what the fuck is going on?' Kirstie cried out in exasperation. 'You come in here wielding a baseball bat, smash up the table and then turn on Lee. But just as suddenly, you let it go?'

'I don't know what you're talking about.' Steph decided to shrug the comment off. She dropped the bat back down to her side.

Lee smirked. 'That's much better, Mrs R.'

'Get out of my house.'

'No fucking way!' said Kirstie. 'This is my house too and I'm not going anywhere until you tell me –'

'Want me to tell your dad what I saw you snorting up your nose?'

'You wouldn't fucking dare!'

'Try me. See what cock and bull story you can come up with. There were two lines, Kirstie. I'm not blind.'

'No, you're fucking stupid,' said Lee. When Steph glared at him, he shrugged his shoulders.

'You're the stupid one,' she told him. 'You brought it in here.'

'Prove it.'

Steph paused, her breathing rapid as she fought to control her temper. She knew that Kirstie would be in deep shit if she said anything to Terry. So what if she didn't have the evidence? That wouldn't make a difference to him. Not where Kirstie was concerned.

Lee took the silence as his cue to leave. He touched Kirstie's arm. 'Come on. Let's get out of here and go back to my place.' His eyes never left Steph's as he continued. 'Finish off what we started.'

'Over my dead body,' Steph told him.

'That can be arranged.'

Kirstie stood between them with arms open as Steph came towards Lee again. 'Stop it!' She turned to Steph. 'You and me, Mum, when I get back, we need to talk.'

Steph roared with laughter. 'You and me, talk? I don't think we have anything to say to each other that would make a difference.'

'You're ill. You need to see a doctor. This isn't rational fucking behaviour!'

'And snorting white powder up your nose is?'

'You owe me for the white stuff,' Lee said before they left the room. 'I haven't finished with you yet.'

Steph ran at them again but they were out of the house before she had time to react. She could hear them laughing when she stopped suddenly as the pain registered. Her feet were bleeding, crimson teardrops sprinkling the flooring. She pulled up one foot and winced as she retrieved a large shard of glass. Seeing the blood drip onto the floor was all it took for her to start wailing again.

It had been two days since Phil had taken a beating from Terry. Still pissed with him for lashing out, he was waiting for his brother's mate, Kenny Webb, to arrive. When Steve had rung from prison after hearing about the murder of Sarah Maddison, Phil had been only too pleased to spell out what had actually happened.

It had been late on a Wednesday evening. Terry had called half an hour earlier to go over some jobs with him. Andy Maddison had knocked on his front door in a mad panic saying he'd killed his wife.

Terry had told Phil to get rid of Andy while he dealt with the situation. But as soon as Terry was out of earshot, Phil had told Andy to sling his hook and lay low. There was no way he was letting him into his house with her blood all over him. He might have incriminated him for something he hadn't been part of.

With Andy gone, he went to see what damage had been done at number fourteen. He got there just in time to see Terry plunge a knife into Sarah Maddison's stomach. Apparently he'd been after a reason to get rid of them both as they were bringing the police to the row too much with all their domestics.

Both clever enough to be wearing gloves, Terry gave Phil the knife and told him to get rid of it. The rain pouring down should have removed anything else, especially as Sarah Maddison had been left in it all night.

Everyone knew there was no love lost between Terry and Steve Kennedy. For the past twenty years, they'd been vying for top dog status in the city. Revenge eating at him, building up every scrap of evidence against Terry had become Steve's mission while he was locked away. Even though the knife hadn't got Terry's fingerprints on it, he'd wanted it anyway.

But it had been with Phil for a week now. With the police so close by, already he'd moved it to three different places as he'd waited for Kenny to collect it. Now it was tucked away in the cellar.

Yet, even eager to get rid of a murder weapon, Phil couldn't stop thinking about the job Terry had lined up for him. He sat in his living room staring into space, the television switched on to some daytime dross. He wasn't watching it. He wasn't even listening. He was still trying to get his head around stuff.

Every now and then he'd take a sip of beer, going over and over the conversation with Terry. 'I want you to kill Steph,' Terry had said. At first Phil thought he'd misheard him. But when Terry repeated it, Phil was sure his heart had stopped for a second. 'You want me to kill Steph?' he'd managed to say, sounding like a parrot. 'Yes, and I want it done this Friday night' had been Terry's blunt reply.

Blood had still been dripping from his lip as he'd listened to Terry running through all the details. After the initial shock had worn off and been replaced by fear he'd realised that, despite his earlier thoughts of him finding out about the affair, Terry must have been planning this for some time.

He took another swig of his drink, wondering if he'd ever have any luck with women. After a failed marriage to Sandra Unwin, Lee's bitch of a mother who had left them both when Lee was seven, Steph had been the only woman whom he'd cared about since. Of course there had been other women – still were, if you counted the young pup who'd given him a shag in exchange for a fix the other day. Jackie Stanton had been the longest to stay, lasting three years before moving out of Stoke when he'd given her one backhander too many. She was a mouthy cow, knew how to wind him up in a flash. She'd deserved what she got.

But Steph had always been around, for as long as he could remember. In the early days, he would see her with Terry in the pub or on a night out. In the latter years, since Steve had been sent down, he'd seen her more frequently, been there to pick up the pieces after her latest fall-out with either her husband or her daughter. It wasn't as if they'd planned an affair. Like many budding friendships, a shoulder to cry on had blossomed into something more. For Phil, it had blossomed into much more. But he'd managed to keep his feelings to himself. He wasn't even sure that Steph knew exactly how he felt about her.

Could Terry have found out about the affair? Steph hadn't seemed to think so when she'd called round yesterday. But this could be his way of punishing them both. Phil cast his mind back, trying to remember when Terry had last lashed out at him. It had been years. And all he'd done was make a joke because he'd been so nervous about Terry knowing where he'd slept the night before, and with whom.

But the real thing he was worried about, that he kept coming back to, was that maybe Terry was planning on setting him up. He wouldn't put it past him to see that he got caught in the act. Yet if he didn't do the job, Terry had made it perfectly clear he would suffer. He'd never said anything like that before – was he calling his bluff?

His phone beeped. It was a text message. Phil cursed as he read it. Kenny couldn't make it today but he'd get to him by the end of the week. And he wanted him to move the knife outside, somewhere he could pick it up whenever he was passing. Damn, he'd have to move it into the outhouse.

He lit another cigarette and glanced at his watch. Fuck, he'd been sitting here for over two hours. Still nothing had become any clearer. Did anyone owe him a favour? Was there anyone he could trust enough to do the job and keep their mouth shut? He trawled his mind for possibilities. Was there anyone willing to do it for a small fee? Or even a large fee, as long as he didn't have to do it? Did anyone owe him a lot of money?

Phil's brow furrowed as an idea came to him. Maybe there was a way he could buy some time.

Chapter Ten

Later that evening, Phil pulled up his collar and threw his cigarette butt to the floor. He stood across the road from The Orange Grove, hidden in a shop doorway. Having the advantage of looking in from the dark, he could see Shaun Morrison coming and going through the large glass window that ran the length of the restaurant. He'd wondered whether to go in but didn't want to draw attention to himself. His nosy bitch of a wife was always moaning about something.

He checked his watch: quarter past five. People were starting to leave for the day from offices and shops nearby. He'd wait another fifteen minutes and then he'd ring the number printed in white letters on the canopy above the window. From his position, he'd be able to see who answered the phone.

But several minutes later, Shaun emerged from the building with two cardboard boxes and loaded them into the boot of a blue BMW parked outside. Rushing over, Phil dropped a hand on the man's shoulder and saw his expression change in an instant.

'I need a word. The Reginald Mitchell, fifteen minutes,' Phil told him sharply before turning and heading into the town.

Next to Waterstones book store, The Reginald Mitchell was housed in what used to be the old meat market. Phil had worked there as a butcher's boy when he was sixteen for a few Saturdays. He remembered clearly the rows and rows of traders, the smell from the stalls, the noise as the men competed with each other to sell their cheapest cuts, the sound of the blade slamming down into the carcass of a pig. Even a glimpse of an uncooked steak or a raw chicken could make him retch now. Often a memory flashed back as soon as he opened the door but The Reginald Mitchell was a good local meeting place.

He took the few steps down to the ground floor. It was a few moments before his eyes adjusted to the gloom but he could see the pub was pretty full. Upstairs a few people sat around the balcony, some enjoying a meal. Downstairs the bar was being propped up by the town's regulars. Young men who hadn't started their working lives through choice stood red-faced with pints in hand; older men who had worked the pots or the pits, the steel workers and the locals, told stories of better times as they knocked back cheap ale. Occasionally a woman would join them, usually dragging some unfortunate away by the ear after one hour too many.

Phil ordered a whiskey chaser. He chose a vacant table tucked away in a corner but where he still had sight of the door. Missing the cigarette he couldn't have due to regulations, he took a large gulp of lager and wondered if Shaun would show. Minutes later, he saw him push open the door and glance shiftily around the large floor. When Shaun spotted him in the far corner, he came over and sat down.

'What's up?' Shaun fidgeted with the black beanie hat he was wearing, pulling it down slightly at the front before he sat down. One side of the collar on his leather jacket was tucked inside the lapel. He was out of breath but he took only a moment before speaking again. 'I can't be long. I have a business to run.'

'Your payment's overdue.' Phil didn't hesitate to get things going.

'You said I could pay double next month!' Shaun protested in a loud whisper. He looked warily over his shoulder, as if he was being set up.

'I changed my mind. I want a grand by the end of the week.'

'I don't have it!'

'I suggest you get it.'

'And how the fuck do you suggest I do that?'

'Call Mr Bank Manager.'

'Don't you think I've already tried that?' Shaun ran a hand through his hair. 'Look, can't you wait until next month? The panto season started last week and we usually rake in a lot from that. I can square up with you in the New Year and try to keep the rest of the payments a bit more regular.'

All the time Shaun spoke, Phil never moved a muscle. It was a trick he'd seen Terry use: put the other person on edge. It worked. Shaun's colour drained. He sat forward, folded arms resting on the table.

'There is another solution.' Phil knocked back the whiskey in one go and put the glass down onto the table with a grimace. 'You could do a job for me.'

Two elderly men walked towards them and then sat down at the next table, shrugging off coats and hats.

Shaun gulped. 'What kind of a job?'

Phil chewed on his lip while he paused. Was he really wise to trust someone who was as close to Terry as Shaun was? His wife and Steph were good friends. What happened if he mentioned it to her and she told Steph? It could all go tits up before it had started.

But seeing no other way out of this, he'd have to chance it. He glanced around again before continuing. The two men next to them were huddled over their pints. Now Phil moved closer to Shaun.

'A hit,' he said.

'What kind of hit?'

Phil sighed. 'What kind of hit do you think I mean, you fucking idiot?'

Shaun's eyes widened. For a moment, Phil thought he was about to leg it. Then he sat forward.

'You mean you want me to *kill* someone?'

'Yeah.'

Horrified but curious at the same time, he asked, 'Who?'

Phil leaned closer and whispered. Shaun stood up so fast that the stool toppled over. The two men on the next table turned their heads quickly. As more people started to look, Shaun stood there until he was old news. Then he picked up the stool, sat back down.

'You can't be serious, man.'

'I'm deadly serious.'

'But I can't do that.'

'One hit and I'll wipe it all out. All twenty grand.'

'But, I've ...' Shaun lowered his voice. 'I've never killed anyone. I wouldn't know how to.'

'I can sort that.' Phil knocked a third of his pint back.

'You make it sound so fucking easy.'

'It is. You do the hit. I'll clear your debt. Simple.'

'Not from where I'm sitting.' They sat in silence for a few seconds before he spoke again. 'I can't.' Shaun shook his head. 'I can't *kill* someone I know.'

'It's your choice.' Phil shrugged before standing.

Shaun was looking pretty sick now. Sweat trickled down the side of his face; his hands had a slight shake. He caught Phil's eye for a moment and looked away.

'I have a choice, then?' His voice sounded weary.

Phil didn't reply. He still wasn't sure this was the wisest thing to do. If he didn't kill Steph, Terry would come after him. But he could take a beating knowing that Steph would still be there for him. Maybe then Terry would forget the whole thing. But for that to work he had to blag himself more time.

He finished the last of his drink and breathed in noisily. 'The job needs doing on Friday night,' he said, seeming not to have a care in the world. 'I'll call again on Friday morning. Go over the finer details.'

'No!' Shaun stood up as Phil walked away. All eyes fell on him again as he shouted after him. 'I didn't mean ... wait!'

But Phil never looked back.

As all around him the punters became merrier, Shaun sat in a daze. Usually when he could spare a night out, he and a few mates would head to The Reginald Mitchell with its cheaper ale and clientele. It would always be their first port of call. He'd started many a good night off in there. The last half hour had tarnished that completely.

An elderly couple asked if the rest of the seats at the table were free. Shaun nodded. He was next to a roaring fire: who was he to begrudge their warmth by hogging the table? As they plonked down a shopper and a few carrier bags, he thought about getting blotto and drowning his sorrows. But he knew the problem would still be there and he couldn't face sobering up to it. Besides, he needed to get back to work once he had his wits about him again.

Fuck, he was in it up to his neck. He couldn't kill Steph – hell, he couldn't kill anyone. What kind of man did Phil think he was? Sure, he was desperate but a killer? No way! It wasn't as if he'd done it before and could get psyched up to do it again when the occasion arose. And what about Carole? He couldn't keep something like this from her. They'd never had secrets in their marriage, not in twenty years. How could he not tell her what Phil had told him to do?

But Shaun could never tell her this. Carole hated Phil, and the fact that he'd scammed them, and that there was nothing they could do about it. Shaun had known when Phil gave them the five grand that he'd probably increase the money each week, making sure they couldn't pay, and landing them in even deeper trouble. If he told Carole, she'd be on the phone to Steph in an instant. Imagine how Phil would react then. And Terry – what would he say? More to the point, what would he do?

Shaun choked back vomit as he wondered how he'd be expected to carry the hit out. Run her over? Stab her with a knife? With a screwdriver? Punch and kick her until she was a pulp? The thought of it turned his stomach and he came over all dizzy. He had to get out of there.

He rushed over to the door and barged through it. Bent over at the knees, he breathed in the air outside like a deep-sea diver with an empty tank. Shit, this couldn't be happening. What was he going to do?

Straightening up at last, he made his way back to the restaurant. With four weeks to go until Christmas Day, there were reams of shoppers hoping to grab an early bargain. As he negotiated his way down through Fountain Square and across Stafford Street, Shaun wondered if he was about to lose his sanity as well as his business.

Back in The Reginald Mitchell, above where they'd been sitting, Lee leant on the balcony and watched Shaun leave minutes after his dad. From his vantage point, he had seen most of the meeting but he couldn't tell if the job had been agreed or not. Although, from Shaun's reaction, it was clear to see that he hadn't taken the conversation lightly.

He took a large swig of his pint. Shaun Morrison wouldn't have been his first choice for the hit but he knew his dad must have a good reason. And Shaun might not be the only person he'd put forward for it. Phil might have chosen a few people to vet. He might even leave it until the last minute so that no one got wind of anything, so that it couldn't be fucked up at the eleventh hour.

Not certain that he'd got the right man, Lee decided to continue trailing his dad and bide his time. See who else he met over the next day or so. Quickly, he finished his drink and legged it back to his car.

In Werrington, Mark parked up in the driveway at home and sighed long and hard. After a successful meeting had turned sour right at the end, he needed to let off steam. Allie would be home soon to hear him out; he knew she'd make him feel better about things. When she wasn't on a case, she loved to smooth things out for him, talk negatives through to positives.

He locked his car and looked over its roof towards where he heard a high-pitched voice shout out.

'Yoo-hoo!'

Mark watched his neighbour, Mrs Simpson, rush up the driveway as fast as her arthritic legs could carry her. If she hadn't been holding a flower arrangement, he might have been tempted to pretend not to hear her. Mrs Simpson had lived in the house next door for over fifty years, the last eleven as a widow, and was the best neighbourhood watch lookout anyone could wish for. Trouble was, she was the best gossip, too, and was forever pushing herself into people's houses to get the latest low-downs.

Mark put on a false smile as she got to him at last.

'Flowers, Mark. For Alison.' She smiled with thin lips, eyelids covered with the brightest of blue powder. 'They came this afternoon but as you weren't in, I offered to keep them until you were.'

'Aw, thanks, Mrs Simpson.' Mark took them from her, wondering for a moment who they could be from.

'Special occasion, is it?' Mrs Simpson asked as he moved towards the house.

Mark tapped his nose with his finger twice. 'Now that would be telling. Bye, Mrs Simpson, and thanks again.'

Despite her protests, he went inside, closing the door with a smile. He could imagine what would be all around the street by tomorrow morning: he and Allie could be expecting a baby, he and Allie could have won the lottery, he or Allie had been promoted again and could be moving out, not good enough for the likes of everyone else living here.

But as he placed the flowers down on the table in the living room, something began to gnaw at him. It was 28 November. He hadn't forgotten anything that he was aware of. Their wedding anniversary was in summer. Allie's birthday was in March. It wasn't a date he associated with Karen.

He picked up the small envelope nestled in the arrangement. Despite his unease, it wasn't his to open. And besides, he had a fair idea who the flowers were from. There had been only one man eyeing his wife up the night before. One man who'd made it perfectly clear that he would have preferred to have Allie on his arm rather than his drunken excuse for a wife.

Thinking of weddings and faced with flowers, Mark cast his mind back to their own big day during the summer of 2001. Allie had taken his breath away as she'd walked through a gathering of their friends to where he was waiting, awestruck by her beauty and the fact that she was to become his wife. She'd worn a floor-length sheath of ivory silk that had made his heart race and started a familiar unfurling in his groin as she'd given him the special smile that said she was totally in love with him. They'd taken ages to choose the right setting for the reception, at last deciding on a country hotel they'd stayed at when they'd first fallen in love. The day had been perfect and he'd loved every minute of it. He'd held her close, never wanting to let go.

He slumped down into the armchair with his thoughts. Sharing her now with another wasn't part of the bargain. But maybe this was something and nothing. Maybe it was someone from work who had sent them. Sam maybe; she was always thoughtful. He really hoped so.

It was nearing six thirty when Allie got home after her shift. She smiled when she saw the outside light on and the curtains drawn. Good, Mark said he'd be home early tonight. She'd popped into the supermarket to get a piece of steak and a bottle of red. After last night's antics, she fancied chilling out tonight.

'Honey, I'm home,' she shouted through from the hallway in a comical fashion. But by the time she'd hung up her coat and emptied the bag of shopping, Mark still hadn't shown his face. Frowning, she went through to the living room to investigate.

Mark sat upright on the settee. He still wore his work suit, his pale blue shirt open at the neck, his tie hanging loose. The television was on but although he was staring at it, she could tell he wasn't watching it. His face was like thunder.

'What's up?' she asked, placing a hand on his upper arm.

Without looking at her, he threw a thumb over his shoulder. Allie twirled round and saw a large display of flowers in the middle of the table, standing in their own water container.

'They're not from me,' Mark spat out.

Obviously.

He handed her a small white envelope.

'Oh,' was all she managed to say. Allie turned it over, thankful that he hadn't opened it. Then again, she didn't want to open it either. She had a sinking feeling about who they would be from. But Mark was looking expectantly at her now. Heart in her mouth, she opened the envelope and slipped out the card.

'Lovely to see you again last night, Allie. Thank you for your delightful company, as always. Terry Ryder.'

Allie held in her fury as well as her shock. Terry Ryder knew that sending them would get her into trouble. They were a spectacular array of festive flowers in colours of red, gold, green and white. She looked at them briefly, picking out red roses, white carnations, holly and pine cones. The florist, Fresh Bloomers, was one of the most expensive in the city.

'Are they from him?'

Mark still wouldn't look at her.

'Him?' she asked.

'That Ryder bloke from last night?'

'Yes, they're from him.'

'What did he mean by seeing you again?'

Allie picked up the arrangement and left the room. Mark followed her out into the back garden. She lifted the lid of the bin.

'You're not going to chuck them away!' He spoke as if it were a baby she was throwing out with the bath water.

'Of course I am,' she replied. 'He had no right to send them.'

'That would depend on what the flowers are for.'

'Mark!' Allie felt a tremor run through her at his tone.

'You have to admit, he was a little too friendly last night. So what did you do to deserve them when I wasn't there?'

'But you were there!'

'I was with my boss for twenty minutes. That was ample time for you to ...'

'That's a great accusation to come home to.' Allie banged down the lid. 'Please tell me you're drunk.'

'I'm stone cold sober.'

Ouch.

'He's playing games.' She touched him lightly on the arm. 'He wants you to react like this.'

'But he knows where you live, can't you see? He has the upper hand!'

'I don't believe we're having this conversation!' Allie stormed back into the house. Of all the things to come home to, this would have been right at the bottom of the list. What was that man playing at? She hadn't encouraged Terry Ryder in any way. And if she had, she wouldn't have got away with it. Not with his bitch of a wife giving her the evil eye for most of the night.

'Allie! Wait!' She heard Mark shout behind her.

She was halfway up the stairs before he caught up with her.

'I'm sorry,' he said. 'But you have to see it from my point of view. If he is playing around, then I feel threatened by it.'

Allie stopped mid-step. She sighed and turned back to face him. He looked so miserable. How long had he been home alone after the flowers had been delivered? How long had he sat in that chair imagining all sort of things? This was madness. Her sweet husband was hurting so much because of someone else's petty actions. She had to put a stop to this.

'Mark,' she spoke quietly. 'Do you trust me?'

'Of course I do. It's him that I don't trust.' He looked away in embarrassment.

'You don't *have* to trust him. Look at me. Look at me!' Allie tilted up his chin so that she could see him properly. 'I love you. I want to be with you and no low life loser like Terry Ryder is going to stop me from doing that. Okay?'

Mark gave a slight nod of his head.

'Now, I have some down time tonight and I want to enjoy it with my man. I don't want to worry about a pesky bouquet of flowers that should never have been delivered. What do you say?'

Finally she saw the tension leave his face. He smiled. 'I'll start on the steaks while you shower. Unless you'd like soaping down....'

Allie managed a smile back. 'Steak. I'm ravenous.' This time she did kiss him.

Going through to the bedroom, she removed her jacket and flung it on the bed. In her haste, she snapped at the buttons on her clothes as she fought to undo them. Naked in record time, she dashed into the shower and scrubbed at her skin, wanting to release the iciness crawling through her veins.

So that's why he had run after them last night, in the disguise of offering a friendly lift. He'd been after their address, the sneaky bastard. She knew it had been a bad idea but hadn't wanted to give the game away that he was under suspicion, that they were watching him.

What was he up to? Was it harmless fun or something more daring that he was after? She let the water run over her head as she struggled to comprehend what he was playing at. Or even what his motive was.

One thing she knew for certain. No one was entitled to mess with her marriage, or her feelings. She'd have to be very careful around Mr Ryder in the future – even though her thumping heart was telling her different.

Chapter Eleven

'Don't you think the world is in enough of a mess without all these threats of cuts and job losses?' Steph said between mouthfuls of food as she tucked into her lunch. She and Terry were at The Orange Grove for a pre-arranged Thursday get-together with Carole and Shaun. Three of their staff were on hand to wait on the owners for a change – something that Carole enjoyed.

Shaun was in an even more unresponsive mood than usual. Carole had tried talking to him earlier but he'd told her to leave it alone, said he wasn't feeling well. She knew there was no point delving any further when he shut himself off like that.

'It's enough to make someone kill themselves,' Steph continued. 'I mean, if I had to work for peanuts and was then told I'd be losing my job – which would result in me losing my home and everything I own in it – I think I'd prefer to hang myself. Leave everyone else to take the flack for it and watch from up there.' Steph pointed her knife up to the ceiling, opened her mouth to speak again and then stopped. 'What?'

Terry burst out laughing. Carole followed suit. Even Shaun sniggered. Steph sat still, waiting for the laughter to subside so someone could share the joke with her.

'What?' she repeated when no one did.

'You are such a card.' Terry wiped his mouth with his napkin before picking up his glass. 'You've never worked a day in your life, never mind had to pay for a mortgage, household bills and things for the kids. You have no idea what a modern couple would go through.'

'And how can you say that killing yourself is an easy way out for anyone?' Shaun joined in.

'Yes,' added Carole, hoping that the others hadn't noticed his harsh tone. 'It's not a clever idea to get yourself out of the shit and then leave everyone else behind to clean up the mess for you. It's really selfish, if you ask me.'

'I wasn't asking you,' snapped Steph.

'But then,' Terry spoke before Steph had the chance to let rip, 'Steph is nothing but selfish. Isn't that right, *darling*?'

Steph gave her husband a tight-lipped smile. 'Yep, that's me. Selfish Steph.'

Terry grinned at her. 'That is so funny. No, really. "Selfish Steph." Now, why didn't I think of that one?'

As Carole joined in with his laughter, Steph got to her feet and grabbed her handbag. 'Need some air,' she muttered before storming outside, practically knocking over the poor waiter who had come to collect the dishes.

Dragging heavily on a cigarette went some way to calming her down, but inside Steph was fuming. Why did they always have to have a go at her? If it wasn't about her opinion, it would be about what she was wearing. About what she had been doing.

Still, at least the meal was free as Carole and Shaun never let them pay. And Steph always made sure she drank lots for that reason too.

She sighed loudly. Usually she enjoyed their lunches, even though Shaun was as moody as ever. But, for once, she'd like to have a laugh with people who weren't laughing at her, who weren't mocking her.

She huddled in the doorway, the rain pouring down outside, dark clouds matching her mood. She hitched her bag onto her shoulder and, in a moment of anger, walked away to join the throng of shoppers. Fuck the three of them: if they wanted to be petty about things, then so could she.

———

After a brisk walk into town, she soon realised it had been a bad plan. With the wind blowing the rain into her face, she stopped off at Walkabout and ordered a double vodka. Two hours later, with a few more inside her, she made her way back.

The restaurant was empty apart from the three of them by now. Terry was laughing at something that Carole was saying, their heads bent together in conversation. Shaun was wiping glasses behind the bar. Jeez, he looked more miserable than when she'd left.

'Well, well, well.' Terry laughed snidely. 'The wanderer returns.' Steph walked past him but he grabbed her arm and pulled her onto his knee.

'You're drunk,' she told him, smelling alcohol on his breath.

'I've only had a whiskey with my coffee, my love. *I* can always stop at one, not like you. Did you buy anything? Maybe something to wear before you hang yourself?'

Steph's body tensed as he and Carole began to laugh. 'Don't start again,' she said. 'It wasn't funny the first time.'

'Get a grip, Steph.' Terry pushed her off his knee. 'You harp on about shit all the time and we sit back and take it. Actually, we've had quite a nice lunch without you running someone or other down.'

Steph leaned forward and poured a large glass of wine. Then, as the background music came to a finish, she filled the silence.

'For your information, dear husband,' she stared at Terry and then pointed at Carole, 'and yours, I had a far better time walking around the shops on my own than sitting listening to you three going on about your businesses and how much money you're making and how everything is hunky-dory in your lives.'

'Don't make me laugh.' Carole folded her arms. 'Our lives are as far from hunky-dory as they are happy ever after. I'm sick of you insinuating all the time that we have money to burn. We don't. In fact –'

'That's enough, Carole,' Shaun's raised voice reached them.

Carole turned to him and sneered. She'd wondered where he'd sloped off to the minute Steph had gone off in a sulk. He glared back at her but, spirit boosted by the wine, she didn't care.

'Someone needs to tell her that things don't only go wrong in Steph Ryder's world.' She pulled herself to her feet. 'Someone ought to tell Steph Ryder that sometimes this friend of hers would like to have a shoulder to cry on instead of listening to *her* woes all the time. Not that she has any woes worth listening TO! Her woes are whether or not she has enough whiskey to keep her occupied for the next few days and whether she has enough fags to choke herself on for the next few days.'

'I beg your pardon!' said Steph.

'You don't care about your family,' Carole continued. 'You have a lovely daughter that you don't give a stuff about. You have a beautiful house – sorry, *mansion* – that you don't care about. You're not even grateful that you're fed and clothed and looked after by someone else. And it's crystal clear that you don't care about him, either.' Carole nodded her head in the direction of Terry. 'All you care about is yourself!'

'Ladies,' Shaun came over then. 'I think you both ought to calm down.' He turned to look at Terry who was clearly amused by the scene in front of him. 'You need to take her home.'

'Giving orders now, are we?' He didn't even look up as he got out his phone.

'No, I –'

Terry ordered a taxi as the two women squared up again. He sighed loudly afterwards. 'Funny how alcohol can change the mood of any happy occasion in the blink of an eye. Come on, Steph. Let's go. We've obviously outstayed our welcome.'

Carole sat down now, the bravado she'd felt earlier disappearing quickly. She rarely fell out with Steph to this level. They had words all the time because Steph always had to be right, or share a heated opinion that had to be agreed to. But Carole, like now, usually backed down. Steph when she was miserable was bad enough. Steph when she was angry? Sometimes Carole couldn't cope with her.

The room was silent except for the music that had started up again in the background, the atmosphere in minus degrees. They heard a horn peep outside.

'Come on, drunkard,' said Terry, taking Steph's elbow.

'I'm not drunk.' Steph shrugged his hand away.

'Yeah, like you haven't been into a pub and knocked back a couple. Let's get you home to sleep that off.'

'Home to bed with you?' Steph's mood changed in a flash. She grabbed Terry's crotch playfully.

'Christ, will you listen to her,' Carole muttered.

Suddenly Steph launched herself across the room. Shaun put an arm in front of Carole and took the brunt of her slug. Terry grabbed Steph around the waist.

'What is wrong with you?' he cried as he pulled her towards the door. 'This is going too far again. What did I tell you the other day?'

Long before the taxi pulled up in the driveway of The Gables, Steph knew she was in for a tongue-lashing. Terry hadn't uttered a word to her all the way back. Once at home, he marched into the house. She dawdled behind him but as soon as the front door was closed, he spun round to face her.

'You are despicable at times,' he screeched. 'How I keep my hands from you, I don't know because I could fucking KILL you right now.'

'I'm sorry,' she said.

'I won't stand for it.'

'Look, I've said I'm sorry. What more do you want from me?'

Terry pushed her away and headed for the stairs. 'It's not me you should be apologising to. I'm not the one you launched yourself at. It's a good job I held you back.'

'You know I'd never intentionally hurt Carole. I –'

Terry started to walk up.

'I'll change.' Steph tore after him. 'I promise. I'll dry myself out. Clean myself up. I will!'

Terry shook off her arm as he went through into their bedroom. He removed his jacket and placed it neatly over a chair. Steph hung back in the doorway, afraid to go in, in case he started on her again. She hated it when he was like this, when he took the moral high-and-mighty because he was right.

Terry slipped off his shoes and moved to the wardrobes. He pulled out a clean pair of jeans and cast his eyes over his shirts before pulling out a white one.

'You're not going out again?' Steph moaned.

'I have to sort out number fourteen.'

'But I've hardly seen you this week!'

Terry rushed across the room and grabbed her arm. 'Have you any idea what happened to Sarah Maddison before she died? She was beaten up and then stabbed. Maybe I should do the same to you.'

Steph looked into his eyes, her fear reflecting in his anger. Panic began to build up inside her.

Then just as suddenly, Terry released his grip and moved away.

'You've pushed me to the limit, Steph.' He whipped off his shirt and threw it into the washing basket. 'You're out of control and you could cause me some serious damage by shooting your mouth off. So for your sake, take that as a warning.'

Once in the bathroom, Terry banged his fist into the middle of a stack of fluffy white towels. Again and again. Grabbing Steph around the neck had been stupid. One mark on her, along with a phone call to the police from a pissed-up wife, and his plans would be scuppered. If the police got wind of anything untoward happening in the lead-up to her death, then he could become prime suspect. He wouldn't have that. She'd ruined his life for as long as he could stand it.

While Terry took a shower, Steph curled up on the bed and cried into her pillow. Her life was going from bad to worse. It was okay for Carole to mock her that afternoon but, really, she knew that everyone hated her. She was screwed, in more ways than one if her visit to Doctor Turner revealed what she thought it might do now that things were more evident to her.

The thought that Terry would throw her out didn't often surface but when it did, she always remembered the snide remarks at the party for their last anniversary. No one had thought they would last one year, never mind two decades. She knew they all wondered why Terry stayed with a drunken bitch like her when he could have his pick of women. And she knew there'd been other women. He was Terry Ryder, the charmer.

But he was also Terry Ryder, the crook. She knew that the police were looking into him and his associates. Occasionally, he'd get a phone call from one of the car washes saying they'd been raided after an anonymous tip-off. They'd never found anything concrete yet because the main business was over in Derby but there was always the possibility that one day someone would slip up. And the authorities were bound to know what went on at Ryder's Row. One day Terry would get his come-uppance and then all this would be hers. After all, it was in her name.

She glanced over at the wardrobes. There were only three people who knew about the compartments hidden away in there. Terry would go mad if he ever found out that she'd let it slip to

Carole one night. But she knew her friend would keep it to herself. No one would ever find them if they didn't know they were there. She wondered....

Terry came out of the bathroom. She watched his every move as he packed an overnight bag and zipped it shut.

'I'm sorry, Tel,' she whispered.

But he walked out without a word.

'Terry,' she screamed after him. 'Terry. Terry!'

Chapter Twelve

On the last day of November and the final morning of her life, well over the downer of yesterday, Steph went to the city centre to do some shopping. Her phone was glued to her ear as she dashed across Stafford Street, heading for Powder and Perfume. She'd snapped off a nail last night when she and Terry had been fighting. But she needed to make up with Carole first. The problem was, Carole wasn't making it easy for her.

'Come on,' Steph pleaded as she walked along the pavement. 'I am sorry. Truly I am.'

'You're always sorry. Empty words, coming from you.'

Steph sighed. 'You know how I get when I've had one too many.'

'So what makes you think that I'd want to go out with you tonight? You'll get pissed again and I'll get insulted again.'

'I'll pay for it all.'

'As if that will tempt me.'

'I will.' Steph raised a hand in thanks at the driver who had stopped so that she could cross over Percy Street. 'I'll even treat you to a curry, if you fancy one.' Silence on the phone. The doorbell tinkled as she entered the salon. 'You still there, girl?'

'Of course I'm still here.'

'Well, what do you say? A night out, all expenses paid and a curry thrown in too. Terry will be over in Derby and even though he might make it back and you know I'd want him all to myself then,

I'll let you kip over at mine and take you home in the morning. Save you forking out for a taxi.'

The silence was still there but a little shorter this time.

'Okay.'

'Great!' Steph grinned, even though her friend couldn't see it. 'I'm having my nail refixed and I want to look for a pair of heels to go with that top I bought last week. I'll ring you later, yeah?'

She disconnected the call before Carole had time to respond. Roberto, the salon's owner, bustled over and dropped into the seat next to her.

'Oh, will you look at the state of you,' he cried out, touching her hair. 'You are going to get these done today? Those roots are so no-no, darling.'

Roberto was slightly on the small side, but what he lacked in height he made up for with flamboyance. His clothes were loud, his jeans were tight and his tattoos colourful. People in the city waited weeks to see him, if they could get in at all due to his top-notch prices, but he'd always squeeze Steph in. Always make her feel like a million dollars, even if he couldn't always make her look like a million dollars.

Self-consciously, Steph ran a hand over her hair. She'd looked at it this morning and thought the dark brown roots were showing a little too much. 'I thought it might wait another week, Roberto? I've come in with a snagged nail.'

'No, no, no!' Roberto pulled her to her feet and clicked his fingers. 'Clara. Clara! Miss Stephanie needs a-fixing.'

Steph smiled gratefully. At least she was treated with respect here!

———

As soon as she'd put down the phone, Carole dreaded telling Shaun of her plans. She knew he wouldn't be too happy after yesterday's fiasco. He'd had a right go at her once the taxi had taken their friends home, saying that she'd be a fool if she ever spoke to Steph again. But Steph was trying to make amends by offering to pay for her and she really could do with a night out, a night away from The Orange Grove. Living above the business had its disadvantages as well as its advantages.

She decided to wait for the last of the midday rush to go. Leaving Stacey, one of the waitresses, in the empty restaurant setting up the tables again, she went through to the kitchen. Shaun was getting things ready for the evening session, preparing salad vegetables and fresh dough for bread and pizza bases.

'Are you mad?' He stopped slicing as soon as she told him. 'Surely you haven't forgotten what she said to you yesterday?'

'Of course I haven't,' Carole replied curtly. 'But you know Steph. She's all mouth and she has apologised.'

'You're so gullible.'

'I just want to get out and have a laugh, that's all.'

'She was downright nasty yesterday. Or have you forgotten that too?'

Carole hadn't forgotten. Every word of the disagreement was still etched at the front of her mind. But the bonus side of it happening was that to make it up to her, Steph had invited her to stay over at The Gables. With a bit of luck, Terry would come home. Spending a few moments with him was worth a night listening to Steph's moans and groans. Better still, she might get a bit of time alone with him in the morning before coming back here. Steph always lay in bed after a session.

'No, I haven't forgotten.' Carole moved past Shaun to unload some of the plates from the dishwasher. 'But you know Steph. Once she's sobered up, she's all sweetness and light. She'll –'

'Steph Ryder will never be sweetness and light,' Shaun broke in.

'Maybe not, but she's footing the bill because she was so awful to me. So it's a win-win situation. I get a night out and it's all on the house.'

'It's Friday and we need you here.'

'It's one Friday night and we're only going into town for a couple and then back to The Potter's Wheel. There's an Elvis tribute band on.'

The door behind them opened and Stacey popped her head round. 'Someone to see you, Shaun. Phil Kennedy?'

'What the hell does he want?' Carole looked at Shaun, who had paled in a flash. 'It isn't time to pay him yet.'

Shaun ignored her as he went through to the restaurant, hoping that Phil wouldn't let it drop that he'd seen him on Wednesday. Carole followed close on his heels.

Phil sat down on a stool by the bar. Unshaven with a tatty scarf around his neck and wearing an old Donkey jacket, Carole thought he looked more like an old tramp than a man Steph would want to bed.

'Chuck us a whiskey over,' he said without looking up at them. 'It's fucking freezing out there.'

'We weren't expecting you.' Carole's tone was icy.

Shaun shot her a look that clearly said *shut up*. She raised her eyebrows questioningly at him.

'I thought I'd pop in and have a quick chat with Shaun about business. You don't mind, little lady, do you?'

Carole hated it when he patronised her. She would never see what Steph saw in him, especially as she had Terry to go home to every night.

Shaun tapped a measure into a glass from the optics and slid it over. Phil knocked it back in one, slamming the glass down. He smacked his lips as the warmth trickled through him. 'That's much better.' He caught Carole's eye. 'I'll have a coffee as well, darling. And make it strong.'

Carole was about to shout Stacey over when Phil raised his hand to stop her.

'Can't you take a hint, you stupid bitch? Get lost.'

As Carole sloped off, Shaun perched on a stool next to Phil, dreading the start of the conversation.

'So,' Phil's eyes flitted across to him, 'that job we spoke about the other day?'

'Yeah, I wanted to talk to you about –'

'No time for talk.'

'But I don't know the slightest thing about –'

'Keep your voice down,' Phil cautioned. 'We don't want that wife of yours getting a whiff of any scandal, now, do we?'

Shaun wondered if the only scandal would be a report of his death sprawled all over the front page of *The Sentinel*. He could see the headlines now – 'Local Man Found with Throat Cut.' Or worse. He'd probably just disappear, never to be heard from or seen again. That's how Phil Kennedy usually worked – so he'd heard.

But despite his anxiety about his life being over, he had to tell Phil the decision he'd come to.

'I can't do it.'

Phil turned towards him slightly. 'You sure about that?'

'I –' Shaun faltered. 'I've never done anything like that in my life.'

A silence fell between them.

'Fine,' Phil spoke at last. 'Get me my money and I'll be on my way.' He smiled at Carole as she joined them again.

'There's nothing like a fancy cup of coffee on a chilly November Day. Biscuits too. You spoil me.'

Carole put down the tray, laden with three cups. 'May I join you?'

'You really are a pushy one.' Phil looked up at her. 'This is business talk.'

'But this is my business, as well as Shaun's!'

'There'll be no fucking business if you don't sort out some cash for me soon.'

'Why don't you take yours upstairs?' Shaun urged, knowing that Phil could spill everything to her in seconds. 'Once I'm done here, I'll come up to you.'

'Yes, run along, that's a good girl.'

After telling Stacey to keep an eye on things, Carole stormed upstairs, looking over for one last time as she climbed. How dare Kennedy dismiss her as if she were a five-year-old child and needed to go to bed! She was a partner in this business too. Both their names were on the lease of the shop; both their names were on the business loan they were struggling to make payments on. But neither man so much as glanced at her. Men! If they thought they'd got the better of her, then they were wrong. She slammed a door then tiptoed back across the landing and sat on the top step, out of view but hoping to catch some of the conversation.

As soon as Carole was gone, Phil grabbed Shaun's wrist. 'So what's it to be then, Morrison?'

'I can't. I've never killed anyone,' Shaun whispered, his face ashen. 'I can't do it to order. And not to someone I know.'

'Look, it's simple.' Phil gripped him harder. 'You do the kill and I'll wipe out your debt.'

Shaun couldn't say he wasn't tempted. To have twenty grand cleared in an instant would be a godsend to him, and to Carole. To get Kennedy off his back would be an even bigger relief. They'd be able to enjoy the business, run it how they wanted, hire more staff so that they could spend more time together instead of one of them upstairs while the other worked downstairs. Maybe they'd be able to rent a place to live in and extend the business like they'd planned to do eventually.

But to kill someone to erase that twenty grand? No, killing wasn't in his blood. Hell, fighting wasn't. Shaun prided himself in being a fair-natured man, level-headed, good to have as a friend.

And what about Terry? Where did he fit into all this? Occasionally he'd heard about him doing his own dirty work but, more often than not, he'd get someone else to do it. That's why he was involved with the Kennedy brothers. Phil and his brothers had a reputation for doing as they pleased. Steve was doing time for murder, a fifteen-year stretch. Phil had been banged up several times but for the past few years had stayed on the outside. Terry seemed to trust Phil far more than he did Shaun, so why wasn't Phil carrying out the hit? He should never have taken the money from him. Damn the recession affecting their business. They should have sold up and cut their losses. Because right now he was so far up to his neck in shit that he wondered if he'd ever get out of it.

His eyes flitted briefly around the restaurant, the business they'd built up from scratch. They'd wanted it to feel like eating outdoors as much as possible but there was a sense of space as well as privacy if required. They'd thought that getting everything done high spec would bring more custom. The ambience had been just right, plus great Italian dishes with no one nearby to compete with. It was their dream – still was their dream. He couldn't let it go in an instant – could he?

'Supposing I did pull it off?' Shaun pinched the bridge of his nose and blinked slowly. 'How would I do it?'

Phil took a flick-knife from his pocket.

Even though they had their backs to the room, Shaun still looked over his shoulder. The restaurant was empty. Stacey had gone through to the kitchen with the last of the dishes. He picked the knife up and turned it over and over. His stomach did the same thing.

'Twenty grand, gone in a second.' Phil clicked his finger. Shaun jumped at the sound it made next to his ear. 'And all this could be yours again.'

He looked up to see Phil twirling round, waving his arms. Then before he could react, a finger was shoved in his face. 'You do want this business of yours to be a success, don't you?'

Shaun put down the knife. 'I can't kill for it!'

'You can and you will.'

'No!'

Phil grabbed him by his collar and pulled him closer. 'Do I have to make myself clearer for you? Either you do the job or your business will go down, one way or another. And you will go down with it.'

'Does Terry know about this?'

Phil stumbled for a fraction of a second before gaining his composure again. 'Of course he does. What do you take me for?'

'I need to talk to him first.' Shaun shook his head. 'He wouldn't allow this to happen. I can't do this on your say-so. I can't!'

'Look, just fucking do it! OKAY?'

As Phil's face reddened enough to erupt, Shaun felt close to tears as his world fell apart around him. If he did the job, Terry would probably kill him. If he didn't do the job, Phil would be after him. Maybe he'd give him a sickening reminder to wake up to every morning too, like a finger cut off with a serrated knife or an eye burnt out with a hot poker. Maybe he'd shoot his knee-caps away. Maybe he'd shoot Carole too or maim her in some way. Shaun had read about what happened to Sarah Maddison. He knew Andy Maddison would never do that to his wife – he, too, was a coward. Someone else must have been involved and he wouldn't put it past Phil Kennedy to have carried out something as atrocious as that. He ran his hands over his head. What a mess.

'If I did it, how would I go about it? I mean, where do I aim for? What's the best ... the best place ... to ...?'

'The best place ...' Phil stumbled over his words too. He cleared his throat before continuing, this time with authority.

'The best place is always the heart. But I doubt you'll be able to do that, sweet boy. You do what comes naturally.'

'Naturally?' Shaun saw Stacey emerge from the kitchen. In a fit of panic, he slid the knife up the sleeve of his jumper. 'How the fuck does murder come naturally?'

'I want it done by the morning.' Phil let go of Shaun's collar and pushed him away. 'You do the job, ring me the minute you've finished and I'll clean up the mess. No one will be any the wiser. Except for you and me.'

'And if I can't?'

'Ever seen how quick a fire can take hold of a place like this? And the damage it causes? I reckon thirty seconds would be enough to get this building going. Maybe you'll both be asleep upstairs? Who knows when I'll strike?' Phil glared at him. 'But one thing is for sure. I will strike. So either you do the job tonight or ... boom!' He raised his hands and spread his fingers out as if he were throwing out glitter. Then he walked out of the building without another look back.

As soon as he'd gone, Shaun felt that familiar build-up of saliva in his mouth. Breaking out into a sweat, he shivered uncontrollably. He raced across to the gents' toilets, dashed into a cubicle and threw up into the bowl. Wiping his mouth, he slid down the wall, head in hands, into a heap on the floor.

What the hell was he going to do now? There was no way he could kill Steph.

But what if he didn't? Would Phil really go through with his threat to burn the place down with him and Carole inside it?

Maybe he should go to the police. Not the done thing – grassers were really the scum of the earth – but was it his only choice? Then again – would they listen to him? Kennedy could deny it all because nothing would happen unless Shaun took action. And then he would be in deeper shit than he was right now.

He couldn't go to Terry either, no way. Terry would find out he'd been borrowing money from Phil and not paying it back. As dire as the situation was, he'd hate to owe money to him: he had ways and means of getting it. If Shaun thought Phil was menacing....

And which one of them had actually ordered the hit? Did Phil plan to get one over on Terry by wiping out his wife? Or was Terry somehow behind this, getting Phil to do his dirty work for him? Maybe Phil didn't want to be responsible in case Terry regretted it later. Shaun had heard stories and seen war wounds of men who had crossed him before.

He checked his watch. Three fifteen. Fuck! He had less than nine hours left of this day before Phil would know that he couldn't do it.

He couldn't!

Even though it wasn't much more than a minute's walk from Piccadilly, Phil knew he wouldn't make it back to his car, which was parked just off Broad Street. As he passed The Potteries Museum and Art Gallery looming up on his left, he darted down the steps from Broad Street and hid underneath the split-level entrance on the floor above. Amongst the grime and layers of dirt from the street, he started to shake profusely. A film of sweat built on his top lip. As a rush of nausea surged through him, he placed a clammy hand on the wall for support and threw up.

Once the sickness had passed, he sat on the curve of the wall. Head in his hands while the bitter wind blew above, he closed his eyes momentarily. But all he could picture was Steph's face. Tears poured down his cheeks and he wiped at them fruitlessly.

Had he gone too far back there? All that stuff about burning the building down. Would it have scared Morrison too much? There was a fine line between lying and being found out. But he'd had his reasons. He'd had to make it seem realistic despite not wanting Shaun to go through with the hit. Shaun would never have the courage to put a knife through someone's heart – especially someone he knew – if he'd never killed before. It was the best place Phil could have told him to attack – such a hard thing to pull off. Much easier to go for the inside groin, far less personal. Oh, God. He ran a hand through his hair and glanced upwards.

Housed over three floors, the museum told the story of an inventive and industrious city, famous for the creation of some of the best ceramics in the world. People from all over the country still came in droves to admire the Staffordshire Hoard, but none of that interested Phil in the slightest. The only treasure he was interested in was Steph.

The brakes of a bus squealing as it stopped at a junction brought him back to reality. He stood up quickly and made his way the few hundred yards to his car. Once inside he lit a cigarette, taking a deep drag to calm his nerves, and prayed his plan would work. He needed to relax until tomorrow, knowing that he'd done what he'd set out to do. With more time for Terry to get used to the idea that the hit wouldn't be carried out, he could set himself up for the inevitable beating coming his way. There was always a price to pay for going against Terry Ryder's wishes.

From the same shop doorway that his dad had hidden in two days earlier, Lee watched Phil disappear around the corner on to Piccadilly. His suspicions confirmed, he lit a cigarette and took a long, deep drag.

This was turning out to be far better than he'd imagined. He'd expected someone much harder than Shaun Morrison to be lined up for the job. Someone who would kick the shit out of him if he demanded money to cover something up. But Morrison? Lee knew he'd come from the Marshall Estate and had known Terry since school days but that was all he'd ever heard about him. His name was clean. As far as he knew he hadn't been locked up for anything. Then again, neither had Terry Ryder. But Morrison had been close enough to be Ryder's right-hand man. So why wasn't he? Something must have gone wrong. He must have bottled something in the past.

Lee finished his cigarette, chucked the butt to the floor and walked back to his car. He wasn't about to bottle it. He had plans to make for tonight.

Trying to piece together the snippets of conversation she'd over-heard, Carole stayed put at the top of the stairs as she saw Shaun dash into the toilets. She hadn't managed to hear much but what she had convinced her there was something going on. Phil had mentioned tonight, and she'd heard him going on about the money they owed. And something had definitely spooked Shaun. Even from here she could hear him throwing up. She went downstairs.

'Shaun!' She knocked on the cubicle door. 'Shaun, what's going on?'

'Nothing. I came over a bit dizzy, that's all.' Shaun opened the door. He walked unsteadily over to the sink and splashed his cheeks with water. 'Daren't say that the soup's off,' he said, trying to make a joke.

But Carole wasn't in the mood for games. 'Whatever he wants you to do, you mustn't –'

'Were you listening?'

'No,' she lied, hoping her expression wouldn't give her away. 'I'm really worried about you. I hate Phil Kennedy and I hate the situation we're in. That bastard has got us eating out of his hand.'

Shaun managed to keep the shake from his voice as he looked back through the mirror at her. 'I'm okay.'

'You sure?'

'I'm sure. But I don't want you going out tonight, do you hear?'

'Something *is* going on,' she cried. 'Tell me, Shaun.'

Shaun paused while he thought of what to say. 'It's nothing. I'm not feeling well and I might need you to –'

'Oh, I get it. This is all because I'm going out with Steph. That's all you think I am, some sort of skivvy. Well, I don't care if you're *dying* on your feet tonight, I'm going out.'

'Carole!' he shouted as she stormed out. 'Wait!'

Fuming, Carole slammed the door on his protests and left him to it. She knew there was no point talking to him when he clammed up. This had nothing to do with her going out tonight. This was all down to Kennedy's visit. The fact they didn't want to include her in any meetings or conversations set her mind racing. But she knew the best thing for now was to keep quiet and let Shaun think things through.

Because something was going on.

———

After a successful shopping spree in the Potteries Shopping Centre, Steph drove to Georgia Road. Not wanting to draw too much attention to herself, she left her car in the next street and ran across to number two.

Even though Phil had told Steph that he'd be out, she banged hard on the front door several times just to make certain. Then she raced around to the back and did the same on that door. When she was convinced there was no one in, she shouldered open the door to the outhouse and searched out the light switch. Pulling on a length of cord revealed no power. She cursed and pushed open the door to let in as much light as possible.

Originally an outside toilet, the cistern had long gone and it was now full to the brim with half-used tins of paint, paint brushes stuck in cans of turpentine, tools and boxes. A pair of stepladders and a rickety ancient Black and Decker Workmate stood in front of an old wooden dresser. Careful where she was treading, Steph climbed over a pile of house bricks and pulled open the second drawer of three on the dresser. Grimacing, she felt about inside it until her fingers curled around a hard, sharp object wrapped in something soft to the touch. She gripped it and pulled it out. Heart racing, she unwrapped a piece of towelling cloth to find what she had come for.

Quickly she covered it up again, put it away in her handbag and legged it out of the back gate.

Chapter Thirteen

Later that afternoon, Steph took a sip of wine and relaxed back in the warm water. She twirled the bubbles around with her toes, relishing the peace and quiet. This was her favourite room in the house. They'd had this bathroom redone only last year. A designer dream of black and white marble, interjected with a flash of bright in the form of fuchsia artwork. The bath had been her choice. She'd wanted one deep enough that she could lie snugly underneath the water with every body part covered and no plug to sit on, a blessing in itself.

Steph recalled the earlier years when she and Terry had shared a bath in the house they'd rented on the estate. She'd always used to end up sitting at the tap end because Terry would race ahead to get in there first, but it had been fun. Not like now; he'd probably want to hold her head under the water until she stopped breathing. She giggled; she did love the stupid bastard.

Still, sometimes she wished she and Terry could go back to that time when they'd first met. Or even as far back as when they'd first moved into The Gables. Ten years ago, things had been much better. Now their relationship was so volatile that she couldn't tell whether he loved her or not. There was such a thin line between love and hate.

Steph knew that she still loved Terry despite the goings-on with Phil, but most of the time she was afraid to show it for fear of rejection. What was the point if she was only going to get abuse back from him? She'd seen the way he looked at her, the waning interest over the years.

No. She shook her head to clear her thoughts and refilled her glass with more wine. Even when things were tough, she knew they'd be okay. They were Terry and Steph Ryder, one of the wealthiest couples in Stoke-on-Trent. They'd get through this rough patch, just like the rest. And then she'd be able to relax again.

Over on the far wall, a flat-screen television was showing *The Weakest Link*, the volume down low. Steph sank further into the water before hearing a door open on the landing outside.

'That you, Kirst?' she shouted.

'Yes. Who else were you expecting?' Kirstie popped her head round the bathroom door. She was wearing skinny jeans underneath an oversized grey jumper, a long purple scarf and Ugg boots. Steph sighed. She wished she'd take her shoes off in the hallway before treading in the dirt.

'Ha, ha.' For once, Steph didn't want to argue. 'Had a good day?' she offered.

'Since when was going to college having a good day?' Kirstie came into the room and sat on the edge of the bath.

'You'll be glad of it when you get a qualification.' Steph stuck up a leg, admiring her newly painted toenails.

'You've never taken an exam in your life and you did all right for yourself.'

'That's because I found your father.'

Kirstie dipped a hand into the bubbles and pulled out a handful. She watched them disappearing on her palm. Steph knew she was trying to pick the right words to say even before she spoke.

'Mum.'

'What do you want?'

Kirstie looked at her with a frown. 'What do you mean?'

'I know that tone, Kirstie Ryder. It is your "can I have" tone. Do you think I'm made of money?'

'How do you know it's money that I'm after?'

'Don't you always want money?'

'Yes, but –'

'You're not pregnant, are you?' Steph's eyes widened in horror, knowing that one of them being in a mess would be bad enough to sort out, never mind both of them. She was dreading going back to see Doctor Turner on Monday morning. She'd cancelled the follow-up appointment twice in the past two days. 'Please tell me you've not slipped up with that Kennedy idiot. Your dad will do his flipping nut!'

'No, I'm not fucking knocked up!'

'I wouldn't put it past you.'

'Mum!'

'Are you sure you're not up the duff?'

'Yes, I'm sure!'

'So what is it, then?' Steph said a moment later. 'You never come and sit with me unless you want something. Or if you've done something you need me to straighten out for you.'

'I want to move in with Lee.'

Steph's eyes narrowed. 'Has he asked you yet?'

'No, but he will.'

'How do you know? You've only being seeing him – even though you're not supposed to be – for a few weeks.'

'I just know.' Kirstie folded her arms.

'No.' Steph sat up and reached for a towel. This was one argument that she couldn't have with her daughter looking down on her. She felt too vulnerable in the water.

'But if you'd listen to me for a moment,' Kirstie cried. 'I want –'

'I said no.' Steph stepped out of the bath and started to pat herself dry. 'You want me to take all the shit so that you don't have to.

You want me to change your dad's mind from "over my dead body" to "go on, give it a shot." Don't you?'

Kirstie's lilac-enhanced eyelids dipped to the floor.

'I'm not stupid. I know what you're after. And you're a big girl now. You're seventeen, not seven. You need to ask your dad yourself.'

'But he'll say no!'

'Precisely. Which is what I say too.' Steph glanced sideways while rubbing her hair dry. 'He's a bad influence, Kirstie.'

'But –'

'No buts. Your dad doesn't even know what happened the other day.'

'And you're so clean on drugs that you can preach?' Kirstie snapped, forgetting that she needed to be in pleasant mode.

Steph ignored her comment, flung the towel into the laundry basket, pulled on her dressing gown and left the room. But Kirstie followed her across the landing and into the master bedroom.

'I know you can't get through a day without a drink of some sort,' she said caustically. 'You're an alcoholic, Mum, whether you admit it or not. And you're a fucking mess. I don't know what Dad sees in you. I really don't.'

At the mention of Terry, Steph turned and slapped Kirstie hard. The sting on her hand stayed with her for quite some time afterwards.

Kirstie's head reared to the right before she turned to glare at her mother. Then she slapped her back.

Steph was so shocked that she stood there, hand on her cheek. It was the first time that had happened. The two women squared up to one another.

'I hate you,' said Kirstie, bursting into tears. 'I hate you with all my heart.'

Steph closed her eyes as tears began to brim in them too. She wouldn't let Kirstie see how upset she was. And it was the only way she knew how to stay calm rather than lash out again. Really, it was high time she learned to live with her daughter's outbursts. Although, thinking back to what she'd put her own mother through, she wondered if, in some bizarre way, this was payback time.

When she opened her eyes again, Kirstie was still there. But Steph really didn't want to fight.

'You're lucky I'm going out tonight,' she told her sharply, her true feelings hidden away again. 'I'll forget we ever had this conversation and I won't tell your dad anything if you just leave me in peace.'

'But –' Kirstie was ready to go again.

'Shut up!' Steph held up a hand to silence her. 'I've had enough of your whining. Close the door on your way out.'

The slam that followed reverberated through every bone in her body. Steph sighed dramatically. What was wrong with that girl?

———

Lee couldn't believe it when Kirstie knocked on his door just after six, barging past him. She knew they weren't supposed to be seeing each other tonight. But how could he get out of it without arousing suspicion?

'I fucking hate her with a passion.' Kirstie dropped onto his settee with a huff when she'd told him all about the fall out. 'I should have hit her harder, the bitch. Lashed out at her good and proper, put her in her place.'

Lee hid his smirk. Kirstie might be a mouthy bitch and able to give someone a slap every now and again but she didn't have it in her for anything more, despite all her hard talk.

'I hate her,' Kirstie repeated. 'I wish she was dead.'

'No, you don't,' he said absent-mindedly, all the time working out what to do now. He handed her a bag of white powder. 'Here, have a bit of this. This should take the edge off things for a while.'

'Ooh, ta.' She took it from him. 'You don't mind me coming over tonight, do you?' She pulled a full bottle of Jack Daniels from her bag. 'I can make it worth your while. I lifted this before I came out. Stupid bitch will probably be too pissed to notice.' She licked her lips. 'Sex on demand as well.'

'I don't have anything better to do.' Lee shrugged a shoulder: he'd just thought of a way out.

Kirstie slapped his leg as he sat down next to her. He piled dirty dishes on top of more dirty dishes at the end of the cheap wooden coffee table and pushed a magazine onto the floor to clear a space. Then he ran a hand over the grimy top before using a nightclub membership card to cut some of the powder into two lines. After taking a note from his wallet, he rolled it up and snorted a line. He held out the note to Kirstie. She quickly followed suit.

'That's so much better.' She sniffed, wiping at her nose.

Lee opened the bottle of whiskey and passed it to her, encouraging her to drink away. 'Where's your old man tonight? Home or away?'

'Away.' Kirstie grinned as she felt the powder take hold. 'I could stay over, if you like.'

Lee grinned back. 'Fucking too right. Let's order some food. What do you fancy? Chinese or Indian?'

'Indian.'

Lee went through to the kitchen. Yes, Kirstie turning up unannounced had made his plan that little bit smarter. A good fuck would work off his pent-up adrenaline. It would take his mind off things and stop the night from dragging until he needed to go out. Then he could slip her a sleeping pill, sneak out to The Potter's Wheel and be back before she even noticed he'd gone.

He poured the liquor into two glasses. To Kirstie's, he added a lot. To his own, he added a little. He didn't want to get booked for drunk driving, especially as the filth would be cracking down for the Christmas party season soon. He topped both glasses up with Coke and took them back through.

He flopped down next to Kirstie on the settee, feet up on the table as she snuggled in next to him. His smile widened manically as the drugs heightened his senses. Oh yes, she would be the perfect alibi.

At the end of her shift that Friday evening, Allie headed off to see her sister.

'Hello, Allie.' Miriam Walters smiled a greeting as she sat behind a desk in the reception area of Riverdale Residential Home. A slight woman in her late fifties, she wore a white blouse with a tiny pink flower dotted here and there and a navy blue, round-neck cardigan. Her grey hair, wrapped up in a bun, and kind eyes behind thick rimmed glasses fondly reminded Allie of a grandmother she'd lost long ago.

'Karen's gone into her room as she was tired earlier on,' Miriam added as Allie signed the visitors' book.

'Thanks, Miriam.' Allie smiled. It was one of the things she loved about Riverdale. How the staff were not only there to welcome her in but they could always tell her where Karen was and how she was doing. If she'd had a bad night, they'd tell her. If she had made a slight bit of progress, they would report it. It gave her a sense of peace that she had made the right choice to move her sister there. 'How's she been?'

'Fine. That cough she developed is slowing down now with the antibiotics she was prescribed.'

Allie continued past the desk and along the corridor, its biscuit-coloured wallpaper and Wedgwood blue carpeting welcoming her as she went through the double doors and into the main area, off where she would find the corridor to Karen's room.

Riverdale felt like Allie's second home, she visited it so often. Always twice a week, more when she could make it. It was a newly built home, complete with all mod cons and technology that made things easier for Karen. Allie had moved her here when their mother, Barbara, passed away seven years ago from stomach cancer. It had been a traumatic time for Allie. Watching someone who had been able to walk and communicate change into someone who couldn't was pretty much like reliving what had happened to her sister.

When Karen was attacked, Allie had been head-over-heels in love with Mark and recently back from university. She'd been waiting for a placement to start with the local council as a trainee social worker. Having got her first car only a week earlier, she'd been late to pick Karen up from Hanley after she'd been out for the night. Parking up outside Flickers in Town Road at eleven forty-five, she'd waited for ten minutes and thought that maybe Karen had stormed off to get a taxi from the rank nearby. She tried ringing her mobile phone but it was switched off. They later found out she'd left it at home. Not thinking any more of it, Allie headed back to her parents' place – something else she'd never forgiven herself for. She should have gone to look for her.

CCTV in the nineties wasn't as prominent as nowadays so there hadn't been many sightings of Karen after she'd left the city centre. All the police could say was that Karen must have decided to walk home alone. Taking a short cut through an enclosed alleyway, she'd been grabbed by the hair – they knew this as Karen had a bald patch as big as a tennis ball at the back of her head – and pulled into bushes. She'd been raped and beaten. The attack was so severe the police said she'd definitely been left for dead. But Karen had survived as such, if you could call needing twenty-four hour care, being unable to talk and needing a wheelchair "survival."

Karen had been moved back in with their parents. There was no way she could live independently anymore. Their father, Roy, had died two years afterwards of a heart attack. He'd never stopped looking for the attacker and campaigned right until the moment he died. When their mother had died too, Allie had had to make the agonising decision to put Karen somewhere she would receive the care that she couldn't provide. She and Mark had been married for seven years then. Even happy to concentrate on their careers and put children off until later, they weren't in a position to look after Karen around the clock.

The decision to admit her sister to Riverdale had haunted Allie for months. She'd visited daily until she realised that Karen was safe and well looked after and that the staff were a caring bunch that made her and Mark feel welcome.

And to this day, Karen's attacker had never been found. Fourteen years later, the bastard who had destroyed all their lives remained at large. Allie had joined the police for this very reason.

'Hey there, Karen,' Allie smiled as she opened the door to find her sister sitting up in her bed. The room was of standard size and set up with the machinery the staff used daily to keep Karen comfortable spread around it. The walls had recently been painted in a shade of lemon that made it feel sunny all year round, even though there were already scuff marks where the wheels of the chair had banged against them. Modern floral curtains were drawn across the window. A single wardrobe held Karen's array of jumpers, cardigans and easy pull-on skirts and trousers.

It always pained Allie to see how similar they were in features but how damaged Karen looked underneath. Her deep blue eyes had a glaze to them, her face hardly any colour. In contrast, she wore a pink pyjama top underneath a deep purple cardigan. Her shoulder-length dark hair had been left loose. Allie noticed her nail varnish was beginning to chip and made a mental note to redo it when she next visited.

'How have you been?' she asked, even though she knew she wouldn't get a reply.

Karen tried to smile.

Allie hung up her coat, wheeled the hoist to one side and pulled a chair nearer to the bed. 'Your hair looks lovely.'

Karen groaned, her only way of communication. Over the years, Allie had learned to read her moods depending on that noise.

'Let's put on some music,' Allie said after a few minutes of one-sided chit-chat. She'd long ago lost the embarrassment of speaking into an empty room and not being answered. She opened the CD cover on the system she'd bought Karen for her last birthday and checked to see what was inside. The nineties compilation CD that they mostly listened to was still there. Allie selected a track and sat down again.

'Ce Ce Peniston, Karen,' she said, taking her hand. 'Do you remember? "Finally It's Happening to Me." 1993. Valentino's, The Pig & Truffle, Flickers and Yates's Wine Lodge. All gone now but we still have the memories, don't we?'

Memories. Yes, that was all they had now. Allie gazed up at the photo frame on the wall. Seventeen individual photos of better times. A picture of the two of them as young girls with their parents. One of them both in roller skates at a caravan park. A strip of photos taken at Blackpool funfair in a booth. There was one of Karen and Robert Machin, whom she'd been engaged to – twice – before dumping him altogether. Another one with Phil Green. Another with someone Allie couldn't remember now.

There was one of Karen at their wedding in 2001. Karen sat in her wheelchair, Allie kneeling down on one side, Mark on the other, holding hands across her lap. Allie's floral bouquet rested there too. There was never any question that Karen wouldn't be invited, despite the extra cost to hire a nurse for the day so that their mum could get a bit of downtime too.

Mark had been her stalwart after the attack. He'd only known Karen for a few months before and was as shocked as Allie when it happened. It had cemented a budding romance into the strong marriage of today. From that moment on, Allie knew he would always be there for her. Without him, she would have crumbled for sure. He tried often to talk her out of her guilt. She had been fifteen minutes late but she couldn't ruin her life because of that, he'd told her over and over. Karen wouldn't want that.

And at least he had known Karen before the attack. Mark could always sense when things were eating at Allie. When a case had been particularly nasty, he'd share memories with her to make her smile. *Remember this, remember that.* And Allie would smile for a while. And then the pain would come back.

Another photo of Allie in her police uniform. Mark had gone ballistic when she'd announced that she was quitting her social worker placement to join the police force. They'd had many an argument over it since, too. Allie would come home distraught as some woman being attacked brought back memories of Karen's assault. A woman's body would turn up and she'd be frantic to catch the killer. It had spurred her on to becoming a detective constable six years after joining the force. Four years after that, she'd passed her sergeant's exam and a few months later, this position had come up.

As Karen's eyes began to close, Allie turned the music down a little and stared at her. Such a fucking waste of life, she thought with bitterness. Karen had had everything going for her. She'd been hoping to move to London and turn a love of photography into a career. Karen had a flair for creating spectacular photographs. She might have made it big if some bastard hadn't come along and tried to end her life.

By far the worst thing for Allie was the not knowing why. Had Karen simply been in the wrong place at the wrong time? Or had the attacker stalked her for a while before pouncing on her? And had it been his intention to kill her from the start or had he slipped up and gone too far?

Why had he never been caught? The question ate at her every day. Had he been sent to prison for another crime before he'd had the chance to rape someone else? Had he died? Was he just passing through? Had he stopped at the one attack? And what the hell had become of him? So many questions left unanswered.

An hour later, Allie kissed her sister lightly on the forehead. Karen was fast asleep now. She put on her coat and slipped out of the room. Just as Karen's attacker had slipped out of her life.

Chapter Fourteen

Ten minutes before the eight thirty taxi was due, Steph poured another gin and tonic. She was glad Kirstie had stormed out after their fight, leaving her to get ready in peace. Even over the sound of the hairdryer, she'd heard the car screeching away. Stupid bitch. Lord knows when she'd be back but she'd show her. She'd double-lock the door tonight so she wouldn't be able to get in until her mother got home. See how she liked sleeping out, even if it was in her car. She'd probably storm off back to Lee's house anyway.

Steph hadn't meant to lash out at her daughter but sometimes, she couldn't explain it, she hit back – literally. Yet, although she took her anger out on Kirstie – like Kirstie took it out on her – she didn't mean anything by it. She lashed out because it was the easy way. She hated hearing the truth.

And despite everything, she knew Kirstie was right. She did need help with the drinking – not that she would ever admit it to anyone. Grinning, she knocked back the drink and poured another.

Her mobile phone rang. Terry's name flashed up on the screen.

'Hey you.'

'Hey, how's it going?'

'Oh, you know, just had the day from hell.' Steph found herself holding the phone close, wanting to hear his voice. 'Are you still mad at me? I'm really sorry.'

'You're always sorry.'

'But I mean it this time. Are you coming home tonight?'

'I'm not sure. It could be tonight. It could be in the morning. You going to The Potter's Wheel?'

'Yeah, me and Carole are going around town first.'

'You and Carole?' She heard him snigger. 'That woman is a sucker for punishment.'

Steph ignored him. 'Maybe go for a curry after or order one and bring it back here. Do you want me to ring you when I'm on my way home, see where you are? I could always order you something?'

'Best not. I'm not sure where I'll be. Look, I've got to go.'

'Love you.'

'Yeah.'

The phone went dead.

Steph tutted. 'Love you too.'

Feeling flat after the call, she topped up her glass with more gin and sat down on the settee. But it wasn't long before her phone jumped into action again. It was a text message this time.

'U got it babe?'

A car blasted its horn as it turned in at the gate. She quickly sent a reply.

'Got it. xx'

Steph tottered through to the hallway, rechecked her make-up in the mirror and then smiled. Telling Steve that she'd got the knife was only half the tale really. Yes, she'd got the knife; yes, he'd told her to hide it in the garage, somewhere it wouldn't be found by Terry but could be found if the police were ever given a tip-off.

But no, she hadn't hidden it in the garage. It was still somewhere that Terry wouldn't find it but it was there for her own purposes now.

The horn blasted again. She knocked back the last of her drink, grabbed her belongings and disappeared into the night.

While his wife was out around the pubs of Hanley, Terry spent a couple of hours dining out with a few of his business associates in Derby. They were in Carlito's Way, a Greek restaurant known for its opulent décor as well as its food. The restaurant had been fully booked that night but Terry had made a call and a table for six had been theirs.

Across from him sat Charles Roberts and his wife, Veronica. Terry was looking forward to catching up with Charles tonight, to see how their latest project was coming on. Charles was a large man in stature as well as in life, his ruddy complexion making him look like a farmer. He was a property developer and the main reason Terry came over to Derby so often. Between them they'd invested in a block of dilapidated flats sold off by a local housing association and were in the process of renovating them into premier apartments. Due for completion in early spring, already there were people waiting to sign when their release date was announced. It felt good to have something legit that he could be proud of.

But tonight Terry only had eyes for Charles' wife, Veronica, whom he'd met on several occasions like these; she was looking as spectacular as ever. She was dressed in a tight, short crimson dress, sleeveless to complement toned arms. Her hair was dyed a snazzy shade of red, cut in a sleek bob and sharp for her age, which he put at late thirties. Terry caught her eye and winked. Watched with a grin as a flush formed over her chest. Putty in his hands.

To his right sat Richard Powers and his wife, Jean. Richard was in his early fifties and the project manager for the site. A short man whose belly always fought to stay inside his shirt, he didn't look the type to haul himself onto scaffolding to spot-check a roof or shimmy up and down a ladder at breakneck speed. But, so far, he'd done a cracking job. For once, Terry had found someone who he would happily take through to his next venture. Charles Roberts, however, he wasn't too sure about.

A hand squeezed his thigh underneath the table and he turned his head to the left. Terry had met Cathryn Mountford at the start of the project, six months ago, and had shared a bed with her only a week later. She was twenty-eight, ran her own accountancy business and was his most dazzling piece on the side yet. Young, fresh and exciting with long, blonde hair and fantastic tits, she also had legs up to her armpits that she loved to wrap around him. He moved her hand to his crotch and gave it a squeeze so that she'd know how much he wanted her. She smiled at him. It was heading to be a good night all round. He hoped his gamble to be with her tonight would pay off.

Terry wiped his mouth, put down his napkin and excused himself. Instead of heading straight for the toilet, he tried to reach Steph on his Blackberry. It was just gone ten and he wanted to see if she was at The Potter's Wheel yet. But there was no answer.

Although he cursed, it wasn't unusual for Steph. She was always forgetting her phone. Or maybe the music was too loud for her to hear its ring. He leaned on the wall, shivering slightly as the front door blew in the cold night before closing quickly again. Thinking he'd try again later, he slid shut the phone and headed for the gents.

He'd been in there a matter of seconds when the door opened behind him. Looking up as he finished off, he grinned at the sight before him.

'Wash those hands, why don't you,' Veronica Roberts purred.

Now that he could see all of her, he realised what a treat he was in for. Below the dress she had fine, toned legs covered in what he hoped were black stockings. He licked his lips as his eyes flicked downwards to four-inch heels. She lowered her hand to the hem of the dress and pulled it up, tantalisingly slowly. Yes, they were stockings. And she was wearing no underwear. He grinned as he felt himself harden.

She followed him over to the basin where she covered her hands with his as he soaped up. He rinsed them under the water, watching her every move through the mirror in front and, not bothering to dry his hands, he turned to face her, pulled down the front of her dress and sank his teeth into her nipple. She moaned loudly. He glanced up to see her neck thrown back.

The wind caught the door to the hallway slightly and as noise filtered in and back out again, Terry grabbed Veronica's hand and led her into the cubicle. They kissed, bodies pressed together as close as possible, hands eagerly exploring bodies. She pulled his buttocks closer as he moved his hand up towards the top of her stockings.

Terry liked to please his women, make them come back for more. Veronica tried to pull his head up as he sucked at her breast and pushed his fingers inside her at the same time. He felt her left knee buckle and smiled. She was definitely his for the taking.

'Fuck me, Terry,' she whispered, along with another moan of pleasure. 'I can't hold out much longer. You have to join me.'

The outside door opened again and this time voices were heard. Terry put his hand across Veronica's mouth and continued to knead her with his fingers. Her eyes pleaded with him to stop. He stared into them, knowing that would turn her on even more.

The men were there for quite some time. The music playing low allowed for the exchange of a hand for his lips and he kissed her, his tongue diving in to find hers. She pulled at the buckle on his trousers, then the zip. It was his time to contain the pleasure. They stopped as the door opened again. If the room didn't empty soon, they would both explode. But the men who had come in minutes earlier both left and the room descended into silence once more.

Terry hitched up Veronica's dress and pushed himself into her wetness. She wrapped her legs around his torso and, steadying herself on the wall, began to move with him. This time she wasn't quiet.

Once it was over, they laughed. They adjusted their clothes and Terry left her in there while he tried to contact Steph again.

When there was no answer he cursed.

'Come on, Terry,' a male voice shouted through from the restaurant. 'You can't spend all night on that bleeding phone.'

Terry raised a hand as he continued to listen to the unanswered ring tone. Damn Steph. If she didn't get to The Potter's Wheel, there would be all hell to pay. He put away his Blackberry and pulled out a pay-as-you-go phone. Quickly, he sent a text message.

'Terry!'

Sighing loudly, he went back to his table.

———

Steph was late getting to The Potter's Wheel because Carole hadn't been ready when she'd arrived at The Orange Grove and she'd had to wait. As she propped up the bar, helping herself to a few more gin and tonics for her troubles, it was obvious that Carole and Shaun had been arguing. She knew he didn't approve of Carole going out with her. But she laughed as she clocked his stony face. He would never dare stop her.

They made it to two pubs before heading to the taxi rank at ten thirty and over to The Potter's Wheel, where the crowd was heaving and the music loud. It was standing room only in the lounge where the band was set up. The crowd the group had brought along with them was huge. Most of the regulars had to stand at the bar, glaring at the non-regulars hogging their seats.

Steph loved it at The Potter's Wheel. Busy or empty, she didn't care. As long as nothing kicked off, it made for a lively atmosphere. And until a curry called, it was where Steph intended staying.

After she'd been served, she squeezed back through the three-deep crowd at the bar and walked towards Carole. Then she squashed herself into a space made for one and budged everyone else up to make room for the two of them. At least Carole was starting to thaw now, although it had taken long enough for her to come on side again. Already it was quarter past eleven and she'd only just started to let go. Now she was telling her how worried she was about Shaun. Well, at least that's what she thought she'd been saying. Steph had zoned out ages ago. She didn't want to talk about men tonight. She wanted to get rat-arsed.

When the band took a break, Carole spoke to her again 'What?' she shouted, pretending that she couldn't hear over the drone of other people.

'You're not listening to me, are you? That's why I said you were a bitch.'

'I know, I know.' Steph wasn't at all bothered by the insult. 'I can't help myself.'

'Huh.' Carole reached for her drink. 'That's a poor excuse.'

'Oh, come on, Carole. When are you going to let up?' Steph whined. 'You've been going on all night.'

Carole grinned and nudged Steph. 'I'm winding you up. I'm all mild and mellow now.'

'Oy!' Steph cried. 'Watch my drink!'

'You and your drink.' Carole laughed. 'I'd get you another but seeing as you're buying tonight...' She finished her Bacardi and rattled the melting ice cubes around the bottom of the glass. 'Another?'

'Already? It's a good job I'm married to Terry Ryder,' Steph sighed as she took it from her, 'or else you'd bleed me dry.' She pulled out her phone and checked for missed calls.

'How many?'

Steph peered at the screen. 'Four,' she replied with a grin. 'Only four attempts to get in touch with me. I must be losing my charm.'

'I wish someone would check up on me like that,' Carole said wistfully. She lurched forward as someone squeezing past her banged into her shoulder.

'You wouldn't if you knew why.'

'Oh?' Carole was intrigued. 'I thought it was to see that you weren't bleeding him dry.'

'Ha bloody ha. You are a barrel of laughs tonight.' Steph's smile was saccharine. 'No, he doesn't trust me.'

'It's a bit late for that. You've been married forever.'

'Yes, I know, but he thinks I'm going to shoot my mouth off and say something that I shouldn't.'

'I don't follow.' Carole looked on in confusion.

Steph moved her head closer to Carole's. 'He's getting into some dodgy things and he doesn't like the fact that I know about some of them.'

'Has he said that?'

'Nope, you know Terry. Keeps thing close to his chest. But just because he shuts himself away in that study doesn't mean that I don't get to hear anything. I'm a dab hand at listening at the door.'

Carole was impressed. 'So what have you heard?'

Steph tapped a finger to her nose, nearly poking her eye out during the process. She grinned. 'I know lots of things about Terry that could put him away for years.'

'But they're things that you wouldn't use against him or else you would have shopped him years ago.' Carole paused. 'Tell me something new.'

'I found a note screwed up in Terry's waste paper bin in his study. Something's going down tonight.'

Carole gulped, recalling the visit that Shaun had received from Phil earlier in the day.

'What did it say?' she asked.

'I'm not sure what it meant but it mentioned Friday night and involves twenty grand.'

'Twenty grand!' Carole nearly choked on her drink.

'Keep your voice down!' Steph hissed as heads started to turn in their direction. They huddled together as she continued. 'I mean, fancy losing twenty grand like that. I'd do my nut.'

'Oh, you mean someone is going to *lose* twenty grand.' Carole blew out the breath she'd been holding as she took in the relevance of Steph's words. 'You mean they're playing cards?'

'I'm not sure if it's that simple.'

'You'd better be careful what you say about it, then.'

'Don't worry about me.' Steph knocked back the last of her drink. 'I have my own security.'

'Really?' Carole raised her eyebrows.

Steph leaned forward. 'Let's just say I have something that links Terry to a murder.'

'Yeah right.'

'It's true!'

'You're winding me up. Terry wouldn't be stupid enough to leave evidence around for someone to use against him. Besides, I don't think he has it in him to do anything that nasty. I reckon Phil Kennedy does all his dirty work for him.'

Steph frowned. It was clear that Carole was off her rocker if she believed that. She picked up her glass and stood up unsteadily, holding onto the table for a moment.

'Another Bacardi?'

Carole nodded. Steph grinned as she heard a phone beep the arrival of a text. 'Ha, he's after me again.'

Carole reached for her bag. 'I think it's mine.'

'Aw, see. He does love you after all.'

Steph sat down minutes later with their refills as the band geared up to start again.

'Well?' She flopped back into her seat.

'Well, what?'

'What did he say?'

'Nothing much.'

But Carole glancing at her watch didn't go unnoticed.

'He's having a go, isn't he?'

'No, he isn't.'

'Yes, he is. Look at you. Your body language says it all.' Steph pointed at Carole's face as the singer tested his mic: one-two, one-two. 'Shaun's given you a hard time about coming out with me again, hasn't he?'

'Leave it, will you?'

'Hey, don't come all bolshie with me!'

'I'm going out to get some fresh air.' Carole pushed past her. 'I'll be back in a while.'

'Be sure to tell him to fuck off from me while you're there, won't you?' Steph shouted. She sloped back in her seat as eyes fell on her again.

Damn that Shaun Morrison. Who did he think he was, demanding that his wife tell him her every move? She knew that was what the text message had said. What else would have made Carole so annoyed?

As the band started to play again, Steph began to get more irate. Carole would probably skulk off now and leave her to make her own way home. Well, stuff her. She knocked back her drink and started on Carole's. Waste not want not.

Someone was trying to catch her attention. She looked up. Phil Kennedy stood at the bar. He raised his glass to her. She raised hers back: at least there was someone she could talk to if Carole continued to blow hot and cold.

At nine o'clock, Lee had been standing in the empty shop doorway opposite The Orange Grove again. He'd been able to see right inside the restaurant, saw that stupid fucker Shaun faffing about being all smiles with the few people at the tables. From there, he'd been able to see when his car left the rear entry of the restaurant car park.

Now, two hours later, lucky not to be given away by the people walking past who'd glared at him suspiciously as he watched a fit piece with blonde hair lock the door, he realised it was time to move to his car.

Minutes later, Shaun and the girl came out of the back of the building and climbed into a car. They drove off and Lee followed close behind. Fifteen minutes later, the girl got out in Milton and walked off with a wave. He picked up Shaun's tail again and they cut through to Leek New Road. But at the junction of Newford Crescent, instead of turning right towards The Potter's Wheel, the car headed left, back towards the city centre.

Lee stopped at the junction. What the hell was going on? Had Shaun bottled it, the stupid knob?

He turned left and followed. Ahead, Shaun pulled into the side. Was he using his mobile? Lee drove past but he couldn't see. He stopped at the next junction, reversed at speed and headed back the way he'd come. Shaun's car was still there but he couldn't see Shaun. Then he spotted him bending over on the kerbside. Fuck, he was puking up. He *had* bottled it.

Lee parked a few yards up and watched through his rear-view mirror. Shaun stayed put for a few more minutes before getting back into his car and driving off in the same direction.

Lee banged his hand on the steering wheel. What a useless piece of shit. His dad would be livid. And his plans had gone to pot in a split second. Unless....

There was only one thing for it. He put his foot down and drove towards The Potter's Wheel.

PART TWO

Chapter Fifteen

Early on Saturday morning, December first, Allie had been waiting for Mark to bring her tea and toast in bed when she'd taken the phone call. It was eight thirty. She hadn't realised yet, but she had much to thank Terry Ryder for as she and Mark had just made love again. Since Tuesday it had been as if Mark, knowing she was desired by another man, had felt the need to prove he was enough for her. And he had proved it again last night – twice, in fact. But the phone call had taken away any cosiness. She pushed away old memories attempting to flood her mind.

'Who was that so early? Has there been a mur-dah?' Mark asked as he rejoined her, plopping one of two mugs down onto the cabinet by the side of her bed.

'There's been a woman's body found over on Brooke Lane.' Allie pulled back the duvet and sat up. 'By The Potter's Wheel pub.'

'Sorry, are you going to be okay?'

Allie smiled at Mark's concern, even though she knew he'd be upset that she might be working all weekend. Then again, maybe he might not be that annoyed. Stoke City were playing that afternoon and it was being televised.

'I have to go.' She kissed him. 'I'm sorry to ruin the weekend – again. Will you ring Ruth and Chris to put them on standby?' Ruth and Chris were friends they'd known since they'd met. They'd recently moved house and had invited them over for a meal.

'Yeah.' Mark nodded and climbed back into bed. 'I might even go on my own if you're going to have a late one.'

'I'll let you know.'

Half an hour later, Allie drove along Leek New Road in the direction of Endon. The car park of The Potter's Wheel had been cordoned off before she arrived, as had the entrance to Brooke Lane. Two uniformed officers stood guard ensuring no one drove in. Another officer a few yards behind them held a clipboard. He was taking note of anyone who came to or left the scene. Allie recognised the DI's car and pulled in next to it. Already there were a few onlookers: an elderly man and a black Labrador sitting at his feet, two teenage boys with a skateboard apiece, a few of the staff who had turned up to work at the pub, a woman gawping across the road as she waited at the bus stop. Allie shuddered involuntarily: that type of thing always gave her the creeps. What did they find fascinating to look at?

Detective Inspector Nick Carter was talking to a man in a suit when he saw her approaching.

'It's a nasty one, Allie,' he said as she reached him. 'The back of her head has been bashed about as if it was a potato. And,' he sighed, 'we know her.'

Allie took a sharp intake of breath. This was a first for her. She followed Nick, unsure of what she was about to witness but knowing that she had to view it for herself. Despite what had happened to Karen, someday she hoped to be faced with being the lead on an investigation like this. A tent had already been erected, covering the area where the body had been found. She pulled on plastic shoe covers and latex gloves and they went inside.

Allie's hand moved to cover her mouth, trying desperately to keep the hurried piece of toast she'd eaten inside her body. The woman was face down, arms at her sides. From where she was standing, Allie surmised she could be anywhere between early twenties and early forties. She was fully clothed in designer boot-cut jeans, black high heels with a slight platform and a turquoise sleeveless top. None of her clothes were torn in any way but she wasn't wearing any jewellery. Blonde hair on what was left of her head was covered in blood and brain matter, the indent of a weapon an impossibility to gauge at this stage due to the force of the attack. Allie carefully moved to the other side to get a closer look at her features, and felt her legs go weak as she recognised who it was.

'Ohmigod! It's Steph Ryder.'

'I can't believe we were with her the other night.' Nick stooped down for a closer look. 'Whoever did this was in a rage. I've never seen anyone hit so many times before.'

'Time of death?'

'Eleven p.m. to one a.m.,' said the man she'd seen talking to Nick earlier. Dave Barnett, the forensic officer on duty, was a tall man with thinning grey hair, glasses perched on the end of a large nose and chubby hands that didn't look fit for the job but were renowned not to miss a trick.

'She was hit from behind,' he continued, motioning with his hand. 'Fell to the floor and then someone kept on hitting.'

Allie swallowed before stooping down too. The eye that she could see was staring ahead at nothing. Never again would she see a summer day, another smile, a beautiful sunset. Allie welled up. No matter how many victims she saw, it never took away the shock. Steph Ryder was someone's mother, someone's wife, someone's friend. She would have been going about doing her own thing, like her sister, Karen.

'There are a few cars left in the car park so one of them may be hers,' said Nick. 'There was a group on here last night by all accounts. We'll get as much as we can checked out but it will be a nightmare to locate everyone. Half of them will be too pissed to remember clearly. Still, there won't be much door-to-door to carry out.'

Allie nodded. Although The Potter's Wheel was on the main road, there weren't many dwellings nearby. Brooke Lane at the end of the car park went at least half a mile before any houses started to emerge. On the other side, open playing fields and two football pitches. Across the road, more fields. The Potter's Wheel was as close as this area got to a village pub.

'Someone must have seen something,' she said, trying not to look down again until she had to.

'I suppose there'll be snippets of information to fit together. But there were also a lot of people around that could have messed up potential evidence.'

'Has anyone found her bag?' Allie glanced around, trying to take in every tiny detail.

'Nothing yet.' Nick stood up. 'We'd better get over to Ryder's address and break the news.'

Allie stood up too. She flipped the door back on the tent and stood for a moment, breathing in the air. Big, huge, icy gulps of the stuff to calm her nerves. Her eyes searched the large crowd now standing behind yellow crime scene tape and wondered if the murderer was part of the group. Some, she knew, liked to come back to taunt their victims, as well as the police.

She wondered if she should mention to Nick about the flower arrangement she'd stuffed in her bin on Wednesday night. Maybe she should just gauge Terry Ryder's reaction when she saw him. Besides, under the circumstances, she could hardly bring the subject up. *Thanks but no thanks; I don't want your flowers.*

And really, in the scheme of things, was it all that important now? Maybe he had acted on the spur of the moment. Back then, it had seemed so pathetic. This morning, it seemed ... sad.

Terry arrived back from Derby at nine thirty after managing to pass the commotion at The Potter's Wheel without having a heart attack. The first thing he did was try Phil again on the pay-as-you-go mobile. He'd been trying since the early hours to get through but the line had been switched off every time. Fuck, he'd told Phil to ring him the minute the cleanup crew had finished. He sat down on the bed with a thud. Something had gone wrong.

He heard a car pull up outside and raced to the window. But it was only Kirstie. Had she been out all night too?

'Do you know anything about this?' he asked as he flew down the stairs.

'Fuck!' Kirstie jumped as she pulled her key out of the lock. 'Let me get in first, will you? Do I know anything about what?'

'Language.'

'Sorry.' Although Kirstie swore like a navvy and had been told not to in front of her father, words slipped out as habit.

Terry tried to calm his rapid heartbeat. Would he normally be this worried if Steph hadn't come home? Wouldn't he try to find out if she had stayed over somewhere?

'Sorry, sweetheart.' He followed her through to the kitchen. 'Your mother never came home last night. Did she say anything to you about staying out with Carole?'

'No, but we didn't exactly split on good terms.' Kirstie pulled back her hair to reveal a slight bruising on her cheek. 'She hit me again last night. And it was only tea time and she was pissed.'

Terry came nearer to inspect the damage. He could hardly see a mark. 'I suppose you were mouthing off at her?'

'No! Why do you always side with her when you, of all people, know what a cow she can be?' Still under the effects of a little white powder, Kirstie felt braver than usual. Lucky for her that her dad's mind was elsewhere or she would have copped it.

'Was it anything to do with you not coming home last night, I wonder?' Terry wanted to know.

Kirstie froze. Shit, she'd thought she'd got away with it. 'I stayed over at Ashleigh's,' she lied.

'You'd better be sure about that. You weren't with Lee Kennedy? I told you not to see him again.'

'I know you did. I'm telling the truth, Dad. I was over at Ashleigh's. Ring and check if you don't believe me.' Calling his bluff, she reached for her phone but he didn't take it from her.

Terry looked towards the front door as if Steph was going to magically appear. Picking up the coffee he'd made, he took it through to his study. With his Blackberry, he sent a quick text to ask what time she was coming home. At least it would look like he was bothered about where she was.

Through the pay-as-you-go mobile, he tried to reach Phil again. But still there was no answer. He threw it down onto his desk and stared ahead, all the time the sense that something had gone wrong growing by the minute. If Phil Kennedy had fucked up, he could have done a runner and left him with the mess to clean up. He knew he wouldn't relax until he'd heard from him.

And, either way, there'd be trouble.

Chapter Sixteen

The address printed on the driving licence was The Gables, Royal Avenue, Endon and was three miles away from The Potter's Wheel. On the journey there, Allie couldn't rid herself of Steph Ryder's image. She gazed through the window at the oncoming traffic but instead saw Steph's head turned to one side, one eye wide and dead, her head a mass of tissue and congealed blood.

Royal Avenue was just off the main road but well hidden from view, a cul-de-sac of individually designed homes set on its own, surrounded by fields and farmland. Allie often referred to it as Millionaire's Row when she went past it with Mark.

'Do you think it was a random attack or premeditated?' she asked Nick as he drove past a few houses, top of the range cars parked in most of the driveways.

Nick pulled into the gateway of the fifth property on the right. 'Seems pretty random to me, but you never know.' He came to a stop and yanked up the hand brake. 'Christ, will you look at this place.'

The Gables stood regal in stature, over two floors, a row of three garages attached to the right. To the left, a pair of wooden doors guarded secrets they might never find out. Above the grand entrance, a large, rectangular stained glass window proudly displayed the crest of the local premier football team. The house looked to be no more than a decade in age, woodwork still in good condition, gardens tidy even though it was the middle of winter. The drive that they swept onto finished the look precisely.

'How the other half live,' sighed Allie, overwhelmed by its beauty.

The front door was opened by a young woman. Allie could tell at a glance that it was Steph Ryder's daughter.

'Hi.' Nick flashed his ID badge in way of greeting. 'I'm Detective Inspector Carter and this is Detective Sergeant Shenton. Is Mr Ryder home?'

'He's in his office. Do I need to get him?'

'Yes, please.'

'You can wait in there.'

They stepped into a large hallway with double doors, parquet flooring and stairs leading to a galleried landing. Nick urged Allie forward first with a nod of his head.

The doors led to a large living area that stretched out in an L-shape at the back to accommodate a dining area and kitchen. On one of the pristine cream walls, a television set dominated the right side of the room. Allie's heels tapped on oak floorboards this time. Three black leather settees surrounded a small coffee table that looked out of place. At the far end were a dining table to seat ten and a bank of glazed doors that led out onto a landscaped garden. Allie could see a pond with a fountain at the side of a large decked area. Several wooden loungers stood in a row, waiting to be sat upon.

'Far cry from the houses we usually visit,' Nick muttered, his eyes unable to rest on anything in particular.

The young girl was back. 'He'll be down in a minute.'

Nick smiled his thanks. 'So, you are?'

'Kirstie. Kirstie Ryder. Would you like a coffee?'

'No, thanks. We're fine.'

Allie studied Kirstie discreetly. Like her mother she was striking, although in different ways. Her hair, dark as opposed to

Stephanie's blonde, was cut into an angular bob. She was of average height, if a little skinny, and had the most dazzling blue eyes.

'Christmas shopping later?' Allie asked, feeling awkward just standing there. Then she cursed to herself. She was about to tell Kirstie that her mother was dead. Stupid fool. She glanced at Nick who, thankfully, remained impassive.

'I'm going this afternoon,' Kirstie replied.

Oh no, you're not.

Nick walked over to the front window and took in the row of cars outside. The black Range Rover he knew belonged to Terry Ryder. The red Mini Cooper S with black and white chequered roof surely belonged to Kirstie. There was a grey Mercedes SLK parked next to it. He wondered if that had been Steph's, which meant that she'd had a lift on her night out.

'Any Christmas parties last night?' he asked Kirstie.

'No, I stayed in, watched a video.'

'With friends?' He turned round quickly with a grin. 'Or with a boyfriend?'

'That's none of your business.' Kirstie's voice faltered a little before regaining its composure. 'I stayed over at my friend's house last night.'

'And who might that be?'

'Her name is Ashleigh Stewart.'

'And is she –?'

'What's going on?' Kirstie's eyes flitted from Allie to Nick. 'Look, what's with all the questions?'

'I was about to ask the same thing,' said a velvet voice from behind them.

———⌣———

It was his eyes that did it for her again. Just the same as they'd done on Tuesday night at the charity event. Just like they'd done when she'd seen him at one event or another through work. Pools of dark liquid sucking her in immediately. Down, down she fell into their depths. Not so much 'come-to-bed' eyes as much as 'fuck-me-here-right-now-up-against-the-wall' eyes. They sparkled with a hint of mischief, yet at the same time gave away the danger behind them.

Allie looked away as they lingered on her, unable to stop herself blushing. What was wrong with her? Under the circumstances, she was mortified.

Nick took a few steps forward. 'I'm afraid we have bad news, Mr Ryder. It's about your wife. Would you like to sit down?'

The confident look Terry had displayed moments earlier disappeared completely. 'What's going on?' he asked.

'Could we speak to you alone?'

'No,' said Kirstie with a frown. 'I need to know too.'

Nick looked at Terry for confirmation and cleared his throat when he nodded.

'We've found a body this morning, on Brooke Lane, at the back of the car park of The Potter's Wheel. We believe it to be your wife, Mr Ryder.'

'No, tell me that's not true!' Kirstie cried, sitting down. 'Tell me.'

Terry flopped onto a settee, his head resting in his hands. 'But it can't be her. I spoke to her only last night.'

'At what time?'

'About eightish. She was waiting for a taxi. I stayed over in Derby last night. I've been staying over there quite a lot recently. I have work there.' His eyes were misted when he looked up. 'What happened?'

'She was attacked from behind and hit over the head. We're not exactly sure what the murder weapon is yet. The forensic officer gave us an estimated time of between eleven p.m. and one a.m. You were in Derby then?'

'Yes, I got back about half nine this morning. I never thought...'

As Kirstie sat crying, Allie took a handkerchief from her pocket and gave it to her. 'I'm so sorry for your loss.'

Terry switched off the television, sat down next to Kirstie and pulled her into his arms.

'Are you sure it's her?' he asked. Then, 'Of course you are. We were with you both on Tuesday.'

'Yes, we're sure,' said Nick, 'although we do need you to formally identify the body.'

Terry nodded. 'I'll get my keys.'

'Don't you leave me!' Kirstie cried.

'I won't.'

'That won't be necessary yet,' Nick told them. 'We need to ask you a few questions first.'

'May I ask who found her?'

'The cleaner at the pub. She spotted the body through an upstairs window.' Allie cast her mind back to the distraught woman. She'd been the colour of Kendall mint cake.

'Do you think someone killed her deliberately?' Kirstie managed to speak through sobs.

'We can't tell as yet,' said Nick.

'How bad was she?' Terry wanted to know.

Nick's silence spoke more than any words. 'Is there anyone we can call for you?'

'I knew something was odd when she didn't come home last night.' Terry said. 'I need to speak to Carole. You met her last week as well.' Allie nodded. 'I sent her a text message earlier – I sent Steph one too – asking if Steph was with her. They were out together last night.'

'You didn't call either of them?' asked Nick.

'No, it was too early.'

'And did Carole ...'

'Morrison. Carole Morrison. She and her husband own The Orange Grove restaurant in Hanley.'

'Did Mrs Morrison get back to you?'

Terry shook his head. 'No, although I haven't checked my phone in the last half hour.'

'Don't worry, we'll speak to her shortly.'

'They only went out for a drink,' Terry continued in a daze, as if they weren't there. 'They usually get back around midnight.'

Allie could see he was struggling to contain his emotions as she wrote down Carole Morrison's details. She touched Kirstie gently on her shoulder. 'Will you be okay until the family liaison officer arrives?'

'Family liaison officer?' Terry's back straightened. 'We don't –'

'It's routine procedure, sir,' Nick explained. 'In cases such as this, we always employ someone to help the family understand what the police are doing. We need to get to the bottom of this, and as quickly as possible, for all your sakes.'

'Do I have to have one?'

'No, but it does look better if you co-operate.'

'Better for whom? Are you suggesting that I had anything to do with this?'

'On the contrary, sir, but we do have to keep an open mind. A family liaison officer is –'

'A waste of money, if you ask me. I'd rather you employed an extra officer to look into my wife's murder.' Terry closed his eyes for a moment. 'I'm sorry. I'm not thinking straight. What I'm trying to say is that Kirstie will more than likely be round at her friends and I'm here alone now that … now …'

'Let's see how things go, then,' Nick offered a compromise.

Allie kept her face straight. She knew they couldn't force anyone to have an officer in their home twenty-four-seven and Terry was right – their time could be better utilised. But it seemed a strange request to refuse. And surely his daughter would want to stay close by her family home after what had happened?

After a preliminary search through some of Steph's belongings, other officers started to arrive. Matt and Perry joined them to take down the first account from Terry as she and Nick made their way back to The Potter's Wheel.

Allie wondered if the killer had left anything behind. Nick had set up a team to sweep the immediate area. Even if evidence had been trampled away on the car park the night before, the area around the body would be quite clean. She didn't envy any of them as they pulled into the car park to check. It was still like the ice age out there, despite it being lunch time.

'What do you think?' Nick asked as he switched off the engine.

'No FLO?' she questioned, hoping that she didn't sound insubordinate. But it had puzzled her ever since he hadn't pushed the issue.

'I have my reasons.'

Allie waited for him to continue but he didn't elaborate. 'You want my honest opinion?' She sighed. 'It's unusual to have two murders around here in less than two weeks. It's even more unusual that Terry Ryder can be linked to both of them. Call it instinct, gut reaction maybe, but something doesn't sit right with me. I think those were crocodile tears back there. From both of them.'

Chapter Seventeen

Shaun hadn't slept on the night that Steph was murdered. How could he when he'd failed to do what he'd been asked to do? Hell, in his pathetic state, on the way home from dropping Stacey off, he'd even driven halfway to The Potter's Wheel, like he was going to get extra courage on the way.

Minutes from the pub, he'd pulled the car across to the kerb and threw up into the gutter. He'd got back in his car to collect his thoughts, turning his mobile phone over and over in his hands until suddenly, with an angry cry, he'd thrown it onto the passenger seat and started up the engine. He'd been in The Orange Grove fifteen minutes later, knocking back the whiskey like no man's business, thinking that his life was over. Or how it would be in a few hours when Phil found out that he hadn't followed through.

He was supposed to have killed Steph Ryder. Put a knife in her heart and watched as she bled to death. He couldn't do that! Murder wasn't in his blood. He may as well top himself now and get things over with rather than wait around for Phil Kennedy to do what he couldn't. He was well and truly fucked.

He kept going over and over how Phil might react when he next saw him. Would he come in to The Orange Grove and have a go at him in front of Carole and their customers? If he chose his moment, after the Regent Theatre emptied and its clientele were hungry, he could lose a fair amount of trade. Or would he do as he'd said, set the place on fire with both of them in it? Shaun swore he'd never sleep a wink again.

Last night, he'd been surprised when Carole had rolled in around midnight. Luckily for her he'd still been awake or she would have had to knock him up. She'd come in moaning, saying that Steph had abandoned her and she'd had to fork out twelve quid for a taxi back and what kind of friend was she, before staggering upstairs to bed. Shaun had stayed downstairs, sitting in the dim light of the restaurant with a mug of cold coffee and a half-empty whiskey bottle.

He'd sat there all night, listening to the sounds of the city outside. For a while it was noisy as people walked home after getting a kebab or a late night drink. Every now and then, he'd hear the faint beeps from the pelican crossing a few hundred yards away.

He woke just after eight with his head on the table and the bottle of whiskey empty by his side. But he stayed where he was and, after more coffee and more time lapsed, the next thing he knew it was past midday. Realising the restaurant should be open by now, he stood up. With heavy feet he went upstairs, wishing he hadn't given up his ten-a-day smoking habit. He could kill for a cigarette right now. Then he drained of all colour. Even a thought about murder could do that.

Carole was in the living room. 'You look like I feel,' she told him as he stood in the doorway.

'I'm fine.' Shaun glanced at her sheepishly. Her face had stains of last night's make-up and her hair stuck up in tufts after a deep sleep. A purple dressing gown was wrapped around her, held together by her folded arms.

'What's up?' she asked.

'Nothing.' He raised his mug, still full of cold coffee. 'I'm making a fresh drink. Want one?'

'Make it black.' Carole sighed. 'My head is pounding. Had a right skinful last night. Oh, I had a text message from Terry earlier.'

Shaun dropped the mug. Coffee splattered everywhere, the mug shattering into tiny fragments with a bang and a whoosh.

'Do you have to be so noisy?' Carole held onto her head with both hands. 'What a mess you've made, you clumsy git.'

'What did Terry want?'

'Apparently Steph didn't come home last night. No wonder I couldn't find her. I bet she's gone back with that lazy...' Carole stopped.

'That lazy who?'

'That lazy tart, Tracy Smithson,' Carole recovered quickly, thankful that she hadn't given the game away. She could take a secret to her grave but she doubted that Shaun would – for the simple reason he would love to tell Terry Ryder that Phil Kennedy was screwing his wife.

'So, she didn't go home? She'll turn up soon though, won't she?'

'Yeah, course she will. I reckon it's because I was supposed to be staying over at her house. He was probably expecting the pair of us to be there this morning. You know how possessive he is with her, with all his texts and phone calls, checking up on her all the time. I'm not texting him back. Can't stand that type of thing.'

Shaun wondered about the scathing tone but he let it go as he bent to pick up the remnants of the mug. Then he took them through to the bin. He almost dropped them again when he heard a news bulletin on BBC Radio Stoke. It was being reported that Leek New Road was closed off temporarily on one side due to a police incident. The reporter spoke of delays in traffic, for the next few hours at least, as a body had been discovered on Brooke Lane. Details were sketchy but more would follow as and when they received them.

But for Shaun, there weren't any sketchy details. It had to be Steph. Blood rushed to his head and he sat down quickly. It must be her. It was too much of a coincidence for it not to be. But what had happened? Who had killed her? And how had they killed her? Fuck, her life could have been ending while he'd sat in the gutter throwing up. How guilty would that make him feel – stupid, spineless shit that he was.

There was no mention of how it had happened yet. Not nearly enough information to tie up the details for someone who should have murdered her to get away with saying that he had. Because that was the next thing he needed to figure out.

Christ, what was he going to do? He hit the heel of his hand on his forehead twice in quick succession. Think. THINK. Was someone trying to set him up as a killer, even though he'd never touched Steph? Or was someone wanting Steph dead more than Phil Kennedy? Could Terry have got to hear about it?

As he stood there, a sickening yet welcome thought struck him. Maybe he could bluff his way through this. He could tell Phil that he'd done it. After all, surely the real killer wouldn't come forward? But what if Phil told Terry that it was him who'd killed Steph? His life would well and truly be over then, for sure.

Shaun choked back vomit. He was in a no-win situation.

If he told Phil that he'd done it, and Phil found out that he hadn't, he'd be dead meat.

If he told Phil that he'd done it and Terry found out, he'd be dead meat.

If he told Phil that he hadn't done it, Phil could burn this place down. Or, worse, he could put his debt up!

Shaun slapped his forehead again. THINK. But he couldn't: he was all thought out. Much worse, he realised that his fate could even lie in the hands of whoever was first to walk through the door – Phil Kennedy or the police.

'Thought you were making a brew?' Carole said, coming in behind him. 'Bleeding hell, what's wrong with you? You look like you've seen a ghost.'

'Nothing.' Shaun pushed past her. He needed time alone again, to think about this new development. 'I'm going downstairs. We're late opening up.'

'Charming,' Carole harrumphed. 'I'll make my own bleeding cuppa.'

———⁓———

Quarter to one. Phil sat in his living room. For hours, he hadn't wanted to switch on the radio to hear the news. Yet he needed to. If there was no mention of anything untoward, then he'd have to get ready to scarper for a few days. He'd checked his phone half an hour ago. Terry had stopped ringing him shortly after ten. Maybe Steph had now got home. Last night at The Potter's Wheel, he'd only had about twenty minutes with her before she'd disappeared. He'd tried to keep her in the pub but when he'd turned back after getting another drink at the bar, she'd gone. Thankfully, her friend was nowhere to be seen either so he assumed they'd gone home together. Soon after that, he'd cadged a lift home with one of the guys he knew.

Shaun Morrison didn't have it in him to do anything, he was sure. And if Steph had come home, he'd be in for it but he didn't care. He'd rather get a good beating than do any harm to her. And maybe Terry would calm down and the situation would blow over.

Yet, ultimately it would have landed him in the shit if Shaun had done anything, and he'd have to sort things out pretty quick or else he could wind up dead himself. There would be questions to answer and somehow he couldn't work out whether he would be around to reply to them. Damn Steph Ryder for getting under his skin. He loved her, the bitch. He cursed himself for it, but it was too late to go back.

He sat there until five to one. Then he switched on the radio. It was headline news.

'Police are making enquires after the discovery of a body in Brooke Lane, earlier this morning. The woman, believed to be in her late thirties, sustained fatal head injuries. Police are asking anyone who was in the vicinity of Brooke Lane, or at The Potter's Wheel public house last night, to come forward.'

Phil frowned. Head injuries? What the fuck ...? But realisation that the job had been done turned to grief and he crumbled. Steph was dead? No, he shook his head and walked through into the living room.

NO!

His hand swept across the fireplace mantel, knocking off everything in its path. Phil picked up the coffee table and threw it at the wall. He covered his ears with his hands at the sound of splintering wood and shattering glass. Breathing laboured and heart breaking, he stood bewildered. Saliva glistened on his top lip; tears poured down his face.

She was gone.

Steph Ryder.

He didn't need to wait for the body to be identified. He knew for certain it was her.

In the middle of the floor of number two, Georgia Road, Phil dropped to his knees and he cried.

Chapter Eighteen

Lunch time was coming to a close when Allie and Nick arrived at The Orange Grove just after two that afternoon. There was only a table of three diners left seated when they walked in to a welcoming smell of garlic. Allie sniffed longingly. All she'd had since breakfast was a chocolate bar and a packet of crisps from a petrol station on the way there.

Allie recognised Carole Morrison as soon as she saw her. She stood behind a long counter situated on the back wall of the room. The restaurant had a Mediterranean feel about it: orange and pale cream walls and dashes of vibrant blue. A large, thick wooden table stood lengthways in the centre of the room for parties of up to twenty to sit around. Amongst several tables for two, six booths were set out specifically for smaller groups. The place reminded Allie of a recent holiday she and Mark had taken in Pathos. As creatures of habit they'd chanced on an old style taverna on their second day and gone back there every night for the rest of the week.

'Hi,' Carole smiled as they approached her, recalling them both from the charity event. Then her face dropped. 'Oh, no. Tell me this is pleasure rather than business?'

Nick showed his ID card. 'I'm afraid not.'

Carole quickly joined them, wiping wet hands on a tea towel.

'There's no easy way of saying this, but your friend, Steph Ryder, has been murdered,' Nick told her.

Carole's mouth dropped open as she looked from the inspector to the sergeant and back to the inspector. She shook her head.

'But she can't be!' she said, 'I was with her last night.'

'She was found in Brooke Lane this morning. What time did you last see her?'

Carole struggled to get any words out as her mind raced ahead. She steadied herself on an empty table. 'Around half eleven, I think. What do you mean, she was found? What happened to her?'

'I'm afraid she sustained fatal head injuries, Mrs Morrison.'

'Ohmigod.' Carole covered her mouth with her hand and sat down. 'I've been ringing her phone all morning and getting no reply. Terry's not answering either. He sent me a text asking if I knew where she was. I don't believe it. No, it can't be true.'

'You say that it was eleven thirty when you last saw her?'

'It must have been around that, I guess. I went to get some fresh air after I felt a bit queasy. I went back in a few minutes later but I couldn't find her. I – I thought she'd gone home.'

'Without telling you?'

'Yes.' Carole's eyes brimmed with tears. 'She'd quite often up and leave if she was drunk. And she'd never remember doing it the following day. I was really annoyed with her last night. I couldn't believe she'd gone. And I had to pay for a taxi on my own. It costs a small fortune at that time of night.'

'And you came straight home?' Allie sat down opposite her, opened her notepad and looked over the details she had been given by Terry Ryder. 'Is that here, too?'

'Yes.' Absent-mindedly, Carole pointed to the ceiling. 'We live upstairs.'

'Have you ever taken a taxi back on your own before?'

'Sometimes, yes.' Carole regained her composure slightly. 'I don't like talking ill of the dead but Steph liked her drink and well … I could never keep up. I have a business to run. I can't stay in bed like she can every morning. Like she could, I mean.'

'What was she like, Steph?' asked Nick.

'Most of the time she was a good friend. But she was also hard work. She was very demanding, very self-obsessed.' Carole looked uncomfortable for a moment. 'Well, you met her. What did you think of her?'

There was a noise behind them. Shaun approached through a door at the back of the room. He stopped abruptly when he saw the police.

'Shaun, Steph's been murdered,' Carole told him quietly before bursting into tears again.

'But you were with her last night.' Shaun gulped, his eyes flitting everywhere but refusing to land on either Nick or Allie. He shook his head fervently. 'How?'

'Head injuries.'

'Head ...?' Shaun sounded puzzled. Luckily, before he could slip up, he noticed the three diners getting to their feet. 'Can I see to them and I'll be with you in a moment?'

Once the restaurant was empty of customers, Shaun joined them again.

'What time did you close up last night, Mr Morrison?' Allie asked.

'The last table went around eleven. No one else had come in since nine. It was a slow night.'

'And you have other staff?'

'Yes, there were five of us last night, with Carole being out. Not that they were needed after all. I gave Stacey – Stacey Richards – a lift home around quarter past eleven.'

'Do you often do that?' asked Nick.

Shaun nodded. Allie wrote down the names of the other staff members as he reeled them off too.

'Where does Stacey live?'

'Bagnall Road in Milton.' Carole sniffed.

'So you would have been on Leek New Road around midnight, after you'd dropped her off?'

'No – no, I was back here by that time.' Shaun's eyes narrowed. 'You don't think I had anything to do with it?'

'They're all routine questions for now.' Allie continued to write in her notebook.

'When you were in The Potter's Wheel, Carole,' Nick asked, 'can you run me through who you spoke to?'

'Oh, I – I was drunk,' Carole faltered. 'I still feel queasy from it now. I doubt I can remember a thing.'

'You must remember the beginning of the night, before you had a little too much?'

'Well, yes. Steph met me in here and we had a couple of glasses of wine. Then we moved on to The Tontine, then The Reginald Mitchell, before getting a taxi to The Potter's Wheel.'

'What time was this?'

'About ten, I think. It could have been a bit later, I'm not entirely sure. When we got there, it was packed.'

'So people must have seen you and Steph together?'

'Of course they must have. I...' Carole faltered. 'I can't remember who we spoke to, who might have seen us. I know the bar staff will have.'

'You can't remember anyone?' Nick said sharply.

Carole shrugged. 'I told you. I was drunk.'

'It doesn't matter yet if you can't remember,' said Allie. Patience was a virtue in this game, especially when someone was trying their best not to slip up. She could see right through the best-friend-for-life act, even if Nick couldn't.

Carole gave a weak smile to show her gratitude.

'No, I don't suppose it does,' said Nick. 'We'll catch you on CCTV somewhere. You think you were in the Reginald Mitchell until ten, you say?'

'About that.' Carole began to cry again.

Allie stood up as Nick nodded his head towards the door. 'If there's anything you *do* remember, Mrs Morrison,' he stared at her as he handed her a card with his details on it, 'please ring and let us know.'

Carole still wouldn't meet his eye.

'Something dodgy going on there, don't you think?' Allie said as soon as they were on the pavement and out of ear shot.

'Yes, she was definitely hiding something,' said Nick. 'What's the betting that Carole Morrison has been having a bit of extra-marital fun?'

Once the police were out of sight, Shaun locked the door and drew down the blind. There was no way they could open up tonight. He'd ring Stacey; she could tell the others not to come in. He checked what bookings they had – five so far. Good job they always took down contact numbers.

Even though he was trying to stay calm and not alert Carole to anything, halfway through dialling the first number he stopped. 'What the hell's going on, Carole?'

Carole started to cry again. 'I don't know. I only went out to get some fresh air and when I came back I couldn't find her.'

'So she never came after you?'

'I don't think so – I can't remember! But if I had seen her, I wouldn't have come home alone, now, would I? And she – she wouldn't be dead.'

'Did you try to call her?'

'N – No, I was in a mood with her. You know what she's like. She'd been harping on at me all night,' she lied, 'picking fault as usual so when she sloped off, I just wanted to go home.'

'So you didn't go and look for her?' Shaun ran a hand through his hair as he paced the room. 'And you're sure you didn't see her again?'

'Yes, I'm sure!'

'Did you see anyone?'

'No! Look, what's with all the questions?'

'I want to know, that's all.' Shaun sat down beside her with a thump.

'Why? You don't think I had anything to do with it, do you?'

'Of course not.' Shaun shook his head. 'I've never been more certain of anything. You wouldn't have the courage.'

'Sometimes I wished I had.'

'Don't speak like that.' Shaun reached for her hand but Carole drew it away.

'Do you think they'll be back to question us again?'

'I imagine so. They said they wanted to interview the rest of the staff. And I suppose they'll want more details from me.'

'Why?'

'I left here at eleven fifteen. I drove Stacey home.'

'But you wouldn't have gone past The Potter's Wheel to get to Milton.'

'No, but they don't know that.' Shaun wouldn't meet her eye. How could he tell her that he'd been nearby without arousing suspicion, even if he hadn't done anything wrong?

'Why would they think that you had then?'

'You heard that sergeant. She said that I would have gone that way.'

'She said you would have been on Leek New Road. She meant somewhere, not outside The Potter's Wheel. Leek New Road is miles long. Besides, I would have seen you, if you were. Would have been cheaper too, if I had.' She paused. 'Why didn't you ring me? You could have picked me up.'

Shaun stood up. 'How the hell was I to know you were coming home? You were staying over at Steph's, remember?'

'Yes, but –'

'Look, stop going on about it now. You sound as though you're feeling guilty. Is there something you're not telling me?'

'No!' Carole replied, her words coming out quickly and determined. 'I've got nothing to hide.'

'Me neither.' Shaun caught her eye for a moment before looking away.

Carole's head felt like mush. What had gone on last night when they'd split up? She hadn't got a clue how long she'd been outside. Had Steph come looking for her? Or had she stayed inside to talk to Phil Kennedy like she often did? Carole wouldn't put it past him to do something in a fit of temper. He was a real nasty piece of work. But, then again, it seemed to her that he obviously cared a lot for Steph. On the odd occasions she'd caught them together, they seemed really into each other, despite the fact they weren't meant to be together.

Suddenly, she rushed upstairs. When she came back down, she was shrugging on her coat.

'Where are you going?' asked Shaun with a frown.

'I have to go and see Terry. He'll be upset and –'

'And what?'

'She was my best friend.' Carole grabbed the car keys and rushed past him. 'He'll need someone with him.'

'You can't just barge over there!'

She stopped at the door. 'Yes, I can. And if you have any sense, you'd be coming with me.'

'Why?'

'We're their closest friends. Well, I am, anyway. The closest thing Steph had to family because she pushed them all away with her nastiness. If we're not seen up at that house, the police will think we've something to hide.'

'Don't be ridiculous.'

'But don't you see, I may have been the last person to see her before she was ... before she....'

'Carole, wait!'

But Carole had already unlocked the door and disappeared.

Shaun ran a hand through his hair. What a fucking mess. Thanking his lucky star he'd had the sense to get rid of the knife that Phil had given him, he raced to the door to follow his wife.

Lee had been pacing up and down the tiny living room since Kirstie had left that morning. Trying to get all his facts in order, he'd gone over and over what had happened the night before. Kirstie had got really drunk so she'd spent the night with him. That part was true anyway as Kirstie had practically passed out after he'd added two sleeping pills to one of her drinks. She didn't think he'd been out at all. So as far as she, or anyone else, was concerned for the moment, he'd been with her.

When a knock came on the door, he pulled back the closed blinds at the window to see his dad at the door. He panicked and paced a little more. Fuck, he didn't dare tell him. What if he was wrong? What if the job had been called off and he didn't know?

The banging on the door continued.

'What kept you so long?' Phil clipped him around the side of his head when he finally let him in. 'And why are your blinds shut? What have you been up to?'

'Nothing. Why?'

'You not heard what's going on, then?'

'Of course I've heard. Kirstie rang me when the cops told her.' Lee's words came tumbling out. He took a deep breath to steady his nerves. 'I need to see her again. I want to see if she's okay.'

'Are you mad? Terry will do his nut.'

'He will do when he finds out she was here.'

Phil sat down on the settee. 'You stupid fuck.'

'It's no big deal. She was upset. She and Steph had a fight and ended up lamping each other. Kirstie came running to me.'

'Steph hit her?' Phil paused, wondering if she had anything to do with this. Could Lee be covering for her? 'That gives Kirstie motive.'

'To cave her mother's head in? I don't think so.' Lee glanced furtively at his dad. That was a stupid thing to come out with. He needed to be careful what he was saying or else he'd land himself in it. 'They reckon she was in a right state,' he continued.

'They'll question Kirstie anyway. She's family. They always question family.'

'They can do what they like. Kirstie was with me.'

'All night?'

'Yes, all night.'

Phil whistled through his teeth. 'Fuck, you are in deep.'

Lee banged his fist down on the coffee table. 'Exactly, man. If I tell the cops she was with me, I'll get a doing over by Terry. You know he can't stand me.'

'But if you took her home, then she wouldn't have been anywhere near The Potter's Wheel.'

'No, but we have to drive past The Potter's Wheel.' Lee bit his bottom lip. 'I need to think about this. I don't want to land myself in it.'

'I think it's a little too late for that, don't you?' Phil shook his head. 'I warned you not to play with fire. Not with Terry's daughter, I told you.' He paused. 'You are telling me the truth?'

Lee gulped and held his eye. 'Course I am.'

'You're not covering something up that happened between Kirstie and her mother?'

'Course not.' Lee shook his head. He couldn't believe how far from the truth his dad was. And at least it gave him time to work out when to tell him what had really happened.

Phil nodded, letting the conversation drop for now. He knew Lee was lying about something. Which made him realise that, since his plans for Shaun Morrison had gone to pot, he couldn't trust anyone now.

Chapter Nineteen

One of the things Nick and Allie removed from The Gables was a handful of receipts from shops that Steph had visited the day before. Allie found it particularly sad when she'd seen the bags piled up in the master bedroom – Steph hadn't even unpacked some of the clothes yet. But as the date and time were stamped on three of them, it helped to trace some of her movements from earlier the previous day.

After leaving The Orange Grove, Nick and Allie made their way up to Hanley town centre and joined the throngs of Saturday shoppers. It was always the same at this time of year, mused Allie as she moved aside to let a woman struggling with several large bags get past. People spending like there was no future beyond Boxing Day. She looked around. Everyone had at least one shopping bag. No financial crisis would stop people having a good time at Christmas, even if it meant paying for it all the following year. And this was only the first day that the Advent calendars had been opened. She sighed, realising it would only get worse over the next couple of weeks.

In Stafford Street, they crossed over to Powder and Perfume.

'These sorts of places give me the creeps,' Nick muttered as he pushed open the salon door with a hefty hand yet trepidation in his step. 'What kind of a woman owns a place like this?'

'It's a man actually, and a colourful one at that.'

Allie grinned as she saw Nick pull his face at the sound of the tinkling doorbell. How could a man of his calibre, who would think nothing of facing a crazed good-for-nothing scrote with a knife or wrestling down a druggie hell-bent on causing mayhem, be afraid of a few women in a fancy shop?

'Hello, hello,' Roberto beamed. 'Is this to do with the body that's been found over at The Potters?'

Nick nodded. 'If I can have a few moments of your time?'

'You mean I might know her?' Roberto looked horrified in a mocking kind of way. 'Please, come on through.'

Nick flashed Allie a weary look as they were escorted through the middle of a group of women in varying stages of beauty treatments and shown through to a tiny office at the back of the salon. Allie smiled again as she watched Nick perch his lanky torso on the end of a lime-green leatherette cube. She sat next to him on a chair covered in blue and white striped material.

Roberto looked as though he would combust if someone didn't tell him soon who the murder victim was. Allie took the lead as Nick clasped hands together in his lap.

'It was Steph Ryder.'

'No!' Roberto's hand shot to his mouth. 'But I only saw her yesterday!' He leaned closer. 'Is it true that her head was caved in? You could have knocked me down with a feather when we heard it on the radio, couldn't you, Clara?'

Clara, a young girl of seventeen with vibrant pink hair, tanned skin and far too much make-up, stood in the doorway nodding.

'There were no such details given out on the radio.' Nick raised his eyebrows.

'I don't doubt that.' Roberto shrugged a shoulder slightly. 'But it was all around Hanley by lunch time. I really had no idea I would know the victim. That's what you call her, hmm? The victim?'

'You said you saw her yesterday?' Allie wouldn't be drawn into Roberto's games.

'Yes, she came over in the morning. She was here two hours, tops. Good job, really. Frankly, I can't stick her for more than that. Any longer and she makes me want to drag my nails down a chalk board.'

'Roberto!' Clara cried out in astonishment.

'It's true!' Roberto flapped a hand in the air before leaning in close to the two officers. 'You know what happens when someone gets murdered or attacked? Everyone comes out of the woodwork so that they can be on the telly. They all say what a lovely person he or she was, "never did anyone any harm, and wouldn't hurt a fly, blah, blah, blah." Load of baloney, if you ask me. So,' he prodded himself in the chest, 'I'm going to tell the truth. Steph Ryder was an out and out bitch. She was always moaning about something or other – though never about the price of my services as she didn't pick up the tab. I –'

'What do you mean, didn't pick up the tab?' Allie interrupted.

'Her bill was always settled by one of Mr Ryder's minions. Once a month, on the dot. A good payer, definitely. I mean, her bill could be huge some months to make her look more than the drunken layabout she really was.'

Allie stifled a grin. She loved a straight talker and Roberto definitely wasn't one to mince his words.

'What did you think of her?' Nick asked Clara as she busied herself sweeping the floor outside, but making sure she was in earshot of everything.

'I thought she was okay,' she said. 'But sometimes she'd be in a right mood. You never knew what to expect with her from one visit to the next.'

'Exactly!' Roberto chimed in, eager to get into the limelight again. 'She was a desperate housewife, if you can have one of those in Stoke-on-Trent. Mind, I think they're all a bit desperate, if you ask me.' He laughed at his attempt at a joke. No one else followed suit.

'Look,' he sighed, before wiping away his fringe with a dramatic gesture. 'She was a nightmare – end of. But good for business and I'm really going to miss her for that. She used to send lots of people my way. I suppose I should give her credit where it's due.'

'So you didn't notice anything unusual about this visit?' asked Nick. He stretched out his legs, struggling to stay upright on the cube.

'No,' Roberto replied. 'She wasn't any more hyper than usual.'

'Did she talk about where she was going later?'

'Of course she did!' Roberto shook his head in disgust. 'This is a beauty salon. We get to know everyone's business. She said she was going to do a bit of shopping – wanted shoes to go with some new top she'd not yet worn – and then she was going to call in to see her friend, Carole, from The Orange Grove. You know the one, off Piccadilly?'

Allie nodded as he continued.

'Then she said she was off around town before going to see some Elvis tribute band at The Potter's Wheel on Leek New Road.'

'And she never mentioned any more than the two of them meeting up?'

'No.'

'Did she mention anything about Mr Ryder?'

'She said he was out of town last night. That sounds a bit too convenient for me, though. What do you think?' He leaned forward again in anticipation. But he was disappointed when Nick stood up and Allie followed suit.

'If there's anything you think of after we've gone,' she handed him a contact card, 'please call me.'

'Yeah, yeah.' Roberto took it from her and then whispered. 'Go on, then. Now I've told you what I know, spill. What was she killed with? Was it brutal? Did her hair look good in the photos? Oh, my. I hope her nails weren't damaged in the struggle.'

Allie could hear him gossiping about it before they'd closed the door on Powder and Perfume.

'He should have been a copper,' Nick remarked, clearly still surprised at Roberto's straightforward mannerisms. 'He'd have you hung, drawn and quartered in court for remembering all of that.'

'Bet he'd look great in the uniform too,' Allie smirked.

***

Both Nick and Allie were thankful that Steph Ryder hadn't been an all-weather shopper as they split up at the entrance to the Potteries Shopping Centre for their calls. Usually, she'd take one of the team with her to gather details of the victim's last whereabouts but because of Terry Ryder's importance, Nick wanted to get into the investigation first-hand. A mere five minutes from their offices at the city's main police station, they decided to walk. Allie headed up to the top floor to her favourite shop, Extravagance.

'Allie, how lovely to see you,' Mary Francis said, greeting her with a warm hug and a kiss on each cheek. 'How did the big event go the other evening? Please tell me that you felt like a million dollars.'

'I did, Mary, thanks,' Allie told her truthfully. She'd felt lovely at the beginning of the evening. Not so much by the end of it.

'So what are you after today? I've had a beautiful blue dress in that would suit you down to the –'

Allie placed a hand on the woman's arm. She told her why she was there and watched her reel as she took in the news.

'What was she like yesterday, Mary?' Allie asked after a moment.

'She was her usual charming self,' Mary said, with a slight hint of sarcasm. She fetched an order book from behind the counter, ran a finger along the page, stopped halfway down and tapped it twice before looking up again. 'Here it is. She put an order in for a new dress for the Christmas Ball. She and Terry – that's her husband – organise one every year.' Mary sighed. 'I suppose she won't need that any longer.' With one fluid move, she drew a line through the name and closed the book with a bang. 'Shame.'

'And she didn't seem upset about anything?' Allie asked. 'Worried? Anxious? Did she say anything in conversation to you?'

'Huh, are you kidding? I don't think Steph Ryder would be worried about anything more than a nail breaking. I'm sure she has – had no heart.'

Allie glanced at her, a little shocked to hear Mary badmouthing anyone.

Mary shook her head. 'I'm sorry but I doubt whether anyone liked her. She was an impossible woman to please. Always moaning about something or other. Hardly ever gave a tip and always asked for a huge discount.'

Hmm, Allie thought. This was getting a little predictable now. Steph Ryder didn't seem to be liked very much anywhere they went. Still, that didn't explain such a brutal attack. She wound up the interview.

'Thanks, Mary.' Allie handed her a contact card before leaving. 'You know where to find me, if you can think of anything else.'

Allie went back to the entrance of the shopping centre to find Nick waiting outside Starbucks with two polystyrene cups.

'I didn't get much,' he said, handing one to her. 'You?'

'Nothing that we didn't already know. Steph Ryder didn't have many friends.' She lifted the lid to find coffee, blew on the liquid before taking the tiniest of sips.

'I hail the day when we can nail Terry Ryder but the bastard always seems so squeaky clean.' Nick moved out of the way before he was run over by a woman with a double buggy. 'And Phil Kennedy too, after getting rid of his brother.'

Phil Kennedy was one of three brothers and a younger sister. The youngest brother, Jay, had never got into trouble but the eldest, Steve, had been locked up five years ago. He'd killed a man over the right to sit on a bar stool in The Burton Stores and had gone down for fifteen years on a murder charge. Steve and the guy who was killed, Derrick Stanton, had been feuding for years prior.

It had been good for the police to get rid of the two men but there were always others waiting to take their place. While he was inside, they reckoned that Phil Kennedy was supposed to be looking after his patch, as well as Derrick Stanton's, but it seemed Terry Ryder had muscled in and made what was theirs into his. None of the force were looking forward to the day when Steve Kennedy was released and wreaked his revenge. Neither too, they surmised, would Phil be. Nor Terry Ryder, come to think of it.

'Steve Kennedy's got too long to go inside before he can make a difference outside, surely?' Allie questioned Nick.

'Not necessarily.' Nick drained his coffee, scrunched up the cup and dropped it into a nearby bin. 'Where are you heading next?'

'Stacey's Shoes in the market and La Senza.'

He groaned. 'Can't do any more of the girlie stuff. Meet you back at the station, yeah? Then we'll pull together what we have so far.'

Allie nodded. She finished her drink as she watched him disappear into the crowds outside and allowed herself a few minutes to think. She liked this part of the investigation most, where the clues unravelled and anything was possible. Later, after the witnesses had been interviewed and they'd drawn up new leads and the phones went quiet due to the hour – that was when it would hit her that, yet again, she was dealing with another senseless death.

This morning as she'd seen Steph Ryder's body for the first time, before she was even identified as Steph Ryder, Allie took pity on her. It was hard not to in her line of work. Apart from sharing a table with the couple last Tuesday evening, she hardly knew anything about Steph. For all she knew, she could have been drinking too much due to nerves. A big charity event such as that took some organising. There was bound to be more than a little stress involved in getting everything just so.

Steph Ryder could be a doting mum with a loving husband and a grade one marriage to boot, but after their investigations dug beneath the surface it wouldn't take long to get a completely different picture. Even now, she was beginning to form her own. And it wasn't pleasant.

She moved inside Starbucks for a moment and sat down while she made a few notes in her pad. There would be a list of people to question who could have seen Steph Ryder out last night. There were people in the town as well as at The Potter's Wheel. There was the rest of the staff at The Orange Grove. Christ, for all she knew, there could have been the whole of the city centre while she was out walking from one pub to another last night. At least CCTV should have monitored most of that.

Allie took one last flick through her notepad before putting it away and heading back into the crowds and up the escalator to the next floor. There was so much to check over but they would get to it all eventually.

After going back to the station to her team, it was past midnight when Allie finally got home on the first day of the case. She half expected Mark to rush at her, telling her to keep away from Terry Ryder, but the house was silent. He'd already gone to bed.

She listened at the bottom of the stairs. If he was awake, he would shout to her. He didn't.

In the kitchen, she made a mug of coffee but couldn't drink it. She couldn't rid herself of that awful image of Steph Ryder. From one side of the body, one blue eye stared back at her. From the other side, she hadn't even been able to make out an eye. There was so much pulp. She shuddered.

Allie hardly ever knew the murder victims. On the odd occasion she did, it was usually because they were already known to the police. Steph Ryder was in a bracket of her own. Allie didn't know her but she felt as though she did. And she would definitely know her inside out by the time the enquiry had finished.

What happened to you, Steph Ryder? She hoped she'd find out soon.

Giving up on the coffee, she tipped it away, locked up and went up to bed. As she brushed her teeth in the bathroom, Mark appeared in the doorway behind her. His eyes full of sleep, his hair stuck to the side of his head, he yawned and leaned on the frame.

'It was all over the news,' he spoke to her through the mirror.

Allie spit out the toothpaste. Tears glistened in her eyes. 'It was nasty, Mark.'

He came behind and wrapped his arms around her, enveloping her in his masculinity. She moulded herself into him and gazed at him through the mirror.

'Are you okay?' he asked. 'Not too many bad thoughts of Karen?'

She shook her head. Keeping busy with the case meant she hadn't time to remember too much. 'I'm sorry about this evening. Were Ruth and Chris okay about it?'

'Don't worry.' Mark kissed her on the cheek. 'I ended up rescheduling it, for a fortnight's time. And then I fell asleep on the sofa at eight.'

They shared a faint smile.

'I bet he did it,' he added. 'It's always the husband in these types of cases.'

Surprised that he wasn't telling her to come off the case, Allie went with the flow. It was good that he was trying to make light of the situation. She paused.

'Mark, I –'

'Shush,' Mark told her. 'I said I trusted you. That's all you need to know.'

Chapter Twenty

It was nearly seven when Allie headed back into work on Sunday morning after having only a few hours sleep. She wanted to get her head around things and see what had come in overnight.

She swiped her card to get into the police station and made her way up two flights of stairs. Nick and the team were crammed into the corner of an open plan office. As she walked the corridor created by the backs of the blue screens that separated the teams, she caught sight of the whiteboards ahead and the map of the city, a black circle around the area where the murder had taken place. The photo of Steph Ryder's body was blu-tacked onto the white background. Even now, the sight of a body could reduce Allie to tears. What right did anyone have to violate or kill another human being? What right had anyone to take a life by bashing someone's brain in? She wanted that board full of leads soon.

During murder enquiries of this size, the team would get together at the beginning and end of each shift and swap details. Sometimes this was when "eureka!" moments happened and a vital piece of the puzzle would slot into place. Other times, like now, at the beginning of a new case, it was a catch-up among Nick, Allie and the staff she managed.

Saying good morning, she sat at her desk and scrabbled around in the drawer for her emergency bar of chocolate that was replaced every two or three days. She bit into it and sighed with relish, wondering if any new leads had come in overnight. She soon found out as Nick came out of his office and joined them all a few minutes later. He stood up as he went over the events from the day before. Apart from the buzz of a few computers, the floor was quiet. Matt and Perry perched on the end of Allie's desk. Sam had wheeled her chair to the edge of hers.

Nick updated them on their findings after informing Terry Ryder of his wife's murder, visiting The Orange Grove and the beauty salon. Allie updated them on her visits to the places Steph Ryder had been shopping and what she wanted them to follow up on.

'Have you started doing door-to-door enquiries?' Nick asked Matt and Perry.

Matt nodded. 'We've spoken to the bar staff and the landlord and they gave us as many names as they could. Obviously it won't include everyone so there's an appeal going out on local radio. Loads of people have come forward for now, so we'll be getting to as many of them as we can.'

'Allie, I want you to head back to the Ryders' residence. I want you to interview Terry again, and his daughter. Go over everything with him. Sam, I want you to go too.'

'Sir.' Sam nodded.

'I need you both to be on your best behaviour,' he continued. 'The DCI wants us to keep this low level. He doesn't want anything to get in the way of the full investigation that's going on.' Nick raised a hand. 'I know, I know. It sounds terrible, like we don't give a toss. But I want to catch Ryder off guard if I can. Let him think we're not doing much while we look into everything. I just need you two to tread carefully. See if you can worm anything out of him.'

Ah, Allie understood now. That was why Nick hadn't wanted to chase up the family liaison officer. She glanced surreptitiously at Sam and they shared a secret smirk. Throughout the years they'd often been used to get close to people, victims and suspects. But Allie wasn't quite as keen this time. Womanly charms were all well and good but not when Allie broke out into an embarrassing hot sweat every time she got near to the person she was questioning.

Nick clasped his hands and then rubbed them together. 'Right for now, that's it. There's plenty to do but we'll start on the mundane things and see where they lead us. Twenty-four hours in – let's see if we can solve this thing in forty-eight.'

After a restless night, Phil left his house to head off to see Terry. He couldn't put it off for a minute longer. He needed to tell him that, despite what he must think, he hadn't taken any part in Steph's murder. Then he'd go and see Shaun.

As he was getting into his car, his phone rang. It was Kenny Webb.

'Where's the knife?'

'You have it. Don't you?'

'I wouldn't be asking if I did.'

Phil paused momentarily. The knife had gone when he'd checked in the outhouse yesterday. 'You must have it!'

'It wasn't there. Did you tell anyone else about it?'

'No one. You did look in the right place? Second drawer of the dresser?'

'Yeah, there was nothing there.'

'But I put it there!'

'Well, it's not –'

Phil disconnected the call and threw his phone down onto the passenger seat. The last thing he needed was grief from Kenny Webb. And despite the urgency, he didn't have time to work out who the fuck had the knife. It would have to wait.

Unbeknown to her dad, Kirstie had gone out that morning on the pretence of picking up Ashleigh and coming straight back again. But instead, she'd gone off route to see Lee. She'd had to knock him up out of bed and he'd been none too pleased.

'I can't believe I've been more or less grounded,' Kirstie stropped as she sat next to him on the settee. 'Once I pick Ashleigh up, I've got to go straight back home for when the police arrive again. I suppose they'll interrogate me. Can't see what they can find out though, when I was here with you all night.'

'You can't tell them that.' Lee turned to her sharply.

'Why not?'

'Your dad will go barmy. I'll never get to see you again.'

Kirstie gave him a huge grin. 'Aw, that's really sweet. I've already told them I stayed at Ashleigh's.'

Lee gave her a faint smile back. He wasn't doing it to be sweet. He was doing it to keep the police off his back. It was all well and good to think that Kirstie could be his alibi but it would be better if no one knew he was with her at all. Then the police wouldn't have any reason to question him. He wasn't at The Potter's Wheel so he wouldn't be on any list to be questioned. And if he wasn't questioned, he couldn't slip up. For now, he had to act natural so that Kirstie didn't suspect anything either.

'Why do you need to bring Ashleigh back to your house? I thought you said you'd be staying with her.'

'That's what my dad told the police so we didn't have some stupid family liaison officer breathing down our necks. It's bad enough that we both have all this finger-pointing going on without having someone there to watch our every move.'

'Are they saying you're a suspect?' Lee was intrigued.

'I fucking hope not.' Kirstie shook her head. 'I'm pissed off with all the attention already. It's interfering with things. Us for starters. I can't just nip out and see you now.'

Lee frowned. Kirstie didn't seem in the slightest bit bothered that her mother had been murdered. All she seemed to care about was the effect it had on her. How her life would change. How the attention had been shifted from her, he reckoned. He hadn't realised quite how self-centred she was.

'I thought you said you hated her,' he said.

'I didn't mean it!' Kirstie sounded exasperated. 'I put on a great act when the police came over yesterday, though, to take them off the scent.'

'The scent of what?'

'Dur. Are you fucking listening to me? If they realise how much I don't like her, I could become prime suspect. Are you sure I can't say I was here?' She moved closer and kissed him.

But Lee couldn't lose himself in the moment. All he could think of was getting her away from him and his house.

'You need to go,' he said, pushing her away.

'Why?' Kirstie looked on in surprise.

'You talking about motive made me remember.' He jumped to his feet, grabbed her arm and practically dragged her across the room. 'She nearly caved my fucking head in the other day, with a cricket bat.'

'She was drunk.' Kirstie understood his panic now. 'She wouldn't have remembered. Besides, only we know about that. And I'm certainly not going to say anything.'

'You better not.'

'What is wrong with you all of a sudden?' Kirstie tried to pull her arm away.

'I don't want you leading the police to my door. If they search this place, they'll find no end of knock-off gear. I'll be sent down in an instant.'

'Relax. I won't say anything.'

'Too risky.' They were at the front door now. He opened it and pushed her out. 'I'll call you later, yeah?'

'But you're not making sense! Lee. I –'

Lee sighed with relief once he'd closed the door. Fuck, that had been close. If anyone saw them together, the police would come and question him. He knew they'd get to him eventually but he'd be better to stay away from her for a while. At least until the rest of his plan fell into place.

Terry stood in the bay window of The Gables, staring out over the front garden to the open fields and beyond. Hands deep in trouser pockets, he thought back to the events of the previous day. Acting all grief-stricken in front of the police had been a doddle. Part of it had been true, anyway. It had taken him by surprise when he'd become emotional after identifying Steph's body. Seeing her had made it real. He'd actually questioned whether it had been worthwhile for a moment, until coming to his senses. Kirstie had sobbed uncontrollably, to the point that he'd wondered whether or not to sedate her. She seemed better this morning, though, almost as if it had washed over her during the night.

Coming back to an empty house had been surreal. He'd walked around for a while not knowing what to do. There had been people to ring, messages left on the answer machine as the news filtered through. And then Carole had turned up with Shaun, saying that she would look after him. As if he couldn't handle it, the stupid cow. But he'd played along, played the grieving husband. Had them completely fooled, even though grief wasn't the whole reason Carole was there.

But he still hadn't heard from Phil; neither had Shane nor Mitch, who were supposed to be cleaning up any mess. He'd tried again several times this morning too, on the pay-as-you-go phone, but nothing. He knew Phil would be laying low until the police had gone but it was a mystery why he hadn't called to see him yesterday evening. A mystery he intended to solve as quickly as possible.

Still, there had been something good about yesterday. It had brought Allie Shenton to his door. Terry could recall every detail about that. The black trouser suit that smacked of authority, the sharp white of her shirt, the neckline open suggestively to allow a little manoeuvre for flirting. Her eyes, pools of lust that she'd tried to hide away from him. She was his for the taking, he was sure. He'd seen enough of her now to realise the change in her skin tone was down to the way he looked at her. She was a good-looking woman, one he'd be happy to have on his arm, or over the kitchen table, any time she was ready. She was due back this morning. He wondered if she would come alone this time.

A van pulled into the driveway. Oh, no, no. Not here, not now! He raced out to meet its occupant.

Phil jumped out of the driver's seat. 'I need to see you, Tel. I –'

Conscious of the CCTV cameras on the house recording his every move, Terry reached out and shook Phil's hand. For the sake of appearances, he had to make it look as if Phil was only here to pay his respects rather than explain to him why he had fucked up the job. 'Come into the house,' he said.

Once the front door was closed, Terry slammed Phil up against the wall. 'What the fuck went wrong?' he yelled. 'I give you one job and you mess up.'

'Look, I can explain!'

'You were supposed to have got rid of her body. I told you to contact the cleanup crew. I wanted her to disappear. I could have coped with that type of investigation. The last thing I need is the police breathing down my neck. And now? They're going to be here every fucking minute. They're waiting for me to screw up! I ought to shop you, you stupid –'

'But I didn't do –'

'I don't want to hear another word.' Terry pointed his finger in Phil's face. 'I'll deal with you when I'm ready.'

'But I need you to listen to me. I –'

Terry wanted to ram his head into Phil's but was conscious of how it could mark him, too. He could quite easily take a knife to his throat but covering up one dead body was enough. Instead, he had to be content with punching Phil hard in the stomach. Phil doubled over.

Terry flexed his fist. He waited for Phil to catch his breath before he spoke again.

'Walk out of here as if there's nothing wrong. If the police question you, you came to pay your respects.'

'But Terry, I –' Phil tried one more time but he got pushed out of the door.

Once he was certain that Phil had gone, Terry paced the family room. He groaned loudly, like an animal in pain, trying to keep his aggression locked inside him. Despite feeling like he wanted to kill Phil, he'd have to deal with him later. The last thing he needed to do now was lose his cool knowing that the police were coming back.

Chapter Twenty-One

No more than twenty minutes after Phil had left Terry's home, Allie headed back to Royal Avenue with Sam to question Terry further.

'What's he like, this Ryder fella that everyone goes on about?' Sam asked, pushing her blonde fringe out of her eyes. 'I can't believe I've never come face to face with him yet.'

'I'll let you make your own mind up once we get there,' said Allie, stopping to give way to oncoming traffic. 'I don't want to sway you in any way.'

'But I've already heard he's a charmer.'

Allie nodded. 'Oh, he's a charmer, all right.'

'Now you have me intrigued. If I hadn't been told he was a looker, I'd guess that he has two heads or something.'

'More like two faces,' Allie muttered.

Even without the dark clouds looming overhead, The Gables had a sense of doom shrouding it. Allie parked the car next to the Mini that she now knew belonged to Kirstie. She tried not to glance at Sam as she was introduced to Terry and they were shown through to the family room. But she couldn't help it. She watched as the younger woman took note of Terry's appearance and everything around her.

Clean-shaven and smelling of something divine, Terry was dressed smartly with not an edge of grief about him. But Allie knew from past experience that that might not mean anything. For all his cool and calm, she wondered how he was really feeling inside. Unbelievably, she felt her cheeks burning as she caught his eye. Damn, that wasn't supposed to happen to her!

'Ladies.' Terry pointed to the dining table and sat down. They sat opposite him.

'Kirstie is upstairs with her friend Ashleigh,' he told them.

'I thought she was staying *with* Ashleigh,' Allie questioned, a little annoyed at his revelation.

'She is, yes. I wanted her to be here for your visit. I thought you'd need to speak to her.'

'Yes, we will.'

'I feel like I'm in a television drama,' Terry laughed, and then coughed awkwardly. 'Sorry, I didn't mean that as a joke. I just feel like I'm taking part in someone else's life. That I'm watching it from my settee instead of living it.'

Allie got out her notebook. 'We'll briefly go through the details you told us yesterday,' she stated. 'You say you last spoke to Steph at eight fifteen, before she was due to go out for the night with Carole Morrison?'

'Yes, that's right. I was working away. I wasn't sure if I'd be home for the night so I rang to see how she was. If I'm away we usually speak once or twice a day. It's good to keep in touch, don't you think?'

'And what did you chat about?'

'This and that, but nothing in particular. She said she'd had a busy day; stressed out, she said she was. I remember laughing it off. Steph's always stressed, according to Steph. She said that she'd fallen out with Kirstie and that she'd stormed off afterwards.'

'Did she say what the argument was about?'

Terry shook his head. 'No, but they were always having words. It wasn't anything out of the ordinary. I have two women in the house. One is a teenager. Most of the time the other acts as if she still is one. There are always lots of hormones and tantrums.'

'And you left Derby at ...' Allie let him fill in the gap so that she could double check it with her notes.

'Eight thirty.'

After confirming this, she nodded. 'And did you come straight back to Stoke yesterday morning?'

'Yes, although I stopped for petrol while I was on the A50.'

'Why were you in Derby?'

'I'm overseeing business. I'm developing an apartment block near the canal side. While I was over there, I caught up with a few associates over dinner.' Allie wrote down the names again as he reeled them off. 'It's always too late to drive home afterwards so I book in a hotel. The Bartley Hotel,' he added, pointedly glancing down at Allie's notepad before smiling again.

'Around what time did you get to your room?' Allie tried not to look at her colleague but was desperate to see her reaction.

'I'd say about eleven thirty,' said Terry.

'Were you alone?'

'Yes, I was alone.' Terry raised his eyebrows slightly. 'I am a married man, Sergeant Shenton.'

'I meant did you have a witness to that effect, Mr Ryder. If you had, we could have eliminated you from the enquiry for now.'

'What do you mean, for now?' All of a sudden, Terry's voice hardened.

Allie let a silence invade the room before ignoring the question and moving on.

'Have you any idea who would want to kill your wife, Mr Ryder? Does she have any enemies, anyone she's upset lately?'

'She was always upsetting people but I doubt anyone would have been angry enough to kill her, Sergeant,' Terry remarked.

'Does she have many friends?'

'Only one close one. Carole Morrison.'

Allie nodded. 'Yes, we spoke to her yesterday.'

'Did she mention that the two of them fell out?'

'When?'

'It was earlier in the week. Wednesday.'

Allie recalled the two of them on Tuesday night at the charity event. They'd been a bit tetchy with one another but nothing had turned nasty. Maybe they fell out quite often, as some friends did. Still, she made a note of it.

'And there isn't anyone else you can think of?'

'No.'

'Did she get on with your daughter? You mentioned they'd had an argument.'

'Yes, they got on as far as daughters and mothers do get on at that age.'

'Meaning?'

Terry sighed. 'I think you should ask her that yourself. You did want to see her?' Terry smiled again as his charm returned.

'May I go up to her?'

'Yes, go ahead.'

Sam went to stand up but Allie placed a hand on her shoulder. 'There's no need. I'll see her on my own.' Leaving her with Terry, Allie was at the door before he spoke again.

'Did you like the flowers, Detective?'

She turned towards him with a frown. It matched the expression on Sam's face. Damn the man for bringing them up now, and how disrespectful.

'I hardly think they were appropriate then, Mr Ryder,' she told him curtly, 'and I certainly don't think they're appropriate now.'

Kirstie and Ashleigh lay on top of Kirstie's double bed. They'd seen the detective from yesterday arrive and were waiting for her to summon Kirstie. Jessie J was playing in the background. Kirstie was twiddling her hair around her index finger, her leg over her knee waggling in time to the beat. Ashleigh lay on her side turned towards her, hands underneath her chin.

'Who do you think did it, Kirst?'

Kirstie sighed. 'I don't know. I bet she had loads of enemies. I hardly ever saw a good side to her.'

'She wasn't all bad.'

'You didn't have to live with her.'

'I know, but as mums go, she gave you a fair bit of freedom.'

'You reckon?' Kirstie disagreed. 'She'd ground me at any opportunity. And she wanted me to stop seeing Lee. There was no way I was doing that.'

'I thought it was your dad who doesn't want you hooking up with Lee. Why doesn't he like him?'

'It's something to do with the families. He's told me over his dead body will he allow me to be involved with a Kennedy. He says he's bad blood and not good enough. But he seems to forget that he came from the Marshall Estate and look how he turned out. Didn't do him any harm. I mean, look at this place.'

'So it has nothing to do with your mum, then?'

'Course it has. I bet it was her who put him up to it. She could never see me getting more attention than her.'

'I wonder if they'll find out who it was soon. Most murders get solved in the first forty-eight hours.'

'You've been watching too much telly, girl.'

'*According* to the telly,' Ashleigh shrugged a shoulder, 'they say it's usually someone she knows.'

Kirstie looked at her as if she had two heads. 'I hope you're not suggesting it was me!'

'Don't be stupid. I didn't mean you! I was thinking more of someone that your dad knows.'

'Or mixes with?'

Ashleigh nodded.

'It had crossed my mind.'

'What will the police ask you?'

'They'll want to know who's been here lately. Where we were when it happened. What mum's been up to, things like that, I suppose. Listen, Ash. You need to say that I was with you on Friday night.'

'What?' Ashleigh raised her head slightly from the pillow. 'Oh, no fucking way.'

'But if you say I was with you, then they won't know I stayed with Lee. My dad will go mad if he finds out.'

'I can't lie to the police!'

'I'd do the same for you.' Kirstie tried for the guilt trip.

'I wouldn't ask you to,' Ashleigh replied sharply.

'Please,' Kirstie begged. 'It's shit enough living here at the moment without me and dad falling out. Please!'

Ashleigh relented. 'Okay. But that's all I'm saying. Don't ask me to lie about anything else.'

'I won't.'

Ashleigh shuddered involuntarily. 'I can't believe your mum's dead, Kirst. I mean, it's too weird. What are you going to do without her?'

'I don't know,' Kirstie replied truthfully. 'But things are going to be different from now on, aren't they?'

'You'll have to be strong for your dad.'

'Are you mad?' Kirstie snapped. 'Do you really think my dad gives a shit that she's dead? He's probably glad to see the back of her.'

'Is that true, Kirstie?'

The girls looked up to see Allie standing in the doorway.

* * *

'Can I come in?' she asked, when no one spoke.

Kirstie nodded but wouldn't meet her eye. Ashleigh sat wide-eyed, her skin reddening. Allie knew better than to ask Kirstie the same question as before. She was bound to deny what she'd said or try to cover up the insinuation. Instead she tried to side with them, show them she was not the enemy.

'How are you holding up?' she asked gently. It was a stupid question, really, but what else could she start with? She stepped a little further into the room and closed the door. The pink curtains and rug, stripy pink and white wallpaper and shocking pink duvet cover surprised her. Apart from the *Playboy* logo on the bed, the room was totally different than the image Kirstie liked to give out. It showed a glimpse of her vulnerable side.

'I've been talking to your dad,' Allie said.

'Questioning him, more like.' Kirstie sat up and folded her arms.

'Yes, I was actually. It's part of the investigation. I need –'

'It isn't him, you know. They used to argue all the time but my dad would never do that to my mum. And besides, he wasn't here. So you're barking up the wrong tree. You should be out there trying to track down the real murdering bastard, not sitting in here drinking coffee.'

Allie ignored the jibes but couldn't help wondering why Kirstie was so tenacious about putting her point forward, especially after what she had just said. She moved a little nearer and took a chance sitting on the end of the bed. When she wasn't told to get off, she started her questioning.

'Where were you on Friday night?'

'I was at Ashleigh's flat, wasn't I, Ash?'

Ashleigh nodded slightly.

Allie took out her notebook and wrote this down. 'Your address, Ashleigh?'

'Why would you want to know that?' snapped Kirstie.

'Routine. I need to check this out.'

'I live off Ivy Road, in those new build flats. 27 Bramble Gardens.'

'And you were there from what time?'

'About half eight, Ash?' Kirstie looked at her pointedly. Ashleigh nodded. 'And I left about nine in the morning.'

'And you stayed in all night?'

'Not all night. We went to The Victoria on the Square.'

'Just to The Victoria on the Square?'

'Yes, we had a drink first and we went out – about ten, Ash?' Ashleigh nodded again. Still she wouldn't meet Allie's eye.

'What time did you get in?'

'How the hell should I know?' said Kirstie. 'We were bladdered.'

Despite wanting to slap Kirstie's legs and tell her to be a good girl, Allie noted down her hostility. Grief could make people act irrationally but she wondered if there was any grief to be had. Kirstie seemed only to feel sorry for herself. Someone should teach her some manners.

'Ashleigh, can you remember?'

As Ashleigh shook her head, it was obvious to Allie that she was holding back on something. She stood up.

'Thank you for your time, ladies.' She handed them each a card. 'If there's anything you need to talk to me about or tell me, any tiny detail that you think might help, call me.'

'Thanks.' Kirstie took it from her and, without looking at it, threw it onto the bed.

Allie smiled at them both before locking eyes with Kirstie. 'A word on your own, please.'

Kirstie sighed loudly and shuffled to the end of the bed. 'I'll be back in a minute,' she told Ashleigh and followed Allie out onto the landing. She stood like an insolent child, one foot in front of the other, arms crossed in defiance.

Allie moved her head forward a little. 'Look, unless you want to get your best friend into trouble, quit messing around. I can see that Ashleigh is worried about something. So I'll ask you once again, while you're on your own. Did you stay at her flat on Friday night or were you with Lee Kennedy?'

At the mention of his name, Kirstie gulped. She looked down at her feet. 'I was with Ashleigh,' she said quietly.

'You're quite sure about that? Because if I find out you're lying, I'll want to know what you're covering up.'

'I'm not!'

'Are you sure?' Allie probed. 'I can –'

'I was with Ashleigh,' Kirstie snapped. 'Why won't you believe me?'

'Because I know you're not telling the truth.' Allie paused for a moment. 'I just don't know why yet.'

Kirstie held Allie's gaze for a moment before sighing. 'Okay, okay. I was with him. But you mustn't tell my dad. He'll kill me.'

'Go on,' said Allie, thankful that she was getting somewhere at last.

'We had a row, me and Mum, before she went out,' Kirstie told her, omitting the part where they'd hit each other. 'I knew that Dad wouldn't be coming back so I stayed the night with Lee.'

Allie took out her notebook. 'What time did you get there?'

'About sevenish.'

'And what time did you leave?'

'About half nine the next morning.' Kirstie chewed on her bottom lip. 'You won't tell him, will you?'

'And you were there all night?'

Kirstie nodded. 'We had a takeaway and a drink in the house.'

'And then what?'

'We ... we had sex.'

Allie frowned. 'I meant did you go out at all?'

'Oh!' Kirstie blushed immediately. 'No.'

'So you were together all night?'

'Yes! But please don't tell my dad.'

Allie walked off, leaving Kirstie in suspense. Of course she wouldn't mention anything to Terry unless he asked and then she wouldn't lie. And didn't he have enough to think of at the moment without worrying about his wayward daughter? Seriously, what on earth was she doing hanging around with Lee Kennedy?

Allie was barely out of sight of The Gables before she was parking up the car again to question Sam.

'What did you think of the wonderful Mr Ryder?' She turned towards her.

'My God, he's hot.' Sam fanned her face with her hand. 'He had me blushing.'

'Why?' Allie gasped. 'What did he say?'

'That's just it. I don't think he said that much. It was the way he looked at me. It's like he ... like he's undressing you with his eyes. And not in a perverted way.'

Allie threw Sam a weird look then laughed as she realised she was winding her up.

'There's definitely something about him,' Sam agreed. 'But he's not my type.'

'I should think so,' Allie said, sharper than she'd anticipated. 'You're married.'

'So are you! But I can see how women fall at his feet. He has a certain magnetism. You do need to be careful, though.'

'What do you mean?'

'Despite you wanting to see my reaction, he only had eyes for you.'

'Don't be absurd.'

'I'm telling you, he followed your every move. Even when you were upstairs, he was watching the door for you to reappear.'

'That's his guilty conscience, if you ask me.' Allie batted away the comment. 'He's worried what we'll find.'

'Maybe.' Sam shrugged. 'Still, I think you should visit him on your own next time. He'll be better when it's just the two of you. And what did he mean about the flowers?'

'Oh,' Allie rattled off the first thing that came into her head, 'some arrangement that I nicked off the table last week.'

'You stole flowers from a charity do?' A look of disbelief crossed Sam's face before she laughed. 'Ha! Nice one, Sarge!'

'Not a word,' Allie warned Sam, thankfully knowing that she could trust her colleague not to say anything.

Sam crossed her heart with her finger.

Allie smiled then. Her secret was safe, even though it was a lie.

Chapter Twenty-Two

Shaun knew it was only a matter of time before he had a visit from Phil. In fact, he wouldn't put it past him to be watching from the shadows for the police to come and go. He knew they'd be there to question Carole. He thought he would have been round first thing on the day of the murder and, for once, had been glad to get up to Terry's for a couple of hours even though the atmosphere had been tense. He'd hardly slept the previous night, getting up at four thirty after Carole told him off for fidgeting and looking out of the window. So although his nerves were shot and he was dreading the outcome, it was almost a relief when he noticed him crossing the road, coming towards The Orange Grove that afternoon.

'Hold the fort for a while?' Shaun said to Carole as he walked past her towards the door. 'I've got business to sort out.'

'What sort of business?'

'Nothing for you to worry about.' He held up a hand to acknowledge Phil as he came through the door.

Phil pointed to the stairs. 'A word.'

As they went from her view, Carole stopped folding up napkins. What the hell was going on? Phil Kennedy was visiting far too many times for her liking. She had never seen so much of him in ages. And he hadn't said a word about Steph. Even without mentioning the affair, all three of them knew her. He could have said something in general conversation.

What was Shaun up to with him? Kennedy only visited when he was after something. Suddenly she froze. Please God, Shaun hadn't borrowed any more money. Or even worse, was just about to. She went to the bottom of the stairs, but fear of what Phil might do stopped her from going up. She'd have to wait until he'd gone and collar Shaun instead. Besides, she had enough on her plate looking after Terry without worrying about him.

Shaun followed Phil up the stairs and then showed him into the living room.

'You have more bottle than I gave you credit for,' Phil said.

Shaun gulped. He couldn't speak. His mouth had gone dry, his lips were sticking together and he could feel sweat erupting in tiny pinpricks over his brow.

'You kept that rage deep within there.' Phil prodded him firmly in the chest.

'It's best kept in there most of the time,' Shaun replied.

And in that split second, he realised there was no going back. He'd made the biggest mistake of his life. If not with Phil Kennedy, it would be Terry Ryder. If not with Terry Ryder, it would be the police. If not with the police, Carole would most probably murder him. He was well and truly screwed.

'What happened to the knife I gave you?' Phil interrupted his thoughts.

'I couldn't use it.' Shaun flopped down on the sofa as he prepared to lie for his life. He tried not to notice Phil's facial expressions becoming darker by the second. 'I knew her too well to see her dying. If I stabbed her, I might miss and not kill her. If I didn't get the right place, I – I might have bottled it and rung for an ambulance. Or run away while she was still alive.'

'So you beat her head to a pulp?' Phil's fist curled into a ball.

'It was quick and easy,' Shaun guessed. 'And it was over for her in no time. Better that way.'

'What did you hit her with?'

'What?'

'What did you hit her with?'

'Does it matter?' Shaun stalled for time.

'Of course it fucking MATTERS!'

The atmosphere in the room changed to arctic cold.

'I used a brick.'

'A brick?' Phil sounded amazed.

'Yeah, it was easier for me to just hit her and hit her.' Shaun had seen this on a recent episode of *Silent Witness*. The girl had run from the murderer and fallen to her knees, and he'd battered her a few times with half a house brick. At the time, Shaun had to look away at the sheer brutality caused by such an inanimate object. Now it served its purpose as a memory rather than a clip from a television program.

'And what did you do with this brick? You didn't lob it, I hope?' Shaun felt queasy as he imagined what the brick would be covered in. Imagining what would be on his hands, he wrung them hastily as if to rid himself of it. Finally, he gained his composure enough to continue.

'I chucked it in the canal,' he lied. 'About two miles from the pub. Along with the knife you gave me.'

Phil nodded. 'But what happened to the cleanup crew?'

'Hell, I don't know. I rang but no one answered. I was shitting it in case someone came out and saw me.' Shaun glanced up and back down quickly. 'I kept trying the number for ages, but still no one answered so I legged it. I didn't have your number and I didn't want to hang around with – with. I – I didn't know what to do.'

Phil stepped nearer, his finger in Shaun's face. 'You should have come to see me, you stupid PRICK! Not leave her there for anyone to find. I would have sorted it!'

'I didn't know that!' Shaun cried. 'I've never done this kind of thing before. I panicked.'

Phil took a deep breath to calm himself down. He wanted to kill Shaun so much right now. He had to get out of there before he did something he'd regret.

'Your debt is cleared – for now,' he told him, shoving his hands deep into his coat pockets to stop them lashing out. 'But if I hear from Shane or Mitch that you didn't ring them, then you're fucking dead.'

<hr>

The more time Shaun and Phil spent upstairs the more Carole worked herself up into a frenzy, wondering what they were meeting about this time. Shaun was going on the other day about the bar bill that had come in and who they were going to fail to pay while they cleared that debt instead. He must have borrowed more money. She'd kill him once she got her hands on him.

By the time she saw Phil come back downstairs ten minutes later, Carole was livid and no amount of reasoning by Shaun was going to make things better. She rushed upstairs but Shaun was already halfway down. She pushed him back up and into the living room again.

'You've sold us out, haven't you?' she hissed, prodding him in the chest sharply.

'No, I haven't,' Shaun replied.

'So what was all the secrecy? And why wasn't I included in the meeting this time?'

'Relax,' Shaun cajoled. 'You have enough to worry about with Steph at the moment. Let's just say that I've sorted things for now.'

'But how?' Carole didn't understand. 'How can you pay off twenty grand just like that?'

'I haven't. Phil wiped it out for me.'

'Phil Kennedy wiped out our debt?' She laughed. 'You don't expect me to fall for that, do you? Phil's a loan shark. He wouldn't let you off unless you had something on –' She stopped suddenly, her hands starting to shake as a ripple of fear ran through her. 'You don't have anything on him, do you? He wasn't involved with Steph's murder?'

'No! I don't know why he did it,' he continued. 'I suppose he felt sorry for us and let me off with a warning.'

'A warning?' She frowned. 'What kind of warning?'

'Nothing sinister, if that's what you mean.'

'This is Phil Kennedy we're talking about. He wouldn't let you off paying back twenty grand.' She shook her head. 'He wouldn't.'

'He would and he did.' Shaun took both her hands in his own. 'Look, I don't see what the big deal is. We're debt free again. Don't you think we should be celebrating instead of falling out?'

'No.' Carole snatched her hands away and walked over to the window. She looked down onto the street below, watching people walking by as if they hadn't a care in the world. She kept her back to him as she tried to figure out what the heck was going on. No matter how many times Shaun would try to convince her otherwise, Phil Kennedy would never drop twenty grand as a favour.

'It's because of Steph,' she said without turning back to face him. 'Isn't it?'

'No!' Shaun walked over and stood by her side. 'It hasn't got anything to do with her. Apart from that he feels sorry for what happened. He feels slightly responsible for her death.'

'Oh?' Carole turned to face him again.

'Look, don't say anything but he was in The Potter's Wheel the night she died,' Shaun chanced a lie. 'He said he saw you two and –'

'I never saw him,' Carole lied too, knowing full well that he'd been standing at the bar before she'd left.

'It was late on. He called in on his way home. Said he saw Steph but he didn't –'

'Did he see me?' It was Carole's turn to look guilty.

'I don't know. He told me about Steph as he felt bad about things. He said if he'd offered her a lift home, then maybe none of this would have happened. It has knocked him about, Carole. So he thought he'd help us out.'

Carole stood in silence, staring at her husband. That was a pathetic excuse. She knew he was lying. She just hadn't worked out why yet.

Phil knew that Shaun was lying too. He hadn't worked out why yet, either. Collar drawn up against the sleet that had started an hour ago, he marched down to where he'd parked his car off Broad Street.

It had taken all his strength not to jump the few strides across the room and ram his fist into Shaun's face. Already, he could imagine returning with a hammer and using it to bash the brains out of him. Shaun must think he was stupid. He'd checked with Shane and Mitch before he'd visited The Orange Grove. They hadn't received a phone call and he knew they wouldn't back down on a job. Unless they were out to set him up too, which was quite feasible if they were in this with Terry.

And what the hell had happened to the knife in his outhouse? Steve's idea to hide it at The Gables would have been fine if it hadn't gone missing. And if it turned up, Steve couldn't look out for Phil while he was in prison. He should have got rid of it and kept his mouth shut.

Phil began to panic. It was all sounding quite dangerous now. He had to get to the bottom of this business with Shaun and quick. He needed to figure out exactly who he was covering up for, before it cost him in more ways than one.

Chapter Twenty-Three

Lee had rehearsed what he was going to say before going to see Shaun Morrison that evening. Yet still, he was as nervous as hell. This was one of the biggest challenges of his life and he wasn't sure he could pull off a mature enough attitude.

For starters, he'd never tried blackmail before. In his eighteen years, he'd tried almost everything else. At twelve, he'd been caught nicking at the local supermarket on numerous occasions and got away with cautions. At thirteen, he'd been caught doing his first TWOC and cautioned again. At fourteen, he'd attacked another lad and ended up in juvie for six weeks. At fifteen, he'd gone down for three months for burglary. At sixteen, he'd been wiser and cottoned onto himself. He'd taken time to watch his dad and his uncle Steve and learn his trade. And despite not being as hard as he'd liked, at eighteen, he wasn't about to go back inside for something he'd done but hadn't yet got away with.

Right now, he was hiding in the back alleyway behind The Orange Grove. He'd thought he'd wait until Shaun came outside and then collar him but his plan hadn't included the rain lashing down. Not knowing the routine of the restaurant, he'd hid behind the stinking bins for over three hours. Soaked through and pissed off, eventually he heard the back door open. Some woman came running out with a load of black bags. Lee ducked out of sight as she threw them into the bins and then rushed back in out of the rain.

Another twenty minutes and he'd had enough. Cursing himself for wasting time, he squelched around to the front, opened the door and stood dripping on the doorstep.

Shaun was alone behind the bar, stocking up the shelves ready for the evening session, when he looked up to see him. His face dropped as he recognised Lee immediately. He hadn't seen him in a while. What did he want? He went over to investigate.

'Yeah?' he spoke sharply.

'We need to talk.' Lee's voice came out hoarse after he'd been quiet for so long. He coughed to clear his throat. 'About Steph Ryder.'

'Oh?' Shaun tried to act nonchalant but Lee saw his hesitation. And when Shaun pushed him out onto the pavement, it gave him courage to continue. The road outside was fairly quiet, office and shop workers leaving for the day. There were a few people scattered in the distance, but the street would be pretty dead until the theatre show finished around ten thirty.

'I know what you did,' Lee told him. He threw his cigarette butt into the road.

Shaun followed its path with his eyes before looking at him again. 'And what would that be?'

'Actually, I think you'll find it's more a case of what you didn't do.'

'So what didn't I do?'

Lee glared at Shaun underneath the street lights. He was medium build, not much to him, easy to handle with one punch. Shaun looked as though he was quaking in his boots. And he kept glancing into the restaurant. What a wuss.

'You didn't kill Steph Ryder, that's for sure,' he said.

'Keep your voice down!' Shaun barged into Lee's shoulder as he pushed past. 'I'm not discussing this here.' Lee followed him to the back of the building and found himself where he had started five minutes earlier.

'What do you want?' Shaun turned abruptly, taking Lee by surprise.

'Money.' Lee took a step backwards and then gained his composure. 'Five grand to keep my mouth shut.'

Shaun nibbled his bottom lip before replying. 'Keep your mouth shut about what?'

Lee made a big deal out of sighing. 'Look, man. You were told to knock off Steph. You didn't. Then –'

'Do you know who did?'

'I might do. But –'

'I need to know!'

'Shut the fuck up, will you? All I know is that you didn't kill her and you told my old man you did.'

'That's got nothing to do with you!'

'I think you'll find it has everything to do with me. Because if he found out that you were lying?' Lee made a cutting motion at his neck. Shaun paused long enough for Lee to gain a little more confidence. 'You're deep in it, my friend.'

Shaun knew how deep he was in it without some teenage thug thinking he could get the better of him. He wondered what his game was and exactly how much he really knew.

'Your old man know you're here, then?' he asked.

Lee laughed snidely. 'Don't fucking play me.'

'Get out of here.' Shaun walked away, then took a few steps back and looked Lee straight in the eye. 'I killed her. That's all you need to know.'

'No, you didn't.' Lee stayed firm. 'I saw you in your car on Leek New Road. You were puking up on the pavement. I drove past you.'

Shaun gulped. 'That wasn't me. You must have been mistaken.'

'It was you. I –'

Lee didn't anticipate the fist that came tearing up towards his chin in a flash. He staggered back at its force. The next punch knocked him to his knees, the kick following it connecting with his ribs. He curled up into a ball to protect himself as another kick caught his back.

Fuck, he hadn't been expecting this. Once down, he couldn't get up. Shaun wasn't supposed to be a fighter. He'd heard his dad talking to Terry, who'd called him a teddy bear. This was more like being attacked by a grizzly bear. There was nothing he could do but cover up as much as possible and ride out the storm. Then he'd get the fucker later.

He felt one more kick and then it stopped as quickly as it had started.

Shaun grabbed the back of his jacket and pulled him up to his knees. 'Don't you ever threaten me, do you hear?' he seethed. 'What I did or didn't do is no concern of yours. Now, fuck off and don't come here again.' He pushed him away roughly.

Lee struggled to his feet and walked off, his steps laboured and shuffling. A few feet away, he turned back.

'You're dead, mate,' he told Shaun, holding on to his ribs. He tasted blood, spat it out. 'Either you get my money or you're fucking dead.'

***

Shaun bent over in the silence of the alleyway. Soaked through, he took a few moments to catch his breath before looking up again. But Lee was nowhere to be seen. The little fucker had scarpered.

He leant on the wall. His right hand was throbbing; already he could feel it beginning to swell. What the fuck had he got himself into? Shaun admired the lad for having the audacity to try something like blackmail but he'd just got rid of one debt. He sure as hell wasn't going to create another.

He stared into the shadows, his familiar surroundings so alien, shrouded in darkness. In the distance he could hear traffic, the odd shout, but here in the alley there was nothing but a ringing in his ears. And stillness, making it all the more sinister. Anything could be lurking in there. He shivered. Fuck, what a mess.

Still breathless, he wondered what to do next. He couldn't go back inside without Carole suspecting something. She was bound to have come downstairs by now to find the front door unlocked with no one in the restaurant. He checked his watch. Some of the staff were due to start the five-thirty shift in minutes.

Slowly, he walked around to the front, wary of the cameras tracking his every move once back on the street. To his relief, Carole was upstairs. But it took one cry from Stacey and she was downstairs in a flash.

'What a bloody mess,' Carole said as Shaun concocted a story about an intruder coming in through the kitchen as he was behind the bar. 'I didn't even know you'd gone outside.'

'It all happened so quickly.' Shaun winced as she placed his hand under the cold water. Underneath the blood, there was some nasty swelling.

'We'll have to call the police and report this.' Carole shook her head in disbelief. What was happening to them lately?

'No, I'll be okay.'

'But –'

'I said no!' Shaun lowered his voice when he saw the hurt expression on Carole's face. 'I don't want any retaliation. He could have been on something. You know what some of the druggies are like around here. And he might come back.' He tried to make light of the situation. 'Besides, you should see the other guy. He didn't get a look in.'

Carole took his hand in hers and ran a finger over his knuckles. She knew he was putting on a brave front. It was the first time she'd seen him hit out at anyone. She ought to be proud of him but instead she felt annoyed that he'd been so stupid as to put himself in danger. She shuddered as her mind went into overdrive.

The alleyway at the back of their property was a haven for lay-abouts hanging around. The property next door but one had been empty for a few months now, and since a group of squatters had moved in they'd had nothing but trouble. Cars had been damaged and broken into, one of the neighbouring businesses had been burgled and they'd had to upgrade their security alarm system. This incident could have been much worse, especially if the attacker had pulled a knife.

'He was stealing the stock.' Shaun covered Carole's hand with his own to reassure her. 'It was an opportunist. I saw red and he got the brunt of it. It's a good job he scarpered when he did or else I'd have walloped him again. It was my fault. I nipped out to the bins with a cardboard box I'd crushed. We need to be more careful about locking the back door.'

Carole still wasn't convinced. 'I still think we should report it,' she said.

'For fuck's sake,' Shaun snapped. 'Don't keep going on about it. He got away with nothing; that's all that matters!'

Carole's eyes filled with tears. She held up her hands in resignation before walking out of the kitchen.

Shaun swore silently. Now he'd upset her as well. He dabbed at a cut he'd noticed, hoping it wouldn't become too prominent over the next few days. He was bound to see those police officers again and they'd want to know what he'd been up. And he could hardly tell them that without landing himself in it too.

'Fuck!' He spoke aloud this time. He'd have to sort something out soon or that frigging Kennedy family would be the death of him.

Later that evening, Allie took a call from the coroner. The post-mortem had been completed yesterday but there were several things to finalise before the report came through. There was only her and Nick left on the floor so she headed over to his office.

She knocked on the DI's open door. Nick sat at his desk, shirt sleeves rolled up by now. Even this late on, the faint tang of his aftershave caught her nose. Nick was always well presented. He wasn't one of those men who got out of bed ten minutes before they had to leave the house, not even bothering to clean their teeth. She admired this in a man. Likewise in ... Damn, she was thinking of Terry Ryder again.

'Steph Ryder was pregnant,' she told him in the tone of an excited five-year-old. She coughed, a little embarrassed about her outburst. It sounded as if she was gloating.

'Pregnant?' Nick looked up. 'I suppose you wondered?'

'Who the father would have been?' Allie moved a pile of paperwork off a chair and onto the floor before sitting down opposite him. 'I did, yes.'

'The daughter. How old is she? Seventeen?'

'Yes, but Steph Ryder is thirty-eight. It is easily possible.'

'I have no doubt of that,' Nick nodded. 'It's just that they've been married since they were teenagers. It hardly seems something that they'd plan. Maybe they were trying to inject romance into a dead marriage.'

'Which is not the way to go about things,' Allie snapped before she had time to think who she was snapping at.

Nick sat back in his chair, eyebrows raised.

'Sorry, sir.' Allie looked on sheepishly. 'I mean, having a child isn't necessarily the thing to stick people together. Normally it seems to be a wedge that drives couples further apart.'

'Lots of couples do it, though.'

'And lots of children end up in single parent families because of it.'

'My, we are cynical today, aren't we, Mrs Shenton?'

Allie smirked at him. Nick knew she and Mark had put off children and now were unsure if they wanted to have any at all. And just because they might not have any, it didn't stop her having strong views on other people's being treated well.

'How far gone was she?' Nick's fingers were in a steeple.

'Thirteen weeks. Puts a different slant on things, don't you think?'

'I wonder if she knew.'

'I wonder if *they* knew.'

Nick paused for a moment. Then he sat forward and went back to his work. 'I assume you can break it to him in the morning? Go by yourself this time.'

Chapter Twenty-Four

When she parked up in the driveway of The Gables at eight thirty the next morning, Allie hadn't expected Carole Morrison to open the door – and certainly not dolled up as if ready to go to a party. She wore black trousers, the highest of patent heels and a red knitted top that accentuated her neckline as well as her cleavage. The curls of her hair were immaculate, make-up perfect.

Her smile didn't reach her eyes when she saw Allie.

'I need to speak to Mr Ryder.'

'He's busy.'

'Too busy to see me?' Allie frowned. What an absurd thing to say.

Carole's guard dropped. 'Yes, of course. Sorry, come on in.'

Allie was shown through to the family room while Carole went to let Terry know she was here. The room was exactly how she remembered. *Exactly.* There wasn't a dirty coffee mug, a magazine, a pair of shoes hanging around. It seemed that chaos didn't rule in the Ryders' residence. It gave the place the air of a show house.

Carole rejoined her a minute later. 'He'll be with you in a moment,' she announced as if she was head waitress. Oh, yes, Allie thought snidely before turning to her. She would be used to that.

'Helping him out with something, are we?' Allie asked, wanting to figure out why she was here.

Carole blushed. 'No, he's catching up on some paperwork. I've been helping to keep things ship shape here since … since … well, you know.'

Allie did know but wondered what part of the sentence Carole wanted her to add on. Since Steph had been murdered two days ago and her best friend felt the need to look after her husband? Since Steph had died and her best friend wanted to take her place?

She checked her out as they waited for Terry to arrive. No, there couldn't be anything going on there. She didn't look his type. It was simply her cynical copper's mind. Or the green-eyed demon she remembered from back in her school days.

'How's Kirstie keeping?' she asked next. If Carole knew how Terry's daughter was, it could mean that she'd been spending a lot of time here.

'I haven't seen her,' said Carole. She sat down on the edge of the settee.

Oh.

'Has she gone to stay with Ashleigh now?'

'She's flitting between the two places.' Carole folded her arms. 'Although if you ask me, I reckon she's staying with that layabout boyfriend of hers.'

'Lee Kennedy?' Allie offered.

Carole nodded. 'Steph told me he'd been hanging around.'

'When?'

'Well, obviously before she died.'

'I meant, when was he hanging around?'

'Oh.' Carole had the decency to blush. 'She caught them in here. Lee wasn't allowed –'

'Caught them doing what?' Allie broke in.

'Lee shouldn't have been in here.'

Allie wondered if Carole had deliberately ignored her question as she continued. 'He isn't welcome at the house. Steph said Terry can't stand him. Reminds him too much of himself when he was younger. Cocky bastard, he calls him. I reckon they think he's not good enough for Kirstie. Steph said she'd told him to sling his hook.'

Allie was about to speak again when she heard the door open and in walked Terry. Wearing grey sweats, a white round-necked T-shirt and leather slippers, it took her by surprise. She had never seen him in casual gear before. She tried not to stare at his toned arms, the dark hair curling at the neckline, the faint outline of a taut torso.

Her stomach involuntarily flipped as he flashed a smile her way.

'Sorry to keep you waiting, Sergeant.' He held out his hand.

It seemed a strange thing to do, shake the hand again of the woman who was dealing with your wife's murder enquiry. To save face, Allie shook it. Terry held onto her but she pulled away awkwardly.

'I'll make coffee,' Carole said brightly. Allie had almost forgotten she was there.

'No need.' Terry kept his gaze on Allie.

Carole gently touched his forearm. 'But it's no trouble.'

'No, it's fine.' Terry looked at her then. 'You can head off home now. Thank you for the lasagne.'

'I'll pop by tomorrow, in case there's anything else you need.'

'I'll be fine.' His eyes returned to Allie. 'I have everything I need right here.' He indicated the settee. 'Shall we?'

Carole was still standing where she had been dismissed when they were both seated.

Terry sighed. 'Bye, Carole,' he said, without looking her way.

'Right.' Carole smoothed a hand over her hair. 'Right then, I'll be off.'

Before she had left the room, Terry leaned back in the settee and crossed one leg over the other. 'Is there something you need to tell me? Or ask me?' he said. 'Whatever it is, fire away.'

Allie felt terrible as she watched a dejected Carole walk away. For all her pitiful behaviour trying to get noticed, Allie could understand her. Despite being married, she'd had her fair share of admirers, flirtatious comments and office banter double-entendres. Most of the time, Allie was able to give as good as she got. But Terry Ryder did something to her. Without trying. Very much in the same way as he did to Carole Morrison, it seemed.

She kept her eyes down, away from Terry's intense stare, so that he couldn't see the reddening of her skin. Couldn't see what he could do to her with just the touch of his hands.

'You wanted to see me?' he said eventually.

Allie cleared her throat. 'Yes, I've had notification from the coroner's office, Mr Ryder.'

'Please,' he said softly. 'Call me Terry.'

Under the circumstances, there was no way Allie would call him Terry. She could be about to shatter his life for the second time in three days. So she didn't address him at all. She just nodded and continued.

'Were you aware that your wife was pregnant?'

For the first time since the murder investigation began, Allie saw Terry flinch. She watched his eyes flit around as if in disbelief.

'Steph was pregnant?' he replied.

'Yes, just over three months. I'm sorry. It seems that you didn't know.'

'What? That my wife of twenty years was fucking another man?'

Guiltily, Allie lowered her eyes momentarily. She'd thought as much herself only a few hours ago.

'I've had a vasectomy,' Terry explained. 'It must be over ten years ago now. We'd tried for another baby but nothing happened. I had no idea she was screwing around. How do you feel about people having affairs, Sergeant?'

The question took Allie by surprise. 'I don't think my personal views are of any relevance at the moment,' she answered.

'Do you think it's wrong?'

'I –'

'Would you never have an affair?'

She shook her head.

'You're telling me that you've never felt the attraction – the magnetic pull of anyone else all the time you've been married?' His eyes were on hers again.

'I'm not condoning those who do but I wish they'd finish one relationship before they wrecked another.'

'People shouldn't have their cake and eat it?'

'Something like that.' Realising the conversation was going off at a ridiculous tangent – why the hell should she justify what she thought? – she got it back on track. 'Look, I know this can't be easy for you after what's gone on, but I have to –'

'You want to know if there's anyone I think she would have been sleeping with?'

'Yes.' Allie nodded.

'Do you realise how cut to the core I am at losing Steph?' The emotion in his voice threw her. 'I –'

'But she was a bitch.'

'Excuse me?' Allie frowned.

'Yeah, you heard me.' It was Terry's turn to nod. 'I didn't know she was having an affair but things weren't that great between us, so even though I hate finding out like this, I can't say I blame her.'

'Do you think she would have been meeting someone else on the night she was killed?'

Terry sat back in the seat, arm stretched along the back. 'It's possible, I suppose. I never kept tabs on Steph. She was a free soul.'

Allie cast her mind back to what Carole Morrison had said. According to her, Terry was always on the phone checking up on Steph. Failing that, he'd be messaging her. Someone was lying.

'And there isn't anyone who comes immediately to mind?' she tried again.

'There are plenty of men who'd want to be where I was,' Terry said confidently. 'How many of them would dare to go there is another question.'

'And why's that?'

'Let's say they'd be lucky to come away with their balls intact if they did.'

Allie kept her expression impartial. For someone who'd lost his wife and had only minutes earlier told her he was cut to the core, Terry seemed rather calm about this new revelation. Maybe he was always this way, kept his emotions to himself. Some men were good at it. She made a mental note to do some more checking with Carole Morrison, and maybe her husband, Shaun. Perhaps they could help her figure out the real Terry Ryder. There was no way she wanted to get to know him any better. She was already too close for comfort. She moved on with her line of enquiry.

'I want to ask you about –'

Terry held up a finger. 'A minute, please.' He crossed the room to the front window. Then he went through into the hall.

Allie heard the front door open and muffled words. A few of them drifted in.

'Let go of me!'

'If you've been with him again, I swear I'll –'

'Is everything okay?' Allie joined them in the hall.

Terry held on to Kirstie's arm. She tried to shrug him off, but his grip was too tight.

'Just a little family disagreement,' Terry replied, turning to Allie. 'Kids. Who'd have them?'

Allie was astounded at his choice of words.

Kirstie pulled her arm away. 'Let me go, Dad.'

'I'll deal with you later,' Terry told her as she walked away. 'You and I need to talk.'

'Want to tell me what that was all about?' Allie asked once she'd heard a door slam upstairs.

Terry shook his head, all smiles and cool composure back. 'Like I said – kids.'

'So there's no truth in the Lee Kennedy thing? She's staying over at her friend Ashleigh's place, like you said?'

'Are you trying to trip me up, Sergeant?' Terry tutted. He waggled a finger in her face. 'I said she'd be staying with friends, not specifically with Ashleigh. And Kirstie has surprised me by wanting to stay close to home. Anyway, Lee Kennedy, you say? Where did you get his name from?'

Allie refused to divulge that to him. 'You do know him, though?' she questioned further.

'Of course I know Lee Kennedy. He and his father, Phil, work for me.'

'Work *for* you?' It was out before Allie could think about what she was saying. She raged inwardly for giving information away. He probably knew they were looking into his background, as well as his links with Steve Kennedy, but still.

'Yes,' said Terry. 'They help out at my car wash franchise. Though a fat lot of good the young one is. Not much work in him, I'm afraid. Now, if you don't mind. I'd like some time alone with my thoughts.'

'Of course.' Allie nodded, annoyed to find herself dismissed but aware she had no reason to stay and question him further at the moment. 'You will let me know if you can think of anyone, please? I know it's hard but it could be really helpful for our enquiries,' she added, trying to keep him sweet.

Terry shoved his hands in his pockets and shook his head. 'I honestly couldn't tell you who the father might have been.'

Allie watched closely as a million thoughts and possibilities seemed to shoot through his mind. At the same time, a million thoughts and possibilities shot through hers too. She dismissed them quickly.

'But,' Terry added with a look on his face that made her gulp, 'I am determined to find that out.'

Chapter Twenty-Five

'Where have you been?' Shaun snapped as Carole came through the front door of The Orange Grove. 'We're due to open for lunch in an hour!'

'Oh, stop moaning. Stacey's here, isn't she?' Carole unwound her scarf and took off her coat, annoyed that Shaun couldn't manage without her for a couple of hours. Honestly, she had more important things to think about than the restaurant right now. She'd planned on staying at Terry's house all morning but after being dismissed so early she'd wandered around the shops to give her time to calm down. The incident had been embarrassing, humiliating even. And at this moment in time, she hated Allie Shenton with a passion.

'That's not the point,' Shaun continued. 'I needed you here too.'

'I told you I was going over to Terry's this morning, see if he needed a hand with anything.'

'But you've been over there for the past three days. I can understand the day that it happened but not every day.'

Ignoring him, Carole went into the kitchen. Shaun followed behind her.

'Hi, Stacey,' she smiled. 'Everything okay in here?'

'Yes, everything's fine, thanks.' Stacey wiped her hands before opening the fridge.

Carole pulled a 'what's-the-problem' face at Shaun and poured herself a glass of water. Her head was pounding for some reason.

Trust that bitch of a sergeant to turn up just as she had Terry all to herself. She could have come half an hour later. She hadn't even had time to coax him out of his office.

'Terry's a big boy,' Shaun told her. 'He can look after himself.'

'For God's sake, Shaun. His wife has been murdered.' Carole fought back a sob. She glanced at Stacey, who was doing her best not to show she was listening. 'She was my best friend. I wanted to see if her husband was okay.'

'And was he?'

'Not really,' Carole fibbed.

'Oh?'

'Stacey, would you check to see if everything is okay out the front, please?'

Once she'd gone, Carole continued.

'He's in a right state. Perhaps you should be more understanding.'

'I suppose so.' Shaun relented a little, enough to let her think he was showing remorse. Of course he didn't give a stuff about how Terry was feeling. He only wanted to know one thing. 'Has he heard anything from the police yet?'

'Yes, plenty.' After she'd been so rudely ousted by Terry, Carole had been putting on her coat in the hallway when she'd overheard some of the conversation. She'd held her breath for a moment but she couldn't hear anything else, and she didn't dare hang around in case she got caught.

'That sergeant came back, that female one. I heard her say that Steph was pregnant,' she told Shaun with the look of super-sleuth pleasure.

'But I thought Terry had the snip?' Shaun looked on in confusion. 'He did, didn't he? I remember him being in agony afterwards.'

'Yes.'

'So she was screwing around?'

Carole nodded.

'Who with?'

Carole marched over to the door and checked to see that Stacey wasn't in eavesdropping range. 'Phil Kennedy,' she told him.

Shaun's eyes widened in surprise. 'You're having a laugh.'

'No, it's been going on for a while.'

'You knew?'

'I had my suspicions,' Carole lied, hoping her expression wouldn't give her away. 'He'd sometimes appear at the end of a night out to give us a lift home. I was always dropped off first because I'm in the town.'

'That doesn't mean he was screwing her.' Shaun shook his head. 'He wouldn't do that. Phil wouldn't cross Terry.'

'Why? Because he's his big mate?' Carole sniggered nastily. 'Don't bet on it. Phil Kennedy would get away with anything if he could.'

'I meant because of what Terry would do to him if he found out. He'd kill him!'

'No, he wouldn't. Phil has his big brother to hide behind. He might be locked up but he could still get to Terry.' Carole sighed. 'Still, at least if Terry did do him in, it would get Phil off your back too. I still think there's something you're not telling me.'

Shaun flinched.

'Men like him don't let you off repaying twenty grand,' she added in the hope of getting him to talk. 'He'll want you for something bigger, you mark my words. And when he does, I hope you'll be ready for it.'

'You've changed the subject pretty quickly,' Shaun accused. 'You know far more about Phil than you're letting on, don't you?'

'I'm just telling you what I heard.' Carole lowered her eyes. If she wasn't careful, she might land herself in it without thinking. She grabbed a box of cutlery in the pretence of something to do to leave the kitchen.

But Shaun wouldn't let it go. 'Was he at The Potter's Wheel when Steph was murdered?'

'I've told you before. I was too drunk to remember.' Carole marched past him but he grabbed her arm.

'I know, you told me that before. But what aren't you telling me, Carole?'

'Nothing!' She shrugged her arm away.

'Then why were you over at Terry's again? Why the sudden interest?'

'I'm trying to help out!'

'You should be helping out here! Come on, spit it out. What's the big secret?'

'I haven't got a secret!' Carole lowered her voice. 'What's wrong with you all of a sudden?'

Shaun folded his arms. 'Nothing.'

'There's clearly something on your mind too. What's your big secret?' Carole glared at him. 'Not willing to share?' she said after a while.

Shaun remained silent.

'Fine.' Carole walked off again. 'Until you can share your secret with me, then I'll go to The Gables as many times as I feel necessary.'

'Fine! I'll run things smoothly this end until you decide to grace us with your presence again.'

As Carole left the room, Shaun sat down with a thump. He wondered if Terry knew about the pregnancy, then cursed himself for not asking Carole. Still, knowing that Steph had been messing about could be his way out of this mess, especially since Phil was sure to be gunning for him once he found out that he hadn't killed her.

While Shaun sat thinking of some way he could use this new information for his own purposes, Carole banged cutlery down on the tables. *One morning*, she fumed. She'd been away for two hours and Shaun was already complaining. She felt like a slave. Wasn't she entitled to a life of her own?

Well, stuff him. Shaun would have to complain a little more because she was going to The Gables again tomorrow. She would make a shepherd's pie. Terry would like that. She might even return to dish it out, prepare some vegetables and a carton of gravy. Maybe she could join him.

She smiled now her thoughts were back on track. Terry needed her and she would be there for him, no matter what.

Allie left the Ryder residence with a jumble of thoughts in her head. As she climbed into the pool car and reversed out of the driveway, she looked up to see Kirstie watching from an upstairs window. She paused for a moment and caught her eye, wondering if she wanted to speak to her. But she didn't acknowledge her in any way so she continued off down the avenue.

She'd been surprised that Terry had no idea who the mystery man his wife was having an affair with might be. Oh, she knew that was the nature of the liaison, the other partner not knowing anything, but even so. Terry Ryder struck her as the type of person who would know everything that went on in his personal affairs. She wondered again if Steph had known she was pregnant before she died. After all, she'd only been thirteen weeks gone. Maybe she hadn't had any symptoms to suggest it by that stage. And if she did know, had she told the father? Had she even had *time* to tell the father? Maybe she knew and the father didn't?

There were so many loose ends to tie up on this case but one thing was certain. Terry Ryder didn't take too kindly to his daughter mixing with Lee Kennedy. In a way, Allie could understand his outburst. If she had a daughter, she wouldn't want her to go anywhere near him.

Back at the station, she started on the mound of paperwork that she needed to action. Across the desk from her, Sam sat huddled over a monitor.

'Any luck with CCTV yet?' Allie asked her.

'Some,' Sam replied, not taking her eyes from the screen. 'I've picked up Steph Ryder with Carole Morrison as they go in and out of the pubs that Carole mentioned. Then they get into a taxi on Stafford Street at quarter past ten. We lose them when they leave the city centre.'

'And there are no cameras to speak of at The Potter's Wheel?'

'There are two dummy cameras and a grainy image on a working camera showing the right side of the car park so I'm mapping out the cars from there. But it doesn't swing round enough to cover the side where she was found. The light was out around the back too.'

'Out or broken?'

'Broken.'

Allie paused for a moment, wondering if the killer had known this or if it had simply worked out in their favour. She sifted through some of the witness statements that Matt and Perry, along with a few uniformed officers, had gathered from anyone who had been in The Potter's Wheel that night. A couple of people had seen Carole leave and also Steph, but they couldn't be certain which one of them had gone first or if any of them had come back in at all. It had been a typical drunken night - lots going on but no one really noticing anything. *A great time for anyone to lie*, Allie realised with despair.

She trawled through more of the statements that had come in from Georgia Road. Despite its location, Nick wanted all the residents questioned. It was a long shot, but maybe one of Terry's tenants had taken a disliking to him over a dodgy deal or an eviction. But she soon realised as she flicked through the paperwork that she could hardly call them witness statements. True to form, no one on Georgia Road had seen Steph Ryder at any of the properties in the few days before she'd died. Number sixteen said he'd never seen Steph down there, or her car. Number six refused to answer the door, on several occasions. Number twenty-four denied knowing her at all. Number twenty-two had been away for the weekend. Perry had checked that out with the custody sergeant and, sure enough, he'd been booked into the custody suite early Friday evening, appeared in court first thing Monday morning and been given conditional bail. And, according to Phil Kennedy, when she came across his statement, he said that he had seen Steph that night but hadn't noticed anything untoward. Allie made a mental note to check that out again and also go over Lee Kennedy's statement when that came in. So far no one had caught him at home.

A text message beeped into her phone. It was from her friend Kate, asking if she fancied meeting for lunch the next day. Allie sighed. She hated letting her friends down but there was no way she could make it, not in the middle of the case. With regret, as this was the third time in a row, she sent a message back with her apologies. Halfway through it, a movement caught her eye. Sam was on the phone waving frantically at her. Allie waited for her to put down the receiver.

'There's been a handbag found in the bushes of an empty property about a mile away from The Potter's Wheel,' Sam said. 'It has a phone – a smart phone – and a purse. And there's a watch with the name Steph engraved on it.'

Allie was in the shower when she heard the door to the cubicle open and close. Steam rose around her. Momentarily, she was shocked when she felt a hand slowly rising up the side of her thigh. But then she turned her body, closing her eyes against the force of the water. Two hands found her waist. Lips found hers. They kissed, slowly, water dripping into their mouths and over their tongues. They broke for air and his mouth moved lower, over her neck, her chest, her stomach and back up again. She gasped as his hand caressed her body.

Letting the hot water flow over her breasts, she arched her back as the waves of passion began to build. She opened her eyes and glanced down ... to find Terry Ryder looking up at her. Flames licked at her insides as his lustful eyes mesmerised her. But then she saw red. Red over her stomach, the tops of her thighs, her breasts. The water diluted it but it kept coming back. She put a hand to it, brought it closer to her face. As she climaxed, she realised it was blood.

Allie woke with a start. She sat up and switched on the bedside lamp. It was three a.m. The house was quiet. With Mark asleep beside her, a slight snore escaping his lips, she wondered why the hell she'd dreamt about Terry Ryder. Until she could prove otherwise, he was a suspect in a murder case. And what the hell was all the blood about?

Could she pass this off as normal behaviour or was there something else to it? Working on a case was all-consuming for Allie. She ate, slept and breathed it until she could do no more about it. Usually that was down to one of two things. Either the suspect was caught and charged or the case went cold as the leads dried up and there was no satisfying conclusion.

Going over individuals' details meant she often knew the victim better than the family. Yesterday, she'd picked up more personal effects from Terry. Along with examining the items found in the bag this lunchtime, yet to be confirmed as Steph Ryder's, the afternoon's job had been to go through everything to see what she could piece together. Finding the phone meant that they could trawl through the phone records. And as technology had advanced, there could be a lot of personal items to search through on there also. Emails, photos, even downloaded applications could build a broader picture. Quite often social media accounts such as Twitter and Facebook could tell you more than any family member. Allie liked to do as much of this as she could. It helped her to get inside the victim's head.

She lay back down again. Thankfully, it had only been a dream. Guiltily, she spooned into Mark's back, her hand reaching possessively around his waist, perhaps to remind her that he was real. She shouldn't be dreaming about anyone but him.

She tried to sleep but still Terry invaded her thoughts. To catch a killer, sometimes Allie had to get near to that killer. Get them to trust her. Get them to slip up. So far, Terry had given no signs that he could be involved in his wife's murder, but still, instinct told her to keep pushing. That meant playing her part. Yesterday, she'd known he was trying to manipulate her with all that talk about affairs. Make her seem uneasy around him so that she wouldn't outstay her welcome. But somehow she had to make Terry think the opposite. She needed to get underneath *his* skin. It was dangerous but she'd done it before to great results. Never with anyone as powerful as Terry Ryder, though.

Allie closed her eyes and up popped Terry's face again. What was wrong with her? Why was her heart ruling her head?

Chapter Twenty-Six

Even though her dream from the night before was still clear in her mind and even though it made her more than a little wary of visiting Terry, after the following morning's catch-up meeting revealed nothing further coming in overnight, Allie made her way to The Gables alone. She'd phoned Terry to tell him she'd be calling but was still taken aback when she saw him waiting in the doorway. He smiled as she parked up, looking oh-so-bloody-fresh in navy jeans and a pale blue shirt, sleeves rolled up to the elbows. She sighed. Wasn't the man ever cold? It was minus two outside and she was sick of scraping the ice off car windows, yet here he was again dressed as if it were summer.

He stepped onto the driveway to greet her. Allie felt her cheeks start to flush as the aroma of his aftershave enveloped her. It had a masculine woody note with a hint of vanilla, definitely something by Tom Ford. She breathed it in then stopped abruptly. She needed to keep her cool to pull this off.

'We've found a few more things we think belong to your wife.' She rummaged in the back seat of the car for the evidence bags.

Terry closed the door for her afterwards. 'I hope you've caught the bastard who did this as well?'

'We're still making enquiries.'

'It's been four days. Don't you have any leads?'

'There are a number of things we're following up.' *Like your every move before the crime occurred.*

They walked to the house. Allie could feel his arm resting on the small of her back, even though it wasn't there. When they went through to the family room, she was surprised to see Carole there again. She was cleaning down a work surface, a tap gushing as it filled up the sink. Looking irritated, she turned off the tap and rushed across the room to join them.

Before Allie could speak, Terry did.

'I'll need to see the sergeant alone,' he addressed Carole. 'This is another personal matter.'

'But I thought ...' Carole turned quickly on her heel. 'I'll make coffee, then.'

Allie felt another pang of pity for the woman but was happy to brush it aside. She passed Terry the first transparent evidence bag. Inside it was the shoulder bag that had been found. It wasn't anything in particular - small, black with a zip opening and a few decorative buckles. Perry had located it in one of the high street fashion stores for less than twenty pounds.

'Did this belong to Steph?' she asked.

'Yes, I think so.'

'You think?'

'I'm not a woman so I don't take much interest in bags. You mentioned something inside it when you phoned?'

Allie passed him another evidence bag. Inside this one was a wrist watch. It was made by Tag Heuer, the model Aquaracer 2000. Its mother-of-pearl diamond dial had a polished steel case, the bracelet scratch-resistant sapphire crystal. Perry had looked it up on the internet. The price tag was just under seventeen hundred pounds to buy it now. And although there were many good counterfeit watches doing the rounds, it certainly didn't look like a knockoff from a market stall.

Terry turned the bag over and peered at the inscription on the back of the watch. It read '*To Steph, all my love x.*'

'I bought her that for our twentieth wedding anniversary,' he said. 'We went to Las Vegas. I surprised her while I was there.'

Allie wished Mark would surprise her with a watch costing that much when they reached twenty years. Next, she passed Terry an evidence bag containing a purse.

He took it from her. 'Where did you find these things?'

'The bag was hidden in the front garden of an empty house in Baddeley Green,' Allie told him. 'The estate agent was showing someone round when she found it tucked in the hedge. Said she'd seen Steph's details on the news, saw the inscription and the photograph on the driver's licence in the purse and handed it in.'

'Other things?'

'There's a diary, a gym membership card and a set of keys. Did these belong to Steph?' She held up another bag containing the items.

Terry nodded but he didn't take this bag from her. She watched as he seemed to drift off into the distance for a while. She left him to it for a moment. A few feet away, she could hear Carole clattering around in the kitchen, determined to make them realise that she was still there.

'She was such a looker, at one time,' Terry said. 'Still was to some extent, but much better before the booze took hold of her. Do you drink a lot, sergeant?'

'We also found this.' Allie ignored his question and moved to the final item. It was a Blackberry Touch smart phone. Apart from a spot of mud, it was intact and in good condition. She held it up in another clear evidence bag.

'We know this is Steph's because it has photos of you and Kirstie on it,' she told him. 'We've got a lot of numbers from it and from the calls stored. Steph seemed to use the same ones with frequency. We're checking them out at the moment. I'll let you know if we see any that need identifying.'

Terry reached for the bag that contained the mobile phone. Allie paused. Had he deliberately touched her hand? She looked at him but he was staring at the phone through the plastic covering.

'She never had this bleeding thing off.' He shook his head. 'Always texting someone or other. Arranging appointments. She lived her life by this phone. Do you think it will hold any clues?'

Allie nodded. 'Yes, it could. Sometimes we find vital information.'

'How?' Terry gave it back and pointed to the settee. Allie sat down, and then became a little uncomfortable when he sat next to her in the vast room. He crossed his legs and turned his body slightly towards her.

'It will tell us when she last used the phone,' she replied, trying not to notice. 'Who she spoke to, where she might have been over the last few days that could prove relevant, and there are emails we can check, too. Yes, you're right. It can often help us with the bigger picture.'

'By that you mean what she gets up to when she isn't with me?'

Allie felt the heat of his stare. 'We all need to spend time alone,' she responded.

'I should have been there for her, don't you think?' Terry leaned forward. 'I should have been a better husband. If I had, maybe she would be here now.'

'Why do you say that?'

'I worked too much. I never gave her the attention she needed when we were together.'

'What is it, exactly, that you do?'

Terry smiled. 'You know what I do, Sergeant Shenton. You've done your homework on my wife, so you must surely know all about me.'

I know all the legitimate things you do.

Allie reached into her bag for her notebook. Terry sat forward and, before she had time to react, she felt his fingers in her hair, moving it away, tucking it behind her ear. She looked up quickly.

'What do you think you're doing?' she asked.

'Your hair seemed to be in the way. I thought I'd move it for you. Besides, I like to see your face.'

He reached his hand out again. Allie moved her head back.

'Drinks!' Carole marched into the room and slapped a tray down onto the coffee table.

For the second time, Terry ignored Carole, not even turning to look at her. But Allie was glad that she'd come over when she did. She could feel herself colouring again. Christ, how must this look to her? She smiled her thanks and reached over for a cup. Terry leaned over too.

'I'll get it for you.' He passed it to her.

Allie refused to meet his eye. Instead, she shuffled to the front of the settee. Most of the time she dressed smart-casual for work, but today she wore a pencil skirt, a fresh lilac blouse underneath a grey pinstriped suit and black knee-length boots with a high heel, despite it being slippery underfoot. She crossed her legs at the ankle and rested the cup and saucer on her lap. Carole, still standing in front of them, wore black trousers and a white shirt. The neck was undone far too low for Allie's liking.

When she eventually looked up, Allie couldn't believe Carole's reaction. Her skin had drained of colour and her hand shook as she reached for a cup. Something then made her pull it back and she stood there awkwardly. Allie looked at Terry and swallowed. No wonder the woman had been spooked. Flashes of evil tunnelled from his eyes. Yet in an instant, Terry turned towards Allie with a smile.

What the hell was going on? Had she walked into a lovers' tiff? Or worse, was Terry trying to include her in some kind of love triangle? Either way, she wasn't joining in with his games.

'Actually, I don't have time for coffee.' She put the cup and saucer down on the tray, smoothing down her skirt as she stood up. 'I'll be in touch soon, I'm sure.'

'I do hope so,' Terry replied.

When she hit the cold air outside, Allie gulped it in as if she were drowning. Had she really been a part of that? Oh, God, what a creep. Half an hour ago, she'd seen his eyes fill with tears when he'd caressed his dead wife's watch. Now she realised that it might have been for her benefit. Maybe she'd been given a true taste of how powerful Terry Ryder really was.

She got in the car and once again looked back at the house as she put her car into reverse. This time it was Terry Ryder who was at the window.

───

As Terry stood watching Allie leave, Carole wiped away a tear that had fallen, hoping he wouldn't turn round and notice. Humiliated yet unable to voice her feelings, she wondered how he'd explain away his actions. He'd made a pass at that bitch. She was sure of it. And after all she'd done for him.... It was a good job she'd walked in when she did.

She blinked away more tears threatening to fall and tried to smile for when he turned round. Terry didn't like his women weak. She quickly gathered herself together and held her head high. But he continued to stare out of the window. What was he thinking about? More to the point, *who* was he thinking about? Her, Steph or Sergeant Shenton? She hadn't anticipated any competition.

'Are you okay?' she asked moments later when she began to think he'd forgotten she was there.

'Clear that stuff away,' he said.

At his harsh tone, she did as she was told. Once she'd loaded the dishwasher, she joined him. By now he was seated again on the settee. He looked deep in thought.

'Penny for them,' she giggled and sat down next to him.

He looked at her with such disgust that she thought she was going to cry again.

'I was thinking about you,' he said.

She smiled. That was better.

'A glorified waitress, that's what you are.' Terry nodded. 'That's what you'll always be. Ready to clean up after someone else.'

'Don't be so nasty.' Carole tried to laugh the remark off. 'I do have other uses.' She placed a hand on his thigh but he smacked it so hard that she drew it away. 'What's wrong with you? You're never usually this hostile.'

'I'm rather amazed that you think you can be a substitute for Steph.'

'No. I –' Carole flinched at his accusation. 'What a horrible thing to say.'

'Okay, then. I'll say this instead. I think it's best if we cool things.'

'Of course. I understand.' She touched his forearm gently, praying he wouldn't slap her hand again. When he didn't, she continued. 'There's too much heat at the moment and, as much as I long to be with you, I can wait.'

Terry said nothing. Carole mistook his silence for emotion and smiled encouragingly.

'It'll be okay,' she said. 'Things will get better once that nosy bitch has completed her investigations. We'll be able to be together again then. I'll be more of a wife to you than Steph ever was.'

Terry pushed her back onto the settee. He held both her arms up beside her head, squeezing her wrists until she cried out in pain.

'Whore!' he shouted, his face so close she could see the hate in his eyes. 'A fucking whore. You'll never be any more than that. I only ever fucked you when I wanted to and how I wanted to. Do you understand?'

'My wrists!' Carole cried out, her heart pumping out a drum beat. 'You're hurting me.'

'You need teaching a lesson on respect, Mrs Morrison.' Terry pulled her onto the floor.

'Ow!' Carole caught her back on the corner of the coffee table.

'Take off your clothes.'

'No!' Immediately Carole's arm moved to cover her chest.

'But you want me to fuck you, right?' Terry pulled her nearer. 'Either you take off your clothes or I will rip them off. Then how will you explain that to your precious husband?'

Crying openly, Carole flipped off her shoes, pulled off her trousers and her shirt. Terry watched her every move. She was down to her underwear.

'Take off the rest,' he said.

Carole unclipped her bra and then pulled down her pants. She stood in the middle of the room trying to muster as much dignity as she could.

'Now lie down on the sofa – here, this one – on your back.'

Carole frowned. Terry grabbed her arm and pushed her down. 'Hurry up!'

When she looked round he was gone. But in a moment he was back, with a digital camera.

'No!' She grabbed for her blouse.

'I wouldn't do that if I were you.' Terry covered her hand with his foot and pressed down hard.

'Smile.'

When she didn't, he yelled.

'I said fucking SMILE!'

In that split second, Carole realised she had no choice but to go along with him. She tried to look happy but how could she when inside she was dying. He took three photos and reviewed them before undoing his trousers.

'Now you can do your stuff.'

Carole kneeled in front of him and took him in her mouth. If panic weren't shooting through her veins she would have bitten the end of his cock off but she knew she wasn't a hard bitch. That was Steph's way, not hers. Steph had often told her how rough their sessions had been, often shown her bruises and welts. It hadn't seemed exciting to her then and it wasn't exciting to her now. She quickened her pace. The sooner she got this over and done with, the faster she could get out of the house.

Wiping her mouth afterwards, she looked up to see a look of satisfaction on Terry's face. Of course she had known that it would always be one-sided. She knew he'd never love her. She knew he'd never leave Steph for her. But right now she'd give anything to be inside The Orange Grove, waiting on tables, with Shaun out the back cooking Spaghetti Bolognese. What a fool she'd been to ever think she was what Terry wanted. She dressed quickly so that she could be on her way.

'I fantasised you were her,' he said as she tucked in her shirt.

Carole's teeth started to chatter. Oh, how could he say that to her now? After what she'd just done. After *everything* they'd done.

'Not Steph,' Terry continued. 'Detective Sergeant Allie Shenton.'

Carole gagged but tried to keep it hidden.

'I could see her when you made me come.' He grinned. 'Fuck, it's making me horny thinking about it.'

'If you start anything with her,' Carole snapped without thinking, 'I'll show the police the text messages you sent to me.'

Terry grabbed the collar of her blouse and pulled her within inches of his face. 'Then I'll show everyone those photos, including that spineless bastard of a husband of yours.'

'Please, Terry.' Carole felt the ability to stand being taken away from her.

'I took one while you had my cock in your mouth,' Terry continued, eyes glazed with rage. Then he pushed her away.

Looking back, Carole was never quite sure why she antagonised him when she was so scared, but she said the only thing she thought she had to stop him in his tracks.

'Then I'll tell everyone about Phil and Steph.'

'What?'

'They were having an affair. If the police knew about that, they'd know you had a motive to kill her. I know you didn't murder her, but what would they think?'

Terry punched her in the face.

Carole staggered and then dropped to the floor. Blood gushed from her nose. The pain was like nothing she'd ever experienced.

'If you say anything to anyone,' Terry came at her again, grabbing her hair and pulling her to her knees. 'If you say ... if ...'

Carole grimaced as he held onto her. She could feel the blood pouring down her face, onto her shirt. Oh, God, he was going to kill her!

'Don't you ever think that you can threaten me or there'll be plenty of what you've just had,' he went on. 'Treat that as a warning. If you open your mouth again, I'll cut out your tongue. Do you understand?'

Ye – yes.'

'I said do you UNDERSTAND?'

'Yes!' she cried.

Terry let go of her then and she fell back onto the floor. He grabbed her bag, searched through it and found her phone. With a press of a few buttons, she knew the text messages had been deleted. He threw everything to the floor and walked away, only turning at the door to say one last thing.

'Get yourself cleaned up, fuck off out of my home and don't ever come back.'

It took all the strength Carole had not to crawl into a ball and sit in a corner crying. Had that really happened or would she wake up in a minute? Find out it was all a bad dream, that she hadn't been punched head-on by a man.

But fear of Terry returning and hitting her again propelled her unsteadily to her feet. Throwing back her head, she pinched the bridge of her nose to stem the bleeding. Then she retrieved her clothes, dressed as quickly as she could and ran out of the house. In her panic to get away, she struggled to get her keys into the door and to start the engine. Crying openly, she finally managed and sped off, wanting to put as much distance between them as possible.

As soon as his fist connected with her face, Terry regretted what he'd done to Carole. Not for the pain he'd caused her but for the stupidity of his actions. He sat down in his study and seethed. Why the fuck hadn't he hit her somewhere that it wouldn't be notice-able? He could have thumped her in the stomach and it would have had the same effect. He only needed to get rid of her. Then again, he shouldn't have hit her at all, really. Shit, he was losing it. Last week he'd lashed out at Phil with the wrench in the cellar and now Carole. But how dare she think she could blackmail him with those text messages? Did she really think she could get one over on him, the stupid bitch?

His hands clenched into fists, nails digging into his palms. He unclenched them suddenly and glanced at his hands. Damn, he didn't need any cuts or bruising on them. Not now.

Calm down, Terry, he chastised himself, or it's all going to go tits up. He opened a desk drawer and dialled Carole's number on the pay-as-you-go phone. Surprisingly, she answered.

'One word of who did that to you and there will be more of it, lots more of it.' His voice was calm but menacing. 'Do you understand?'

Chapter Twenty-Seven

After taking the phone call from Terry, brute strength must have got Carole home to The Orange Grove. She parked the car around the back of the building as best she could but, braking too late, she clipped the front bumper on the wall. Gasping for breath, she didn't even register it. Now that she was safe, relief engulfed her and she started to cry again. Tears poured down her face. She dared to look in the rear-view mirror. Already her right eye was beginning to close, bruising appearing almost as she looked. What the hell had she done to deserve that?

She'd thought Terry was ringing to apologise but all he'd been interested in was saving his own skin. Now all she could think about was saving her own. What the hell was she going to tell Shaun? How could she explain what had happened and why? She'd have to make something up. There was no way she could tell him the truth. She sat there until she thought what to do.

Seeing that the back door was unlocked, despite their good intentions, she went in that way. One look and Shaun flew across the kitchen towards her. 'Ohmigod, what's happened?'

'I – I –' Even though she'd worked out something to say, she still couldn't lie to him straightaway.

His concern and shock made Carole cry even more. Not for herself, but for deceiving him. Shaun was her saviour. In the twenty years they had been married, she knew he'd never strayed.

Lord knows she'd pushed him away often enough to give him the chance. And what had she done? Screwed someone they both knew. Which made her a selfish, thoughtless, heartless bitch and she had no one to blame but herself.

She clung to Shaun as he helped her upstairs, fearing that if she let him go, he would leave her. Guilt overrode her usual ability to feel safe in his arms. She knew if he found out what had really happened it would break his heart. Not only would their business be ruined but also their marriage.

Shaun pushed the bedroom door open and helped her onto the bed.

'I'll get you something to wipe yourself with,' he said and disappeared.

As she waited for him to return, Carole wondered what had got into Terry to attack her in such a violent manner. Oh, for sure she knew about his 'hard man' reputation but she assumed that would be against other men. In all the years she'd known him, she'd never thought he was capable of this type of behaviour with a woman. How could she ever have slept with that – that beast? Worse, how could she ever have been so taken in by Terry Ryder the Smooth Guy?

'What happened?' Shaun asked again when he returned a minute later.

'I'd called into the Spar shop on Granville Road and was getting out of the car when someone tapped me on the shoulder.' Carole let him dab away at the blood gently. 'I – I turned round and he – someone punched me in the face.'

'Someone?'

'I – I think it was a man.'

'Did he take your bag?'

'Yes,' she lied, having hidden it in the boot of the car for now. She'd have to remember to shift it as soon as possible and hope Shaun would be too concerned about her to go looking through the car. 'But my keys were in my coat pocket. He took my phone, my money and my credit cards. There was nothing I could do.'

'Did you get a good look at him?'

'No,' Carole started to cry. 'I know it was light but he – he –'

'Shush, you're okay now,' Shaun soothed. 'Did anyone else see him?'

'I don't think so.'

'You mean you didn't report it?' Shaun frowned. 'Why ever not?'

'I was too shocked, I guess. I just got back in my car and drove. I wanted to get home.'

'Well, I've rung the police. They're sending someone over.'

Oh God. 'No!'

Shaun cried out in exasperation. 'Some bastard robs and assaults you and you want him to get away with it?'

'No, but I – I don't want to talk about it yet. If I talk to the police, I'll have to relive it and I – I can't.'

'But you'll have to do it at some point.'

'But please, not now.'

Shaun paused. Carole's right eye was swelling by the second, already the bruising coming through; it looked so painful. Despite him wiping away dry blood from her face, there was more down the front of her blouse. And all the time that bastard Lee Kennedy would be laughing at him. That stupid fucking bastard! Not only was he insistent on blackmailing him, even after a kicking he was determined to get one over on him by hitting him where it hurt. Or more to the point, hitting the one that he cared about the most. Well, he wasn't going to let him get away with it.

As Carole's heart sank, Shaun's sank even further. He caught his reflection in the dressing table mirror. His face was grey, his hair a mess where he'd run anxious hands through it. Carole's blood was all around the collar of his shirt too. His eyes filled with tears as he touched it. Fuck, what a mess.

And all because of his lies.

'You need to see them now,' he insisted.

Allie had called in at The Potter's Wheel to see if any more witnesses had come forward. The landlord was taking a list of telephone numbers and the team had been working through them. So far it had proved fruitless, but she knew everything could change with one tiny detail coming to light. She sat in her car, trawling through the names.

Surprised to hear the shout go out for The Orange Grove, she called in to say that she'd deal with it and headed off. She was there ten minutes later.

Shaun stood waiting on the doorstep. 'Carole has been mugged,' he said, his face etched in angst.

'When did this happen?' Allie asked. It wasn't an hour since she'd seen her at Terry's house. She wondered if Shaun knew that.

'About half an hour ago.' Shaun ushered her in. 'She's really shook up, can't remember much but I wanted someone to come as quickly as possible. I'm really worried but she won't let me take her to the hospital.'

Allie followed him upstairs to the bedroom. Shaun tapped on the door.

'Carole?' Shaun spoke gently. 'DS Shenton's here.'

Carole started to cry. Taking her tears of self-pity for those of fear and shock, Shaun held her close and shushed her again.

'I won't keep you long.' Allie sat down on the side of the bed. 'But I really need to ask you a few questions while everything is still fresh in your mind.'

Shaun moved away. As Carole turned her face towards her, Allie tried not to flinch at the state of it. Carole's eye was a swollen mass, so much so that she seemed to be having trouble seeing through it. Her nose was swelling. Whoever had done this had hit out in temper. Then she frowned. Had Terry Ryder got anything to do with this?

'What happened?' she asked, getting out her notepad.

'I didn't see who it was,' Carole told her sharply. 'I can't give you a description.'

'It's okay. Take your time and we'll run through it all. Let's start with where you were.'

'I went to the Spar shop to pick up a few things.'

'Which one?'

'Granville Road.'

'Had you been anywhere else before this?'

'No.'

All the time she lied, Carole willed Allie not to give her away. Shaun stood beside them, his arms folded, face like thunder. She had to contain the lie or else he'd find out about her affair.

Thankfully, Allie made no mention that she'd seen her over at Terry's that morning.

'So you got out of your car and then what?'

'I – I felt someone tap me on the shoulder. I turned around and he – he –' She glanced at Shaun. 'Do I have to do this now?'

'A few more questions and I'll leave you in peace. Mr Morrison – Shaun – would you mind if I had a few minutes with Carole alone, please? I'm sure she's upset because you can see her like this.'

Shaun nodded. Allie waited for him to leave the room, waited a few more moments to make sure he was out of ear range and then moved closer to Carole.

'Right, then, *Mrs* Morrison. Cut the bullshit. Why don't you tell me what really happened?'

Carole's heart sank. She knew the minute the police were called she would be found out. Maybe Shaun wouldn't think anything of the attack at the Spar shop. She'd only lifted a story from *The Sentinel* that had stuck in her mind ever since she'd read it. But this was Allie Shenton. She knew she wouldn't be able to fool her too.

'What happened?' Allie prompted.

Carole had two choices. She could either continue to lie and look stupid, or she could admit what had happened to the police and tell Allie how scared she was that Terry would kill her. But then that would get back to Terry. And she had those photographs to think about. She couldn't let anyone see them, never mind Shaun.

'Did Ryder do this to you?' Allie asked.

At the mention of his name, Carole flinched.

Allie placed a hand gently on Carole's forearm. 'You have to tell me what happened. You can't let him get away with this.'

'Would you get me something, please?'

'Look, I really need to –'

'Please.' Carole pointed to the dressing table. 'Would you pass me that?'

Allie looked behind her. There was a small hand mirror. She picked it up and gave it to Carole.

Carole took a deep breath and held it up. She cried out loud when she saw the damage done with one punch. Tentatively, she ran a finger over the swelling in her nose. Her right eye, puffy and closing, had shades of red and purple appearing. She put a hand to it and drew it away quickly when it hurt.

'How could he do this?' she looked at Allie, trying not to cry again.

As Allie remained silent, Carole realised she was beat.

'It was him,' she said quietly.

'Excuse me?' Allie couldn't believe her ears. She hadn't thought for a moment her notion would be true.

'It was Terry Ryder. I'd seen him a few times before Steph died. It was when he fancied a quick fumble and Steph was either too pissed or not around. But it's not as if it's a full-blown affair.'

'Is there any difference?'

'Don't you dare judge me!'

Allie lowered her eyes for a moment. If Terry hadn't been on her mind so much, she wouldn't have said that. Annoyed that she'd let her private feelings into the conversation, she turned back to professional talk.

'Look, I need to get the facts,' she said. 'I want to find out who killed Steph as much as you do and what you've just told me needs further investigation.'

'All I can see is his face after he punched me and knocked me to the floor,' Carole sobbed. 'I'll never forget it.'

'You're saying that Terry Ryder did this to you?' Allie had to corroborate that she was hearing right.

'Yes.'

She wrote it down in her notebook.

Carole put a hand on Allie's arm. 'Please don't do that. I don't want to press charges.'

'I don't care. I still want all the details.'

'But he'll find out!' She sat up further. 'What happens if he comes after me again? Look at me! Look what he did with his hands! Imagine what he'd do with a.... You have to help me.'

'I'll help you if you tell me the truth. Were you with Terry the night Steph was murdered?'

Carole nodded slowly. There was no point lying now.

'He texted me while I was in the pub with Steph. He said he was back in town and wanted to see me. I sent him a message to say where we were and he said he'd be in Brooke Lane at half eleven.'

'Brooke Lane?' Allie looked up from her notepad at the mention of it. 'What time did he send the message?'

'Just after ten.'

'So you met him outside? At half eleven?'

'Yes. I got into his car and ...' Carole turned her head. She felt cheap and stupid enough as it was.

'Can you remember how long you were with him?' Allie felt her heart racing as she wrote down the details.

'Twenty minutes at the most. When I went back to the pub to find Steph, she wasn't there. I asked a few people who had sat near to us but no one had noticed her leave. I stayed for a while but then I assumed she'd gone home without me. That's when I left on my own.'

Allie sat with her thoughts for a moment. 'Did you see anyone else there that you knew, someone who could be associated with either Steph or Terry?'

'Only Phil Kennedy. He was often around at the end of nights to take us home.' Carole stopped to see if Allie had made the connection. 'You know that Phil Kennedy was having an affair with Steph?'

Allie looked up from her notes again. If that was true, could Phil Kennedy be the mystery father?

'Did Terry know?' she said.

'He asked me about it a couple of weeks ago. Said he had his suspicions. I was so taken aback by his question that by not saying anything, I suppose I gave it away.'

'Did you know Steph was pregnant?'

'Not until I overheard you telling Terry.'

'You were listening?'

'I hadn't quite gone! And don't come all innocent with me. He only had eyes for you as soon as you showed up.'

Allie stopped writing again. 'I hope you're not insinuating anything with that comment.' She frowned but Carole wouldn't elaborate. 'So Steph hadn't told you about the baby?'

'No.'

'Strange, considering what good friends you were.'

'It's pretty convenient too that Terry does this to me right after the murder, don't you think? He sees me for a few weeks, Steph's murdered and then he dumps me with a punch?'

Allie paused for a moment, to regroup her thoughts. 'Do you think he would have harmed Steph?'

'If you'd asked me yesterday, I would have said no. Now, after what I've just been through, I'd say anything was possible. He just went crazy in a flash.'

'So why do you think he stayed with her for so long?'

'I don't know.'

'Do you think she had some sort of hold on him?'

Carole screwed up the tissue in her hands before nodding. 'It's something that she didn't confide in me, before you ask.'

'Did you try to find out more?'

'Of course I did.' Carole laughed rudely. 'I mean, come on. You know by now that their marriage was a sham. Normal married couples don't act like they did.'

Allie thought back to the charity event at the beginning of the month. She'd seen Terry trying to keep his cool as his wife became more and more intoxicated. Maybe he was bothered that she would say something that would land him in it one day? She had to dig deeper.

'Do you have any idea what it might be?'

'No. But there's a compartment in the master bedroom, behind her wardrobe. She kept her jewellery and stuff in there. You wouldn't find it if you didn't know about it. Terry paid a fortune for it not to be traceable. Steph told me that too. Maybe there might be something in there?'

Allie could hardly contain her excitement. A secret compartment? She'd have to get a warrant to search it out but if this was true, there could be anything inside it. Terry certainly hadn't mentioned it when they'd been looking through Steph's belongings.

When Carole lay for a while in silence, Allie stood up.

'Get some rest,' she told her. 'I'll come back or send someone over tomorrow to get a full statement.'

Carole groaned. 'I don't want to press charges.'

'I'm not talking about that. I need a statement about the night Steph Ryder was murdered.'

'I can't.' Carole looked up at her and began to cry again.

'You can and you will.' Allie leaned in closer. 'If all these fragments fit together, don't you realise that Terry Ryder could have murdered his wife?'

'No. He wouldn't do that.'

'How can you be so certain after what he did to you?'

She paused. 'Would he?'

'I need you to make a statement.'

'But then Shaun will find out that I've been having an affair!'

Allie was losing her patience. She wanted to say that it wasn't her problem but she stopped herself. It wasn't her job to break up relationships. But Carole would have to tell Shaun at some point. She relented a little. The woman had been through enough over the past few days.

'Look,' she said. 'If he asks me questions about the attack, then I'll either tell him to check the details with you or if he asks me anything I can't reply to without landing you in it, then I won't lie. But if I were you,' she shrugged, 'I'd come clean.'

'I can't do that,' Carole sobbed.

'It's up to you. But you saw his face. He wants revenge. From what I've seen of your husband, he's a good guy –'

'He is.'

'So he'll want the perpetrator caught. I'm not certain he'll let this rest. I'd have a good think on it because it isn't going to go away.'

———

Shaun was waiting when Allie came downstairs.

'What did she tell you?' he asked.

'Not much, I'm afraid.' Allie decided to give Carole a little time. 'She's obviously disorientated, confused.'

Shaun nodded. 'I'll go and check on her.'

Allie stopped him. 'Maybe you could leave her be for now? She'll be clearer in the morning.'

Forgetting all about her visit to Georgia Road, on her short journey back to the station, Allie's head was ready to explode. If what Carole told her checked out to be true, she could put Terry Ryder at the scene of the crime at the time of the murder. She needed to talk to Nick about getting a warrant and sussing out that secret compartment.

Chapter Twenty-Eight

When Allie got back to her desk, only Sam and Perry were in the office.

'I've heard from The Bartley Hotel, where Terry Ryder said he was staying,' Perry told her before she'd even taken off her coat. 'He does use the hotel quite regularly but he didn't have a booking that night.'

Allie paused. Surely Terry would have known they'd check up on that? Why lie?

'Could he have used another name?' she asked, sifting through the messages on her desk and finding nothing that needed dealing with immediately.

'It's possible, I guess. But if they know his face, wouldn't he have been better booking another hotel? I doubt Ryder would get caught out that easily.'

'Hmm.... Thanks, Perry. Any luck with the CCTV footage, Sam?' Allie placed her coat around the back of her chair and switched on her computer.

'I'm almost done piecing it together.'

'Good, because I have a witness who can put Terry Ryder in Brooke Lane at the time of the murder.' Quickly, she told them about her interview with Carole.

'But if Carole Morrison was with Terry Ryder at the time of the murder, then it could have been her,' Sam piped up.

Allie pressed two fingers either side of her temple. She'd been so hell-bent on linking the murder to Terry that she hadn't thought about the implications of Carole being there too. Missing important details was a no-no. How could she have overlooked that little gem?

She stood up. Suddenly an image of Terry ramming a fist into Carole's face attacked her vision. Then it changed to the image of Steph Ryder. Again. And again. Bile rushed into her mouth. She barely made it to the ladies' loos before throwing up.

'Are you okay?' Sam rushed in after her.

'I'm fine. Must be coming down with something.' Standing up, she took the handful of tissues offered and wiped her mouth.

'You sure that's all it is? Because I think –'

'I'm fine,' she repeated.

Sam shrugged. 'You don't want to talk anything through?'

'No.' She looked up quickly. 'Just give me a moment, yeah?'

Once she'd gone, Allie tasted fresh vomit rising. She swallowed rapidly a few times, trying not to smell it on herself, knowing this would start her off again. Then she swilled her face and hands.

Ashen and nauseated, she held onto the sink for support. Her face in the mirror said too much. What had made her react like that? Was it fear that she felt or a delayed reaction to the brutal act itself? Did she really think Terry Ryder would kill his wife now that it was a possibility? It could just have easily been Carole Morrison who dealt the fatal blow.

She shuddered. Terry Ryder had made a pass at her earlier. And if she wasn't careful, it could be her lying in bed with half her face swollen like a melon, like Carole.

It took her a few minutes but finally colour came back to her cheeks. Allie returned to her desk; everyone around her was working and, thankfully, oblivious to her plight. Shaking now, she switched on her computer. Time to get back to work. Until she could talk to Nick, she had things to think through.

———————

Unable to face seeing his dad since he'd taken the beating off Shaun the day before, Lee had been keeping a low profile while he tried to work out what to do next. His mind kept whirling over the things that could happen to him if Terry found out that he had done his wife in. And taking that beating off Shaun Morrison had surprised him too. He'd expected him to bow down gracefully and give it up.

Fuck, he should never have killed Steph Ryder. What had he been thinking? The simple idea of blackmail had turned into full-blown murder in a matter of a few hours. He knew he shouldn't have taken all that cocaine last Friday.

The more he thought about his predicament, the more he realised that he had to get out of Stoke. But he still needed money before he left. He'd have to visit his dad.

When Phil opened his front door it was nearing three in the afternoon. His sigh was loud and exasperated.

'What the fuck happened to you?' he asked, surveying the bruises on Lee's face.

'Just a bit of trouble last night.'

'What kind of trouble?'

'This and that.' Lee shrugged and followed Phil through to the kitchen. 'Have the pigs been round here?'

'Someone questioned me, yeah.'

'What?' Lee's voice shot up an octave. 'When? What did they want?'

'You're a bit jumpy,' said Phil. 'What's up?'

'Nothing.' Lee shrugged again.

'Look, I could do without the hard boy act right now.' Phil pinched the bridge of his nose and closed his eyes for a moment. 'What have you done?'

'I'm in trouble, Dad. I need to get away.'

When Phil's eyes met his this time, Lee knew he had to come clean. But his stare got to him. He gulped away his nervousness. 'You must know that stupid prick Morrison didn't kill Steph. Well, I've been trying to get money out of him to keep quiet.'

'I'm not with you.'

'I was going to get some money off him to keep my mouth shut about him knocking off Steph Ryder. But the stupid bastard couldn't kill her when push came to shove. I went –'

'How did you know I asked Morrison to do it?'

'I followed you.' Lee could barely meet his dad's eye now, sensing his mood change. 'I saw you meet him in The Reginald Mitchell and then again on Friday. I was going to watch him at The Potter's Wheel then tell him I saw everything and get some cash from him.'

'Blackmail?' The vein in Phil's temple started to twitch. 'I told you to keep your mouth shut about what you heard between me and Terry!'

'It was too much of an opportunity to miss.' Lee tried to explain. 'But on the way I saw him puking up at the side of the road. I knew something wasn't right. When I turned back, he'd gone. He bottled it! So I thought if I . . .' he paused for a moment, 'if I did the job I could still get money out of him because no one would know who did it.' Another pause. 'I finished her off instead.'

Phil jumped across the room in one swift movement and drew his fist up in the air. 'You stupid fucking idiot!' he screamed.

'I'm sorry, Dad. I didn't think it through.' Lee's hands went up to protect himself. 'I thought I was doing you a favour when he wouldn't do it. You'd be in deep shit, right, if the hit on Steph wasn't carried out? I always thought Morrison was gutless so I took a hammer with me, thought if I used the claw side, it would be over and done with in one swing. When I got there, Steph was sitting outside the entrance. I thought I'd have time to wait for her round the back but she saw me. As I drove past, she started yelling, followed me in the car, giving me right fucking lip across the car park. I was coked up, Dad, and I lashed out. I hit the side of her head. When she fell down, I heard her head crack on the tarmac and she never got back up.'

'That's not right.' Phil shook his head. 'The police said it was a brutal attack. Her head was *smashed in* with a hammer.'

'I know what the police said but I –' Lee pushed his arm away but Phil held on tight.

'Don't you see, you stupid idiot? That wouldn't have killed her!'

'She went down like a deck of cards. I saw her.'

'No, you're lying. She took a right beating.'

'She didn't!'

'She did!' Phil screamed into his face. Then he pushed him away.

Lee straightened out his jacket. He didn't understand. He'd seen Steph go down and she sure as hell hadn't got back up again. He'd nudged her a few times but she hadn't moved. He must have killed her! And if he hadn't killed her, then how was she dead?

'It must have been me!' he said. 'How else –'

'Get out! I've had as much as I can take of you for now.'

'But, Dad, you've got to help me!' Lee pleaded. 'Terry will be after me. I need some money so I can leave Stoke, stay away for a while until the heat dies down.'

'OUT!'

'Can't you see? I messed up but it's Morrison who's in the wrong. He told you he'd done her over. He's the one taking the piss. Why should I get all the blame?'

'Oh, he'll get what's coming to him,' said Phil. 'But you? I can't trust you. You're a liability.'

The word *liability* hung in the air. A liability could mean there'd be a hit out on him. A liability could mean ... Lee shuddered at the thought.

'Dad?' Lee reached out to Phil. 'I need your help, Dad.'

Phil pushed him away again. 'Fuck off out of my sight or I'LL KILL YOU MYSELF!'

After leaving number two, Lee ran back to his house. The silence did nothing to welcome him; soon it was ringing in his ears. He sat with his head in his hands. Fuck, this was all going wrong. Why had Phil been so angry? He wasn't at fault here. It was Shaun Morrison who had bottled out. Shaun was the one who should have killed Steph and didn't.

Fuck, fuck, fuck.

Was his dad really in love with Steph? He knew they'd been screwing around for some time and he knew Phil screwed around with other women too. But what if that was the reason he hadn't been able to kill her?

He wondered if Terry knew about the affair. Or maybe he'd found out? Was that the reason he'd wanted Phil to kill Steph? Some kind of fucked-up sweet revenge?

He began to pace the room. Fuck, he was in deep shit now. Without his dad to help him out with money, he didn't have a chance of getting away. There was no alternative but to try Shaun Morrison. See if he could call his bluff. Without a second's thought, he was off again.

On double yellow lines outside The Orange Grove, he gathered up his nerve and got out of his car. Trying to fit in and look casual amongst the shoppers walking by, he leaned back against the driver's door and stared through the large glass window into the restaurant. He could see Shaun stocking up behind the bar. He lit a cigarette and waited. It wouldn't be long before he spotted him.

Sure enough, Shaun appeared outside a few minutes later. Lee stepped back slightly as he came hurtling towards him.

Shaun pointed a finger into his face. 'Stay away from me and my wife or you'll get more of that bruising.'

Lee stared him out. 'Don't think you can knock me to the floor again, big boy.'

'You touch her again and I swear to God, I'll kill you!'

'Touch who?' Lee frowned. 'What the fuck are you going on about?'

'I'm talking about my wife.'

'I haven't done anything to your wife.'

'Listen here, you little fucker. If it wasn't for the cameras, I wouldn't be held responsible for my actions.'

Unable to work out what he was on about, Lee continued. 'Give me some money and then I'll be on my way.'

'You're getting nothing from me.' Shaun shook his head and then took a step back. 'Not a fucking penny.'

'I want five grand by lunchtime tomorrow or else my old man gets to know the truth.'

'Like who really killed Steph Ryder?'

Lee took a deep intake of breath. It didn't go unnoticed by Shaun, who moved in closer.

'You thought I wouldn't work it out? I must admit, it took me a while but it was so obvious when it did click.'

'What do you mean?'

'I didn't kill Steph. You know that I didn't kill Steph. And if you know that I didn't kill Steph, then how the fuck would you know who did?'

Lee began to blink rapidly.

'The only way you would know is if you were there.'

'Five grand.' Lee looked Shaun straight in the eye hoping to get the better of him. He couldn't fuck up again. 'Or everyone will know.'

'How about you keep your mouth shut for nothing or everyone will know that you killed Steph.'

'Five grand.' Lee repeated.

'Two words. Fuck. Off. You've done enough damage hitting out at my wife and –'

'I haven't done anything to your wife,' Lee interrupted.

'Shaun, what's going on?'

Shaun swung round as he heard Carole's voice behind him. Shit, trust her to appear now. He gave her a false smile, hoping it would pacify her. 'I'm sorting something out. You go in. I won't be long here.'

Shaun speaking to Carole gave Lee enough time to wriggle out of his grasp and get back in his car. He screeched off before he could threaten him again.

'That was Lee Kennedy, wasn't it?' Carole asked as she joined him on the pavement. 'Christ, we'll have had the whole family on the doorstep soon.'

'I got in touch with him to see if he could put the word out. See if he could find out who attacked you.'

Carole sighed. 'Let it drop, now.' She wrapped her arms around his waist. 'I'm okay. That's all that matters, surely?'

'You could have been killed.'

'That's a little dramatic coming from someone who let rip on one of the druggies. And besides,' she kissed him gently on the cheek, wincing slightly in pain. 'It got us to sit down and talk, didn't it?'

Shaun hugged her. Yes, for once, it had served its purpose. Last night they'd cleared the air. Steph's death plus the assault had made both of them think about what they had and what they could lose. Like a lot of couples in long marriages, they'd taken each other for granted. Together they realised they'd been given a second chance.

'Yes, you're right,' he said. 'Come on. Let's get you in out of this cold weather.'

Before he went back inside the restaurant, Shaun took one last look up and down the street to make sure that that freak had gone. He couldn't see him anywhere.

But, one thing was certain. He knew Lee Kennedy wouldn't give up. If he'd killed Steph and come back to see him after a good beating, either he had to come up with the money to keep him sweet – which he couldn't – or he would have to sort him out.

———

At four p.m., Allie was in Nick's office updating him with their findings. 'We need to check out this secret compartment, sir,' she said. 'We need to interview Phil Kennedy again, see what his take is on him screwing around with Steph Ryder. It could be his baby. We need to question Terry Ryder about the alleged assault. And we need –'

'Of course Carole Morrison could be lying to cover up her own tracks,' Nick broke in.

'I doubt –'

'If she is having an affair with Ryder, she could want him for herself. Maybe she saw an opportunity to do away with the competition.'

Allie shook her head. 'Maybe Ryder assaulted her because she knows too much? Maybe she was about to say something that would land him in it. I'm not sure but we'll need to question them both again – Carole Morrison to see if she knows any more than she's telling me and Ryder about the alleged assault. We need to dig deeper.'

'Allie.' Nick hung up his coat before turning back to her. 'I know I told you to use your womanly charms but don't you think you're taking things a little too far?'

'Excuse me?' Allie raised her eyebrows.

'You seem to be on some personal vendetta.'

'But you asked me to –'

'What? You haven't got a mind of your own?'

'I believe my instincts are –'

'Sometimes what we want to believe is not always the truth. Carole Morrison could be a suspect just as much as Terry Ryder. You still need to stay objective, Sergeant.'

Allie couldn't believe her ears. It was Nick who'd told her to get under Ryder's skin, to find out everything she could about him. What was this tack, all of a sudden?

'I thought I *was* being objective,' she pointed out. 'I've been going over things from every possible angle. If you're questioning my integrity, sir, then I –'

'If *I'm* questioning?' The warning look on Nick's face told her she was going too far. 'Close the door for a moment, Allie.'

Allie did as she was told, the same when he motioned for her to sit down.

'What is it about Terry Ryder?' said Nick.

'I'm not sure,' she replied, hardly daring to look at him. Even the sound of Terry's name was enough to make her blush. 'There's something about him.'

'Something about him?'

'I can't explain it but it's like he has this . . . power.' Nick waited for her to elaborate but she couldn't. 'There's just . . . something.'

'So, you think he attacked Carole Morrison? She's now telling you there's a compartment hidden in a wardrobe. Did you see anything when you looked through Steph's clothes on Saturday?'

'No.'

'And did any of the other officers?'

'No.'

'But you chose to believe her over Terry Ryder. Why?'

'I don't have any reason not to. And from the sound of it we wouldn't have seen the compartment anyway. It was built to be missed.'

'But what makes you certain that she isn't involved in this too?'

'I saw what he did to her!'

'So –'

'Do you think I'd put myself in danger for that … that bastard!'

'Are you asking me or was that a rhetorical question?'

Allie felt tears of frustration brimming. She tried to calm herself. 'I saw what he did to Carole Morrison,' she repeated.

'You don't have the proof that it was him.'

'Then let me get it for you.'

'How?'

'Let me question him about this compartment first before getting a search warrant. If he won't let me look, it could mean he's got something to hide.'

'So when we go back with a warrant and he's moved whatever is supposed to be in this compartment to somewhere else, what will happen then?'

'There might not be anything in there!'

'Exactly!' Nick drummed his fingers on the desk for a moment. 'Have you any idea how long the investigation into his affairs has been going on? I already have the DCI breathing down my neck to solve this case and move away from Ryder so we can continue surveillance on the car washes and his dirty money. One false move from you and that could all be put in jeopardy.'

Allie thought Nick was going to refuse her request. She breathed again when he nodded.

'Okay, but do it with a warrant and only search that room. And I sincerely hope you find something. If Ryder thinks we're on to him, he could go to ground. And Allie?'

Already at the door, she stopped.

'No mention of the alleged assault either. We'll play this nice and calmly.'

———

Head held high, Allie left Nick's office and walked to the only place she knew she would find a minute's peace. She locked the cubicle of the toilet and slapped her hand on the wall a few times, hoping to rid herself of her excess energy. Fuck. Fuck. FUCK!

How dare Nick say that she was getting too close! Damn him. Couldn't he see that she was using it to her advantage and not simply for her advantage?

But his insinuations made her wonder if she was really behaving in a professional manner. Had she got too close in the hope of finding out the truth? Or had she let Terry Ryder manipulate her, like she knew he intended?

Damn that man for getting underneath her skin.

'Allie, are you okay?' Sam asked as she knocked gently on the door. 'You're not feeling sick again?'

'Sick of this case.' Allie opened the door and glanced at Sam sheepishly. 'Do you think we should always follow our gut feelings, Sam?'

'Of course we should.' Sam frowned. 'Why, you're not doubting yourself, are you?'

'I don't know.' Allie sighed. 'I'm not sure I know anything right now.'

Chapter Twenty-Nine

'You look tired,' Mark said when Allie finally got home that evening around eight. 'I have a glass of wine with your name on it and I've ordered in some food.'

They sat at the kitchen table. The conversation flowed but she couldn't tell Mark about her day. They both knew she couldn't discuss certain aspects of it at any time but Mark sometimes added another dimension that she'd missed, especially when working so closely. And she had been working too closely on this one.

Her eyes brimmed with tears as she recalled what happened to Carole Morrison. 'It's such a mess, Mark,' she told him, unable to tell him about the assault. 'I should be used to the sights that I see all the time, but everyone is still an individual. I don't understand people at times.'

Mark reached across the table for her hand.

'I know you think I'm mad because I want to do this job,' she continued. 'But it's because I'm able to get to the bottom of such atrocities that I want to do it. I want to hunt down the bastard who murdered Steph Ryder and ask them,' she paused and shook her head trying to rid herself of the images within, '"why did you hit her again and again? Twice may have been enough, once even because of the force. But why over and over and over again? Why had she made you so mad?"'

'Do you have any leads?' Mark asked. 'Is it Ryder?'

'Anything's possible at the moment.' Allie sighed and sat back in her chair again. 'It all seems so … so pointless.'

They moved through to the living room. But at half past ten, Allie's mind still refused to switch off. She sat on the sofa, feet curled up underneath her, wine glass at her side. Mark sat across from her on the armchair, feet up on the coffee table, slippers cast aside. He was laughing at some sitcom. He glanced over in her direction and she smiled as if she'd caught the joke but she wasn't listening. She was trying to pick holes in Carole Morrison's story. Each time she came back to the same conclusion. Terry Ryder was covering something up and it was only a matter of time before they put together the rest of the clues.

Checking out the hotel room had been a minor detail that she'd been thankful for but she couldn't yet rule out that he'd used a different name. Or that he had checked in with someone else, using their name. It would take time to figure out but she'd put Matt onto it first thing in the morning. Get him down to the hotel in Derby and also get him to check with any known associates of Terry's from the list he'd given to them.

What she couldn't get out of her mind was what Terry had done to Carole. Surely Carole couldn't be lying? She had seen her at The Gables barely an hour earlier. And if she was telling the truth, there'd be evidence, blood to check in the family room.

Was Terry Ryder really capable of lashing out at a woman like that? It had been obvious that he didn't love Carole, that he thought of her as a piece of meat that he could use and abuse on his say-so. And what about this so-called secret compartment? Could they have missed something? And did Nick really think she'd cocked up?

Mark sat watching Allie while she was deep in thought. He half expected to hear the whirrs and clicks inside her brain as she worked through things. Sometimes he didn't mind so much that she'd chosen to go into the police force after the attack on her sister. The majority of cases involved men or victims of domestics and were sewn up pretty quickly. There had been one case involving a serial killer in Stafford and Allie had worked on that as part of a larger investigation, but most of the time she was able to cope – if the killer was caught.

If the killer wasn't caught, that was when Allie became unbearable. He'd lost count of the friendships she'd ruined over the years as she'd put off her social life to sift through another pile of case notes, revisit another witness in person. She would work her fingers to the bone going over and over old ground until there was nothing else to check. Only then would she admit defeat.

The first time it had happened was when a seventeen-year-old girl was strangled and dumped on wasteland off the Tunstall bypass. Allie had only recently moved over to the murder squad as a detective constable. Mark had come home to find her in a heap on the bathroom floor, crying inconsolably and wishing she could do more for her family. She wanted to catch the bastard, couldn't understand why they hadn't. Even as he'd held her, he'd known she was crying over losing her sister.

She'd been like that on several occasions since, could be like that for days, a black cloud hanging over her when she was at home. Nothing he did could shake it, not until she was ready to accept there wasn't anything more to be done. He bore the brunt of it, whatever. Because he loved her. Because he'd known Karen before the attack and had seen what it had done to her, ripping the dreams of life away. He'd seen their father, Roy, die of a heart attack, brought on by the constant fight to find the monster that had left his elder daughter for dead. It had consumed him as much as it consumed Allie now, for when he'd died, she'd taken on his burden. Every new case, every new DNA sample, every new attack was a reminder because she questioned everything, checked everything constantly, waiting for the attacker to slip up. What she really needed was closure, to rid her of the guilt of being late. Mark doubted she'd get it now. Not after fourteen years.

He watched her again, biting at the skin around her nails. She was still deep in thought, still staring at the television. Mark worried about her when she was like this. He couldn't protect her. She locked him out. And he hated her for it at times.

Even though he knew he'd always be there to pick up the pieces, it still didn't stop him responding angrily every now and then.

'Allie?' he said.

She didn't hear him.

'Allie!'

Allie jumped and looked over at him in a daze.

'I've been talking to you, trying to get your attention for the past few minutes. Do you want to watch the news or grab an early night?'

'You go on up. I still have things to work out.'

'Great.'

Allie caught the sarcasm in the word. 'What's that supposed to mean?'

'Nothing.' Mark sulked. 'I bet you made time to speak to *him* today though, didn't you?'

Allie looked up. 'If by *him* you mean Terry Ryder,' she replied haughtily, 'then yes, I have.'

Mark mumbled something.

'I'm sorry, what was that?'

'Nothing.' Mark switched the television over to the news and folded his arms.

'Christ, give it a rest,' Allie chastised. 'Sometimes the only peace and quiet I get is when I'm at home. I could do without you moaning about it.'

The television went off. Mark threw the remote down next to her. 'I won't bother you any more then. Seeing as you haven't got time to turn me on, turn off the light when you're done thinking.'

'It's not all about us,' she snapped. What was it with him this week? All he seemed to think about lately was sex. She sighed. But that was hardly fair if she dared to think about it. He'd asked her if she'd seen Terry. She'd told him she'd been with him today. Was it obvious how much it was affecting her or was he feeling threatened again?

'It's not all about you, either,' Mark answered back before standing up. 'Here we go again, like a broken record. You work yourself too hard and no matter what you do, it'll never make Karen better. Sometimes I wish you'd realise this and move on.'

'Move on to what?'

'I don't know! You could have a cushy job somewhere in an office.'

Allie sighed and closed her eyes as he continued.

'Sensible working hours – safe working hours. Posh clothes, long lunches!'

'Do you really think that would suit me?' she challenged.

'Anything's better than having to watch you torture yourself, push yourself to the limit to get a result.'

'But my job is important to me!'

'I'm important to you! Karen's important to you!'

At the mention of Karen again, Allie flinched. She hadn't found time to see her this week and already it was Tuesday.

'When was the last time you saw her?' asked Mark.

'I visited on Friday.'

'And when do you intend seeing her next? Have you even thought about her once during this investigation?'

Allie looked away guiltily. In actual fact, since Steph Ryder's body had been found she'd hardly thought of Karen at all. She'd hardly thought of anyone except . . . She felt her skin reddening.

'Of course I have!' she lied, hating herself for it. 'You know she's never far from my thoughts.'

'No, she shouldn't be. She'll be waiting to see you.'

Tears welled in her eyes. 'I can't do everything.'

'It's okay,' Mark relented. 'She was fine when I saw her.'

Allie felt relief and annoyance in equal measures. Relief that Mark had gone to see Karen so she'd had a visitor. Annoyance that he'd taken it upon himself to go to see Karen because he knew she wouldn't find the time. She hardly knew which route to follow to reply. The annoyance won.

'So now you think you can make up for me, is that it?' she challenged. 'And why didn't you mention it?'

'I did. You were obviously a little preoccupied to take it in,' he told her sarcastically. 'I called in for half an hour this evening.'

'I – I . . .'

The fight had gone.

'How was she?'

'She was fine. I took a copy of *Hello!* magazine and read some of it out to her.'

Allie's eyes brimmed with tears. She couldn't be mad at him when he was only looking out for them both.

'I'm sorry,' she spoke softly, reaching forward for his hand and pulling him near. 'I don't mean to let it take over. It just happens.'

'I know. That's why I'm here to pick up the pieces. But I can't keep doing it.' Mark ran a hand over her hair. 'It tears me apart to see you like this.'

'But this is me, Mark. Yes, I do this because of Karen, but also because I want to help other people too.'

'Fine.' Mark sighed. 'You go ahead and help everyone. In the meantime, I'll head up to bed. By myself.'

Allie heard him stomping around upstairs before finally settling down. She had intended to go through a few more statements, check a few more details but, unable to concentrate knowing she had upset him, she followed him up a few minutes later.

'Brrr,' she snuggled into his back. 'It's brass monkey weather out there.'

'Don't expect me to warm you up,' he retorted.

Allie turned away from him and lay on her back. What was the point?

Chapter Thirty

Wednesday morning. Even though her officers were right behind her as she drove up the driveway of The Gables, Allie's heart was pounding at the thought of what they were about to do. They were searching a property on someone else's say-so. Okay, most leads came through from someone who gave them information but she couldn't help wondering if Carole Morrison was telling the truth. Had she been blinded by the charmer too?

Matt and Perry stood either side of her when she knocked on the door. Sam stood behind them.

Terry came to the door. 'What's going on?' he asked.

'We have a search warrant for the master bedroom,' Allie told him, waiting for him to show his true colours.

'But you've already searched it a few days ago!' Terry's face was ablaze with fury.

The officers moved in and past Allie. In the blink of an eye, the charmer was back.

'I suppose you'd like a cup of tea and one of those biscuits that you love, Sergeant?'

Allie saw Sam turn back at the remark. She glared at Terry. Still his cool remained. He was taking the piss out of her, a smile on his lips that didn't reach his eyes. *Let's see how calm you are in twenty minutes.*

'Well?' Terry was waiting for her to reply. 'What's it to be?'

Allie marched past him. Following the officers up the stairs and into the main bedroom, she snapped on plastic gloves before opening a wardrobe door. She pushed the clothes apart like a pair of curtains. Men's clothes: trousers in every colour, shirts in every designer name. Shoes at the bottom, heels placed neatly on two rails.

As Terry stood behind her, she knocked on the wall. It didn't sound hollow. She opened the next wardrobe, full to bursting with women's clothes in no particular order. Grabbing a handful to make room, she slung them onto the bed.

That wall sounded solid, too, as she felt around it. She moved closer, examining the edges for any possible signs of a handle or a hinge. She pressed every inch of both walls to see if anything would push open. But there was nothing.

After a minute or two, she stood up. She paused. If she was wrong about this, it could be a hell of a blot on her career. But if she was right, who knows what they might find in there.

Behind her, Perry stood poised with a sledgehammer.

'Look,' Terry said, 'if you're hell bent on getting in there, why didn't you ask?'

Allie glared at him. *What?*

He took a remote control from his trouser pocket and pointed it at the wardrobe. A click was heard and, at waist height, a door opened as if on a timer switch.

'How the hell?' Allie frowned.

Perry put down the sledgehammer with a look of admiration. 'Nice,' he muttered.

Inside the compartment, Allie could see some kind of metal container. It was the size of a shoe box. She placed it onto the floor and looked for a lock but it didn't have one. She lifted the lid. Inside, it was lined with purple velvet. The first thing she saw was a passport. Confused, as they already had Steph's passport from the previous search, she took a quick flick through but it was out of date. Steph Ryder stared back at Allie from the photo, the only glaring difference the eight-year age gap.

There was a roll of notes that Allie estimated at five hundred pounds and a few rolls of purple velvet. She opened the first one and found a stone-encrusted locket attached to a gold necklace. Given Steph Ryder's penchant for the best of everything, Allie could only assume they were diamonds.

'We've been robbed quite a few times when we were abroad on one holiday or another,' Terry said in way of explanation. 'Steph wanted something secure fitted at home to ensure she didn't lose anything precious to her. I commissioned a job from Burslem.'

Allie wondered. 'Is there one in your wardrobe, too, that I couldn't find?'

Terry nodded. Another click of the remote control and a second compartment was revealed. Allie thrust a hand inside but there was nothing there.

'My wife had impeccable taste, Sergeant. Whereas I have nothing of value.'

Allie realised he was mocking her once more. She stooped over the box on the floor again. There were a further three rolls of velvet. She laid each of them out in a line and opened the first one. It contained a vast array of jewellery in the form of necklaces and bracelets. She set it down with the contents on view and unrolled another.

A knife with a wooden handle fell onto the floor. Its blade, approximately five inches in length, was covered in dried blood. Allie pulled an evidence bag out of her pocket, slipped the knife inside and held it up to gauge Ryder's reaction. At first, his face was a look of confusion, but it quickly changed to calm.

'I have no idea where that came from,' he told her.

Allie held his stare.

'I'm serious. Allie, if you think for one moment that I'd leave anything behind in my house to incriminate me in anything, then you hardly know me at all.'

Allie took a step closer to him. 'That's right,' she said quietly. 'I hardly know you at all. And it's Detective Sergeant to you.'

Terry smiled back at her. 'Believe me, Detective Sergeant,' ridicule dripped from the last two words, 'I never forgot your rank. But maybe once or twice you might have.'

The words were like a smack across the face. Oh, she would get him for that.

'I think you and I need to have a chat in private,' she said.

'Another one?'

Aware that her team were watching, Allie turned to Sam.

'Get him out of here.'

Once everyone left, Allie sat down on the bed before her knees gave way. Her rapid heartbeat felt like it was banging out her fright. Panic began to overwhelm her and she breathed long and hard, in through the nose, out through the mouth. She had to keep her cool here. There were too many people who had heard Terry's allegations and she knew before she could get into her car, word would be out all over the station if she let on how much she had fucked up. What the hell had got into her? And what the hell was her DI thinking in allowing her to get so close?

But she couldn't blame Nick for this one little bit. This was all her fault. She had been in the same house as a killer. She'd let Ryder get under her skin. What was she thinking?

She held up the knife inside the transparent bag. The weapon inside it couldn't be connected to the murder of Steph Ryder because she had been attacked with a hammer. So whose blood was this?

Chapter Thirty-One

At the police station, Terry was placed in an interview suite on the ground floor. As he hadn't been arrested, he said there was no need for his solicitor to be present, unnerving Allie immediately. What wasn't he telling them that made him so cocksure of himself?

Nick wanted her and Sam to conduct the interview.

'Make him feel that he's only helping us with enquiries at the moment,' Nick said as they went downstairs. 'If he gets too much, I'll come in to you.'

Despite Allie's protests, he sounded her out. 'I'll watch from the next room. It'll all be monitored. I want to see his reaction.'

'I was hoping no one else would be joining us, Sergeant,' Terry remarked coolly as they went into the room.

Although his words were loaded with meaning, Allie ignored his jibe. She pulled out a chair and sat down opposite him. Sam sat by her side.

'Tell me about the knife, Mr Ryder,' she said.

'I have no idea what you're talking about, Detective Sergeant.'

'So, am I to assume you've never seen it before?'

'Yes, assume away.'

'Considering your wife has recently been murdered, don't you think it's a bit of a coincidence that it was found in a secret compartment in your bedroom?'

'I don't see how that can be a coincidence at all, especially since my wife didn't die from stab wounds. Like I said, I've never seen this before.'

'Would Mrs Ryder ever have had cause to keep a knife covered in blood for anyone?'

'You're asking the wrong person. I'm not my wife's keeper.'

'Whose blood do you think is on the knife?'

'I have no idea.'

'She didn't tell you about it?'

'No.'

'So you had no idea that it was there?'

Terry shook his head. 'She could have used it herself for all I know.'

'You think so?'

'Steph was a volatile woman. It was common knowledge that she liked a drink.' Terry smiled affectionately as if remembering something about Steph. 'She was always a handful. I've had to clear up lots of odd things for her in the past.'

'*Odd* things?'

'Yes. The odd ruined suit or dress she's spilt drink over. The odd pub mirror she's smashed in the ladies'. The odd woman she's ripped a dress off or a bracelet that she's broken in a tiff.'

'You paid people to keep quiet about your wife's crimes?' Allie was astounded.

'I'd hardly call them crimes.' Terry stared at her. 'Just a few misunderstandings. I helped keep people sweet by paying for the damage Steph caused.'

'The night Mrs Ryder was murdered, you said you were out of town. You got back at half past nine the following morning.'

'That's correct.'

'I have a witness who says otherwise.'

Terry's eyes went from one woman to another. 'I very much doubt that,' he replied.

'I have someone who can put you in Brooke Lane at midnight.'

Terry shook his head. 'That's impossible.'

'What makes you so certain?'

'What makes you so certain that your witness is more credible than I am?'

Allie shuffled in her seat. She glanced at Sam uncomfortably. Terry was right. They had no evidence yet.

'We spoke to Carole Morrison and she said –'

Terry laughed before she'd finished the sentence.

'Do you have to be so rude?' Allie refrained from reaching across the table and slapping him. God, the arrogance of the man!

Terry put a hand up. 'I'm sorry but you said a *credible* witness. Not some bunny boiler that can't leave me alone since my wife died.' He pointed to his temple. 'Sick she is. She's got it into her head that she can waltz into my life and take over from Steph. In her bed, if you catch my drift. You've seen her, Detective Sergeant, haven't you? Did she always seem rational to you?'

Allie paused before she said something that would damn her. She couldn't let him get the upper hand.

'Were you aware that she had been attacked?'

'No. I saw her early yesterday – we both did – and she was fine then. I hope she isn't too badly hurt?'

'Oh, just scared about saying the wrong thing about the attacker and getting further repercussions.'

'That is a shame. She and her husband were good friends of ours – are good friends of mine. For some reason she's got the wrong end of the stick. Thinks I need looking after, but I don't. Does she really need to be here?'

Allie looked up to see him staring at Sam.

'Yes, she does. Why, do you object?'

'She doesn't say anything.'

'She doesn't need to say anything.'

Terry shook his head. 'Waste of public money, two of you being here. I prefer it when you come alone, Allie.'

'As you've already told me several times.' Allie knew he was trying to wind her up. Truth be told, he was winning. But she'd be damned if she would show her hand. She, too, could play games.

'Carole was attacked after I last saw you and her together,' she continued. 'Shortly after I left your property. You're certain you didn't have anything to do with it? She had some horrific injuries.'

'Of course it was nothing to do with me.' Terry frowned. 'Maybe I should send her some flowers. Flowers always cheer a lady up, don't they, Sergeant?'

Another stare in her direction. Then Terry held up his hands. 'Okay, I'll come clean. But only because I'm here and being questioned about something I haven't done and I need to clear my name.'

'Go on,' said Allie.

'Carole Morrison has had a crush on me for years. I wasn't going to tell her husband – we're all really close friends but it was an embarrassment the way she threw herself at me before Steph was killed. It got to the point that Steph actually thought there was something going on and got quite angry about it.' Terry raised his eyebrows. 'Now that was a time when I had to pay for damages. Steph went ballistic in The Orange Grove when she saw Carole try to kiss me.'

Allie hadn't heard that before. She wondered if it was true and made a mental note to check it with Carole when she visited her later. She closed her eyes for a long second and squeezed the bridge of her nose. 'Let me get this straight. Carole Morrison tried to kiss you.'

Terry nodded. 'We – Steph and I – we laughed it off. But she was becoming a bit of a liability. Carole was becoming so obvious that Shaun started to put two and two together, coming up with five.'

'And you chose to do nothing about this little … obsession she had with you?' Allie looked at Sam long enough for her eyes to ask *do you believe this shit he's coming out with?*

'I didn't want anyone to get hurt,' Terry explained. 'But since Steph was killed, Carole has called every day. You saw her, didn't you, dolled up to the nines? If you hadn't shown up when you did, she'd have stayed for ages. Of course I could put it down to grief but, well, if I thought it was obvious, then what the hell might Shaun think?'

'So you punched her in the face and threatened her, to get her off your back?'

'Of course not.' Terry shook his head. 'That day you visited, you brought with you some of Steph's belongings. Well, Carole went mad once you'd left. She accused me of having an affair with you, can you believe that?'

Sam cleared her throat as Allie felt the heat rise to her face.

'I had to put things straight, no matter how much it was going to hurt her. I couldn't let things continue this way. I told her that whatever she thought was happening wasn't and that she should leave me alone to grieve in peace. That was when she lashed out at me and lost her footing. She fell over and caught her face on the coffee table. There was blood everywhere.'

Blood. Damn that man, Allie groaned silently. If they found blood now, it would be his word against Carole's. With no witnesses, there would be no proof.

'Why didn't you ring Shaun Morrison and let him know what had happened?'

'Are you crazy? I've already told you that the guy's a good friend of mine. I wasn't about to tell him that his wife is obsessed with me. I thought if I kept quiet about things then Carole would come to her senses, make up a story about how she had got hurt and hopefully the nightmare would be over. I told her, once I'd cleaned her up, that if she didn't stop coming around I would tell Shaun everything.'

'Nice try, Mr Ryder.' Allie had to stop from applauding him. She knew he was lying.

'It's Terry to you, Detective Sergeant. It always has been.'

She stared at him pointedly. 'I suppose you've had enough time to get things straight in your head,' she told him. 'Now, let me tell you what I think happened. Carole Morrison told me that you attacked her. Carole Morrison also told me that you texted her last Friday night and asked to meet her in Brooke Lane. At approximately eleven thirty she said you met and you had sex. Now there's quite some difference between the two stories, wouldn't you agree?'

Terry nodded. 'Absolutely. Do you have any evidence to back up her alleged story?'

The room dropped into silence for a moment.

'Or any proof that Carole didn't have a hand in what happened?'

'You seem very calm about the situation, Mr Ryder,' Sam tried to get into the conversation, 'if you don't mind me saying so.'

'Yeah, I do mind,' Terry snapped.

'Why did you tell us that you stayed at The Bartley Hotel?' Allie questioned. 'We checked. You didn't.'

Terry let out a defeated sigh. 'Look, I really didn't want to do this. I wanted to keep her out of the investigation. But now, I'm afraid you leave me no choice but to tell you who I was really with the night my wife died.'

Allie raised her eyes to his. Internally, she shuddered at his stare. Externally, she held his eye. But she could read nothing.

'On the night Steph was murdered, I was out of town,' Terry acknowledged. 'I had a meeting in Derby and afterwards I took my business partner and a couple of clients out to dinner at Carlito's Way. One of the guests was Cathryn Mountford. Once the dinner had been consumed we went back to Cathryn's apartment and I stayed the night with her.'

Allie sighed. No, no, no. Please don't say any more.

'I stayed the night at her apartment, Detective Sergeant.' Terry looked at her triumphantly. 'The woman I'm having an affair with is Cathryn Mountford.'

———

At her desk, Allie tried not to flop over it with weary resignation. She had to hand it to him. Terry Ryder was a cunning bastard. Not once had she thought he'd have an alibi after all this time. And another woman? Jesus, how many women did this man control?

While Sam tried to contact Cathryn Mountford, she spoke to Nick.

'I don't know what to think now.' She sighed loudly. 'I wasn't expecting him to say there was another woman involved.'

'Terry Ryder's a player, with the ladies as well as the men,' Nick reasoned. 'There must be crimes he's committed that have been covered up. He has an army of blokes that will do anything for him. Do you really think he'd let someone like Carole Morrison get the better of him? He would have covered his tracks.'

Allie nodded in agreement, realising again that she had jumped to conclusions. She really was losing a grip on this case. 'I'll get off to Derby as soon as possible. See what this Cathryn Mountford has to say – although I can guess already.'

'Allie.' Nick looked directly at her. 'Why do you think he had anything to do with his wife's death?'

Allie paused. What could she say? Because she had fallen under his spell too? Because he had manipulated her into thinking she was wrong? Because he was charm personified and could talk his way out of anything?

No, it was the way he had dismissed Carole Morrison when she had clearly been upset by the attention he was giving over to her. But she couldn't tell him that either.

She looked up at the inspector. 'Maybe he didn't have anything to do with it, sir,' she replied unhappily.

'Exactly,' said Nick.

Allie frowned.

'Go and see what you can find out in Derby. Other than that, we wait it out until forensics come back with whose blood is on the knife. I doubt it will be Steph Ryder's and if it is, we can't link it to her murder anyway.'

'It's someone's blood, sir,' said Allie.

Chapter Thirty-Two

It took Allie and Sam forty minutes to get to Derby and a further ten minutes to park somewhere near to the address they were after. Hargate Court was situated in a residential area, a few minutes from the city centre. Although the street alongside it was full of cars, they were upmarket vehicles. Top-of-the-range Porsches, four-by-fours, convertibles. The whole row was worth a small fortune. Allie wondered which of the cars in allocated parking spaces within the court railings belonged to Cathryn Mountford. Even though she'd yet to meet her, her eyes rested on a year-old BMW convertible in bullet grey.

'Weren't you surprised that he didn't tell us about his other woman earlier?' Sam asked as they crossed the road towards the entrance. 'It would have made things a lot smoother for him. And it would have saved us a lot of time.'

'That's Terry Ryder for you,' Allie said sharply. A little too sharply, as she saw Sam scuttle off in front of her.

'Nice place.' Allie tried to change the subject. 'Must cost a bob or two. I bet he pays for it all.'

Sam spun round to face her, a look of bewilderment etched on her face. 'What is it with you and him?'

'What?'

'What Ryder was implying? It's none of my business but –'

'You're right. It is none of your business.'

Allie sighed. It was only because she knew what Sam was going to say that she'd interrupted her. But Sam continued regardless.

'It's . . . well, you light up at the mention of his name.'

'That's absurd!' Allie pressed a buzzer with Ms Mountford's name on a tiny brass plaque by the side of it.

'And you denying the fact makes it even more obvious that you have feelings for him.' Sam continued as Allie tried to speak again. 'Hang on a minute. I know you won't act on them, but all the same, don't you think that it might cloud your judgment?'

'Look, whatever I've done has been purely on a professional basis. And you were there when Nick told me to get close enough to find out the truth.'

'Yes, but we all know Terry Ryder's a smooth operator. I did blush when he first spoke to me and I –'

'I did what I had to do,' Allie insisted. 'You're a good-looking woman, Sam. Don't tell me you haven't flirted that little bit extra to get someone to tell you more?'

A female voice spoke through the system.

'Come on up, Detectives.'

Allie yanked open the door, determined to get in the last word with Sam. 'The thing you don't get about Terry Ryder, is that he likes to play games,' she said.

Leaving behind the icy atmosphere, they entered a lobby and took the lift to the third floor. The young woman waiting for them as they emerged took them both by surprise. She was tall, with long blonde hair, straightened and neat. A heavy fringe framed the deepest of blue eyes. She wore the best of clothes on her tanned, toned body. Apart from the ageing of time, she was virtually the image of Steph Ryder.

'Cathryn Mountford,' Allie held up her ID. 'I'm Detective Sergeant Allie Shenton, and this is Detective Constable Sam Markham. I'd like to ask you a few questions about Terry Ryder.'

Cathryn Mountford indicated the way with her hand. They were shown into a room suitable for any interior design brochure. Two white leather settees set up in an L-shape stood in the middle of a large room; there was a deep red wool rug on top of the dark wooden floor. A fire and television were sunk into the far wall; a huge artwork in pink, red and purple swirls hung to the right. Allie wondered what went on in here after hours. Was it all parties and razzmatazz or cosy dinners for two? A pang of jealousy alarmed her.

'Would you like coffee?' Cathryn offered. 'I expect you're thirsty after your journey.'

Allie nodded. 'Thanks.' She and Sam perched on the same pristine settee as if scared to contaminate its whiteness. Despite their disagreement minutes earlier, both women smiled as they realised they shared the same thought.

'I assume you know why I'm here?' Allie started when they were all settled.

Cathryn nodded. 'Yes, I've been expecting you. Things often have a way of getting out, although we had tried to keep things quiet as long as possible.'

'We?'

'Terry and I.' Cathryn paused for a moment to clear her throat. 'I assume you're here about me being his mistress?'

Allie thought the word *mistress* was so antiquated. Then again, what was worse? *Whore*? *Tart*? *Bit on the side*? Yet glancing at Cathryn, it was hard to imagine that she would take second place to anyone. She certainly seemed as though she could handle her own. But then again, Allie surmised, Terry could easily have used his charms on her too.

'I know what you're thinking.' Cathryn picked up a cup. 'Why am I having an affair?'

'I was thinking far from that,' Allie replied. 'I'm here to check out the facts. I'm interested in the night of Friday November thirtieth in particular. Could you tell me where you were and who you were with, please?'

'I was at Carlito's Way, an Italian restaurant, with Terry, Terry's business partner and his wife and another couple.'

'What time were you there?'

'I arrived at ten past seven. I went straight from work – I run my own accountancy firm in the city centre. I met Terry there.'

'Had you met any of the other guests before then?'

Cathryn nodded. 'Yes, I know the Roberts's – Charles and Veronica – very well. We dine with them often when Terry stays over. The other man was a business associate, Richard Powers, with his wife, Jean. I was tagging along, really.' She lowered her eyes. 'Terry never likes to dine alone.'

'Did you notice anything different about that night?'

'No.'

'Did Mr Ryder go missing for any length of time?'

'No.'

'Did he send –'

'He hardly had time to drive back to Stoke and commit murder, if that's what you're suggesting,' Cathryn interrupted sharply.

'I'm not implying anything, Ms Mountford,' Allie spoke back. 'Was he talking to anyone on his phone?'

'He's a businessman. He would talk to people on his phone, surely. I take calls when I'm not in my office.'

Allie changed tack, aware of the hostile yet polite front of the woman. 'Was he missing from the table for a long time?'

'No.'

'Did he seem agitated in any way?'

'No!'

Cathryn said that too fast for Allie's liking. She tried to dig deeper.

'Do you know if he spoke to Mrs Ryder on the phone while you were there?'

'I can't say I remember. I can't say I'd want to know, really.'

'So as far as you were aware, Mr Ryder wasn't acting any differently to how he normally acts, wasn't away from the table for any period of time or –'

'He did spend time outside while he tried to contact his wife on the phone.'

'What time was this?'

'About half seven, quarter to eight. Then again about ten.'

Allie nodded. That tallied with what Terry had told her.

'Do you know if he spoke to her then?' she asked next.

'That's another no, I'm afraid.'

Allie feared she was getting nowhere fast. 'What time did you leave the restaurant?'

'I'd say around ten thirty.'

She sat forward. *Exactly enough time to drive back to Stoke.* She tried something else. 'And he dropped you off at home before he left to go back to his hotel?' By her side, Allie saw Sam look up from her notes.

'Left?' Cathryn frowned too. 'He didn't leave, Sergeant, as he will have told you, no doubt. He stayed here overnight. He left around eight fifteen on Saturday morning. Shortly after, I headed out to do some shopping.'

Allie studied Cathryn for a moment, hoping to see some sort of giveaway that she was lying, or indeed covering up for Terry. If he treated Cathryn with the same respect that he gave Carole Morrison, she might say anything to cover up for him.

Allie knew she was done for now. She and Sam stood up.

'Thanks, Ms Mountford.' Allie gave her a contact card. 'I think we have all we need for now. I'll have to check a few details to verify your statement. If there's anything amiss, I'll be in touch. Or you can call me if you remember anything else.'

'What did you make of that conversation?' Allie asked Sam as soon as they were out of hearing range.

'I'm not sure.' Sam replied. 'It seemed a bit polished for me.'

Allie nodded, glad that Sam had picked up on that too. Still, this time she was going to examine every possibility. They walked back to the car.

'Do you think she could be telling the truth and that Carole Morrison is lying?' Sam continued.

'It is possible.' They crossed over the road. 'But then again, maybe Terry Ryder has been telling the truth all along about Carole Morrison. Maybe they'd had an argument at The Gables and Carole ran at Terry and injured herself. I mean, if she was scorned, she'd hardly go running home to spill her guts to Shaun. "Sorry love, I tripped at my lover's house and fell. Oh, didn't I mention that I was screwing someone else?"'

Sam smirked as they fell in step beside each other. 'I'm not sure I believe any of them,' she said. 'They could both be covering for him. No wonder you fell under his spell. He certainly has some kind of magnetic pull. I'm sorry for what I said earlier.'

'It's okay,' said Allie, although it wasn't really.

'No, it isn't.' Sam turned towards her slightly. 'I of all people should trust you. I've worked for you long enough to know when you're using your better judgement and you're a fantastic mentor. I should have realised you were stringing him along.'

Allie looked ahead, hoping that Sam couldn't read her mind. Right now she was thinking quite the opposite. She was wondering if she *could* trust herself. They got to the car and set off for Stoke.

'Something doesn't ring true,' Sam said as she gazed out of the window at the shadows of the late winter afternoon.

Allie nodded her reply. If Cathryn Mountford was telling the truth, then Terry would be in the clear. It would also throw doubt on Carole Morrison's statement. Both women appeared to be in love with Terry, so which of them was lying for him?

'I think we need to clarify a few things with Carole Morrison,' Allie said, after some more thought. 'I said I'd head over there today.'

When they arrived at The Orange Grove, Shaun showed them upstairs to the living room. Carole was lying on the settee wrapped in a duvet. The swelling to her face was more prominent today, angry bruising that looked painful to the touch. Her nose had scabbed over slightly where it had split.

Allie told her as much as she needed to about their meeting with Cathryn Mountford.

'That's not true!' said Carole. 'He rang me and I met him at the end of Brooke Lane. We drove down out of the way and we ... we had sex. Then I left and went back to the pub. I couldn't find Steph so I called a taxi and came home.' She looked up at both of them with pleading eyes. 'You have to believe me. Terry Ryder was not in Derby at the time Steph was murdered. He was here, in Stoke.'

'If what you're saying is true, that puts him right at the place where the murder happened, and at exactly the same time,' said Allie.

'It's true!'

'Well then, you must agree that it puts you right at the place where the murder happened also – and at exactly the same time.'

Carole paused for a moment. 'I didn't have anything to do with it!'

'But I have a witness that puts Terry Ryder in Derby at the time you say he was with you. If that's the case, then you could have had time to commit the murder, go back in to look for Mrs Ryder so that people saw you afterwards, and then get a taxi home to make it look more authentic.'

'No.'

'Did you have sex with Mr Ryder and then see Mrs Ryder in the car park as she came to find you?'

'No!'

'Did she see you getting out of Mr Ryder's car? Was there some sort of altercation on the car park and you hit her and left her for dead?'

'No.' Carole began to cry. 'How could you say that? Steph was my friend.'

'Friends don't screw their best friends' husbands, Mrs Morrison.'

'I – I know but I – I loved him.'

'Right, you loved him.'

'Just because I want to be with him doesn't mean I would KILL her!'

'So you stand by your previous statement that you were with Mr Ryder at midnight on Friday November thirtieth?'

'Yes.' Carole nodded through her tears.

'And you'll stand up in court and say that, will you?'

'Yes!' Carole pointed to her face. 'Look what he did to me!'

'Sarge,' Sam tried to intervene.

Allie held up a hand to quieten her. 'You told me that you couldn't see your attacker. Then you changed your statement to say that it was Mr Ryder. How do I know you're not going to change your mind again?'

'Because I'm telling you the truth!' Carole looked for some sort of sign that they believed her. 'The bastard that did this to me was Terry Ryder!'

'Terry Ryder?'

All three women turned to see Shaun standing in the doorway with a puzzled look on his face.

'Terry Ryder did that to you? I thought you said you didn't see your attacker,' he spoke to Carole. 'What's going on?'

<hr>

As soon as the police left, Shaun charged up the stairs and back into the living room. Carole sat with tears pouring down her face.

'It was Terry Ryder that hit you?' Shaun looked stunned. 'But why?'

Carole caught his eye for a moment. 'I'm sorry. We ... we were ...' was all she managed to say before bowing her head.

But in that split second, Shaun filled in the gap.

'You and Terry?'

'I'm sorry!'

Shaun took two steps away and then turned back. 'Did you chase him after Steph died or were you already fucking him?'

'No – we –'

Shaun didn't wait for her to find the words. He raced over and pulled her up to her feet. 'If you weren't in such a state, I would give you a good slapping. How long has this been going on? Tell me!' he demanded.

'Not long, I –'

'HOW LONG?'

'A few weeks!' Carole blurted out as the anger in his voice invaded the room.

Shaun dropped her arms as if they were too hot to handle.

'But it's over now,' she added.

'Because he hit you?' Shaun snorted. 'Oh, that's okay, then. The fact that he beat you half to death and the fact that his wife was murdered doesn't come into things?'

Carole said nothing. Despite her initial thoughts around telling the truth, she deserved what she got.

'I don't believe this,' Shaun said quietly. Tears glistened in his eyes as he looked at Carole. Then he frowned. 'Why did he hit you?'

'Because I was with him when Steph was killed.' Not wanting to keep anything from him now, she explained what had happened.

'You're covering up for him!'

'No! Why won't anyone believe me?'

'So what happened? Did Steph interrupt you while you were screwing? Did she see you and did she have a go?' Shaun's face drained of any colour. He pointed at her. 'Ohmigod. Did you kill her?'

'No, I didn't! Surely you know me better than to think I'm capable of that?'

'I didn't think you were capable of fucking someone else,' he said with so much venom in his voice that Carole flinched.

'I didn't do it.' She reached towards him. 'You have to believe me. I didn't kill Steph.'

Shaun pushed her away and walked towards the door. 'This is all too convenient. One of you must know something.'

'Where are you going?' she shouted after him.

'To see Ryder.'

'You can't!' Carole ran to him, grabbing hold of his arm. 'Please! I don't want you to go.'

Shaun pushed her away. 'You should have thought about that before you ... before you ... How could you?'

Carole looked up to see the pain she had caused. He was right. How could she have done this to him?

'It's over,' was all she could think to say.

'And that's supposed to make me feel better? Punching his lights out will do that instead.' Shaun left the room.

Carole followed him onto the landing. 'Please don't go,' she sobbed. 'I'm sorry. I'll do anything to make it up to you.'

'Do you really think I'd want anything to do with you now?' He glared at her. 'You disgust me.'

Carole threw herself at him and wrapped her arms around his waist. She buried her head in his chest but he pushed her away again.

'If you go after Terry, I'll tell the police everything. I know something is going on with the Kennedys.'

They stood facing each other like two animals ready to pounce. All that could be heard was Shaun's shallow breathing as he fought with his emotions and Carole's sobs as she let hers go.

'I know something dodgy is going on,' Carole said through her tears. 'When Phil came to see you before Steph died, I told you that he wouldn't just wipe out your debt. Then his lowlife of a son came round threatening you.'

'He didn't threaten me.' Shaun tried to deny it.

'I heard him. And maybe I can't figure out what's going on, but I bet the police will.'

Shaun pointed his finger into her face. 'You think by setting me up you can get yourself off the hook, is that it?'

'No, but you know something, don't you?'

'NO!'

'So why all the secrecy? WHAT DID YOU DO?'

Shaun pushed her to the floor and ran down the stairs.

'Shaun!'

Chapter Thirty-Three

At The Gables, Shaun screeched his car to a halt by the side of Terry's Range Rover. He ran to the front door and banged on it.

'Ryder! I want a word with you.'

When Terry opened the front door, Shaun landed a punch on his chin.

'You bastard!' he shouted.

Terry stepped back from the force of the hit. Hand to his mouth, he wiggled his jaw about. 'What the fuck was that for?'

'Funny you should mention the word *fuck*. I can't believe you of all people would screw my wife.'

'What?' Terry looked agog. 'I've never screwed Carole!'

'LIAR!'

'I haven't!'

Shaun eyed Terry suspiciously. He certainly looked shocked by his accusations. If he was telling the truth, then Carole could be putting Terry at the scene of the crime to cover up for something she had done. He shook his head. He didn't know whom to believe.

Terry placed a hand on Shaun's shoulder. Shaun shrugged it off.

'Come through to the kitchen and we'll sort this mess out,' he said. 'I need to know what's going on.'

'I don't know what to say,' Terry said when they'd sat down and Shaun had explained everything. 'I've never slept with Carole and

I've certainly never laid a finger on her. I mean, surely you know I'd never cross that line?'

'But if you weren't there,' Shaun paused for a moment, 'then Carole was the last one to see Steph alive and I – oh, fuck. I don't know what to think.'

'There were a lot of people in The Potter's Wheel that night. It could easily have been someone who had it in for me. Strange Stevie, Monty, Dave Shuff, Phil Kennedy, Pete –'

'Phil Kennedy was there?'

'Yeah, why?'

'Oh, nothing.' Shaun thought back to his lie to Carole about Phil being there. It seemed it had actually been true. 'And you were in Derby, you say?'

Terry nodded. 'I was with someone but it wasn't Carole. Her name is Cathryn. I stayed with her that night, which is what I told the police. I have no idea why Carole would make up such serious allegations. It goes beyond belief after we've known each other for so long. Have you any idea why?'

Shaun suddenly felt embarrassed. Shit, what was wrong with him? Why hadn't he come to Terry when Phil told him to do away with Steph? If he'd come clean, then maybe Terry would have sorted things out so that he wouldn't have to look over his shoulder forever. He wondered if it would be too late to tell the truth now.

'Phil Kennedy asked me to kill Steph,' he blurted out in the end.

Terry's chest rose up.

'I didn't do it.' Shaun held up his hands. 'I owed him money and he said if I killed Steph he would wipe out my debt.'

'But that's mad. Why would he do that?'

'I don't know. But if he was in The Potter's Wheel that night –'

'Phil said if you kill her, he'd wipe your debt out?' Terry sat forward.

'Yes.'

'Why the fuck do you owe Phil money?'

Shaun lowered his eyes for a moment. 'We got into a mess with the business. Phil bailed us out.'

'Why didn't you ask me? I would have helped you.'

'How could I when I'm such a failure at everything I do?'

'And did he wipe out your debt?'

Shaun nodded. 'Not sure I believe him, though.'

'Not sure I would either.' Terry paused. 'Look, I need you to go home to Carole. Don't let on that you've seen me. Don't let on that you know she's lying. And don't say anything to Phil either. Something isn't right but I don't know what yet. I need to think through what's best to do next.'

'You do believe it wasn't me who killed Steph, right?' Shaun needed to know before he left.

"Course.' Terry patted him on the shoulder before showing him to the door. 'Now remember, keep quiet about this, yeah, until I've asked a few questions and done a bit of digging? I need to get to the bottom of this mess.'

———— ————

Once Shaun had gone, Terry went back to the table and sat down. He banged his fists onto its surface. Why the hell had he involved Carole Morrison in this? He should have known that stupid bitch wouldn't keep her mouth shut. Sure it was easy to fool Shaun into thinking he hadn't known anything of what was going on. But Allie Shenton? He should have given her more credit. She must have wangled all that stuff out of Carole. And Cathryn had rung him to say she'd been over to Derby to question her. Luckily for Cathryn, she'd backed him up.

Hearing what Shaun had to say about Phil only confirmed what he'd been thinking too. The money Shaun had borrowed was his money, not Phil's. He'd been making enquiries, checking the books over the past couple of days. There was money being siphoned off every week from each car wash. Little amounts some weeks, larger amounts other. Different amounts from each car wash, but a considerable amount over time. When he'd finished with Phil, well, he wouldn't be able to talk again, that was for sure.

He frowned. Mostly he blamed himself for the mess, for wanting to stand in the shadows and watch Steph die. Make sure the bitch was really out of his life. Payback time for all the shit she'd put him through and all the mess he'd had to clear up for her. He couldn't have her blabbing her mouth off about things, bringing him down. He certainly wasn't going to put up with any bastard child either.

Terry punched in a number on his phone. First things first. Phil Kennedy could wait. He needed to make sure that Cathryn would keep her mouth shut, even if it meant shutting it for her.

'Cathryn,' he spoke when she answered. 'We need to talk. I'm heading over.'

Shaun parked his car behind The Orange Grove. By this time it was seven thirty and he knew he should have been back for the evening session. But tough. Let the staff sort it out for once. Or Carole would have to look after things, despite the way she looked.

He heard a noise behind him as he locked his car. Phil Kennedy came out of the shadows. Great, just what he needed.

'What do you want?'

'Your debt's not clear.' Phil took a step closer and then another. 'You didn't kill Steph. The deal's off. I want my money by tomorrow. All of it.'

Shaun shook his head. 'I haven't got that kind of money. Your lad is after me too but he's not going to get any either.'

Phil smirked. 'I know what Lee did but it doesn't change things.'

For a moment, Shaun was thrown. Had Lee told Phil what he'd done? Or had Phil worked it out like he had?

'Your dickhead of a son says he wants five grand off me or else he's letting on to you that I didn't kill Steph. So if it wasn't me, then it must have been him. Unless,' he smiled cockily. 'Unless it was you.'

'You don't know anything.' Phil came closer.

'I know that I didn't kill her.' Shaun threw his trump card. 'And what's more, Terry knows that I didn't kill her.' Sure enough, he had Phil's attention now. 'Yeah, I told him everything.'

Phil head-butted him in the face. 'I want my money back. All of it or I'll fucking kill you, do you hear me? You're lucky I don't do it now, you useless piece of shit.' He turned to walk away but as an afterthought, rammed his fist in Shaun's stomach.

Shaun doubled over and dropped to his knees.

———————

After catching his breath, Shaun got into his car and drove over to Georgia Road. Now that he knew Terry had his back, there was no way either of the Kennedys would get the better of him. How dare Phil threaten him too! Time to sort out this fuck-up once and for all.

He banged on the door of number twelve. A heavily pregnant girl answered. She looked him up and down and then squinted at him.

'Yeah?'

'Lee Kennedy. Which house?'

'You the pigs?'

'Do I look like a pig? Which house?'

'Number eighteen.' The door slammed shut before he turned away.

Shaun banged on Lee's door next.

'I hope you've got it all,' Lee said once he answered.

Shaun pushed past him into the house. He walked down the narrow passageway and into the kitchen, not impressed with what he saw. The place was a dump. A loaf of bread left open, one fallen slice already drying up. A butter tub, its lid tossed to one side, sat with a knife stuck in it. There were beer cans and dirty dishes on every surface. The stench of something rotting assaulted his nostrils.

He turned to Lee who was hanging back in the doorway. 'This place is a shit hole. How do you live like this?'

'Quite easily,' Lee replied. 'What's with the nose?'

Shaun put a hand to it. It stung but it came back dry. 'Nothing you need to worry about.' He pointed a finger at Lee. 'You need to concentrate on what I'm going to tell you now. The same thing I've just told your father. I've been to see Terry and I've told him everything.'

Lee's cocky attitude disappeared.

'I told him how your dad set himself up as a loan shark, too. I bet Terry's worked out how he could get so much money. He's obviously been taking from somewhere he shouldn't.'

'Fuck! What did you say about me?'

'He knows, Lee.' Shaun folded his arms and smiled triumphantly. 'He knows that it was you who killed Steph.'

'No.' Lee shook his head. 'My old man says that I didn't hit her hard enough. That I –'

Shaun paused. 'So you admit to being there?'

'He says –'

'Don't hide behind your old man! Act like a grown-up for once.' Shaun couldn't keep the disgust from entering his voice. 'People like you make me sick. You swan around as if you own the place, never bothering how many lives you wreck in the process. Fuck, you even live off your family's reputation. You're a loser.'

'You'd better be winding me up or else I'll –'

'Or else you'll what?'

Lee lunged for Shaun, catching him on his chin. But it wasn't enough to have an impact. Shaun punched him on the side of his face. Lee staggered back into the kitchen. Glancing at the knife in the butter, he pulled a drawer open, grabbed a larger one and turned, slicing it through the air.

'Don't come near me, you bastard!'

'Watch out, you idiot!' Shaun dodged the blade. It came at him again. 'Watch out!'

'This is all your fault.' Lee moved round the floor after him. 'If you'd had the bottle to kill her, then I wouldn't be in this shit.'

'I was never going to kill her.' Shaun held up his hands in surrender. He stepped backwards towards the door. 'Christ, put the knife down!'

Lee charged at him again. Shaun dodged to the right but Lee anticipated it. He thrust his arm forward and the knife went into Shaun's stomach.

'I said you're not telling anyone anything!' he cried, the knife going in again and again.

'Stop.' As blood rushed from him, Shaun tried to push Lee away but the knife seared his flesh once more.

Lee's eyes glazed over. 'You're not taking me down, you bastard.'

'Stop.' Shaun tried again but it only came out as a whisper.

'Bastard!' Lee shouted with every thrust. 'Bastard! Bastard!'

Shaun clung onto Lee's arms as his legs gave way. He slid down his body, pawing at his hands, his thighs, his knees. He grunted in pain as he sank to the floor.

But Lee continued with the attack. Screaming out in rage, he kicked Shaun in the stomach, then in the head over and over. Blood from the wounds splattered across the kitchen units; blood from his stomach pooled onto the floor.

Shaun gave one last groan as Lee's boot came down on him again. Moments later, his life slipped away.

Chapter Thirty-Four

Lee waited for his breathing to slow down enough to think straight. The knife clattered to the floor as he loosened his grip. He held shaky hands palm up. They were covered in blood. He glanced at the floor, at the mess he had created. Nudging Shaun with his foot, he said his name. He knew he wouldn't answer. Half of his face was unrecognisable. His ear was probably perforated. But he insisted on trying again.

'Shaun!' When there was no response, his legs buckled and he dropped down on the floor next to him.

Fuck, he'd done it again. What the hell was wrong with him? Trying not to look at the place where Shaun's face had been, he rummaged through his pockets. There were a few notes in his wallet, which he threw to the ground in disgust. He hadn't come with his money! Damn. That wasn't enough to cover the petrol to get him out of Stoke.

He leaned back on the refrigerator and closed his eyes. This couldn't be happening. If Terry Ryder got to him before he did a runner, he'd be for it. Not only had he killed his wife, he'd done in his mate as well. And this one wasn't going to be so easy to cover up.

He opened his eyes. Fuck, he had to hide the body. Trying not to gag, he dragged Shaun across the floor. Slipping in the blood, it took all his might to get him up and over the step into the hallway.

Sweat pouring off him, he opened the cellar door and hurled him down the steps.

He grabbed a towel to wipe up the blood but there was too much of it. All he managed to do was swirl it around. Realising it was hopeless, he pulled off his T-shirt and wrapped the knife inside it. At the bottom of the stairs, he took off his boots and socks and left them there. Then he ran upstairs with the knife. There was no time to spare but he couldn't go anywhere until he'd had a shower. There was too much blood. He'd have to swill himself down.

After a frantic scrub, he quickly threw on another T-shirt, jeans and trainers. All the time expecting someone to knock on the door and catch him in the act, he bundled a few clothes into a holdall, followed by the knife. Then he grabbed his phone. The last thing to do was call his dad. Phil answered on the third ring.

'I've killed him!' he cried. 'Shaun Morrison. He's dead.'

'What are you talking about? Hang on, let me pull over.' A pause. 'Where are you?'

'Listen to me, will you?' Lee paced the room. 'I've killed him. He told Terry that I killed Steph.'

'I know.'

'I couldn't let him get away with – what do you mean, you know?'

'Word gets around Stoke. You should know that.'

'But you told me that I didn't kill her!'

'Where are you?' Phil asked again.

'I killed him, Dad. I need to get out of here.'

'Lee, where are you? Wait!'

Lee disconnected the call and legged it.

⌣‾‾‾‾‾‾⌣

Phil flipped his phone shut and threw it onto the car seat. Half-way home, he turned back and parked up just off Broad Street again. Wanting to keep his car away from the city centre, he walked quickly to the alleyway behind The Orange Grove and sneaked in. There was no sign of Lee or his car. Shaun's car wasn't there either. After a few minutes searching the shadows, he left. Lee must have arranged to meet Shaun and then something had gone wrong. It wasn't even an hour since he'd thumped him right here.

Back in his car he sat for a moment to calm down, trying not to think of how this might have implicated him too. Of all the people to kill, why did Lee have to choose Shaun? Now that Terry knew everything, he was bound to think it had something to do with him.

He banged his fist on the steering wheel. This was all Lee's fault. If he hadn't interfered, Shaun wouldn't have had the guts to go through with the job. And he would have had time to tell Terry that he couldn't do it either.

He started the engine. No matter how much he thought about it, this didn't look good. Ryder would be after his blood for sure now – and his son's. He needed to find Lee and quick – before Terry found either of them.

And if he didn't find Lee within the next twenty-four hours, then he was leaving Stoke without him.

Allie never gave a second thought to the state of Carole Morrison's relationship debacle once back at her desk. Her head was buried in paperwork when Nick shouted to her.

'This has been sent over from the path lab.' He handed her a file. 'You're never going to believe this.'

Allie read a line and frowned. She read it again and looked up at Nick.

'What the ...?'

As they'd predicted, the report stated that there was none of Terry Ryder's DNA on the knife. But the name of the person the blood belonged to was familiar to them.

'It's Sarah Maddison's blood?'

Nick nodded. 'The blades have been compared and it's a match. This is the knife missing from the set in their kitchen. Sarah's and Andy's fingerprints are present but none belonging to Terry Ryder.'

'So why would it be left at his house?' Allie sighed. It didn't add up. What were they missing? 'A bloodied knife is found in Terry Ryder's house, in a secret compartment, and it has the blood of another victim on it. Sarah Maddison was killed by her husband and he's locked up awaiting trial because his blood and prints were everywhere, despite the knife.'

'They would be. He definitely killed her. He confessed.'

'But what if it was made to look like he'd killed her?'

Nick sighed. 'Now you're talking utter bollocks.'

Allie held up her hand. 'Hear me out. The Maddisons rent a house from Terry Ryder. Maddison butchers his wife there but the murder weapon is found at the Ryders' home? Why?'

'But there's none of Ryder's blood or prints on the knife.' Nick perched on the edge of her desk. 'So we can't charge him.'

'What if Maddison started it and then Ryder finished her off without him knowing?'

'But why?' Nick stared at her. 'Why would he do that?'

'Maybe to see if he could?' Allie paused dramatically. 'What if he was going to kill Steph and decided to kill someone else first?'

'As a trial run, you mean?'

'Yes. I know the Maddisons fought a lot, and we didn't like Andy that much, but he did love his wife. And his kids.'

'That's ridiculously far-fetched.' Nick wasn't too keen.

'But, sir. If –'

'If that was the case, why would the knife be at Ryder's property? Surely he would have got rid of it or left it with Maddison at the scene?'

'I don't know.' Allie slapped the desk in frustration. 'But that knife was in there for some reason. According to Carole Morrison, aside from Terry Ryder there are only two other people who knew about the compartment. One of them is dead and the other is her. But what if Steph told Phil Kennedy about it? You know, pillow talk?'

Nick paused. 'Do you think Kennedy could have planted it?'

Allie nodded, stifling a yawn. 'But why would it be in Steph Ryder's wardrobe if it hadn't got his prints on it?'

'Kennedy might not know it didn't have Ryder's DNA on it.'

Allie's eyes widened and then returned to normal. 'Oh, I don't know.'

'Go home,' Nick told her.

Allie looked up, a little startled. 'Sir?'

'Go home, sleep on it. You'll have your answer in the morning.'

Allie glanced at the clock on the wall: it was nearing nine thirty. 'As if it's that simple.'

Nick stood up. 'It is. You're a good investigator, Allie, but everyone needs rest to think straight. Go home, sleep on it.'

Allie texted Mark to say she wouldn't be much longer. She finally packed up and headed for home twenty minutes later. As she passed through the city centre with its array of partygoers getting into the Christmas spirit, she switched on the radio to try and rid her mind of Terry Ryder. But all she could see was the state of Carole Morrison, her battered face, her bloodied nose and clothes. One of them was lying about what happened yesterday morning after she'd left. The clues were there, every piece of the jigsaw. She just wasn't looking hard enough. She mentally laid out all the facts.

Carole Morrison had so much to lose if it was her. Now that Shaun knew about the affair – the *alleged* affair – with Terry she might have lost him anyway. And why cover up her assault by lying about an attack on a small car park?

Could Phil Kennedy have planted the knife at The Gables to get Terry into trouble and if so why? No DNA on the knife proved that Terry hadn't committed the crime. But could Nick's suggestion be right? Did Kennedy think that Terry's DNA was on the knife? Had he intended on setting Terry up? Had *Steph* intended on setting Terry up, even?

She indicated right at the top of Bucknall New Road and headed towards Limekiln Bank, thinking then of the bit on the side, Cathryn Mountford. It had puzzled Allie as soon as she'd stepped into her plush apartment. Cathryn had a business of her own. Why would she risk her reputation and livelihood to lie for the likes of Terry Ryder? They'd checked the deeds to the property. He didn't keep her. Ms Mountford had owned it for six years. Why would she cover for Terry if he had committed murder?

She pulled up at Limekiln traffic lights waiting for the red light to change. This whole thing was a mess. Why couldn't she work it out?

'Stuff this.' On impulse, Allie flicked her left indicator on and headed towards Endon. Ten minutes later, she pulled into the driveway of The Gables and got out of her car. She banged on the front door and stepped back onto the driveway.

As she waited for someone to open it, panic set in. Shit! She hadn't thought further than him being home alone. What if Kirstie answered? How would she explain her actions?

The relief must have shown on her face when Terry appeared. She tried not to take in his casual clothing of jeans, loose white shirt open at the neck. His hair was wet, his feet bare.

'You should have got here a few minutes earlier,' he smiled. 'I was in the shower.'

'I need to talk to you,' she told him sharply, ignoring his insinuation.

'Sure, come on in.' He moved to one side for her to pass by.

'No, I'm staying outside.' Allie pointed at him. 'I don't trust you.'

'You don't trust me?' Terry feigned hurt.

'Don't play games with me, Ryder. I can see right through your bullshit.'

Terry held up his hands. 'You let me go.'

'Only because we don't have anything to charge you with.' *Yet.*

'That's because I didn't do anything.' Terry slipped his feet inside his slippers and stepped onto the porch. 'I didn't kill Steph. She was the apple of my eye.'

Allie snorted. 'People I've spoken to say that your relationship was a sham.'

'You mean Carole?'

'No, just –' Allie stopped for fear of breach of confidentiality.

'They let me go,' Terry repeated. 'What does that suggest to you, Detective?'

'It's Detective Sergeant,' Allie snapped childishly.

'Okay, then, Detective Sergeant,' Terry put emphasis on both words. 'It means that I didn't do anything.'

'It means that we haven't got enough evidence to nail you, you bastard.'

With a nifty move, Terry grabbed her arms and pinned her to the side wall of the porch. She struggled to get away but he was too strong. Her legs flailed trying to knee him in the groin, but he blocked her at every attempt.

'Let me go!'

'Not until you calm down. You have to trust me, Allie.'

'It's Detective Sergeant!' Terry relaxed his grip but not enough for her to break free. 'Let me go.'

'Tell me why you're here if you're so threatened by me.'

'I'm not threatened by *you*.' Allie's breath let him think otherwise as it became shallow. Her heart pounded inside her rib cage. She wasn't certain if it was through fear or lust.

'I know you're not. Because, deep down, deep down in there ...' He gazed at her chest, his eyes lingering. 'You know there's nothing to be threatened by.'

Allie gasped as she felt his hardness pressing up against her when he eased his leg in between hers. For some reason, she resisted her urge to fight anymore.

'I – I've seen what you do to your women,' she spoke softly, his intense stare hypnotising her into submission.

'All lies,' he whispered, his breath close to her cheek.

Allie shivered. It wasn't the December air that made her skin break out all over in goose bumps.

'Let me go.'

'If you calm down, I will.'

She didn't move.

He smiled, hypnotising her that little bit more. 'I mean you no harm. I'm just scared of what you might do.'

'What *I* might do?' Allie laughed incredulously.

'You seem a little agitated.'

She could feel her resolve slipping away but she had to go through with this. He loosened his hold, stepped away and in seconds was back in the doorway. She clutched her chest while her breathing returned to normal.

He held her stare for an agonisingly long few seconds.

'You're welcome to join me for coffee,' he threw over his shoulder as he walked the length of the hallway.

Allie knew he was offering more than coffee and wondered if her nerve would desert her. It was an open invitation.

How far would he go to keep her sweet?

She followed him in to find out.

Chapter Thirty-Five

While Terry was busy in the kitchen, Allie went through to the living area of the family room. The house seemed empty, clinical, still a little too tidy. When had Steph become so disorderly, she wondered?

Her heels clicking on the wooden floor, her eyes flitted around looking for . . . looking for what, exactly? Did she expect to see Carole's blood? Or the hammer that had brutally taken Steph's life? A giveaway clue that would tie him to the murder of his wife? She sat down with a sigh.

The television was tuned to Sky News, the sound button on mute. It screened pictures of some deal gone wrong in the Middle East. Allie watched the yellow ticker tape go across the bottom of the screen with familiarity. Christ, what the hell was she doing here?

Barefoot again, Terry padded over to her and slid a tray onto the table. Two coffees, two small whiskeys.

'I don't drink when –'

'On duty? Surely you're off duty now?'

Allie knew what he was referring to but he was wrong. 'I was actually going to say that I don't drink a drop when I'm driving. Seen too many accidents caused by only the one – occupational hazard.'

'Ah, fair point.' Terry knocked back one measure and picked up the other glass. 'Do you mind?' he asked. When she shook her head, he downed that too. Then he sat down beside her on the settee.

'How's Kirstie?' she asked, not out of concern but wanting to know if she was here alone with him.

'She's at Ashleigh's,' he replied. 'What did you really come here for?'

'I needed to know things.'

'Things?'

'Tell me more about Terry Ryder,' she stalled. 'Who is the man inside?'

'I'm not who you think I am.'

'And who do I think you are?' Allie taunted. She stared at him, wondering exactly what he had to offer her. What information she didn't have already.

He turned his body slightly towards her. 'You think I'm a killer, don't you?'

'I have my theories.'

'You think I murdered my wife?'

'You tell me.'

'I wouldn't do that.'

'How do I know?' Allie paused momentarily, trying to find the right words. 'You give me mixed vibes. I don't know whether to trust you or not.'

'You mean my reputation precedes me?' He bit his lip as if wanting to say more, but he didn't.

'Yes and no,' she responded.

'Meaning?'

'I saw the way you were with Carole Morrison. She was scared of you, but somehow you get me to believe that everything she told me was a lie?'

'It was. The woman is delusional.'

'Why, because she fell under your spell?'

'Are you under my spell?' Terry moved closer. 'I wish to God that you would be.'

She shivered as he ran a finger over her hand. 'Why did you send me flowers?'

'Why does a man usually send a woman flowers?'

'But you knew they'd cause me grief at home. I'm happily married and –'

'Are you?'

'Am I what?'

'Happily married?'

'Yes, I am. Like I said –'

'I know you're married so why say *happily*? It kind of defeats the purpose. Makes me think that you're not.'

'Well, I am.'

'That's okay, then.'

Allie looked away, felt his stare on her. 'What do you want from me?' she whispered.

'I want all of you.'

'And do you always get what you want?'

His laughter made her stomach turn over. Her eyes rested on his neck as he thrust his head backwards.

'Of course I don't,' he smirked. 'I'm not invincible.'

No, just unbelievable.

'Tell me about this knife.' She changed the subject quickly.

'There's nothing to tell.' He kept his eyes on hers.

'Everything has a story. No prints on it. A murder victim's blood on it. Found in your house.'

'It wasn't found. It was planted.'

'Ah.'

'Have you ever thought it could have been Steph's?'

Allie laughed then. 'So you're saying that Steph could have used the knife to kill Sarah Maddison and then use it to frame Andy?'

'It's possible.'

'Anything's possible.' She moved away slightly. He was too close for comfort. Her heart racing, she spoke again.

'How much do you trust Phil Kennedy? He's a bit different from normal employees, from what I've heard.'

'Pray tell me more.'

Allie didn't elaborate. He knew what she was getting at.

'Don't you find it strange that someone was trying to frame you?' she asked.

'That depends.'

'On what?'

'On what *you* believe. Your opinion is highly respected. Surely you can work it out?'

He was mocking her, she was certain. He was mirroring everything she was saying, doing. But she couldn't work out why. And she was all out of questions. The room fell silent.

'I could use a knife right now,' he said.

Allie froze.

'To cut through the sexual tension in this room. You must feel it too, Allie.' He moved closer again. This time his hand went behind her head. She didn't stop him when he gently pulled her towards him and pressed his lips to hers. His touch was light, inviting yet inquiring. Allie closed her eyes as a thousand feelings of lust and wonder invaded her senses. Then she pulled away.

'I have to go,' she told him, the only sound their shallow breathing.

'No one's forcing you to stay,' he whispered into her hair. 'But you know how much I'd like that.'

His lips caressed hers again, light to the touch, then more urgent. She waited for him to stop. It had to be him who stopped.

His hands moved over her back. She mirrored his action. She felt his tongue searching out hers. Oh, no, what if he didn't stop? Her body began to respond in ways it shouldn't.

'Stop. Please,' she whispered.

Terry stopped immediately. 'Really? You want me to stop?'

Those eyes again. *I want to fuck you. Let me fuck you*, they pleaded.

Could she resist them one more time?

Allie left The Gables knowing she'd stepped way over her professional boundaries. She could lose her job if Terry so much as breathed a word. Shit, what had come over her? She could lose everything.

She texted Mark to see if he was still up. It was half past eleven. There was a slight possibility.

She couldn't ring him. She couldn't hear his voice yet. Not after what she'd done. But she needed to see him, feel his arms around her, reassure him of her love.

She fought back tears. She hadn't thought of the consequences of her actions. One look, one touch, one word. That's all it had taken for her to get too close. She was supposed to be manipulating him, not the other way round. Had the same thing happened to Carol, to Cathryn – indeed, even to Steph? Nick was right. Terry Ryder was a charmer.

Mark was in the kitchen when she got home.

'Where have you been?' he asked. 'I thought you'd be back ages ago when you sent your first text.'

'Sorry. We had to check CCTV footage after we thought we'd spotted something,' she lied, kissing him and avoiding his eye.

He pulled away sharply.

'No, really. Where have you been?' His eyes gave away his anger.

'Nowhere. I . . . I told you. I was –'

'I can smell him,' Mark spat. 'I can smell his aftershave. It's all fucking over you!'

'Don't be ridiculous.' Allie moved passed him and flicked on the kettle. She reached into the cupboard for a mug.

Mark slammed the door shut. '"Don't be ridiculous"? You haven't even asked me who I can smell.'

'I work with men all day, Mark,' she bluffed. 'I'm always with men. That's why I smell of aftershave.'

'You never smell that strongly of it at the end of the day.'

His hand was still on the cupboard door. 'Move aside, please.'

'Have you slept with him?'

Allie glared at him. 'Is this where I'm supposed to ask who you're referring to?'

'Ryder!' Mark shouted. 'Have you slept with Ryder?'

'No, I have not slept with him!'

'Then why do you reek of his aftershave? I smelt it, last week at the charity event.'

Allie didn't know what to say.

'I'll ask again, have you slept with him?'

'No!'

Mark stood silent, tears pricking his eyes. Allie put a hand out to touch his face but he moved away. She followed him as he ran upstairs.

'Mark!' she shouted after him. 'Mark, wait! Please!'

He stopped halfway and turned back to her. 'The other night, when you were deep in thought, you were thinking about him, weren't you?'

'Of course I wasn't!'

'No wonder you didn't visit your sister. And all the time I thought you were fretting about the case!'

'I was!' Allie replied truthfully. 'I wouldn't –'

Mark continued upwards, slamming the bedroom door in her face as she got near to. She stopped behind it for a moment, unsure whether to barge in and continue with the fight or leave him to it until he calmed down. That was, if he did calm down. She could hardly blame him for reacting that way.

But the more she stood there, the more she realised she had to talk to him. If she said nothing, he could sit there thinking the worst. And she was only stalling in case she slipped up, said something she'd regret.

She knocked on the door. 'Mark, can I come in?'

He didn't speak as she pushed it open. There was only one thing she had to ask him. Their relationship was built on it – before today, at least.

'Mark, do you trust me?'

He looked back at her in amazement.

'Do you?' She raised her voice. 'Do you trust me?'

'I can't believe you're even asking me that.' Mark sat on the bed with a thud. 'Of course I trust you. I've always trusted you and I always will. But really, don't you think you should be asking yourself that question?'

Allie frowned. He had that look on his face again. The anger, the fear, the mistrust that she had caused all rolled into one.

It was her time to question. 'What do you mean?'

'It's simple,' Mark replied. 'Do you really trust yourself?'

___

A few miles away, hidden from view behind a row of council-owned garages in Bucknall, Lee sat huddled in his car, trying to keep warm. He switched on his phone and checked the missed calls that his dad had left. There were at least two every hour since they'd last spoke. He switched it off again. He didn't want to talk to him. He didn't want to see anyone. He just wanted it to be light.

It was nearing midnight but he wouldn't go home. He couldn't stay in the house knowing there was a body in the cellar. And he knew it was only a matter of time before the police came after him. Once they'd spoken to Shaun's wife, they'd call at his house. He needed to be gone by then.

For now he was going to lie low. First thing in the morning he was going to ring Kirstie. She was the next part of the plan.

———

Midnight. Allie had left half an hour ago but still Terry sat going over things that she'd questioned him about. He had known all along what her game was, why she'd come round to see him. Why she'd left when she did. She couldn't fool him. He, too, could play games.

One thing he should have done was give her more credit. She had a shrewd mind, able to make something out of nothing to enable it to work in her favour. She'd started off with the knife, casually moved on to Carole and then to Phil before he'd won her over.

For the life of him, he couldn't work out why Phil had planted the knife in the secret compartment or how it had got there in the first instance. It irked him that he couldn't. As far as he was aware, only he and Steph had known of the compartment in her wardrobe. Steph wouldn't have known about the knife unless Phil had given it to her for safekeeping. Had Phil been blabbing to Steph before she was killed? Or had Phil planted it without Steph knowing? The more he thought about it, Phil could have slipped over when he was with Cathryn in Derby. But, still, why would he hide the knife? He knew it didn't have his DNA on it. And why the hell hadn't he checked properly when he'd looked after the police had gone? He'd immediately checked out the box but hadn't thought to check inside the rolls of jewellery. Why would he? He hadn't thought anyone would hide anything in them. And there hadn't been time to check everything. He'd been well and truly had by someone.

Terry's fists curled into balls as he fought back the urge to punch the nearest wall. This was all Phil Kennedy's fault. And that fuck-up of a lad of his. He grabbed his phone and dialled a number. He was going to put a stop to this.

Chapter Thirty-Six

Back at his home, Phil tried Lee's mobile again but still the phone was switched off. It was after two a.m. – where the hell was he? He peered through the front window but nothing had changed in the darkness. There was no sign of Lee's car parked anywhere along the road.

Finally, he shoved on his boots and went upstairs. Maybe there'd be some clues as to his whereabouts at Lee's house. He pulled down the loft ladder and took the shortcut through the loft spaces, dropping gently down into number eighteen. It was deathly quiet.

'Lee?' Phil said loudly, switching on the landing light.

There was blood on the bathroom door handle. Phil paused before pushing open the door and stepping back in horror. The room was awash with it. Smears on the shower cubicle, a diluted puddle in the tray. There weren't any footprints but there were patches of blood on the taps, in the basin. A damp bloodied towel was thrown to the floor.

Phil turned around but there was no blood outside the room. He checked the two bedrooms quickly and then made his way downstairs. It was on the second step down that he could see Lee's discarded boots. He leaned over the banister and gasped. Through the open kitchen door, he could see thick swirls of blood on the floor in the shape of a number eight. Bloodstained towels lay dumped in a pile on the work top. Phil surveyed the floor. From where he stood, he couldn't see a body. Not that it really mattered. Lee would be the first suspect in his own home.

He needed to get out of there fast.

His mobile rang as he ran back up the stairs, scaring him so much he wondered if his heart would stop. He checked the caller display to see Terry's name flash up. Fuck! He ran a hand over his chin. Should he answer it and see what he wanted? Terry wouldn't be able to see where he was. He could say he was anywhere, really. But his courage deserted him. He rejected the call and switched off the phone as he made his way back to his house.

Halfway through the loft spaces, he searched out the holdall where his stash of emergency money was hidden and threw it over his shoulder. Once at his own loft opening again, he threw the bag down onto the landing and climbed down the rickety ladder. He heard a noise, turned sharply. He listened but he couldn't see or hear anything. Laughing nervously at how freaked he was, he pushed the ladders into the loft and secured the hatch.

He bent to pick up the bag but it had disappeared. He turned full circle. Where the fuck had it gone?

'Looking for something?' Terry appeared from behind the bedroom door.

Every ounce of courage in Phil's body deserted him instantly but he never showed it.

'Alright, Tel?' he nodded a greeting with his head. He was about to make the speech of his life when he spotted Shane Flint and Mitch Casey behind Terry. The cleanup crew.

Phil made a run for it. Trying desperately not to stumble, he legged it down the stairs. But when he was nearly at the front door, a hand on his shoulder pulled him back, then spun him round. Phil felt a punch in the stomach. He bent over with a groan and a knee brought upwards rammed into his face. Dazed, he fell to the floor as an elbow slammed into his back. But the worst was yet to come. A dark sack was pushed over his head.

'No.' He tried to shout but it came out as a mumble. Gasping for air, he tasted the fear of other men. He'd used this bag previously to do exactly what Terry was doing to him now. The end results had never been good. Before he could protest, he was dragged to his feet, marched through the back of the house and bundled into the boot of a car.

Terry had thought long and hard before deciding to do the hit on Phil himself. And after speaking to Allie earlier, he knew he needed to move fast. He could have relied on the crew to do it for him but he wanted the satisfaction of watching Phil die. He wanted to be the last person he saw and the last person he heard when he took his final breath.

In his Range Rover, he drove out of the city towards Leek. After a few minutes, he turned off into a lane. Another left and a few more and he pulled up outside a gate. Behind he could see the headlights of another car. He opened the gate and let the driver go through. Once he'd driven his vehicle in, he secured the gate again, switched off his headlights and drove forward slowly so as not to make too much noise.

He parked behind a row of dilapidated garages, hidden mostly from view by overhanging trees and unruly moss on top of a corrugated roof. He'd bought them and the land a few years ago at a pittance from a local farmer. The four acres weren't a prime development site. Lots of locals with horses to stable had offered numerous prices for it over the years. But Terry wasn't interested in selling it to anyone.

Except for the odd lights in the distance from the lane, the site was in darkness. During the day, the area was fairly secluded.

The farm in the next field ran a boarding kennels for dogs. The howls of lonely pets crossed the quiet fields at regular intervals. At night, Terry would be really unlucky if more than a handful of cars passed by. There was a four-foot-high hedgerow in between that and the garages. And the dogs howled more during the night. It was the perfect place. No one would hear Kennedy screaming.

Terry undid the lock on the first garage and pulled open the door. He switched on a florescent tube light to reveal an open space. A shelving unit along one wall held cans of paint, steel boxes, tubs of screws. At the far end, a stained wooden chair stood next to a pile of tyres. Shane and Mitch dragged Phil, awake but groggy, across the floor, shoved him down onto the chair and tied him up.

'Let me go, you bastards,' Phil said from underneath the sacking.

The two men remained silent as they worked. Once finished, Terry chucked a bunch of keys at Shane.

'Take my car; be seen around town in it and I'll call you when I'm done.' Only when he heard them drive away did he pull off the sacking.

Phil blinked profusely as his eyes adjusted to the light. Although he'd guessed where he was from the noises he'd heard, seeing it made real panic set in. He pulled at the binding on his wrists and feet but all he ended up doing was tipping over the chair, knocking himself to the floor. His face scraped against the broken tarmac. He was sure he'd cracked his cheekbone. But that didn't upset him as much as the next thought that shot through his mind. There was so much blood on the floor already that forensics would be lucky to spot his amongst it.

Terry dragged Phil back to sitting with an exaggerated sigh.

'Please, you don't want to do this, Tel.'

Terry walked round to stand in front of him. Under the pale overhead lighting, Phil caught a glimpse of his eyes. They looked like the eyes of someone possessed.

Terry shook his head, as if the sight before him was painful to see. 'I never thought I'd see you in that chair. I thought I could trust you with my life.'

'You can!' Phil's eyes pleaded with the dark and nasty soul of a Ryder. 'Look, whatever I've done, I'm sorry. I'll put it right.'

'Like an eye for an eye?' Terry punched him full on. His fist caught Phil's nose. Blood flowed from it at an alarming rate.

'Please, Tel. I –' Phil spit out blood.

'Or maybe a tooth for a tooth?' Terry moved to a side bench, held up a retractable knife in his right hand and watched Phil recoil. He held up a lump hammer in his left hand. 'Or maybe even a life for my WIFE?'

In one step, Terry stood in front of him again. Phil shouted out as the blade sliced his skin from the outside corner of his eye down to the bottom of his nose. Flesh and blood oozed out of its thickness.

'I know everything, you bastard.' To more screams of protest, Terry repeated the action on the other side of Phil's face.

His breathing coming in panic-induced spurts, Phil closed his eyes for a moment, trying to escape the pain and the mad look in Terry's eyes. To hell with it. He might as well put up a fight the only way he knew how.

'You're talking shit, man,' he said, every word accentuating his pain. 'You don't know the half of it.'

Terry pulled his arm back as far as he could and with brute force, brought down the hammer on Phil's right shin. Phil screamed this time. Terry left it a full minute before he smashed the hammer down on his left shin.

When Phil's screams had lessened, Terry began to talk. 'You are some stupid fuck, you know that?' To maximise the pain, he grabbed Phil's chin and squeezed it hard. 'You're a fucking loser. You and that layabout offspring of yours.'

Phil continued to spit out blood. Terry wiped his glove with distaste on the sleeve of Phil's jacket. 'You should never have thought you could get one over me. I gave you the job of doing Steph in because I knew you'd been fucking her. And what did you do? Give the job to someone else – someone who fucked up.'

'You gave me the job because you couldn't kill her yourself,' Phil told him through gasps.

'You think so?' Terry's laughter sounded menacing. 'Hell, no, I wanted to watch her die. Kinda cool that your lad didn't finish her off in the end, don't you think?

He rested the tip of the knife in between Phil's eyes. Then he drew it up his forehead.

'And if fucking my wife wasn't enough, you were stealing my money.' He drew the blade across horizontally next. 'Everyone takes from a player, it has to be recognised. And I wouldn't have minded that. But to then take my money and use it to gain more money? And then to use threats to get it back? Twenty grand, wasn't it? Well, that's just not acceptable.' The knife scored Phil's forehead in the opposite direction.

Phil groaned through clenched teeth. The pain was unbearable, especially since he'd seen Terry do all this before. He was going to die, he was certain.

'And then there's this business around Sarah Maddison. How exactly did the knife that I finished her off with – the knife I told you to get rid of – end up in my house for the police to find?'

'I don't know what you're talking about.' Phil was having trouble concentrating on anything through the pain. Then it dawned on him. It must have been Steph who had taken the knife from the outhouse. But how would she know it was there? Had Kenny told her? Or had it been Steve? Had his own brother set him up?

'It was the baby that was the last straw,' Terry said. 'There was no way I was having your bastard child running around my house, reminding me of you.'

'Baby?' Phil managed to say.

'Oh!' Terry beamed. 'You didn't know Steph was pregnant? Well, that's hardly surprising because she didn't know either unless she guessed. She didn't get the chance to find out her results. You see, I know this bird, Pamela Ruston. Works at the doctor's surgery. She told me the happy news as soon as it came in.'

Phil could hardly see Terry through all the blood. Although determined to keep talking, he wasn't going to let on about the knife. If he was going down, he was going to hurt Terry too, even if he did have to bend the truth a little.

'You think Steph got one over on me?' Blood bubbled between his lips as he spoke. 'She didn't. She screwed us both. She couldn't stand you anymore. She put up with you because she wanted the big house, the lifestyle, the money. Steph was the smart one. She had to keep you sweet. And you fell for it. But me? I'd been fucking her for ages. And all that time, I knew. She didn't love you. She loved me.'

Terry took a flick-knife from his pocket and plunged it into Phil's heart, twisting it for one final act of revenge.

In that split second, Phil knew his time was up.

Terry pulled out the knife and stood back to admire his handiwork. 'No, you're wrong,' he said, watching as Phil's head lolled to the side and his eyes glazed over. 'Steph only ever loved herself.'

___

Shane and Mitch were back fifteen minutes after Terry called them.

'Never to be seen again, yeah?' said Shane, handing Terry his keys.

Terry nodded.

'Same with his car?'

'Yeah. Take it as far away as possible.'

Chapter Thirty-Seven

As Thursday turned into Friday, Allie lay in the dark shadows of the early morning trying not to wake Mark, who was asleep on the far side of the bed. She wished she could manage to drop off again. She'd flitted in and out of sleep for most of the night.

Mark's words lay heavy on her heart. Apart from him moaning about the long hours she worked when a murder case came in, nothing had ever come between them in terms of work. The statistics were high for failed marriages for police personnel so she knew she was lucky to be part of something good, something so strong.

But then again, despite the issue of her sister, wasn't the problem here caused by her and not Mark? Weren't Mark's insecurities down to her recent behaviour?

As she turned onto her back, a hand reached over and touched her thigh, gently resting on it as if it were an apparition.

'I'm sorry,' said Mark.

Usually this was the time that Allie would turn to him and say, 'Yeah me too.' But she didn't speak.

A gentle tap of the hand on her thigh. 'I didn't mean to go off on one.'

'Yes, you did.'

The hand was pulled away abruptly, followed by a sigh and a silence that spoke a thousand words. Then, 'Your work consumes you at times, Allie. It's what I love about you but it's what I hate about you too.'

Allie pinched the bridge of her nose. 'It's six o'clock in the morning and you want to continue where you left things last night?'

Silence again.

'I'm tired of this,' he replied. 'We've always been so good together.'

Allie pulled back the duvet and marched across the room. 'That's funny, because I thought we still were.'

'Allie!' Mark shouted after her.

She went to the bathroom to stew over his words. With the door firmly shut, and water rushing over her, she cried secret tears of frustration. What was wrong with her? Was she losing her mind? How on earth had her life changed so much in the space of a few days?

Minutes later, she heard a tap on the door as she dried herself. Mark pushed it open slightly. Standing there naked made Allie feel vulnerable. She wrapped the towel around her body, but as his gaze travelled lazily from her eyes to her chest, she felt a longing so deep that it scared her. God, she needed to feel loved by him.

'Let's not fight,' she whispered, her hand reaching for the elastic waistband of his pyjama shorts. She drew him close, felt the frustration dropping as sexual tension built up. He pulled her into his arms, kissing her long and hard, hands tugging at the towel that then dropped to the floor.

Allie groaned as his hands moved over her. She needed to feel him inside her, needed to assert her oneness with him after allowing Terry to get so close. She arched her back as he kissed her neck.

See, this is where I belong, she thought as he lifted her up by her thighs and her ankles clasped together behind his back. Here, in the arms of my husband.

This is my rightful place to be.

Lee woke up when a lorry rumbled past in the distance. He switched on the interior light and checked the time. It was half past seven. The image of what was left of Shaun's head swam before his eyes every time he closed them so he hadn't had much sleep. Moving his neck from side to side, he stretched his back. Jeez, that was aching too. For a minute, he got out of the car to stretch his legs but it was too cold to stay outside. His stomach rumbled away. It was ages since he'd eaten. After lighting a cigarette he got back in, started the engine and kept it idling while he warmed up.

As the good people of Stoke-on-Trent awoke to another chilly day, Lee sat and contemplated his future. That is, if you could call it a future. Eighteen years old and already he'd killed two people. What else was going to go wrong?

He wondered if he would get away with his plan – if indeed it was a plan and not a suicide mission. But he had to get money from somewhere. And two sources were better, even if one was pretty damn risky.

At eight, he tried Phil's phone but his dad didn't answer. He disconnected it, wondering if he'd got the hump with him now for not getting back to him the night before. But what could he do? He couldn't chance anyone going near his house, not yet.

He waited another half hour before trying again but still no reply. Then he called Kirstie. It was time to talk smooth and put his plan into action.

'Lee! Where have you been? I tried your phone forever last night. I was over at Ashleigh's. I could have come to see you.'

'Sorry, babe.' Lee put on his best soothing voice. 'I didn't feel too good so I went to bed early. Didn't realise my phone was off.'

'But if you were ill I could have come round to look after you. I could have given you some T.L.C.'

'Actually, I wondered if you fancied catching up this morning. Can you get away?'

Lee heard her catch her breath. 'I can't.' She sounded disappointed.

'Why not?'

'I need to be close during the day, in case the police find out anything about Mum. It's easier at night to slip out and pretend to be at Ashleigh's. That's why I was after you.'

'Can't you pretend that you have to hand some work in at college? I can meet you somewhere and we can come back to mine. No one will be any the wiser.'

'I'm not sure.'

'I'm dying to see you, Kirst,' he lied. 'I can meet you at the Festival Park in half an hour. We can leave your car there and it'll look like you've been in Boots for something, headache tablets or the likes, if you do get caught. Better to get a bollocking for that. What do you say?'

A pause.

'Okay, just for a bit, then.'

Lee sighed with relief. Part one of his plan had worked. Leaving Kirstie's car at the Festival Park would mean that when Ryder started looking for her, he wouldn't find it anywhere near his house.

Allie had been at her desk since seven a.m., running through her team's findings from the day before. All around her, people had started to drift in. Trying to put her personal life in a box until her shift was over, she concentrated on her work. The missing persons call Carole Morrison had made regarding Shaun landed on her desk an hour later as a hunch from a young police constable who recognised the name. After the morning's briefing, she headed over to The Orange Grove.

'I didn't think anything of it at first,' Carole said, indicating for Allie to sit down at a table downstairs. 'We'd been arguing since he'd found out about ... me and Terry.'

'What time did you last see him?' Allie opened her notepad.

'He left here shortly after you yesterday. We had a sixtieth birthday party booked in for four o'clock, with eighteen guests to attend to. I'd been preparing for it for most of the day – can't stop working even when I look like this.' She pointed at the bruising now prominent on her face. 'So I got on with it. But after the first few guests arrived, I knew we'd be understaffed without him. I rang him but his phone was switched off. I had to greet the guests telling some story that I'd tripped up the steps in the kitchen.'

'What time was that?'

'Half five, sixish, I guess.'

'Did you try his mobile again?'

Carole nodded. 'Every ten minutes or so but it was still switched off. By the time they'd all gone around nine, there was still no sign of him. I called the station at eleven. Some bloke told me to ring again if he was still missing this morning. Well, he is and I haven't slept a wink all night.'

'It does seem strange,' Allie started, 'after everything that's gone on recently.'

'You don't think he's in trouble, do you?' Carole's hand rose to her chest.

'Probably not – Shaun seems like a nice guy. But sometimes people have secrets and –'

'We don't have secrets,' said Carole sharply. 'There's nothing wrong with our marriage.'

Allie decided not to comment on the obvious. 'Has anyone been to see him lately? Someone who wouldn't see him usually? Or Terry. Has Terry Ryder been about?'

Carole scowled at the mention of his name. 'I haven't seen him since he attacked me. But I do know that Shaun said he was going to see him.'

'Shaun was going to see Terry?'

'Yes, that's what he said.' Carole paused. 'But Terry wouldn't have done anything to him.'

'Yes, I agree,' Allie soothed. Terry Ryder wouldn't do anything to get himself into trouble, not when things were too close to home. 'Anyone else?'

'That Kennedy has been snooping around.'

Allie raised her eyebrows. 'Phil Kennedy?'

Carole nodded. 'And his son.'

'They came together?'

'No, at different times. I thought something funny was going on but Shaun told me not to worry.' Carole glanced up at Allie. 'You're right. Things did start to happen but it was before Steph was murdered. Phil Kennedy called to see Shaun the day before she died. We owed him money and a couple of days later, Shaun told me that everything had been sorted. That the debt had been wiped out.'

Allie sat forward. 'Didn't you find that a little odd?'

'Definitely. Even I'm not stupid enough to believe that. But Shaun was insistent. Then we had an intruder in the kitchen that Shaun saw off – he didn't want me to report it. Maybe that was one of them but we do have trouble with squatters. I did ask Shaun what Phil wanted but he didn't say. But I clearly heard him say he needed him to take care of something for him.'

'Take care of something?'

Carole nodded. 'Shaun denied anything was going on. Then the day before yesterday, Lee Kennedy was parked outside. I was upstairs and I saw Shaun go out to him. They were arguing but I couldn't hear about what so I went downstairs. When I got to them, they stopped. Young Kennedy got in his car and drove off. Shaun told me not to worry then, too.' She looked at Allie, desperate for her to make sense of things for her. 'One of those Kennedy bastards has done something to him, haven't they?'

Allie placed a hand on the woman's arm. 'Let's hope not.' She turned to go as Carole began to cry. But as she got to the door, she stopped.

'Carole, did Steph ever cause damage to The Orange Grove?'

Carole paused for a moment. 'Not that I can recall,' she sniffed. 'She used to break the odd glass when she was drunk but that was about all. Why?'

'No reason.' Allie decided not to tell her of Terry's accusations. The woman had enough to worry about with Shaun going missing. She didn't need to make things any worse.

She needed to find Shaun.

Chapter Thirty-Eight

After Allie had left, Carole started to go over everything again. Shaun had never gone missing before. He would always ring her if he was going to be late. He'd text if he hadn't time to ring. And since they worked so closely together, she wasn't far from him at all times. It was so unlike him to stay out and not contact her.

She started to wonder if Terry could be involved. Surely he wouldn't do anything to harm Shaun? It seemed too close to home after all that had gone on recently. But the more she thought about it, the more it seemed possible. In the end, she rang him.

'Shaun's missing,' she sobbed down the line. 'Have you done something to him, you bastard?'

'Missing? I haven't done –'

'You've done something to get your own back on me, haven't you?'

'I haven't done anything to him. Look, shut up a minute and let me think.'

But Carole went on. 'I reported him missing to the police this morning.'

'What did they say? Who did you speak to?'

'Allie Shenton's been round. She asked me who had been to see Shaun lately. I told her he'd gone to see you. I told her about Lee Kennedy and Phil –'

'Lee Kennedy?' Terry forgot all about the mention of Allie or himself.

After Carole filled him in with the details, Terry disconnected the phone and felt the hairs stand up on his neck.

———————

After ringing Kirstie, Lee called his dad again but still no answer. Fuck! Where was he? He'd have to chance it and call in at number two. But if the police were at his house already, he'd have to leg it without seeing his dad first for some cash.

Everything was quiet when he drove past. He parked in the side entry and, using the key he had to the house, opened the door and let himself in.

'Dad?' he shouted. 'Dad?' He went through to the living room, the kitchen, ran up the stairs to check the bedroom but the house was empty. He rang him again; still no answer. His shoulders sagged. Where was he? Surely he wouldn't do a runner without him? He checked his watch. There was no time to see if he had. He'd have to collect Kirstie and bring her back here. He could tie her up while he thought what to do next. Jumping down the last few stairs, he dropped into the cellar. He found a piece of rope and shoved it into his jacket pocket. It would have to do for now.

Kirstie was waiting for him where he'd arranged to meet her. She slid into the passenger seat.

Lee pulled her into his arms and kissed her. 'I missed you,' he lied.

'I missed you too.' She moved his hand to her breast.

'Plenty of time for that later.' He started the car engine. 'Come on, let's get out of here.'

On the short drive back, Lee quizzed Kirstie about Steph's murder enquiry. What the police were up to. What they'd asked since he'd last seen her. From what she told him, it looked like he was safe for now, at least.

He parked on the dirt track down the side of number two again. 'I need to call at my dad's first,' he said. Making sure the rope in his jacket pocket was well hidden, he grabbed her hand and ran. 'Come on. He wants to see me about something.'

'Wait up!' Kirstie tottered as she tried to keep up with him. 'My heels.'

Once at the door, he opened it and stepped aside. 'After you.' He threw out his arm.

Kirstie giggled and tottered into the hall. Lee banged shut the door, grabbed her hand again and ran upstairs.

'Hey!' Kirstie protested. 'We can't go up there!'

He took her into the back bedroom and threw her onto the bed. She sat back up again but he pushed her down. He reached for the rope. When she saw it, Kirstie flipped.

'What the fuck's going on, Lee?'

Lee cracked her hard across the face.

'What was that for?' she wailed.

'I want you to shut up. Do you think you could manage that for now?'

Kirstie tried to nod through her panic.

'Good.' Lee pulled one of her hands up and tied her wrist to the end of the metal headboard. Then he grabbed the other and pulled it across the bed to the opposite side, intending to tie it there so that her arms were outstretched. But the rope wasn't long enough. He cursed loudly. Not thinking straight, he tied the rope tighter around the one wrist that was fastened and added a couple of double knots. He pulled at them to reassure himself that she couldn't slip the wrist free. She wouldn't be able to do much with one hand, especially after he'd finished with her, anyway. He took a small clear bag from out of his jeans. It contained several sleeping pills, the ones he'd used to ensure she was out of it last Friday night. He waggled the bag in her face.

'There are lots of things you don't know about me, Kirstie Ryder,' he said. 'So I'd think about that while you keep your mouth shut.'

It was nearing mid-morning when Allie left The Orange Grove. She radioed through to Sam and picked her up outside the station. Then they headed over to Georgia Road. On the drive there, she filled Sam in with what Carole had told her.

'We'll visit both Kennedys,' she said as she drove around Potteries Way, 'and see what they have to say.'

'How well did Lee Kennedy know Shaun Morrison?' Sam asked.

'Not well at all, according to Carole.'

'Do you think he was trying to prove himself to his dad?'

'Possibly.' Allie negotiated a roundabout and then changed to the left lane. 'It could be why he was visiting Shaun so soon after Steph's murder and straight after his dad paying a visit too.'

'Maybe he heard his dad telling Shaun something?'

'It's all circumstantial, though.' Allie sighed.

Sam turned to her suddenly. 'You don't think Phil Kennedy was arranging for Shaun to murder Steph?'

Allie shook her head. 'Why would he do that?'

'Think about it.' Sam paused as she tried to work things out. 'Maybe Lee heard his dad telling Shaun to do it and Lee was pissed about it. Maybe Lee thought he should have asked him. He could have killed Steph instead to prove himself to his dad. Or even followed Shaun and tried to blackmail him.'

'You think Shaun killed Steph?'

'Well, don't you think it's strange that he's gone missing now?'

'I suppose so, but there's no logical connection that Shaun would kill her. And no evidence to connect either him or Lee Kennedy as being present at the scene.'

They continued in silence as they each tried to make sense of their thoughts. Allie knew Sam was on the verge of something. Damn, why wouldn't the last piece or two of the jigsaw slot into the puzzle?

'It's a good theory,' Allie added, indicating right into Georgia Road. 'But why wouldn't Phil kill Steph Ryder rather than get Shaun to do it for him?'

'And what was his motive for killing Steph, or arranging to have her killed, in the first place? I reckon ...'

Allie slammed on the brakes. Checking in the rear-view mirror to make sure nothing was behind her, she reversed back slightly. 'Look.' She pointed at a car parked a few houses away from where Lee Kennedy lived. She located her notepad and flipped through the pages until she found what she was looking for. *Yes*! She almost punched the air. The make and model matched: BMW 5 Series. The colour matched: midnight blue. The registration number matched.

'That's Shaun Morrison's car,' she told Sam. 'Surely that's not a coincidence? And it's parked nearer to Lee Kennedy's than to his father's. We'll try there first.'

Allie parked the car and they ran over to number eighteen. She pounded on the door. No reply. She banged again. Still no answer. She lifted the letterbox and peered through. She could see a narrow hallway, stairs to the right and a door at the far end. But it wasn't the first thing she noticed. Allie could see blood. On the banister, all over the laminate flooring, on the walls here and there. And on the door handle leading to what she knew to be the kitchen. The door was ajar but she didn't need to see anymore. She stood upright and reached for her phone.

'There's blood everywhere,' she told Sam. 'We need backup to force this door.'

'What about round the back?'

'No point. Every door is reinforced to keep us out. Just keep an eye out to see if those curtains twitch. I doubt Kennedy is inside but you never know.'

Fifteen minutes later two squad cars drew up. Allie and Sam stood back while a uniformed officer used a battering ram to gain access. After a few minutes, the door finally gave way.

Allie searched out latex gloves, shoe covers and batons from the officers. 'Wait out here,' she told them, cautious of contaminating a crime scene. 'Don't let anyone follow us unless we shout for backup.

Allie and Sam stepped in.

Allie's baton sliced through the air as Allie snapped it open and held it high. They moved forward stealthily. As she got to the living room door, the blood on the kitchen floor became more prominent. Her eyes flitting everywhere, she pushed open the living room door first and peered round. 'It's clear,' she said. 'So is the kitchen from where I'm standing.'

Sam paled at the sight of the blood. 'What the hell's gone on in there?' She covered her mouth with her hand and gagged.

'Let's check upstairs first.' Allie backed away. 'If anyone does come out of the kitchen, the uniforms will nab them if they make a run for it. We'll hear them if they go out the back way. And remember, try not to walk over anything.'

Holding batons aloft, Allie and Sam went upstairs. But apart from lots more blood in the bathroom, the rooms were clear. Allie surveyed the state of the bedroom. It looked worse than some of the burglaries she'd attended. The bed was unmade, clothes on the floor, drawers open and empty. A three-drawer cabinet had been swept and cleared, she assumed of toiletries, maybe aftershave.

Allie dropped the baton to her side. What had happened here? Had there been a fight? An argument gone wrong? Had someone been taken to hospital? Or was Kennedy the victim? And if so, which one? It could just as easily be father or son.

They went back downstairs. Allie heard Sam catch her breath, a moment before she did the same. To the right was a door that led down to the cellar. There was more blood on its handle. In an instant, all the horror movies she'd ever seen flashed before her eyes. Pulse pounding in her ears, Allie rested her hand on the metal knob for the briefest of moments before taking a deep breath and opening it. She gasped at the sight before her.

The body of a male lay face down at the bottom of the stairs. His neck was at a displeasing angle, the back of his head beaten to pulp, the side of his face caved in. There was more blood underneath his torso. Allie rushed down but before she got to the bottom of the stairs, she could see it was Shaun Morrison.

Chapter Thirty-Nine

Although Terry hadn't gone to bed since he'd finished off Phil Kennedy, he felt a bizarre sense of calm. Phil had had it coming to him for a long time. Not only because he'd been screwing Steph but because he'd been screwing him over, too.

It was ten thirty the next morning. He sat in the family room, looking but not seeing the rear garden. Over coffee and a cigarette, he realised there would be all hell to pay for his actions once Steve Kennedy found out that he'd killed his brother but he'd deal with the consequences later. For now, it was good riddance. Phil could have got him into a lot of trouble and he wasn't going to let any man do that. Or woman.

His Blackberry rang. He didn't recognise the number. 'Yeah?'

'I have your daughter.'

Terry felt the blood drain to his feet as the caller continued.

'I have Kirstie and if you don't give me what I want, I'm going to hurt her. Hurt her real bad.'

'Lee, if that's you, I swear to God I'll –'

There was a pause down the line. 'Never mind who it is. I want money and I want it fast. Ten grand. Do you hear me? I'll ring again in two hours.'

'Hello? HELLO!' Terry cursed as the line went dead.

What the fuck did Lee Kennedy think he was doing with Kirstie? And how the hell had he got hold of her? She'd been home last night – or had she? She could have slipped out when he was over in Leek.

He grabbed his car keys and headed out. But as he arrived at Georgia Road ten minutes later, Terry didn't stop. He drove straight on. There were two police cars outside number eighteen.

Allie rang the details through to the control room. She told the officers outside to cordon off the property with tape.

'No one in or out without my say-so until the Forensics team or DI Carter get here, okay?'

Careful of the blood in the hallway, Allie sent Sam to look upstairs while she searched through the living room. A half-drunk cup of tea, a plate with crumbs and a third of a slice of toast left on a plate were atop of a cheap, beech-effect coffee table. It looked like someone had disturbed Lee, but for what reason?

So many questions came racing into her head. Were Sam's first thoughts heading in the right direction? Why wouldn't Shaun have got Lee to meet him at the restaurant? Was there something else that Shaun didn't want Carole to know? Did he really have something to do with the murder of Steph Ryder?

She flicked through a stack of magazines on the floor, sifted through a pile of clothes on the armchair. She opened a drawer, saw untidy contents pushed in willy-nilly. She leafed through bills, most unpaid. There were a few takeaway leaflets, a programme from a recent concert to see Muse, used train tickets to Birmingham. There was a brochure for holidays in Greece and Turkey next summer. Kos or Crete seemed to be first choices, by the look of which pages were turned over at the corners.

Allie closed the drawer. There was nothing in there to indicate a killer.

Over on the far wall, there was a framed photo of Lee with Kirstie. It looked pretty recent. Allie stared at it as if willing either image to speak to her. Tell her what had been going on. She continued checking the room, behind the settee, underneath the chairs, behind other photo frames ... but nothing. What had made Lee Kennedy flip and kill Shaun Morrison? Assuming that it was Lee, she reasoned with herself. It could easily have been his father, Phil, or even some other thug. Just because there was a body here, it didn't necessarily mean that Lee was the killer. She wouldn't jump to conclusions until the evidence was in – not after the last time.

She glanced in the kitchen, glad to leave it for the forensics team. She didn't want to go in anyway. Once was enough. No doubt that blood on the floor would haunt her dreams for a few nights to come. She shuddered. How did humans do that to others? It went beyond her belief.

'Sarge!' Sam's shout had Allie rushing to the hallway. Sam came down to the bottom of the stairs. 'There's an air rifle in the wardrobe upstairs but it doesn't look like it has been used in a while,' she told her. 'And then there's this.' She held up a plastic evidence bag. Inside it was a hammer. She gave it to Allie. 'There's blood on it.'

Allie's heart began to pulsate out of her chest. She thought back to what Sam had been thinking aloud. Had Lee Kennedy been involved in the death of Steph Ryder?

'I'll see if we can get it fast-tracked,' she said. Then she stepped outside the house for a moment. She breathed in cold damp air like it was going out of fashion, trying to make sense of everything. If the blood on the hammer matched Shaun Morrison's, they had their murder weapon. But if it was Lee Kennedy who was the murderer, wouldn't he have slung it away? He wouldn't leave it at his house for anyone to find, surely?

Allie's shoulders sagged in frustration. Questions, questions, questions when what she really needed was answers, answers, answers.

Then she thought of another.

If Lee Kennedy had killed Shaun Morrison, he was more than capable of having done the same to Steph Ryder.

Chapter Forty

While Lee was on the phone, Kirstie had tried to work out if there was anything she could do. She wondered if she should try talking to him. All the films she'd watched said that kidnap victims stayed alive longer if they built up a rapport with their kidnappers. She gulped as she thought of her situation. No one knew where they were.

'Lee,' she said. 'Please don't hurt me. Whatever trouble you're in, it doesn't matter. You and me, we can work this out. We can sort anything out if –'

'You and me?' Lee glared at Kirstie as if she had lost her mind. 'There is no you and me.'

'But, I thought –'

He took a step towards her. 'You thought I enjoyed what I did with you? Then you must be mad. I fancied some fun, that's all. I don't give a fuck about you. You're a selfish bitch.' He took another step closer. 'I could waste you, right now, if I wasn't so scared of your old man. He'll kill me in a flash if I do anything to you. But he knows too much so I – I need to keep you sweet. For now.'

Kirstie started to cry. 'I want to go home.'

Lee rushed across the room towards her. Kirstie scrambled up the bed and pressed her back to the wall.

'Leave me alone!' she cried.

'No. You're going to tell the police that you did it.' Lee grabbed her free wrist and held it tightly.

'Tell them I did what?' Kirstie looked on in confusion.

'Tell the pigs it was you who killed your mother. Tell them you were pissed and angry. Tell them she mouthed off and you hit her with a hammer.'

Kirstie frowned. Why would he want to put the blame on her? Then suddenly she realised.

'You!' She shook with fear. 'You killed my mum!'

Lee nodded.

'Did someone pay you?' A sob caught in her throat. 'Did you do it for money?'

'Nope.'

'Then why?' Kirstie's tears were back again. 'Why would you kill her?'

'Why would you care? You told me you hated her.'

'I don't – didn't hate her. We didn't get on at times, but I wouldn't have done anything to her.' Kirstie pulled away again but it only made Lee squeeze her wrist harder.

'If you say that you killed her, they'll go easy on you.' Lee nodded. 'The cops are waiting for me to do something stupid like this; they're expecting it. But you? Squeaky-clean Kirstie Ryder? It's perfect.'

Kirstie still didn't want to believe him. 'You were with me all that night.'

'Can you actually say that I was?'

'What?'

'You conked out after two of these.' Lee pulled the bag of sleeping pills from his pocket again and dangled them in her face. 'I crushed them up and put them into your drink. You slept like a baby. My perfect alibi when the police called – not that they caught me in.'

'Oh, God. You killed my mum.'

'Stop your whining. You wanted me to anyway.'

'I NEVER!'

'Yeah, you did. You were always going on about how you wished she was dead.'

'NO!'

'So, you were drunk. I was taking you home. I saw Steph sitting outside the pub and stopped to give her a lift. But you got out of the car and started to argue with her.' Kirstie shook her head as he continued. 'You two were going at it and you got so angry that you grabbed a hammer from out of the car and *wham*! You hit her over the head.'

'No!' Kirstie cried. 'And you can't prove that. The hammer doesn't have my fingerprints on it.'

'But it does.' Lee smirked nastily. 'Remember putting up that photo of you and me, in the living room? The one you insisted on showing off on the wall?'

Kirstie remembered. But so what?

'The only prints on it are mine and yours.'

'But it has your prints on it too!'

'Your word against mine. I took it off you without thinking afterwards. Then I covered it up because I loved you so much.'

Kirstie was beyond inconsolable. How could this have happened? She remembered taking great pride in hanging that frame, even though it was only putting up a picture hook. She'd felt so grown up, like she belonged at Lee's house, like she was part of it now there was a photo of the two of them. She felt like she'd stamped her mark on his territory. And now Lee was prepared to use it to get away with murdering her mum. *Oh, God*, she realised, *he must be mad.*

'Please don't do this to me,' she whispered.

'If you don't go along with it, I'll kill you too.' Lee pushed her hand into his groin. Kirstie recoiled at a hard lump. 'Don't worry. I'm not pleased to see you,' he laughed, pulling out a lock knife.

He flicked open the blade. 'I killed Shaun Morrison yesterday so don't think I won't use it.'

'Sh – Shaun?' Kirstie glanced at it quickly, the enhanced state of her mind making her expect to see blood dripping from the blade. But it was clean.

Lee nodded and grinned. 'He bled like a pig.'

'No, you never!'

'I hacked at him with a knife and then finished him off with my feet.'

At that moment, Kirstie knew she was beat. Lee was either mad or dangerous and she didn't wish to find out which one.

'I'll do it,' she said, knowing that agreeing could be her only way out.

Lee held the knife to her throat. 'Don't think you can sweet-talk me now into letting you go and then you say something different to the pigs.' He spoke through clenched teeth, spittle flying everywhere.

'I won't!' Kirstie gasped for breath as his weight crushed her down onto the bed. With no room to manoeuvre, her bound wrist started to chafe.

Lee's phone rang. The word *Dad* flashed up on the screen.

'Dad?' he almost yelled. 'Listen to me. I –'

'No, you listen to me, you piece of low life.'

Lee hesitated. It was Terry Ryder. What was he doing on his dad's phone?

'Where are you?'

'How did you get this phone?' Lee covered Kirstie's mouth with his hand. She struggled, trying to speak, but one look from him and she quietened.

'Where are you?' Terry repeated, his voice a little louder.

'Tell me how you got this phone!'

'How the fuck do you think? Do the maths. No one crosses me and gets away with it.'

'Wha – what?'

'You have one hour to get my daughter home safe and sound or I'm coming after you.'

'Ten grand.' Lee tried to sound confident.

'You little shit! Do you still think you have the upper hand? I'm calling the shots right now.'

'You can't threaten me! I know everything. I'll tell the pigs and you'll go –'

'Will you listen to me, you stupid FUCK! You have one hour to get Kirstie back home. If I have to find her myself, so help me God, I will kill you when I find you.'

Lee's eyes raced around the room as if expecting Terry to come running out at him. He had to keep calm. Talk was all he had right now to put his point across.

'I'm not scared of you,' he taunted. 'And I'm not scared to kill. I've already killed that friend of yours, Morrison.'

The line went quiet.

'Yeah,' Lee continued. 'Knifed him I did and then kicked the shit out of him. So don't think I haven't got it in me to do it again. You come anywhere near me and Kirstie gets the same.'

'Dad!' Kirstie broke free for a moment. 'Help me!'

Lee slapped her. She whimpered, holding onto her cheek.

'What was that?' Terry wanted to know. 'If you lay one finger on her, I'll –'

'I'll wipe her out in a second.' Lee played what he thought was his trump card. 'Remember what happened to your fucking wife?'

'Yeah, I remember. Didn't quite go to plan, though, did it? The way I see it, you're as gutless as your father. And I finished him off last night too.'

'You're lying,' said Lee. Then louder, 'you're fucking lying!'

'Put Kirstie on the line.'

'No … No, I won't. You killed my dad? You – fuck! I'm going to put a knife through her heart.'

Kirstie screamed.

'Shut the fuck up!'

'Lee,' said Terry. 'You'd better not do anything rash. Do you understand?'

Lee tried to keep his emotions in check. He clenched his teeth to stop himself from screaming out too. He fought back tears as he held onto the phone. Was Terry bluffing or had he really killed his dad?

'Let me speak to Kirstie,' said Terry.

'Fuck you.' Lee disconnected the call.

Kirstie screamed louder.

'Shut up!' he yelled. 'Nobody can hear you and nobody would come anyway. You're in Ryder's Row, remember? Your old man created this row so that no one sees or hears ANYTHING. You got that?'

Lee paced the room as he wondered if Terry was telling the truth. Was his dad really dead? Maybe this was a trick, Terry's way of getting him to let go of Kirstie.

Fuck, his dad couldn't be dead. Terry wouldn't kill him, no way. But why hadn't he answered his phone that morning? And where was he now? His car had gone too. He ran a hand over his chin. His plan to get cash from Terry would never work now. He needed to get the emergency money stashed in the loft and then get the hell away. It was only a grand but it would have to do. But how the hell was he going to keep Kirstie quiet? Although he knew no one would call the police, one of the nosy fuckers could come and investigate. If they found out he had Terry's daughter tied up, they'd grass him up to make themselves look good.

'Lee,' Kirstie started, bringing him back to reality. 'I –'

He stepped towards her, clocking the fear in her eyes. For a moment, he did nothing. Then he took out the bag of sleeping pills, held her chin and tried to force one into her mouth.

But Kirstie was stubborn. She moved her head quickly to the side and the pill dropped to the bed.

'Help! Someone fucking help me!' She cried out in panic.

'Shut up!' Lee slapped her hard but it didn't stop her. She screamed again so he hit her harder this time. Kirstie cracked her head on the wall and she dropped forward onto the bed.

'Kirst?' Lee nudged her but there was no response. Fuck, had he killed her too? He felt for a pulse on her neck, almost crying when he found one. Making sure the rope around her wrist was still tight, he went through to the landing and pulled down the loft ladder.

Chapter Forty-One

Kirstie came round after a few minutes. Disorientated, she sat up. She felt a pain at the back of her head, winced as she held a hand to it. It came back bloody. Panicking, she stood up quickly, nearly wrenching her arm out of its socket. Trying to slow her breathing, she looked around the room but Lee was nowhere to be seen.

'Lee?' It came out as a whisper. Then again, louder this time. 'Lee!'

She repeated his name several times before bursting into tears with relief. A few seconds later, she pulled herself together. If she was going to get out of this mess, she needed a level head. Lee might be gone for now but he could come back at any second.

'Help!' She banged on the wall behind her. 'Help! I've been kidnapped.' She listened with her ear against the wall. But nothing. 'Help!' She tried again and again and again before slumping down on the bed and pulling on the rope. But she couldn't budge the knot. It was tied too tightly to loosen.

A flash of orange caught her eye. Her bag! It sat on the floor at the far corner of the bed. Maybe she could reach it with her feet. Carefully, she tried to hook the handle of the bag around her foot. She stretched out. The loop went over her shoe but slipped as she brought it up. She flicked it off and tried again barefoot, missed completely. And again. But on the fourth attempt, she managed it.

'Yes!' She pulled it up the bed and quickly located her phone. Laughing with relief, she switched it on and pressed the speed dial.

'Come on!' she said but there was no answer.

She clicked on her contact list. The first name was Ashleigh. She answered after a few rings.

'Ashleigh! Oh, Ashleigh, thank God.'

'Kirstie? Where are you? Your dad called me. He's frantic. Oh, you'll be in deep fucking shit if you're with –'

'Listen, Ash,' Kirstie interrupted her. 'You have to call the police. I've been kidnapped and I tried to call my dad but there's no answer. I'm at –'

'Yeah, yeah. Pull the other one. I am not covering for you and getting into trouble again. Your dad will do his nut with me.'

'Ashleigh! Please, this isn't a game. Lee has gone mad. He's threatened me with a knife and I'm tied up in his dad's bedroom. Ash, you have to believe me. Lee killed my mum.'

The line went quiet and Kirstie began to cry. 'Please, Ash. This isn't a joke. You kept the card that Sergeant gave us, didn't you? You have to call her, tell her where I am!'

'What's the number of the house?'

Kirstie cried even more with relief. 'Number two, Georgia Road. I'm in the back bedroom. My dad will have a key.'

She heard a noise and jumped. Shit, Lee must be back. She slid the phone underneath the pillow.

A small crowd had gathered outside the gate of number eighteen when Allie came outside. While she waited for Nick to arrive, she wanted to see if Phil Kennedy was at home and find out the last time he had seen his son. She knocked on the door of number two but there was no answer. She flipped up the letter box but everything seemed as it should be at this address – thankfully no more blood to invade her dreams. Well, not in the hallway at least. The downstairs curtains were open so she looked through the window. The living room was tidy, too. She was about to knock again when her phone rang.

'Hello. Is that Allie Shenton?' a female voice enquired.

'Yes.'

'It's Cathryn Mountford. You gave me your card yesterday and told me to call you. I've been assaulted and I want to press charges.'

'I'm sorry, Ms Mountford,' Allie replied, not really wanting to make time to talk to her right now. 'You need to report something like that to your local police station. I can't –'

'It was Terry Ryder who assaulted me.'

Allie was walking back to Lee Kennedy's house but she stopped. 'When did this happen?'

'Not long after your visit. He broke one of my ribs with one punch. He said that if the police came around asking questions again and I didn't continue to lie for him, that he would do more than that the next time.'

'Continue to lie for him?' Allie held her breath. 'What do you mean?'

'I wasn't telling you the truth. I'm so sorry. Terry wasn't with me for all of the night his wife was murdered.'

'But you said he was in Derby with you.'

'He was in Derby and he did come home with me, like I said. But he was called out just before half ten, more or less as soon as we got through the door of my apartment. He said one of the alarms was going off on site. He told me to go to bed, not to wait up for him.'

'And what time did he get back, can you remember?'

'About three a.m.'

Nearly five hours. Allie knew it was more than possible that Terry Ryder could have driven to Stoke, lain in wait for his wife, murdered her and driven back to Derby. She held the phone between her neck and shoulder as she wrote the details down.

'What about his clothes?' she asked next. 'Were there any stains on them? Did he show any signs of being in a fight or a struggle?'

'I noticed he came back in a fresh shirt.'

He'd changed his shirt? Allie's mind threw a million questions at her. Why had he changed his shirt? And where? At work? At home after he'd killed Steph but before heading back to Derby? Had he gone somewhere else other than where he worked? Where was the shirt he'd changed out of?

'Why did you cover for him?'

'I'm not sure how much time you've spent with Terry but he can be a very charming man. He can spin a great tale. I believed his story about the alarm because I didn't know too many of the details.'

'Even when you knew he hadn't been with you all night and his wife had been murdered?'

'I know how pathetic it sounds, Sergeant. Like I said, he can be a charmer when he wants to be. The seed of doubt was planted when you came to see me. My mistake was not doing anything about it.'

Allie could hear Cathryn crying down the phone. Was it possible that she was right after all? That Terry really had killed his wife? She needed to get back to work, think things through. But first she needed to know one more thing.

'What made you change your story, Cathryn?'

'It was the look in his eyes.' Allie heard Cathryn's voice waver.

'And you're prepared to make a statement?'

'Yes, I am. Believe me, Sergeant. Terry Ryder is not going to touch me ever again.'

Allie disconnected the call and stood for a moment. That had been a turn up for the books. She'd thought Cathryn would have stood by Terry, no matter what. But she had sounded frightened on the phone and it looked like he'd left her in the same mess as he'd left Carole Morrison.

Was everything that Terry had told her a lie? Had he gone to Vegas with Steph or had that been a ploy for her to think their marriage was better than it was? Had he bought her the watch? Or could it have been Phil Kennedy? She could have worn it out on nights when Terry was away and she knew she'd be meeting up with Phil. After all, if he had bought it for her, when would she have had time to wear it?

She looked again at number two. She'd have to come back to it later.

Kirstie held her breath but all was quiet. She picked up the phone again but Ashleigh had gone. She disconnected the call. Seconds later, the phone rang.

'Dad!'

'Kirstie! I tried to call you. Who were you talking to?'

'Dad, you have to call the police. Lee's kidnapped me. He's tied me up and I can't undo the rope.'

'Do you know where you are?'

'He brought me to Phil's house. He said he needed to see his dad but he tricked me,' she sobbed. 'He said – he said he killed my mum. It was Lee. You have to call the police.'

'Is he there?'

'No, but I – I don't know when he'll come back.'

'Are you upstairs or downstairs?'

'I'm upstairs, in the back bedroom. Come quick, Dad. I'm so scared.'

'I'll be with you in no time. I'm just around the corner. Stay put and don't worry. I'll sort that bastard out.'

Chapter Forty-Two

Up in the loft, once his eyes accustomed to the darkened area, Lee trod carefully, walking over to the far wall. He climbed through the hole where the bricks were missing at the side of the chimney and stepped into number four. He walked across the loft boarding and through into the next space until he came to number six. He was about to search out the bag hidden in number eight when a beam of light pointed in his direction. He stooped down quickly and stayed as still as possible.

'I thought I heard something,' a female voice said a few moments later. 'These shadows give me the creeps.'

The torch flashed in the opposite corner of the space. Lee groaned inwardly; he needed that money. Cautiously, he crawled forward on his hands and knees. One shuffle, then another. The sole of his boot scraped against a wooden rafter. The torch beam shone back again. He froze. On all fours, he was vulnerable. One slip and he could find himself falling down into the room below.

'I'm going to walk them, see how far I can get.' That voice again.

Lee shimmied back slowly and stooped down, hidden behind a pile of boxes. His hands felt around for anything to use as a weapon. Fingertips reached out into the dark, finally clasping around a thin plank of wood. The torch and footsteps came nearer.

He held his breath when someone climbed through into the loft space he was in.

The woman stood inches away from him. Having the element of surprise, Lee smacked her across the shin with the plank and made a run for it.

'Argh!' The woman shouted out in pain but it didn't stop her giving chase. Lee felt a hand grab at his jacket as he tried to scramble to his feet. He threw his fist back, punching at her arm until he was free. Hearing another female voice shout behind him, he retraced his steps back to number two. Fuck, that had been close. And he wasn't out of danger yet. They were on to him. There was no time to get the money. He had to get out of there and fast.

There was so much going on at the front of Georgia Road that it was easy for Terry to slip into the yard of number two and in through the back door of the house unnoticed. Surprised to see them searching Lee's house, he wondered if what he'd told him about Shaun Morrison could be true. Had he killed him? If he had, Terry had vastly underestimated the younger member of the Kennedy clan.

He stepped into the kitchen. The house was in silence, nothing out of place. He crept along the hall, checked the living room. Quietly, he opened the cellar door but still no noise. Then, keeping his back to the wall and his eyes upwards, he went upstairs.

Back at number eighteen, Allie had been coming up the stairs towards the loft hatch when she heard the commotion. She climbed halfway up the tinny ladders so she could see into the gap.

'Sam? Sam? Are you okay? What's going on up there?'

In the far corner, Sam stepped through the hole in the wall and back into Allie's line of sight. Allie climbed up next to her.

'There was someone back there,' Sam said, taking a moment to catch her breath. 'Took a crack at me but I'm okay.'

'You sure?'

'Yes.' She brushed Allie's concerned hand away gently.

'Was it Kennedy? Did you get a good look at him?'

'No. I grabbed his jacket but he punched back at me.'

Allie's phone rang again. 'Hello?' She listened intently. 'What? Are you sure? Look, don't worry. We're already there. Yes. Thanks.'

Allie looked at Sam. 'That was Ashleigh Stewart. She's had a call from Kirstie. Lee Kennedy has her. She's here, at number two.'

Sam gasped. 'It *was* him, back there, wasn't it?'

'Yes, quick. Let's get after him.'

———

'Sarge, after seeing what was left of Shaun Morrison, do you think Kirstie will still be alive?' Sam's voice was low as they made their way through the loft spaces.

'I'm not sure.' Allie stepped over a box and pushed another to one side. 'Let's hope their love is sweet and innocent.'

'And Ryder? Do you still think he's innocent in all of this?'

Allie quickly filled Sam in on the phone conversation she'd had with Cathryn Mountford.

'But if he wasn't in Derby,' said Sam, 'that could mean –'

'That he could have been here in Stoke.'

'Which means that Carole Morrison might not be lying.'

Allie agreed. In all honesty, she had always believed Carole Morrison's side of things.

'It still doesn't make sense,' Sam continued. 'Why would he want to be here? Wouldn't it have been better for him to be in Derby rather than near to where the murder took place?'

Allie stopped abruptly and shone her torch round at Sam. Sam squinted and shielded her eyes.

'He didn't come back to kill her, did he?' said Allie.

'Ohmigod,' said Sam. 'He came back to –'

They spoke in unison.

'Watch her die.'

Chapter Forty-Three

Slowly, Terry inched up the stairs. He could see the loft ladder pulled down. He peered up but couldn't see anything. Directly in front, the bathroom door stood open. He could see that the room was empty. The door next to it was ajar. He pushed it open with the side of his shoe, inch by inch until he could see the bottom of the bed. Another few inches and he could see Kirstie's feet. He pushed the door open with his hand and it hit the back wall. A step forward and he could see all of the room. Lee wasn't there.

Relief washed over Kirstie as she spotted him. He put a finger to his lips.

'He hasn't come back,' she told him and burst into tears.

'Did he say where he was going?' Terry dropped to the floor beside his daughter.

'No.'

He saw dried blood on her hands and checked her over quickly with his eyes.

'Did he hurt you?'

'Not really,' she replied.

'He didn't . . .'

'No, he didn't touch me,' Kirstie reassured him. 'But he's psyched up, Dad. He really scared me. We have to go. Right now.'

Terry pulled a knife from his pocket, flicked out the blade and began to hack at the rope.

'He killed my mum,' Kirstie sobbed as he worked to free her. 'He told me to take the blame. He set me up and ...'

They heard a noise. Footsteps down the ladder. Kirstie froze with fear. Terry stood up and quietly pushed the door back to its previous position. Then he hid out of view.

Lee walked in and Terry smashed a fist into the side of his face before he had chance to speak. The force of it slammed Lee onto the bed. Kirstie moved out of his way. Then she grabbed the knife and hacked at the rope.

'You!' Lee ran at Terry, fists flying. 'You killed my dad, you bastard!'

Terry dodged him. 'Don't be so stupid,' he cried.

'But you told me you had!'

'That was to get you to tell me where Kirstie was.'

'Then where is he?'

'What does he mean, Dad?' Kirstie asked.

'You're lying!' said Lee.

'No, you're the liar!' Kirstie shouted. 'You were only out for yourself. You tried to set me up.'

'I never! Kirst, you have to tell him that it was you! You were the one who killed your mother.'

Seeing that Kirstie was now through the rope, Terry snatched the knife from her. He pushed Lee up against the wall and held it to his throat.

'Leave me alone!' Lee pawed at Terry.

Kirstie screamed. 'No, Dad!' Free at last, she grabbed Terry's arm.

'It's okay,' Terry tried to calm her. 'I know better than to cut him up. Go downstairs and grab one of those nice police officers outside on the fronts.'

'Police?' Lee struggled even more.

Terry laughed at the young lad's expression. 'They're all over your place at the moment. I wonder what they're searching for. Or even what they've found.'

Kirstie ran to the door.

'You see,' Terry glared at Lee. 'I'm not going down for some scrote like you.' His head cracked into Lee's. 'But I am going to give you a good hiding for the things you've put my family through.'

———

Hearing a kerfuffle, Allie and Sam quickened their pace. Allie dropped down into number two first and waited for Sam. She prayed they wouldn't be too late. She could hear male voices. No, wait. There was a female voice too.

'Stand in there,' she whispered to Sam, pointing to the bathroom doorway. 'I'll go this side and –'

The door opened and Kirstie Ryder ran out. Allie pushed her towards Sam, who covered her mouth with her hand to stop her from screaming. Once she was calm, Allie moved Sam's hand away.

Kirstie held up her bloodied wrist. 'Lee tied me up and –'

'Who's in there?' Allie had no time to listen.

'Lee.' Kirstie's teeth started to chatter. "With ... with my dad. He killed my mum, he killed Shaun and he ...'

'Is he armed?' Allie took hold of the girl's shoulders when Kirstie didn't speak. 'Does he have a gun? A knife? Anything?'

Kirstie shook her head. She didn't want to get her dad into trouble.

'Run downstairs,' Allie told her. 'You'll be safe when you get outside.'

As Kirstie disappeared, Allie moved forward.

'Aren't you going to wait for backup?' asked Sam.

'There isn't time. You've seen what Ryder's capable of.'

Allie pulled the baton out again and held it up. She gave the door a swift shove. From her position, she could see Lee lying on his stomach on the floor. Terry sat astride him, his hand pushing Lee's face down into the carpet.

When he saw Allie, Terry loosened his grip a little.

'Thank God, Sergeant, I was about to call for the police. He had a knife. I grappled it off him and threw it over there.'

Allie followed the direction of his finger. The knife was in the far corner of the room, far enough away not to pose an immediate threat.

'Gerroff me, you mad bastard!' Lee shouted as he squirmed. He kicked up his feet but Terry stayed firm.

'Now, now, it will be much better if you don't struggle,' he said calmly.

'He's fucking nuts,' Lee told Allie. 'He's killed my dad. Get him off ME!'

Allie and Sam kneeled down beside Terry. Sam pulled out handcuffs. Once they'd clicked into place around Lee's wrists, Allie pushed Terry off him.

'Lee Kennedy,' she said. 'I'm arresting you on suspicion of the murder of Stephanie Ryder and Shaun Morrison and for the kidnapping of Kirstie Ryder.'

'But you have to believe me!' Lee shouted. 'He told me he killed my dad. You check. You'll see he's missing.'

'You do not have to say anything. But it may harm your defence if you do not mention when questioned something which you later rely on in court. Anything you do say may be given in evidence.'

Just then Matt appeared in the doorway. 'Aw, Sarge, I always miss the party. Everything okay?'

'Yes, everything's fine,' Allie nodded. 'I've cautioned him. Now get him out of here.'

To protests, Lee was dragged to his feet.

'You're dead, Ryder,' he shouted over his shoulder as he was ushered out by Sam and Matt. 'When my Uncle Steve hears what you did to my dad, you're fucking dead. He can still get at you, even when he's locked up.'

Once the room was quiet, Allie turned to Terry. 'Care to enlighten me on what really happened?' she demanded.

Terry held up his hands in mock surrender. 'I acted in self-defence. He was coming at us with a –'

'I'm not talking about that. I'm talking about Phil Kennedy.'

Terry gave her that charming smile. 'The lad's talking nonsense.' He moved closer, ran the tip of his finger gently down her cheek. 'Surely, you of all people know me better than that?'

'That's where you're wrong.' Allie knocked his hand away defiantly. 'I don't know you at all.'

Chapter Forty-Four

Eight thirty-five a.m. Allie closed the file on her desk with a satisfying tap, stretched her arms up into the air and let out a huge sigh. In front of her, Perry was messing about with Sam, purposely walking past her and twirling her round in her chair before dodging as she tried to cuff him around the head. Matt was reading last night's *Sentinel* while stuffing his face with his breakfast of bacon and cheese oatcakes. Over in the far corner, Nick was hunched over his computer. Oh, happy days, she smiled to herself, knowing far too well how that could change in an instant with one phone call. But this morning, early into their shift, they had had a few precious moments to relocate as a team again.

Today was going to be a difficult day in some respects, yet highly satisfying in others. It had been nearly a month since Lee Kennedy's arrest. The murder of Steph Ryder had been nothing different for her team but it had been particularly tough for Allie. Several times, her gut feeling had backed her into a corner as she'd tried to get the details that mattered. Several times, she'd risked her marriage for the sake of a man with no morals. Worse still, several times she'd been close to letting a killer get away.

Since the arrest, she and her team had gone over everything again but there was no physical evidence to put Terry Ryder at the scene of his wife's murder. They'd searched The Gables from top to bottom despite assuming they wouldn't find anything there.

Lee Kennedy had been remanded for the murders of Shaun Morrison and Steph Ryder as well as charged with keeping Kirstie Ryder against her will. Kirstie had corroborated her father's story and added her own statement to the mix. Cathryn Mountford had made a statement, too, and left Derby, she hoped temporarily.

The knife found in the compartment turned out to be something of a mystery. Although the blood belonged to murder victim Sarah Maddison, as Terry's fingerprints weren't on it, they'd had to draw a blank on why it was hidden away. The two people who might have solved the puzzle were unable to tell them why.

Terry Ryder had been questioned on several occasions, all informal but documented. Still, they had drawn a blank.

But not everything had gone against them. Phil Kennedy's disappearance and the last words from his son before he'd been taken into custody made Allie take a look over Phil's house. And as she'd walked around the empty place, checking for signs of foul play, she'd found the magic missing ingredients. After all, forensic evidence never lies.

'Ready to go, Sarge?' Sam asked. 'It's nearly time for showdown.'

Grabbing her jacket from the back of her chair, Allie nodded at Sam. 'Abso – fucking – lutely!'

As a mark of respect, they'd dressed in black that morning. At Carmountside Crematorium, Allie and Sam sat away from the family in the chapel, hoping to blend into the crowd of mourners that had arrived for Steph Ryder's funeral. There was quite a turnout. Allie reckoned there must be near a hundred and fifty people sitting around them. The Mayor and Lady Mayoress wore full regalia. Local politicians and councillors, businessmen and charity representatives. Across the aisle, Allie spotted Mary Francis, come to pay her respects, and Roberto and Clara, come to gather the gossip. No doubt Steph would be the local most talked about in Powder and Perfume that afternoon.

So many mourners made Allie realise that Steph might not have been liked by some in real life but she was held in high esteem by many. Or maybe that was because of Terry. She would never know for sure.

She searched the crowd for a second time, not sure if she'd missed Carole Morrison the first. But after scanning it all again, there was no sign of her. She suspected she'd still be grieving for the loss of her husband – Shaun's funeral had taken place the week before. But most likely, Allie assumed, she wouldn't feel comfortable anywhere near Terry since the assault. Even though Allie believed what Carole had told her, Carole still refused to press charges. She wanted to get on with her life now and forget it all.

It wasn't until a third of the way through the service, as the second hymn was being sung, that she looked up to see Terry trying to make eye contact. She stared back for a moment, seeing the faint sign of a smile. She turned her eyes back to the words on the hymn sheet, choosing not to look his way again. How could he smile at her – now of all times, the bastard? It was as if he were taunting the dead.

Twenty minutes later, the mourners came out of the chapel and congregated at the side of the building. A few feet away, Perry and Matt sat in an unmarked car.

'Nervous, Sarge?' Sam asked as they stood under the canopy. 'Or looking forward to it?'

Allie tried not to smirk at the young woman's implications. But actually she couldn't wait a moment longer.

'Mr Ryder!' she called out as Terry shook hands with a few people. 'Might I have a word?'

Terry excused himself before walking over with a polite smile. 'Yes, of course.'

She pointed over to a quieter area. 'Shall we?'

They walked along a gravel path and sat down on a bench dedicated to Mary Brian who had died in 1997, aged 72. Ahead of them, an elderly man knelt at a grave, changing water, a bouquet of flowers by his feet. A young woman with a child skipping by her side walked over to another, the woman close to tears as the little girl leaned forward and kissed the stone. Over in the distance, three ground workers leaning on spades huddled together as they waited for mourners to disperse.

Allie didn't want to break into the peaceful silence but she spoke at last.

'You haven't exactly been straight with me, have you, Mr Ryder?'

Terry feigned shock. 'I don't follow, Sergeant.'

'I think it's time we did away with the small talk.' She used her fingers to count on. 'I know that you set up a meeting with Carole Morrison to try and incriminate her in the murder of your wife. I know that you're lying about an affair with her. I know that you told Phil Kennedy to kill Steph and something went wrong.' Her eyes locked with his. 'I know that you went to The Potter's Wheel purely to watch her die, thinking that you'd covered your tracks sufficiently.'

'Very impressive, Sergeant.'

Terry crossed his legs and swung his body around to face her a little more, just as he'd done on numerous occasions during the times she'd spoken to him. It didn't bother her. She knew all of his tricks now.

'Well,' Allie gave a little shrug, 'we both know that she wouldn't have died with that one blow from Lee Kennedy. So when you had to finish the job off, you were still under the impression that everything would be cleared up for you. And that's when it all started to go wrong. What happened with your timing? Did it take you too long to get it up with Carole Morrison? Didn't she turn you on quick enough to finish the job in time? Or was it something to do with your age?'

She felt Terry's eyes burning into the side of her face but she refused to look at him. Instead, she stared straight ahead as she continued.

'Of course you couldn't hurry her. So by the time you ran across to the car park, it was all over. You were too late to watch. What happened then? Did you find Steph lying on the ground? Did she make a noise, you sick bastard, and then you bashed her head in to finish her off good and proper?'

'I assume you're telling me all this because you have proof? Vital evidence that places me at the scene?'

Allie pursed her lips. Terry was right. Unfortunately, she hadn't been able to find his clothes or his murder weapon. But she could suss out his car later. There might be a tiny fragment of something left behind in there, although unlikely.

'Well?' Terry probed.

Allie could see Matt and Perry standing with Sam now, mingled in with the crowd. She gave them a nod, watched them move towards her.

'I thought not.' Terry sniggered. 'You haven't got anything on me.' When Allie remained silent, he added, 'Have you?'

'You seem a little surprised that I continued with my investigations.' Allie turned back to him with eyebrows raised. 'Surely you know me better than that?'

'Or maybe I don't know you at all,' Terry said quietly.

'Yes, that's right. You *don't* know me at all.' She took great pleasure in his look of irritation as he tried to work out what was going on. 'When Lee told me that you'd killed his father, I didn't believe him at first. You and Phil were known to be as thick as thieves, yes? But then I got to thinking, maybe there was some truth in it. After all, he disappeared quite conveniently, don't you think?' She took a moment to beckon her team over. 'So I stopped by at his place and once inside I had a good shifty around and came across a toolbox. More importantly, I found a wrench. After testing, it came back with Phil Kennedy's blood on it. It also came back with your fingerprints.'

Terry smiled icily. A moment in time where he'd lost control in the wrong place.

'You think a few spots of blood on a wrench will be enough to charge me for something without a body?' His tone was belittling. 'You need to come up with far more than that.'

'I have,' she assured him calmly. 'While you've been a free man, we've been trawling through the CCTV cameras throughout the city. As we were gathering evidence against Lee Kennedy, checking who went in and out of number eighteen Georgia Road before the murder of Shaun Morrison, I asked my officers to keep on checking. Now I know the cameras only cover the front of the row but we came up with footage showing Phil's car on Leek New Road, a few hundred yards away, during the early hours of December sixth. It also clearly showed you in your car driving right in front of it.'

Terry was staring at her now but his eyes didn't do it for her this time. Sadly, she wondered how they ever could have.

'We tracked the two cars as far as we could out of the city centre,' she continued. 'Although we never saw Phil's car again, we did see yours once or twice during the hour afterwards. But enlarging some of the frames showed that you weren't driving it. Shane Flint was. Mitch Casey was in the passenger seat.

'I got to wondering if you had any property beyond the areas of the city. I trawled through the land registers but I couldn't find anything registered to you. I did find a four-acre plot in Steph's maiden name.' She turned to him. 'Do you need me to continue?'

'You can't prove any of this.' Terry shook his head in disbelief. 'You don't have a –'

'A body.' Allie played her trump card. 'Oh, but you see, I do. Because late last night, Shane Flint and Mitch Casey told me where they'd disposed of Phil Kennedy, as well as his car.'

'Where *they* had disposed of him? But that still doesn't –'

'Along with the clothes that they took from you. Along with the gloves that you wore. Along with the knives you used. Along with the hammer you used. Apparently they've done that at every place that you asked them to dispose of a body. Steve Kennedy told them to.' She stood up as her officers approached. 'I was surprised that they coughed up so easily, given your reputation, but I suppose everyone has a tipping point. Or perhaps they were more concerned about what will happen to them once Steve Kennedy finds out they were involved in the murder of his brother. This way they can hang it all on you.'

'They did a deal?'

Allie turned to smile at him now. 'Let's say they're still helping us with our enquiries.'

'You fucking –' Terry lunged at her but Matt and Perry, steps away by now, intervened. Allie moved to one side as Terry was handcuffed and cautioned. Then, with a heavy heart but one full of satisfaction, she made her way back towards the mourners. She beckoned Kirstie over. Before she lost both of her parents, it was the least she could do to explain everything to her.

'You okay, Sarge?' Sam asked just before Kirstie drew level.

'Yes,' she told her. 'I do believe I am.'

Allie smiled. Was it poignant that she had done this at Steph Ryder's funeral? She would like to think so. She held her head high and felt the icy wind blow over her. Thank God she'd been strong enough to resist the charmer. Things could have been so different.

Epilogue – New Year's Eve

Allie pushed open the reception door of Riverdale Residential Home and bustled in out of the cold. Music played low in the background and the lights on the Christmas tree sparkled as if trying to keep in time with the music. She'd left behind the smell of snow in the air and the sky looking full of it but for now it was only a mere promise and she relished the heat that engulfed her as she entered the building.

Miriam Walters wasn't on reception duties today. It was Mick Irvine's turn. Mick had been at Riverdale for a couple of years now and her sister's face always lit up whenever he came into her room. He was a tall, gangly man in his late twenties but with the swagger of a teen. His dyed black hair suited him far more than it should and, although cut into a funky style, most of it was hidden today underneath a beanie hat. He smiled a welcome.

'New Year's Eve, already,' he said. 'Where do the years go? Karen's in her room. She was a bit tired from her physio yesterday but apart from that she's been fine.'

'Thanks, Mick.' Allie smiled back before heading down the corridor.

Karen was awake when she entered the room. Sat in her wheelchair, she'd been positioned to look out over the garden. She was wearing a jumper that Allie had bought her that Christmas.

Her freshly washed hair was held back by an Alice band and she had a tiny bit of pink lipstick left.

'Hey, chick.' Allie leaned forward to kiss her forehead. 'How are you doing?'

Karen smiled and blinked her eyes rapidly, trying to make a sound that was recognisable as a word. But Allie finished off for her.

'That good, hmm?' She checked the CD in the player, selected a track and sat down opposite her. 'Let's have a bit of Wham before we can't play it again until next year. "Last Christmas." What do you reckon?'

She hung up her coat before pulling up a chair.

'So, how's tricks? You been out gallivanting with Mick lately?' She took her sister's hand in her own.

A knock on the door and Mick popped his head around the frame.

'Talk of the devil,' Allie grinned at him.

'This has just been delivered, Allie.'

Mick handed her a white rectangular box. It was tied with red ribbon. She noticed the name Fresh Bloomers woven into it here and there and frowned. That was the florist Terry Ryder had used to send her the bouquet of flowers after the charity event. A quick examination of the box revealed no addressee on it. There was no card, no tiny envelope.

'How did you know it was for Karen?' Allie shouted to Mike, who was disappearing out of view. He popped his head around the frame again.

'It had the room number on the delivery note.'

'Thanks.' She nodded and let him go on his way. Karen made a noise. Allie lifted the box for her to see. 'It's for you, Karen. It looks a strange shape for flowers, though.'

The ribbon slid off easily and she placed the box onto Karen's bed. She shrugged off the lid. Wrapped in white paper tissue was a single red rose. Allie lifted it out to show her sister, careful to watch for the thorns. It was then she noticed the blank envelope underneath it. She pulled out the card inside and read the message.

Karen, until we meet again, my fallen angel.
One day you will be all mine.
And you, little sister, Allie.
Don't you ever stop looking for me.

Allie gasped. She dropped the rose and it fell to the floor. Delicate petals came away from its base, scattering the carpet at her feet like confetti. She shuddered as realisation sank in. The rose must be from Karen's attacker. Why now? Why, after all these years? How did he know that Karen was here? And how did he know that she would be here, too?

She raced to the window, her eyes scanning every car as it drove past. The car park to her right showed no signs of movement. On the pavement in front, a man walked past with his dog. Was it him? Would he look up? In the grounds below, a man was balanced on a ladder, pulling down Christmas lights on the outside tree. Was it him? Would he look up?

Allie stared for ages but there was nothing to be seen. It was hopeless anyway. Even if he was watching, he wouldn't have known she would look out of the window right at that very moment.

No, he wouldn't be watching.

Would he?

Acknowledgments

Thank you to my treasured friend, Alison Niebieszczanski. For listening to me, encouraging me, believing in me and for never being able to get a word in edgewise at times. Who stuck by me every year, through thick and thin, and makes me proud to know her. Same too, for my wonderful friends, Talli Roland, Sharon Sant and Maria Duffy. For comfort and reassurance, chats and laughter. For always being there. I really can't thank you enough and I hope there is much more to come.

My crime gang for their continuous friendship and support – Mari Hannah, Rebecca Bradley, David Jackson and Pam McIlroy. For murderous conversation during the many get-togethers as well as over the phone. Nothing is too much trouble.

Thank you to everyone at The Sentinel, Stoke-on-Trent. Nothing makes me prouder than to see my column in your newspaper every month. Thank you for taking me under your wing.

Also everyone at Amazon Publishing and Kindle Direct Publishing, especially Vicky, Emilie, Thom, Daniel, Amy, Mel, Heidi and Maura, who have been a dream to work with.

For my mum – for being the strong woman that made me into what I am today.

For my fabulous agent, Maddy Milburn, a wonderful person to know and a joy to work with. Thank you for your support, friendship and belief.

For all the writers and authors who have helped me in any way. For all the readers who have sent me messages, whether it be by email, tweets or Facebook, thank you so much for your kind words. Each one makes me believe a little bit more.

Finally, to my husband, Chris. Thank you for your unwavering support, love and honesty. For raising me up when I'm feeling down – and for twisting my twists that little bit further. And for not complaining too much at the amount of times I burn our meals. I could never do, and wouldn't want to do, anything without your love.

About the Author

 Mel Sherratt has been a self-described "meddler of words" ever since she can remember. After winning her first writing competition at the age of 11, she has rarely been without a pen in her hand or her nose in a book.

Since successfully self-publishing *Taunting the Dead* and seeing it soar to the rank of number one best-selling police procedural in the Amazon Kindle store in 2012, Mel has gone on to publish three more books in the critically acclaimed *The Estate* Series.

Mel has written feature articles for The Guardian, the Writers and Artists website, and Writers Forum Magazine, to name just a few, and regularly speaks at conferences, event and talks.

She lives in Stoke-on-Trent, Staffordshire, with her husband and her terrier, Dexter (named after the TV serial killer, with some help from her Twitter fans), and makes liberal use of her hometown as a backdrop for her writing.

Her website is www.melsherratt.co.uk and you can find her on Twitter at @writermels.

44412015R00228

Printed in Poland
by Amazon Fulfillment
Poland Sp. z o.o., Wrocław